LARRY BOND'S
FIRST TEAM

SOUL OF THE
ASSASSIN

**Forge Books by
Larry Bond and Jim DeFelice**

Larry Bond's First Team
Larry Bond's First Team: Angels of Wrath
Larry Bond's First Team: Fires of War
Larry Bond's First Team: Soul of the Assassin

LARRY BOND'S FIRST TEAM

SOUL OF THE ASSASSIN

LARRY BOND AND JIM DEFELICE

A TOM DOHERTY ASSOCIATES BOOK

NEW YORK

LARRY BOND'S FIRST TEAM: SOUL OF THE ASSASSIN

Copyright © 2008 by Larry Bond and Jim DeFelice

A Forge Book
Published by Tom Doherty Associates, LLC
175 Fifth Avenue
New York, NY 10010

www.tor-forge.com

Forge® is a registered trademark of Tom Doherty Associates, LLC.

Library of Congress Cataloging-in-Publication Data

Bond, Larry.
    Larry Bond's first team : soul of the assassin / Larry Bond and Jim DeFelice—1st
hardcover ed.
       p. cm.
    "A Tom Doherty Associates Book."
    ISBN-13: 978-0-7653-0714-9
    ISBN-10: 0-7653-0714-6
    1. Americans—Italy—Fiction. 2. Assassins—Fiction. 3. Terrorism—Prevention—
Fiction. 4. Intelligence officers—Fiction. I. DeFelice, Jim. II. Title.

PS3552.O59725 L38   2008
813'.54—dc22

                                                                          2008005130

First Edition: May 2008

Printed in the United States of America

0 9 8 7 6 5 4 3 2 1

We'd like to thank all of the men and women fighting for our country, especially those who have been injured or wounded in the line of duty. In the past year, we visited Walter Reed hospital, where we were deeply moved by the courage of the patients and the efforts of the staff to help them toward recovery. This book is dedicated to all of them.

Note

The First Team and the Joint Services Special Demands Project Office are entirely fictional. While Special Forces units and the CIA work together on a variety of unique and difficult missions, their operations are conducted within a framework and chain of command that provides for extensive review of their actions. In no case do real-life personnel or their units operate beyond the limits of U.S. law. Nor would such operations be authorized or condoned by counsel in employ of the President of the United States, much less the President himself.

Dramatis Personae

FIRST TEAM

Bob "Ferg" Ferguson
Thera Majed
Sgt. Stephen "Skippy" Rankin, U.S. Army
Sgt. Jack "Guns" Young, U.S. Marines

SUPPORT PERSONNEL

Col. Charles Van Buren—commander, 777th Special Forces Group
Jack Corrigan, mission coordinator
Lauren DiCapri, mission coordinator

WASHINGTON

Pres. Jonathon McCarthy
Jackson Steele—Secretary of State
Corrine Alston—counsel to the President
Thomas Parnelles—CIA Director
Daniel Slott—CIA Deputy Director of Operations

MI6—BRITISH SECRET SERVICE

Nathaniel Hamilton—senior officer at large

SISDE—ITALIAN SECRET SERVICE

Marco Imperiati—special agent in charge

FSB—RUSSIAN FOREIGN INTELLIGENCE SERVICE

Col. Kiska Babev—supervisor, special science
    projects, Moscow office

IRANIANS

Anghuyu "Atha" Jahan, businessman in service of Iranian
    Revolutionary Guard
Dr. Navid Hamid, scientist

Dr. Artur Rostislawitch, Russian biologist
T Rex, assassin
Arna Kerr, "preparer" for T Rex

ACT I

O Muse! the causes and the crimes relate;
What goddess was provok'd, and whence her hate;
For what offense the Queen of Heav'n began
    To persecute so brave, so just a man;
Involv'd his anxious life in endless cares,
Expos'd to wants, and hurried into wars!
Can heav'nly minds such high resentment show,
    Or exercise their spite in human woe?

—Virgil, *The Aeneid* (Dryden translation)

1

Death had never particularly interested Bob Ferguson as a subject of study. It was a fact in and of itself, without nuance. His religious instruction—Ferguson had gone to parochial schools and a Catholic college—taught him to view death as a necessary passage, but the nuns, brothers, and priests who had instructed him tended to focus on either side of the gateway, rather than death itself.

As a CIA officer assigned to the Agency's covert Special Demands team, Ferguson had had a great deal of experience with death; he had often been its agent and provocateur. Still, his relationship was purely professional; he remained neither intrigued nor moved by any aspect of the subject itself. The end of life was simply the end of life. The manner of its coming rarely interested him.

Ferguson's nonplussed expression as the video played on the small screen at the end of the study bothered his host, CIA Director Thomas Parnelles. Unlike Ferguson, Parnelles contemplated death a great deal. It bothered him, especially in its most brutal forms, and particularly when it involved someone he knew. The fact that the death on the screen involved both was particularly upsetting; it had happened to a man who worked for him, and required justice, if not vengeance.

Parnelles had known Ferguson for a very long time—since Ferguson was born, in fact. He had been Ferguson's father's closest friend, and on more than one occasion served in loco parentis when Ferguson Sr. was out of the country. Parnelles assumed because of these things not only that he knew the young man well, but that Ferguson shared his feelings on any matter worthy of having one. So the half smile on Ferguson's face, the completely unmoved expression that was characteristic of the young man, annoyed Parnelles greatly. He finally reached over and clicked the laptop key to end the video just as it focused on the dead man's battered skull.

Unsure why the video had stopped, Ferguson took a sip of bourbon from the tumbler Parnelles had given him earlier. The liquor burned pleasantly at his throat as it went down.

"Technical problems, General?" Ferguson asked.

"There's not much more," said Parnelles. He flipped off the laptop, momentarily shrouding the study in darkness. When he turned on the light, Ferguson had the exact same expression on his face. "Are you feeling all right, Bobby?"

"Never better."

"North Korea was difficult, I know."

"Change of pace." Ferguson tilted the glass. The bourbon was Johnny Drum Private Stock, a well-aged small-batch whiskey more distinctive than such standards as Maker's Mark or Jim Beam. That was one thing about Parnelles—he did not have standard anything.

"Ordinarily, I would tell you to sit down for a while, and take some time off," said Parnelles. "More than the few days you've had. But this is a priority. This is important."

"Not a problem."

"After this, maybe you should take two or three months off. Lay on the beach."

"I'll just get bored." Ferguson leaned forward, stretching his back and neck. "So Michael Dalton was killed in Puys, France, two years ago. Then what happens?"

"Then we spend two years trying to figure out who did it." Parnelles took his own drink from the edge of his desk and walked over to the chair near Ferguson. He told himself he was seeing the younger man's professional distance, nothing more. "We found this video from the bank's surveillance camera. We re-created Dalton's movements. We checked everyone who had stayed in the hotels nearby for up to two weeks before."

"Why was he there?"

"Vacation."

Ferguson smirked.

"No, really, he was taking a vacation," said Parnelles. "This is an out-of-the-way town on the Channel. He liked France, and he'd just spent a year in Asia. So it was different."

"What did the French say about the murder?"

Parnelles settled down in his seat and took a sip of his drink—Scotch—before answering.

"The local police, of course, were incompetent. They believed it was a terrorist attack."

"Just because a car blew up?"

"I really don't know why you're being sarcastic, Robert. You're not taking this seriously."

Ferguson took another sip of the bourbon. Generally Parnelles wasn't quite this worked up. In fact, Ferguson couldn't remember the last time Parnelles had briefed him personally on a mission—let alone asked him up to Maine to do so.

"Yes, it did look as if it were the work of terrorists," admitted Parnelles. "But why terrorists would blow up a car at that place and time—of course the police had no answers. A small village on the French coast? Terrorists would never operate there. Clearly, Dalton was the target. We went to the ministry, of course, but they got it into their heads that we were lying."

"About what?"

"That Michael was working, instead of being on vacation."

"Was he?"

"You're being very contrary tonight, Robert. I just told you he wasn't."

Bad publicity about the CIA's secret rendition program had caused a great deal of friction in Europe just prior to Dalton's death. The French believed that the Agency was withholding information about what Dalton had been working on—they thought it involved something in France—and in Parnelles's view had been less than cooperative out of spite.

Ferguson—who admittedly had never cared much for anything French, let alone their spies—knew that the French security service seldom displayed anything approaching alacrity, even when pursuing their own priorities. But he let that observation pass.

"If Dalton was targeted, then something must have happened in Asia," Ferguson told Parnelles. "What was it?"

"Unimportant, Bob. The point is, what I'm getting to—we know who killed him. He was a contract killer known as T Rex."

"Like the dinosaur."

"Exactly. He kills everything in his wake. He's extreme. T Rex."

Actually the name had been used in a text message intercepted by the National Security Agency just before another assassination, this one of a wealthy businessman visiting Lisbon. Ferguson had already seen the information in the text brief of his mission. There had been other "jobs" as well: T Rex had been implicated in the murder of a Thai government minister and a suspected fund-raiser for Hezbollah, to name just two. Parnelles ran down the list of known and suspected victims, impressive in both length and variety.

Tired of sitting, Ferguson began bouncing his right leg up and down. His foot was just touching the fringe of a hand-woven wool rug Parnelles had retrieved from Iran toward the end of the shah's reign—bad days, Parnelles had said once. It was all he said, ever, on the subject to Ferguson.

"You seem distracted, Bobby." Parnelles glanced at Ferg's foot, tapping on the carpet.

"Foot fell asleep." Ferguson bounded up from the chair. "Can't sit too long."

He did a little jig in front of the chair. "So what's the real story, General? Who is T Rex?"

"We don't know."

"The Israelis hired him, and we can't figure it out?"

"The Israelis *didn't* hire him," said Parnelles. "Hezbollah has a lot of enemies. Including Hezbollah itself."

"So what do you want me to do?"

"Figure out who he is. Apprehend him. Bring him here for trial."

"That's what Slott told me this afternoon." Ferguson glanced at his watch. "Yesterday afternoon."

He got up from the chair and walked around the study. It was as familiar to him as his own condo—more so. He'd played hide-and-seek here as a kid.

Taking T Rex in Italy was sensitive. The Agency was still smarting over a well-publicized trial of several of its members, fortunately in absentia, for the rendition of a suspected terrorist a few years before. The Italian court had found that the man was not a terrorist and had been kidnapped by the CIA, albeit with help from the Italian secret services. The political situation argued for the use of the elite First Team—officially, the Office of Special Demands—a small group of highly trained operatives headed by Ferguson and occasionally assisted by a Special Forces army group.

But the job might have been done by other CIA agents, including a special paramilitary team trained in renditions.

"So when I bring back T Rex," said Ferguson, "what happens? You put him on trial?"

Parnelles frowned.

"If a situation develops where he can't be brought to trial," he said, picking his words very carefully, "that would be something we could all live with."

2

ROME, ITALY

It was simply and finally about the money, nothing else. Early on the assassin believed it was about the challenge, the chase and kill, but that was a lie. There was an element of that, certainly, but it was no more than an element, a small part, not the main motive.

The real motive was greed. Money. There was no denying that, not after all these years.

Many people lied to themselves; it was necessary in this business. But growing older, the assassin made it a policy to be honest when assessing personal motives and vices. Once begun, the practice had been liberating. It saved considerable time, and created clarity.

And clarity was of the essence.

The person they called T Rex pushed back the curtains, watching the dawn come over the city. Bologna would be the perfect place. The assassin already knew it well, spoke Italian fluently, and envisioned an easy time at the borders.

Everything was already moving toward its resolution. It was like an opera, complicated and beautiful.

But again, it wasn't about aesthetics; it was money.

This one would be the last. The payoff would be sufficient to guarantee that. Retirement waited in Thailand. The papers were already prepared.

There was more risk here than in any of the other jobs he had done, but that seemed only fitting. A capstone, a challenge at the endgame.

But really, it was about money, not the pleasure of killing people.

3

NEAR HAMPTON FALLS, MASSACHUSETTS

Ferguson woke around five a.m., and helped himself to the coffee the night watch team protecting Parnelles had made in the kitchen. The coffee was bitter and burnt, but it was enough to get him going. He went out onto the deck, nodding at the surveillance camera before carefully closing the door behind him. The high-tech security gear—not to mention the CIA detail—had been added only in the past two years, necessary precautions, though Ferguson knew Parnelles chafed at them.

As did he. If he'd been in a different mood, Ferguson would have spent a bit of time goofing on them—making faces for the camera, whispering Russian and Arabic curse words to the listening devices. But last night's unofficial briefing had left him in a serious mood. He ignored the sensors and walked to the beach, guided as much by memory as the gray twilight. He wasn't exactly alone—two low-light cameras and an infrared recorded his every move—but it was as close as he could get.

Kill an assassin?

Morally, Ferguson supposed, there was plenty of justification. He hadn't known Dalton but assumed he was a good officer, on the right side. Probably not perfect, but good enough to be hated by the bad guys. Getting T Rex would mean doing justice for Dalton. And surely that was what Parnelles wanted; clearly Ferguson had been assigned the case not so much because of his ability, but because the Director of the CIA knew he could talk to him freely without fear of repercussion.

Yet he hadn't spoken freely, had he? Even Parnelles, who wanted it done, had hesitated to speak openly of murder.

Would it be murder if T Rex resisted?

That would depend on the circumstances, thought Ferguson.

He laughed at himself. "I'm thinking like a Jesuit," he told the waves.

There was plenty of reason for that, as he had been educated by them.

What would Father Francis have said? *Intention, boys. That makes the difference. And it is known by God.*

Yes. The Jesuits were always with him.

"Rest easy, Father Francis," Ferguson told the waves.

He intended to take T Rex alive, if possible, despite his unwritten orders. He'd bring the bastard to justice, but in his way.

Ferguson looked out at the water and sky. He loved the ocean in muddy gray—"fisherman's dawn," his father called it, and though he wasn't a fisherman, it was the elder Ferguson's favorite time of day.

"Anything is possible then," he used to tell Bob. And then he would smile, smirk really, and add, "Not really. But it feels that way."

Ferguson walked toward the dock, intending to go out on the long pier. But he tripped a sensor as he climbed up the three steps; the lights switched on, destroying the mood. For a long minute, he stood staring at the edge of the darkness on the water, waiting impatiently for the floodlight to turn itself off. Finally he gave up and went back to his car.

That's what you get for being nostalgic, he told himself, waving at the CIA bodyguard as he drove through the gate.

Three hours later, Bob Ferguson pulled off the highway to look for a diner and a pay phone. A place right off the interchange advertised itself with a flashing neon, but he didn't want to make the call from a phone so obviously close to an interstate. He took a right onto the local county highway, following it for about ten miles before finally coming to a village. There was a diner on the main drag, a fifties-era bullet building that called itself The Real McCoy. It was a bit too self-consciously cute, but it also looked like the only place to eat in town. Ferguson parked in the lot, then went inside, where his instincts were confirmed—the old-style diner fronted a consciously kitschy place with a fifties theme. But it was too late to turn back.

"Good hash browns?" he asked the girl at the cash register as she retrieved a menu.

"Best. Booth or table?"

"Booth."

Ferguson ordered breakfast, then took his coffee to the phone booth near the men's room. He took a phone card from his wallet, checked his watch, then dialed the number of his doctor in suburban Virginia.

"This is Bob Ferguson," he told the receptionist. "I'm looking for Dr. Zeist."

"He's with a patient."

"I can wait a bit. He wanted to talk to me. I'm out of town and may not get a chance to call back."

The receptionist clicked him onto hold. Ferguson took a sip of coffee. He suspected that she'd told a white lie; the doctor generally didn't see patients for another half hour.

"Hey, Ferg, how are you?" said Zeist, coming on the line.

"You tell me."

"The results are the results," said the doctor. "You know. My suggestion would be to have another treatment. The odds are good. I've only had two patients since I've started practice who, um, had flare-ups."

Ferguson hadn't heard Zeist use the word *flare-ups* before. Ordinarily, the doctor was extremely precise, even clinical, when talking about cancer. He was also generally upbeat, at least about thyroid cancer. The odds greatly favored a positive outcome—even for third-stage patients like Ferguson whose cancer had "escaped the thyroid capsule before detection," the statistics favored a "full, or close to full, lifetime survival rate without recurrence."

Problem was, the cancer didn't seem to be listening. A recent set of tests had discovered the cells in different parts of his body.

"So the treatment here is to poison me, right?" said Ferguson.

"Well, not precisely, Ferg."

"I swallow the baseball and sit in the hotel room for a couple of days," said Ferguson. He'd undergone the treatment before.

"It's not that bad, is it?" said Zeist.

"Nah, it's not that bad," Ferguson said. "Just was the worst five days of my life."

Ferguson, who hated to be cooped up, wasn't exaggerating, though Zeist thought he was.

"We have to do a little surgery first. Take out the adrenaline gland."

The adrenaline gland was where the most cancer cells had been located on the scan; it was also relatively easy to remove and to do without.

"That's really the best odds," said Zeist. "The combination—a one-two punch. You'll beat it. Let's see. I'd like to set this up for next week—"

"Next week's not going to be good."

Zeist sighed. "Listen, Ferg, waiting a few days, even a few weeks maybe, won't be a big deal. But we really do want to move ahead. The best—"

"Yeah, I'm not putting it off. I'm just kind of booked for the next week to two or three. Hard to tell right now. How much advance notice do you need?"

"I can get you to see the surgeon at the end of the week."

"Too soon. What about Ferber?"

"I was thinking of Dr. Ferber since he knows you."

"Good. Tell him I'll be in touch."

"Ferg, he's going to have to see you himself. You know that."

"I trust him. I've seen his work." Ferguson turned toward the glass door to the restroom area, glancing at his neck in the reflection. "As a matter of fact, I'm looking at it now. Very nice work. No scars."

"Ferg, this has to have a high priority. Really. As optimistic as I am, realistically, the sooner the better."

"Looks like I have to go," Ferg said, spotting the waitress carrying his food.

"Ferg—"

"Gotta run. Have a date with the world's best hash browns."

———

Ferguson had finished the home fries—decent, though the coffee nearly made up for it—and was just about to ask for the check when his secure satellite phone began to vibrate with a call. He took it out and slid against the wall at the end of the booth.

"The Real McCoy," he answered. "Home of the world's best hash browns."

"Ferg?"

"Talk to me, Corrigan."

"Where are you, Ferg?"

"On the road again," sang Ferguson, slightly off-key.

"The GPS says you're in Massachusetts."

"Just paying my respects," said Ferguson.

"Oh, I'm sorry," said Jack Corrigan. "Your father's buried up there, huh?"

Jack Corrigan was the First Team's desk officer, the mission coordinator who spent most of his time in a bunker known as "the Cube." His job was to support the First Team while they were in action, providing them information and arranging for assistance when necessary. He'd probably just been briefed on the mission.

The waitress came over with the coffee, but Ferguson waved his hand at her, adding, "Just the check."

"Look, I have the plane all arranged. I have you going out of JFK instead of Logan, though. I didn't know you were up there. I figured you'd want a direct flight to Bologna so—"

"Don't worry about it. When's the flight?"

"Three o'clock. Rankin should be there tomorrow night. Thera and Guns are going in through Rome so they can bring more equipment in."

"That's good."

"You're all packed? You need more gear?"

"I'm good, Mom, thanks. Even have a new toothbrush."

"Rankin's going to come with extra clothes."

"He needs them. Never takes a shower."

"How can you be so flip this early in the morning?"

"That's what happens when you start off the day with great hash browns," said Ferguson.

4

Stephen Rankin watched as the blonde pulled the strands of hair back behind her ear, pretending to preen in the hotel lobby's mirror. She was actually checking to see if she was being watched.

Of course she was. Every male eye in the hotel lobby, including those of the overtly gay man at the front desk, was staring at her. She was just too gorgeous not to.

Which ought to be a liability in her line of business, Rankin thought.

The blonde finished playing with her hair and swept toward the doorway. Rankin watched from the corner of his eye—then nearly jumped as he saw her collide with someone and fall to the floor.

It was Ferguson.

Rankin had worked with the CIA officer long enough now that he shouldn't have been surprised, but he was. They were supposed to be shadowing the blonde, who'd been identified as T Rex's "preparer," a kind of advance man who made sure things were ready for the assassin to do his job when he arrived in town. Shadowing generally meant staying far in the background, but Ferguson had his own way of handling things.

"*Scusi, signora,*" said Ferguson in Italian, bending to help her up. "I hope I didn't hurt you."

"*Merci,*" said the woman in French.

"I hope you're OK," said Ferguson, first in English and then in Italian.

"Yes, OK," she said, her English heavily accented. She pushed down her skirt, scowled at him, then went back toward the door, hesitating ever so slightly before pushing it open.

Ferguson, meanwhile, strolled across the lobby. Seeming to spot Rankin for the first time, Ferguson greeted him in a loud voice. "*Ciao,* my American friend. How is the studying going today?"

"Just fine," said Rankin, remaining seated. He still had no idea what Ferguson was doing, except that it wasn't what they had planned just a half hour before.

"It is a fine day, *si,*" said Ferguson. "You will join me, yes, for a coffee?"

"Yeah, sure," said Rankin sourly. He rose.

"If you're busy—"

"Am I?" asked Rankin.

"Of course not. Come then," said Ferguson, and he swung around toward the doors.

"Should we be watching the mistress?" said Rankin once they were outside.

"I keep telling you, Skippy, she and T Rex aren't like that. My bet is that not only has she never met him, she doesn't even know what he does. Not specifically, anyway."

"Like she couldn't figure it out, huh?"

"He probably sends her on a couple of gigs a year that are just blinds. But maybe she does. The hair color's a dye job."

Ferguson glanced to his left. The taxi was just turning to the east, out of sight.

"We're not going to follow her?" asked Rankin.

Ferguson smiled without answering. Rankin knew Ferguson was acting this way partly because he didn't like explaining himself, and also partly because he liked to annoy people, especially Rankin. Some days Rankin could let it slide without saying anything; today he couldn't.

"Why do you have to be such an ass when we're workin', for cryin' out loud?" he snapped.

Ferguson just laughed and continued toward the mopeds he'd parked nearby. He grabbed the brown one, stepped over it, and got on.

"We're going toward Via Zamboni, I think," he told Rankin. "Stay back. Remember she's seen you."

"Hey—"

"And get your radio on. Channel eight—louder the buzz, the closer you are to her. I'm on channel two."

Ferguson revved the bike's small motor, then helped it get moving by pushing his feet along the pavement. Rather than turning in the direction the cab had taken, he went right; after glancing behind him to make sure Rankin was following, Ferguson reached into his pocket and took out the GPS receiver, glancing at the screen, which showed where the bug he'd placed in the cab was. The taxi had become bogged down in the narrow one-way streets. Ferguson continued to the north, then turned onto Via San Giacomo.

"You with me, Rankin?"

"I guess."

"She said she was going to one of the university administration buildings. Probably bull, but we'll see how patient she is."

"You sure we got the right girl, right?"

"Got me, Skippy. Depends on how far we trust Corrigan."

"Yeah. That makes me feel *real* confident."

One of Rankin's redeeming qualities, in Ferguson's opinion, was his deep distrust of Corrigan, largely because of the fact that Corrigan had been an army intelligence officer before joining the CIA. In this case, however, Ferguson believed that the identification of Arna Kerr as T Rex's "preparer" was probably correct; he'd followed her the night before when she arrived in town, and watched her do the sorts of things Ferguson and the others did before they set up a mission—renting cars, casing buildings, getting the lay of the land. She'd originally been ID'd by matching various credit card and other records against T Rex's known assassinations. Arna didn't seem to work them all, but she had been around for the flashiest ones, including Dalton's.

Though she had come in from Paris and was apparently claiming to be French, they had traced her credit cards to Stockholm, Sweden. If they decided they wanted her—which they might—they could get her there. Taking her now would tip off T Rex and ruin the entire operation.

As would letting her know she was being followed.

The GPS device beeped.

"Uh-oh," Ferg said. "Getting out of the cab. Low traffic tolerance. Stay with me, Skippy."

"That's *not* my name," growled Rankin.

Ferguson pinched his elbows close to his body and ducked down a side street. He turned left and cruised onto Via Bel Belmbro. In the process he cut off a delivery truck; the Italian driver responded with a blast of his horn and a stream of curses. Under other circumstances, Ferguson might have stopped to listen—his Italian was not particularly deep—but he was a little farther from Arna Kerr than he wanted to be. So he merely hunkered down on his bike, pushing his head toward the handlebars and dodging a small car that shot out of a private courtyard. He turned onto Via San Vitale, where he remembered a parking lot; he was off his bike and trotting in the direction of the church before Rankin caught up.

"Go up two blocks; find a place to park. We'll keep her between us," said Ferguson.

"I thought you weren't putting a tracker on her."

"I didn't. It was in the cab. Come on."

Ferguson went far enough up the street so that he could see the next intersection, then leaned back against the facade of one of the buildings. The bricks were arranged in a way that made it look like the wall was a fireplace; for hundreds of years, there had been a marble relief on the lower panel and a statue in the upper niche. Now, though, the niche was empty, and the stone was covered with a thick, oily grime.

"Where is she?" asked Rankin.

Ferguson was just about to say that she was a slow walker when he realized that he had made a mistake: she'd be doubling back, not going ahead. That way, she could check the cars behind her to see if she was being followed.

Well, good for her, he thought.

"Come down the block, slowly," he told Rankin, getting back on his bike. "I think she's backtracking."

"You lost her?"

"Not even close." Ferguson went down toward Via San Vitale, then circled around and passed Arna Kerr as she walked toward Via Rizzoli at the center of the old city. Bologna's two towers stood nearby.

"She's just doing the tourist thing," Ferguson told Rankin.

Ferguson found a place to put the bike. Pulling on a pair of sunglasses, he began walking down the street, considering what to do next. The brief predicted that Arna Kerr would stay in Bologna for one more day or perhaps two. Following her around all that time would be easy, but Ferguson was never one to take the easy way on anything.

"Ah, you again," he said, spinning as they passed on the street. This time he didn't bump into her. "The lady from the hotel whom I knocked to the floor. I am still sorry for this."

Displeasure flickered on her face, the slightest hint of uncontrolled emotion.

A good sign, thought Ferguson.

"I hope you have forgiven me," he told her in Italian, pulling off his glasses. "Here I see you are a tourist, but I thought you were a student."

Arna Kerr was used to men trying to pick her up. She smiled condescendingly, and continued taking photos of the square with her small camera.

"I can tell you're not Italian," said Ferguson, switching to English. "But I don't think you are American. Too pretty."

"*Allez oust*," she said in French. "Get lost."

"*Ah, oui.* But my French is so poor, I don't know what you are saying. I wouldn't have guessed French. Scandinavian."

"I can call a policeman," she said, this time in English.

"Let me," said Ferguson. He swung around, held his hand up, and said in a soft voice, "*Polizia, polizia.*" Then he spread his arms in a gesture of apology. "None seem to be nearby. Which is good—I wouldn't want to share."

"You act like an Italian," said Arna. "But your accent sounds American when you speak English."

"*Grazie,*" said Ferguson. "But it's more Irish, don't you think?"

Arna shrugged, suppressing a smile. If she weren't working, she might find him attractive in an amusing way. He was good-looking, and glib of course, with a sense of humor. But she was working, and wanted to get rid of him as quickly and painlessly as possible.

Without calling the police, certainly.

"I can pretend to be American, if that will help," said Ferguson. "I have been to Boston and New York. And as it happens, I have all morning free, and can give you a guided tour of the city."

"You live here?"

"Just arrived. But in a past life, I must have lived here. Every street is familiar."

"Really, signore—"

"Ferg. Everyone calls me Ferg."

She shook her head. And yet she couldn't help herself. He was attractive, with a certain air about him. "What do you do?" she asked.

"Art. I look at very old paintings and tell people with too much money whether to pay ridiculous prices for them or not. And you?"

"I'm a drug pusher," she said in French. "A vicious woman who sucks the blood from obnoxious Americans."

"Irishmen, too, I hope."

Something about him struck her wrong, and it wasn't just the fact that he so effortlessly figured out what she had said. Arna Kerr took a step toward him, then threw her right hand onto his back, reaching for his wallet pocket.

Ferguson caught her hand. She was quick, and strong. He thought it was possible she was on to him.

"I usually wait for the second date," he said, but then he let her hand go; she reached in and took out his wallet and EU passport.

"Dublin?" she said, reading.

"Don't you think that's a good photo for a passport?" he asked.

Arna Kerr thumbed through the passport, noting that Ferguson *had* been to America several times over the past year—and to Russia, China, and Thailand besides.

His wallet had a few euros and some British pounds, along with a Presto card and American Express—black, so he wasn't exactly poor.

Cute and rich. Well that *was* a good combination.

"Take a business card while you're at it," said Ferguson. "Do I get to feel up your wallet, too?"

"Don't get fresh." She handed the wallet and passport back.

"So, this means you want a tour? You see I can use the money."

"You seem to have plenty."

"Then I'll pay for lunch."

"I have to work," she told him. "I'm late now."

"Where's your appointment?"

Arna Kerr blushed at the stupid lie. No harm done—but still, to be tripped up so easily.

"So dinner," said Ferguson. "Nine?"

"Dinner. I don't know."

"You have to eat, right?"

He didn't look like he was going to leave.

"I—"

"I'll be at the hotel at nine." Ferguson started away, then whirled on his heel. "Meet me in the lounge."

Arna Kerr froze, sure suddenly that she had miscalculated, that he was Interpol or something.

"You never told me your name."

"Arna," she said.

"Arna what?"

"Just Arna."

"Just Arna. It has a nice ring to it," said Ferguson, bowing and walking away.

Rankin had joined the First Team from the Special Forces; he was in fact still a soldier, even if it had now been nearly two years since he'd worn fatigues. Surveillance wasn't really his specialty. He did know the basics, however, thanks to several weeks at the advanced spycraft school the Agency had sent him to when Special Demands was formed: change your appearance often, don't be predictable, and above all else, don't get too close.

So he was more than a little surprised to spot Ferguson talking to their subject.

Rankin almost stopped. He knew it would be the wrong thing to do, though, and he forced himself to look away, concentrating on the reddish brown bricks he was rolling over.

Rankin found a coffee shop about a block away. It was late November, and while not cold for Rankin—he'd recently spent some time in North Korea, where your sweat froze in its pores—it was well past the season when waiters would prowl outside. Needing some sort of reason for sitting there, he went in for a coffee, struggling to remember how to ask for milk until the woman behind the counter smiled and told him in Texas-accented English that it was right behind him.

When he came outside, Ferguson was waiting for him.

"What the hell were you doing?" Rankin asked.

"Getting a date. How's the coffee?"

"Aren't we following her?"

"She's in the Commune. Give her a few minutes, then slip inside and make sure she's still there." Ferguson looked at his watch. "I'm going to run up to the train station and grab Thera and Guns. Watch her until I get back, all right? Then we'll get those guys on the case."

"Just me?"

"And don't get too close. She's already spoken for."

5

BOLOGNA, ITALY

Thera Majed stared out the window as the train made its way through the mountain valley toward Bologna. Her eyes weren't focused so much on the landscape as the blur of the brown fields she passed. She'd put her mind in a kind of holding pattern; the train was white noise around her.

She could have used a vacation. She hadn't thought so; when Corrigan had called and asked if she was up for a mission she'd agreed without hesitation.

"Your option, totally," he'd told her.

And meant it, she thought, though you couldn't really be sure. The CIA was like a big corporation in a way—*what have you done for me lately?*

Risked being arrested and God knows what else in North Korea and then South Korea, but that was two weeks ago; we're on to something new now.

So what the hell. Yeah, she was up for it. Whatever. It was only now, looking at the beautiful countryside, longing to be *just* looking at it and not thinking about the mission, that she realized she was a little burned-out.

She looked forward to seeing Ferg. He could be difficult to deal with, but she liked him. She admired the hell out of him—they all did, even Rankin, who would put a pitchfork through his head rather than admit it.

Ferguson was good, really good. He'd spent pretty much his entire life as an op and so much of what he did just seemed to come naturally. That was a downside for having him as a boss—he didn't understand that not everyone was like him, that other people were human.

He didn't seem to be himself. He'd spent several days in a North Korean jail, probably been tortured, certainly been starved, but of course he wouldn't say. Here he was, back in the middle of something new, undoubtedly gung ho about it.

He had another side to him. He was actually concerned about people. That was something *he* didn't admit, but she'd seen something in the way he interacted with a kid on their first mission together. Something real, beyond the mask he manipulated as part of his job.

"You ready?" said Jack "Guns" Young, sitting across from her. "I figure we're about ten minutes away."

"I'm ready," said Thera. She kept her gaze out the window.

"You look spacey," said Guns. He was a Marine Corps gunnery sergeant, which accounted for his nickname. Originally he'd been chosen for the team because of his skills with weapons and demolitions, but he'd become adept as an all-around op. As Ferg put it, Guns had found his inner spy. There were still some rough edges, but Ferguson had taken a liking to him—partly, he suspected, because he didn't talk that much.

"I'm with you," she said, tapping his knee and getting up as the train began to brake. "It's just a beautiful place to be."

Ferguson stood at the end of the platform, hands dug into his pockets, sunglasses on though the day was overcast. The bright white earbuds of an Apple iPod were in his ears—though the music player was in reality a radio.

He could be a movie star, Thera thought.

"Hey," said Guns, surprised Ferguson had come to meet them.

"Hey yourself," Ferguson told the Marine. Guns was actually a couple of years older than Ferguson, but the CIA officer thought of him as the younger brother he'd never had. He was tall and on the thin side, with a face that could have belonged to a sixteen-year-old.

"Ms. Majed, you made it," Ferguson told Thera.

"You could have warmed up the weather," said Thera, feeling a chill as the wind blew through the platform. "Rome was warmer."

"Next time, Italy in the spring." Ferguson took one of the suitcases she was carrying and began walking toward the taxi stand. Cars needed a special pass to get into the central city. He'd rented three vehicles with the proper paperwork, stashing them in parking garages in case they were needed. In truth, bikes and scooters were much more practical. He and Rankin had placed a dozen around town, along with a pair of motorcycles.

"Where are we at?" Thera asked.

"We're doing a surveillance. We could use you and Guns to switch off," said Ferguson. "She came right in on the plane that Corrigan said she would. Even intelligence guys get things right once in a while."

Ferguson had spent about an hour and a half the day before scoping out the surveillance cameras at the station, and fell silent now, not wanting his lips to be caught on the camera. He doubted the security people studied the video very closely before it was erased, but discretion now might pay off later.

"I'm going to need the video bugs," he told Guns as they reached the cab. "Do you have them?"

"This suitcase," said Guns, lifting it slightly.

"All right. We swap in the cab. I want you to go to the Oxford Hotel. It's about two blocks from where I left Rankin. Once you're checked in, switch your radios to channel three and tell him you're his relief. I'm getting out first at the Borgia. That's where she's staying."

"What are you doing there?" Thera asked.

Ferguson saw a carabiniere walking in a bored circuit not far from the cab line. He waited until the man turned in the other direction to answer her.

"I have to seed some of these around where I'm going to be with her tonight. If we get a chance, we'll all meet back at the Bene around seven. Two-eleven. If not, I'll talk to you when I can. Get rid of the phone cards from Rome. Keep switching, OK?"

The Bene was one of several hotels in the city where they had reserved rooms for the operation.

"Did you say you're going to be with her tonight?" asked Thera.

"We have a date. Jealous?"

Thera felt her face flush.

"Strictly business," said Ferguson.

He was tempted to lean over and give her a kiss on the cheek, but didn't, afraid he wouldn't be able to hold himself back.

6

BOLOGNA, ITALY

The Hotel Borgia traced its roots to a stable in the early Roman era, though even the hotel's Web site admitted that any traces of that building or the two dozen that had occupied the grounds before the present one was built were long gone, probably carted away to form the rubble foundation of one of the local palaces. During the Middle Ages, the property had been used as a sculptor's workshop, then razed and made into a set of houses for well-off artisans. In the sixteenth century, a distant relative of the Borgias—probably serving a semi-exile in the city—had the apartments consolidated into a minipalace. While it would have looked plain on the outside, inside its walls were covered with glorious frescoes and paintings exquisite enough to have earned the jealousy of Bologna's leading citizens—one possible explanation for the owner's untimely death. He died a few hundred meters away from the front door, killed by a knife wound—accidental, according to the available records, which neglected to explain how the weapon could have been thrust accidentally fifty-eight times into the man's abdomen, chest, arms, and neck.

The building had fallen into disrepair and was razed during the beginning of the nineteenth century, not quite in time to see the birth of Italy as a modern nation. Its successor was destroyed during World War II. Its owner had been a notorious Fascist, and it was still said that when it was blown up—there was general agreement by an Allied bomb, though some held partisans had dynamited it—a thousand rats escaped from the cellar. The replacement building was a large, dull brown apartment building that was never successfully rented. In 2005, a German real estate investor bought the building and the rest of the block; he razed the interior and constructed what he called Italy's "most modern accommodation." This was a bit of poetic license, but the place was handsome, all polished wood and marble, accented by gleaming steel. The bar had plush carpet and material in the ceiling that deadened the acoustics—a plus for Ferguson, since it meant he could use a standard bug and not have to worry about background noise.

He ordered a drink from the waitress, then slid back in his seat, watching the doorway.

Arna Kerr might be T Rex, Ferguson thought. It didn't fit the analysts' profile, but she had that kind of vibe—danger lurking beneath her veneer.

She walked into the bar, her pace easy but her eyes darting back and forth, sweeping the room ahead of her, wary of an ambush.

She's good, Ferg thought. He liked that.

Thera hunched over the coffee table in Rankin's suite several stories above the bar, as if changing the angle she was watching the television from would change the aim of the small video bug Ferguson had planted at the edge of the booth.

Next to her, Rankin sighed and shook his head. "I hope he knows what the hell he's doing. It looks to me like he's just going on a date."

"It's supposed to look that way." Thera shifted uneasily.

"He just wants to get in her pants," said Rankin.

"She dyes her hair," said Thera. "And that ain't all that's fake."

"You jealous?"

Thera ground her back teeth together, listening as Ferguson and their subject played verbal footsie in three languages. Ferg had once said he wasn't very good in French or Italian—his languages were Russian and Arabic, which he'd grown up with—but he seemed fluent, joking easily, mentioning Rome, saying he'd spent a lot of time there as a kid.

"That's true, isn't it?" Thera asked.

"What?" said Rankin.

"Ferg. He spent time in Rome when he was a kid?"

"Got me. Half of what he tells us is bullshit. Who knows what he's making up for her?"

Thera turned back to the screen as Ferguson suggested they leave for the restaurant.

"Which one?" said Arna Kerr.

Thera felt her heart jump as Arna Kerr put her hand on Ferg's.

"I knew she wouldn't go for it," said Rankin as the woman made an excuse about not wanting to eat at the restaurant Ferg suggested.

"She's just suggesting another restaurant," said Thera.

"He'd better watch his ass or he's gonna blow the whole thing."

As they got up from the table, Thera reached for the radio to tell Guns they were coming out.

The restaurant Arna Kerr suggested was a Moroccan place perched on the edge of a semi-bohemian area; the clientele seemed to be mostly younger professor types from the University of Bologna, whose schools were scattered around the city. After suggesting the Limone— a contemporary restaurant that he had already checked out and bugged—Ferguson had let her choose. She didn't seem to have scoped out the place beforehand; more likely she was being careful to keep him away from wherever it was she was scouting.

Ferguson wondered how she had become T Rex's preparer; it wasn't the sort of job that you found on Craig's List. She didn't seem like the type to have a military background. He knew a few women who'd gotten into arms dealing through family connections; maybe this was the same thing.

She was prettier than most of those women, good-looking enough to be a model.

"You seem pensive," she said, noticing that he'd fallen silent.

"Beautiful women do that to me. And couscous."

"Couscous?" Arna Kerr looked at the food on her plate and laughed, telling him in French he was one of a kind.

"*Merci.* So are you. A very beautiful one of a kind."

"You're beautiful, too."

"Handsome." Ferguson winked. "Men are handsome. The English word."

"Not pretty?"

"Pretty's a different thing."

They spent a few moments working out the linguistic nuances. Ferguson ordered more wine.

"I don't think I need any more," she said, putting her hand over her glass when the waiter arrived with the bottle.

The waiter smirked. Ferguson asked him if he was Russian.

"No, no."

Ferguson reeled out some Russian, testing not the waiter but Arna Kerr. If she understood what Ferguson said, she didn't let on.

Neither did the waiter.

"What did you tell him?" Arna Kerr asked.

"I said you were a beautiful woman and I was wondering if you would go home with me," said Ferguson. He'd used saltier terms, but that was the gist.

"Home?"

"Home away from home. Bologna."

"Where is your real home?"

"Near Dublin. Where's yours?"

"Paris."

We're a pair of incredibly good liars, Ferguson thought, sipping his wine.

7

While Ferguson was wining and dining Arna Kerr, Rankin went up-stairs to the floor where her room was. Breaking in was too much of a risk; even if she hadn't left a detection device behind, if she was good enough to be working for T Rex most likely she'd be good enough to figure out if someone had been inside. Rankin intended on doing everything but.

Ferguson had already planted a video bug to cover the hallway. The size of an American dime, the unit sent a signal to a transmitter hidden in a fire hose box two floors below. The transmitter boosted and relayed the signal to a satellite system used by the First Team. The ops could tap in via laptops and small purpose-built viewers that looked like video iPods to see what was going on. The deskman also monitored the feedback in the Cube, giving the team another set of eyes and ears. They had installed a series of bugs, both video and au-dio, along with transmitters around the city to help them monitor what was going on. The major drawback to the tiny devices was their limited batteries; they had an average life of only eight hours, though occasionally could last for as many as twenty-four. Larger units had greater capacity, but were correspondingly easier to detect.

Rankin wanted to place one of the larger video bugs in the base of a fire extinguisher at the end of the hall. But first he had to make sure that Arna Kerr hadn't placed her own devices here. He walked down the hall swiftly, holding what looked like a handheld computer in his hand; it was actually a bug detector.

Rankin had almost finished his sweep when one of the doors opened. He stopped at a room at the far end of the hallway as if he was going to knock. Two women and a small child came out and began milling around. The kid was watching Rankin, so he went ahead and knocked at the door he'd stopped in front of.

No one answered—perfect, he thought. He mimed being puzzled, knocking again, calling for a friend named Maurice. To his surprise, the door suddenly opened. A man big enough to be professional wrestler stood inside.

"*Chi è Maurice?*" said the man.

"Gotta be the wrong room," said Rankin. "Made a mistake. Sorry."

"Who's Maurice?" repeated the man, angrily.

"Relax," said Rankin. He didn't know much Italian, and in fact couldn't be sure that was what the guy was speaking. "Sorry I woke you up, all right? Sorry. *Scusi.*"

The man took a threatening step into the hallway. For a moment Rankin worried that the guy was going to start a fight. The last thing Rankin wanted to do was start a commotion—especially with someone who actually looked big enough to give him a serious fight.

If not beat the crap out of him.

"It's OK; it's OK," Rankin said, holding his hands up. "Just relax. I made a mistake. Wrong floor."

The women and kid by now had taken the elevator downstairs. Rankin waited by it, the anti-Maurice watching him the whole time, his eyes flickering with an unspoken threat until the elevator finally came back and Rankin got on.

Was he connected to Arna Kerr? No, thought Rankin—it was just an unlucky coincidence.

"Why doesn't this shit ever happen to Ferguson?" he mumbled as he got out of the elevator on the floor above and walked to the stairs.

Thera was shown to the worst table in the house, a tiny half-moon squeezed between the waiters' station and the ladies' room. She couldn't quite see Ferguson from where she was, but she did have a good view of Arna Kerr. The blonde was exactly the sort that turned men's heads: perfect nose, thick lips, oversized breasts. Her arms looked sculpted.

Probably tennis muscles, Thera thought; all show, no power.

Thera pushed her jealousy away as the waiter approached. She had a little trouble with her Italian, confusing it with the Greek she'd learned as a child and still spoke with her relatives. Her pronunciation was so far off she had to repeat her order several times before she was understood.

Thera suffered through a limp pasta dish before Arna Kerr finally excused herself and headed for the ladies' room. Thera waited until she passed, then rose and walked toward the lobby, taking her phone out as if intending to make a call. She detoured to her left, avoiding a party of eight and walking right next to Ferguson's table. As she passed, he moved his chair back and bumped into her.

"*Scusi, scusi*," he said in Italian, jumping to his feet. "I'm sorry."

"It's nothing," she said, pushing away.

"I hope I didn't hurt you."

"*Mi ammazzi*," she said. "You kill me."

Thera went into the foyer, grabbed her coat from the rack, and then left the restaurant.

"I thought you were going to eat," said Guns when she found him in the car down the block.

"I didn't feel like it." She pulled a pair of rubber gloves from the glove compartment and opened her pocketbook, where Ferguson had tucked Arna Kerr's wineglass when he accidentally bumped into Thera.

"Think we got prints?"

"We'd better. I'm not going back in there."

Thera put her hand inside the glass and then wrapped what looked like a thin electric blanket around it. Instead of an electrical plug, the blanket connected to a USB port in the team's laptop, which was under the foot mat in the car. After fiddling with the sensitivity setting, she got an image of the glass on the screen. There were two smudges, a thumbprint, and what looked like the print of a middle finger.

It figures, she thought.

Ferguson suggested they go back to Arna's room, but she preferred his.

"You don't even know where it is," he told her.

"It's not at the Borgia?"

"I was there to see a friend. Who turned out not be in. Luckily for me. Or I wouldn't have met you."

"You look like the kind of man who would have a nice room. Sauna, right?"

"No sauna," said Ferguson. "The marble sink is on the large size, though."

"That sounds nice." She brushed his cheek with her finger.

"Then let's go," said Ferguson, rising.

Arna Kerr ran her hands across his back as they waited in the lobby for the taxi, making sure he didn't have a gun.

Maybe he was what he seemed—an attractive, well-off but somewhat lonely man about her own age. Maybe he'd seen her in the lobby of the Borgia and decided he wanted to sleep with her. Or maybe something else. She couldn't be sure; the way he looked at her didn't *quite* suggest lust.

She had never once been made while on a job. Would it go down like this? Would Interpol send some smooth Irishman—or whatever he was—to romance her?

No—that happened in movies. In real life, they arrested you. Or shot you.

Most likely shot you.

Which he might be planning to do when he got her to his room.

The wine she'd drunk was making her take chances she shouldn't, Arna Kerr thought. She should just tell him good night, go up to her room.

But part of the attraction was the danger, or its potential.

"Here we go," said Ferg as the cab pulled up. "Are you with me? You're so quiet you might be sleeping."

"I'm awake," she said, and leaned up to kiss him.

After Rankin planted his video bug, he left the hotel and walked around the block to a building subdivided into apartments. He reached for one of the buttons, as if he were going to ring to be buzzed in. Instead, he pushed a thin plastic card into the jamb near the lock. The door opened easily.

Inside, the place smelled of boiling greens; the pungent, spinachlike smell reminded Rankin of his childhood, but not in a good way—he used to gag at the smell of spinach.

The building was five stories high. Rankin trotted up the steps to the top, stopping at the top landing to make sure no one was around. Then he moved quickly down the hall to a window that looked onto the side alley. He reached to the top, making sure the latches he had checked yesterday were still undone, then pushed the window up and stepped out onto the ledge.

When he'd done this the night before, the moon had been out and there was plenty of light to see the narrow ledge by. Tonight, however, it was cloudy, and damp besides; he felt his feet slip as he pulled himself up onto the narrow lip outside the building. He took a breath, holding himself against the old brown bricks. Then he gently pushed the window closed and began sliding to the right, where a small hip roof led to a wide, nearly flat roof overlooking the back of the hotel where Arna Kerr had her room.

Even at this hour, there was still plenty of traffic in the city. Rankin could hear the dull boom of stereos and smell the stink of exhaust as he moved sideways across the building. If she had gotten a room on the other side of the hotel, his job would have been easier—there was a bar with a broad terrace overlooking the street on that side; he could have gotten a drink and pretended to be copping a smoke.

If Ferguson had had this job, that's where the room would have been.

Rankin made it to the hip roof and pulled himself over, knees scraping on the hard ceramic shingles. They were a lot more slippery than he remembered. He pushed on, got to the flatter roof. There he took his water from his backpack and took a long pull, resting for a moment. His breath back, he took out the small dish and screwed what looked like a boom mike into the center. The device worked by feeding an infrared laser onto a window and using it to "read" the vibrations, translating them back into sound waves. Rankin put on a pair of glasses tuned to the laser's frequency and began aiming the device. He had just figured out the correct window when he heard Guns talking to him on the radio.

"Hang on," he said, adjusting the volume. "What's up?"

"Ferguson is going over to the Orologio," Guns said. "How are you doing there?"

"Almost set."

"You can take your time. She won't be going back to her room to-night."

"No shit."

Ferguson had made love to the enemy plenty of times before, but tonight he was off-balance. He went through the motions smoothly, fingers gliding gently down the buttons of her blouse, undoing each one with a simple push, pulling the silk away from her shoulders, letting the shirt fall back and away from her torso. He ran the backs of his hands over her bra—black and silky—then around to undo the clasp.

He pushed his lips against hers. They gave way easily. Her tongue met his, rolling around it. Ferguson slipped the bra from her shoulders and cupped her breasts gently, her nipples hard.

But it wasn't about sex. It was a job, and as smooth as his hands were, his mind felt as if it were watching through a peephole from another room.

He reached the zipper on her skirt and slipped it downward. The skirt caught against her hips but then gave way, falling to the floor.

It might not be about sex, but it wasn't just the job, either. Power was involved: getting it, having it, keeping it. That was what spying was. Not that Ferguson considered himself a spy in the classic sense—it was rarely his job to simply get information, and he never had been a "runner of men and women" as his father had been for most of his career. A spymaster manipulated people—sex had probably been one of his tools, though until this moment Ferg had never really thought about that.

"The bed's in the next room," said Ferguson when Arna Kerr was down to her panties.

"The couch is right here."

She leaned backward toward it ever so slightly. He took the hint, pushing against her gently, moving down with her as she gave way.

8

Thera had heard enough. She reached for the handle of the car door. "I'll be back," she told Guns.

"Where you goin'?"

"Time to run a check," she said, though she had been around the block making sure they weren't being watched only a few minutes before. She slapped the Fiat's door closed and began walking away from the hotel—away from Ferguson and what he was doing with the blonde.

She shouldn't care—she *didn't* care—and yet her whole body vibrated with anger.

Something moved in the shadows at the edge of the street. Thera slipped her hand inside her jacket pocket, wrapping her fingers around the small pistol there. But it was nothing—a young man and woman, making out near the portico's pillar.

Thera continued around the block, her sneakers rubbing on the pavement. She needed a mission, a mind-set: she became a tourist, coming home after dinner. She quickened her pace, slightly worried about the unfamiliar surroundings.

She turned the corner and saw a small crowd of people gathered near a café at the far end, spilling out into the street, laughing and having a good time.

Ferguson was just doing his job, Thera told herself. It shouldn't bother her. It really shouldn't bother her.

He fell asleep after they were done. Arna Kerr pretended to doze herself, then got up and went to the bathroom, grabbing his pants along the way.

No keys, a few euros of change, an Irish pence.

The license looked genuine, but that wasn't much of a trick—her own documents, after all, were phony. She repeated the number to herself three times, enough to memorize it: Arna Kerr had always been good with numbers. She slipped the credit card receipt out, thinking she would take it as well, but most of the account number was x'd out.

The license would be enough. She fingered the wallet. There wasn't much in it besides money: the credit cards she'd seen earlier, a few business cards. No photos, no phone numbers of lovers, just the bare essentials. Very businesslike.

The sex had been businesslike as well. She sensed he was holding back. Maybe he was married, despite the lack of a ring.

Arna Kerr flushed the toilet and ran the water, purposely making enough noise so he could hear and stir if he was awake. She cracked the door to see, but he was still lying motionless on the bed.

Reaching for the light, she caught a glimpse of herself in the mirror. Arna didn't like to see herself naked. Being naked meant being without defenses.

That was what sex was, wasn't it?

She turned off the light and tiptoed into the room, went to the bed, and ran her fingers across the side of his face, tickling his ear and neck. He didn't move. Between the wine and the sex, he was totally out.

She went back around to the other side of the bed and picked up her underwear. Pulling on her panties, she went to the bureau and eased open the drawers. The top one was empty; the bottom held a pair of pants and a sweater. She slipped her hand in and checked: nothing.

There were more clothes in the drawer to the right. Underwear—silk boxers—a soft, thick T-shirt, socks. A pair of jeans.

In the closet, she found a leather briefcase and a suiter. These she took, one at a time, into the bathroom so she could search them thoroughly. The suitcase was empty, except for some tissues and a disposable razor. The briefcase had four yellow folders, some pens, and two pieces of paper that had addresses and phone numbers, all in Bologna. At least two belonged to galleries, and from what she knew of the locations she guessed the others were galleries as well.

Wouldn't a man like this have a laptop with him, or a PDA? If so, it wasn't in the luggage. She put everything back the way she found it, then searched some more. Finally satisfied that her lover was at least roughly who he said he was, she got dressed to go.

Arna Kerr hesitated at the door. There would be no possibility of seeing him ever again.

No?

No.

Outside, she saw someone in a car half a block from the hotel. He seemed to be looking at her. But then she saw a woman coming along the street behind her, crossing to the car—he'd been waiting for a girlfriend.

Well, she thought to herself, that was a nice diversion. Now it's time to get back to work.

Ferguson gave Arna Kerr ten minutes to change her mind and come back, then pulled on his pants and a sweatshirt and crossed the hall to the safe room where he'd left his gear. Inside, he powered up his laptop and entered the surveillance program, checking to make sure she wasn't down in the lobby. Then he turned on his radio and asked the others what was going on.

"Looks like she's taking a midnight tour of the city," said Guns.

"Going back to her hotel?"

"Doesn't look like it. Walking to the east. Maybe she's got another date."

"Jeez, I would've thought I wore her out." Ferguson pulled out his map, trying to psych out where she was going. "She might be trying to make sure she's not being followed," he said finally. "Be careful."

"We don't need you to tell us our jobs," snapped Thera.

"I'll try to remember that," said Ferguson, reaching for his shoes.

The more Arna Kerr walked, the more she sensed someone was following her. And yet, whether she turned suddenly or double-backed or used the mirror in her compact case, she couldn't see anyone.

Subconsciously I'm expecting to be punished for having sex, she told herself. Like a schoolgirl who's stayed out late.

The night had turned cold. Arna Kerr circled the block twice more; finally, failing to see anyone—and yet still not entirely free of the sensation of being watched—she went to the parking garage of the Hotel Borgia and found the small Ford she'd rented earlier in the day. She slipped the key into the trunk and opened the lid. Reaching to the side, she checked the small motion sensor, making sure the trunk hadn't been opened. Then she took out the backpack, reset the alarm with her key code, and checked the interior of the car.

Upstairs in the hotel, she mussed up the bed in her room, and then she slipped out, this time taking the stairs to the lobby. Before going back out she pulled an American-style baseball cap over her head, tucking her hair up until it was hidden. The security cameras at the outside door would see her, but her face would stay in the shadows.

Outside, Arna Kerr walked quickly to the piazza three blocks away. When she reached it, she pulled a laser measuring device from her pocket, then stood against the wall and began taking the measurements she needed. She recorded the measurements on a small voice recorder, adding Ferguson's driver's license number.

It would take her an hour to get the measurements, and another half hour to check the security systems on the street. The rest of what she had to do could easily wait until daytime.

Plenty of time to go back to Ferguson's hotel and slip back into bed with him.

A foolish thought, she told herself, pocketing the laser and walking to the next piazza.

Ferguson grabbed hold of the portico's smooth stone pillar and pulled himself upward, wedging the sides of his sneakers against the stone and shimmying to the top of the archway. Bologna was filled with porticos and covered walkways: a climber's paradise.

His grip slipped as he scrambled up onto the fake balustrade of the building. Ferguson grabbed the side of the window above and pushed himself up, trying to regain some balance. The building rose several more stories, and the climbing would be relatively easy—the blocks were spaced almost like ladders in a decorative pattern at the corner of the building—but first he had to get by the windows on the second floor. Fortunately the Bolognese—or at least *these* Bolognese—believed in sleeping with their windows open; Ferguson was able to get a grip between the window and the ledge and then swing his legs across to the next. A few minutes later, he was on top of the building.

Manually adjusting the magnification on his lightweight night glasses, Ferguson scanned the block, trying to see where Arna Kerr had gone. He spotted the light from her laser device before he saw her; when he finally saw her he thought she was being targeted by the infrared laser sight on a gun.

His heart jerked, his impulse to help. Then he realized that she was the one with the laser, and that she was taking measurements—maybe distances for a sniper. Ferguson settled down against the tiles, watching her continue her work.

Pretty, but not as beautiful as Thera. Thera had an attraction that other women couldn't match.

Ferguson leaned back as Arna Kerr began walking up the street in his direction.

"She's moving," he said into the radio as she passed. Then he yawned.

"Tired, huh?" said Guns.

"She wore me out." Ferguson laughed, then went to find a place to climb down.

SARATOV, RUSSIA

Artur Rostislawitch set the culture dish down next to the microscope, then reached for the tray with the slides. He could feel his hands starting to tremble inside the thick rubber gloves that were built into the protective glass case enclosing his work area.

Rostislawitch's nervousness had nothing to do with the bacteria he was examining, even though the dish contained an extremely deadly and contagious form of E. coli—so dangerous, in fact, that the amount in the dish could kill hundreds of thousands if judiciously deployed. Handling it through the sealed work area, Rostislawitch knew he would not come into direct contact with it. Indeed, one of the bacteria's assets was that it was relatively safe to handle if certain precautions were taken. Placed in a sealed glass container and suspended in the proper growth medium, the bacteria was essentially inert.

Rostislawitch was nervous because he intended on taking some of the material out of the lab. Getting the bacteria to this workstation without arousing suspicion had been difficult; he'd had to make it appear as if it were a harmless form of E. coli rather than the superbug he had created some years before. Creating a false paper trail, preparing the transit vessels, establishing plausible alibis, studying the security system—he had worked for weeks to get ready. Now he needed five more minutes' worth of patience until the cameras watching the lab went off-line before he could proceed. The video system went off-line every Tuesday at exactly 4:45 a.m. while the main computer that ran it backed itself up automatically. That would give him a ten-minute window to take the material without being seen.

Rostislawitch pretended to be studying a specimen, twitching in his seat. He'd waited so long for this day; surely he could wait for a few more minutes.

He rehearsed what he would do—separate two grams of the material, insert it into the medium dishes he'd positioned on the left. Return the material to its safe. Dispose of the other dishes by putting them into the incinerator bin.

Put everything away. Go downstairs, retrieve the dishes from the bin, which he had disabled earlier.

Remove his ID from the security lock. Punch the sequence to erase it.

All within fifteen minutes.

After that—the train, the conference in Bologna, the Iranian. Freedom.

Rostislawitch knew he could do it. He had rehearsed it several times.

He glanced at the clock. Four more minutes.

10

Arna Kerr didn't go back to her hotel until close to eleven a.m. Since she didn't sleep, the team didn't sleep. It didn't bother Ferguson, but Guns' eyes were sagging when they met at the Cafe Apollo just down the block. Thera felt stiff and was noticeably cranky. Rankin just frowned at everyone, one hand over his ear. He was monitoring the bugged transmissions from Arna Kerr's hotel room, listening to the capture from the mike he'd planted on the opposite roof. All he could hear was the sound of drawers being slammed and then the shower being started in the bath.

"So she takes the measurements of three public squares, and visits three different buildings belonging to the University of Bologna," said Guns, trying to prop his eyes open with a long sip of coffee. "What's the target?"

"Movie star," said Thera. "The university is hosting a film festival next month. She went to a theater."

"Who kills movie stars?" said Rankin.

"There's too much time in between," said Ferguson. "It has to be within a few days. Maybe even tomorrow. The cars were rented for two weeks."

"I think he's going after some Italian politician," said Rankin. "Maybe the mayor."

"T Rex costs too much money to bump off a mayor," said Ferguson. "Besides, nobody takes politicians seriously in Italy."

"Like you know how much he charges, right?" said Rankin.

"Has to be a lot if he's got an advance man. Last I heard, taking down a CIA officer cost a million."

"I'll do it for half," said Rankin, locking eyes with Ferguson. "Free, if I can pick the target."

Ferguson laughed.

"All the spots she checked out were tourist spots," said Thera.

"Not all," said Guns. "There was the university art building."

"Maybe some kid who flunked out of the university figures he got a bad deal," said Rankin.

Ferguson put his coffee cup down as the waiter approached with a fresh one.

"Why don't they just refill the cup?" said Guns.

"The dishwasher's a union guy and gets paid on a per-cup rate," said Ferguson.

"Did Corrigan get anything from the fingerprints?" asked Rankin.

"Nada," said Thera. "They were narrowing down the credit card information when I last talked to him, but they hadn't come up with anything significant. They have that address in Stockholm, but nothing else."

"How does T Rex contact her?" asked Guns.

Thera shook her head.

Rankin realized the shower had been turned off in the room and pressed his hand against his ear. He heard some shuffling, and then Arna Kerr began speaking.

"It's Italian," Rankin said, handing the earphone to Ferguson.

"She's getting a taxi to the airport," Ferguson told them, getting up. "Pardon me while I go bid her a tearful good-bye."

11

BOLOGNA, ITALY

Arna Kerr was just putting her bag into the back of the cab when she heard Bob Ferguson calling her.

"You," she said, before even turning to look at him.

"They say you're checking out."

He took her in his arms, kissing her gently. She resisted, but only for a moment.

"On your way over to my hotel, I hope," said Ferguson.

"I have to go."

"Didn't sell enough drugs?"

"Plenty."

"Stick around, you'll sell some more. Maybe I'll buy a few."

He really was cute, she thought, cute enough to change her plans—a few more hours here wouldn't bother anyone.

Or better, she could suggest they go down to Rome, or somewhere farther south, some little village somewhere that was still warm and sunny.

She had to go. He was too tempting.

"Duty calls," she said, pushing him away gently.

"It's almost lunchtime. Come get something to eat."

"I have to go. I'm sorry." She put her hand on the car door.

"A little *vino*?"

"*No, grazie.*"

"Your Italian's getting better."

"*Prego.* Another time, Bob." She started to get into the cab.

"Well, give me your card and tell where you're going to be," said Ferguson.

Arna Kerr hesitated. "I don't think so."

"No?" Ferguson ran his hand along the back of her arm. Even though she was wearing a winter coat, she felt a tingle all the way through to her spine. "Come on. Hang around."

"If you give me your card," she said, "maybe I'll call you."

"Didn't I give you one already?" Ferguson asked.

She cocked her hand slightly, gesturing that if he had, she had lost it. Ferguson pulled one from his pocket.

"Call me," he said, sliding her the card. "It's a service. But they'll get in touch."

She took the card and smiled, then got in the cab. Ferguson gave it a friendly pat as it left—placing a small global positioning device on its rear fender to make it easier to follow.

12

Thomas Ciello paced back and forth in his small office on the second floor of Building 24-442. It was a relatively large office—thirteen paces by eleven and a quarter paces—and he had arranged the furniture so that he could stride in more or less a straight line. Building 24-442 was primarily located underground, so being on the second floor meant he had no windows. But this wasn't a drawback as far as Thomas Ciello was concerned. On the contrary. The very blankness of the walls helped him focus.

Thomas Ciello was the chief analyst for Special Demands, a somewhat nebulous job title that matched his somewhat nebulous job description. In theory, he liaisoned between the team and the CIA's "regular" research and analysis side, digging up background and other information necessary for missions. The reality was considerably more complicated, as Ciello often found himself gathering information on his own, through whatever source he could think of.

But analysts liked to say that the problem wasn't so much obtaining information as making sense of it. Ciello was living that saying right now, as he tried to puzzle out what Arna Kerr's work in Bologna meant.

She'd left vehicles and taken rooms in several parts of the center city; obviously T Rex's target was there. Most interestingly, she'd taken measurements of three public squares in the city of Bologna. From what the First Team had reported, she had documented the distances between the buildings as well as their heights.

Why?

A sniper would want to know distances. But Ciello thought it was unlikely a sniper would plan an assassination in the public squares; the buildings that surrounded them were mostly open to the public, which meant there would be a lot of people who might see him coming in and out. It would certainly be possible—Ciello had to admit that T Rex might know much more about the buildings and the business of assassination than he did—but he thought it unlikely.

Besides the public squares, Arna Kerr had visited three university school buildings, math, computer science, and the Art School Annex, a temporary building being used while the main art buildings were renovated. None of them seemed likely to attract the sort of high-profile victim T Rex was generally hired to target.

After a search of their faculty and student lists failed to turn up anything interesting, Ciello had set out to compile a list of conferences and lectures they were hosting. Getting information on the mathematics school was easy; it posted a calendar online. But the public lectures it listed weren't exactly major hints: "The Evolution of Euclid" and "String Theory" were the highlights. "Computer Science" was equally esoteric; the focus seemed to be on graphic compression routines and video. The Art School Annex listed no guest lectures or conferences until after the Christmas break, when "Fresh Thoughts on Medieval Brushstroke Techniques" would start the new year off with a bang.

Ciello put his thought process on hold and lay down on the floor. The ceiling tiles had a very interesting pattern. Probably they involved a code, but not being a cryptologist, he couldn't decipher it.

That wasn't an excuse, though, was it? Cryptologists were just mathematicians, and everyone knew mathematicians were crazy.

"Thomas, what are you doing?"

Ciello looked up and saw Debra Wu, his executive assistant, standing by the door. She made a show of putting her hands over her dress, as if he were trying to look up it. A faint odor of perfume wafted from her. It tickled his nose and he stifled a sneeze.

"Mr. Slott needs to talk to you," said Wu, shaking her head. "He's having a conference call with Ms. Alston."

Wu continued to talk, but Ciello had stopped listening. His mind was back at the piazzas.

Arna Kerr was making a scale model of them.

"Thomas, are you listening to me? Mr. Slott needs that report. Mr. Slott. The DDO. Your boss's boss. Thomas?"

"Uh-huh."

T Rex's preparer was measuring the space between the buildings, which was another way of saying she was measuring the air.

Air.

Hadn't the UFO sighting in San Diego in 1953 involved some sort of similar measuring devices? No one had figured out what that meant, either.

Bad example.

In his spare time, Thomas Ciello was working on a book that would be the definitive study of UFOs in the twentieth century. So far, he hadn't worked on a case where UFOs were part of the solution—though there was always hope.

"Thomas, are you going to have something or not?" she said finally.

"Don't know," mumbled Ciello.

She turned in disgust. Her sharp twist sent a fresh whiff of perfume in Ciello's direction.

"Oh!" said Ciello loudly. "That's why she took the measurements!"

"What?" demanded Wu.

"Now I get it."

"You know who T Rex is?"

"Of course not. But I know what they're up to."

Wu waited for the answer as Ciello jumped to his feet and started pumping his keyboard.

"Well?" she said finally.

"Perfume."

13

Guns picked Ferguson up in the car two blocks away.

"Ferg, you're slipping," Guns told him. "You couldn't even get her phone number."

"I couldn't even get her e-mail address," said Ferguson in mock amazement. "Next time you take the romance angle and I'll watch."

Guns laughed. Ferguson could always be counted on for a joke.

Rankin and Thera were on Vespas ahead, following the cab as it headed out to the airport.

Ferguson took out his sat phone and called the Cube.

"Yes, Bob?" said Lauren DiCapri, the relief desk person.

"Hey, beautiful, what happened? Corrigan went home?"

"Something about working thirty-six hours straight got to him."

"Tough sitting in that chair, huh?" Ferguson leaned back in the seat. "You tracking us?"

"Of course." All four of the ops had GPS sending units in their satellite phones, showing the Cube where they were.

"Find Arna Kerr's flight yet?"

"The flight for the round-trip ticket she bought doesn't leave for another two days," said Lauren. "So if she's going to the airport, she used another credit card for the flight."

"And different ID," said Ferguson.

"Maybe, maybe not. We're not working with the Italians, remember? I don't have direct access to any of the booking systems, let alone their security lists. I'm working with the credit card companies."

"How could I forget?"

Slott, the CIA Deputy Director in charge of covert action, had told Ferguson in the briefing that they wouldn't work with Italy because of the rendition case. Indeed, Ferguson had a relatively low regard for the Italian intelligence agencies and preferred not to get them involved, either. If he got T Rex—*when* he got T Rex—the plan was to knock him out, bundle him in the trunk of a car, and take him directly to the U.S. air base at Aviano. He'd be in a federal lockup, waiting for a grand jury to indict him, within twenty-four hours.

"Listen, Lauren, I gave Arna Kerr my card. Maybe she'll call; maybe she'll send an e-mail or check the Web site."

"Don't worry. We're ready."

"Good. I wouldn't want to miss a date."

The thin wall separating caution and paranoia had melted by the time Arna Kerr cleared the ticket counter. A kind of panic regularly accompanied this stage of a job—when the fieldwork was done but before she returned to Sweden and safety.

Arna Kerr forced herself to remain calm as she went through gate security, fiddling with her hair and fussing with her makeup to hide her jitters. Once through, she went into a washroom and checked her bags and clothes for a bug or tracking device, by going over them first with a detector and then painstakingly by hand, visually inspecting everything. She'd done this already at the hotel before leaving—and also examined the footage on the two digital cameras she'd left running on the desk—yet she still felt as if she had missed something.

She told herself she was overcompensating for spending the night with the Irishman.

God, what a mistake.

Arna Kerr leaned back against the toilet stall and pulled out his card. She started to throw it into the toilet, then stopped herself. She'd already had the license checked by e-mailing the number to one of her associates; a few speeding violations were the only blemish on the Irishman's record. But he deserved more thorough scrutiny.

Scrutiny? Or did she really want to contact him?

She couldn't.

Her body nearly trembled, remembering how they'd made love.

No, she told herself, dropping the card in the toilet. Not worth the risk.

Thera waited until Arna Kerr's plane had taxied to the runway before she left the terminal. Outside, the air smelled wet, heavy with moisture, as if it were going to snow. Thera zipped her jacket tighter. She was glad Arna Kerr was gone. Maybe now she could get some sleep.

"Hey," said Ferguson, appearing beside her. "You with us?"

Thera jumped. "Jesus, Ferg. You scared me."

"You have to pay attention to where you are," he told her. He was serious.

"I am."

"You were daydreaming. Somebody could have snuck up on you like I did. Are you being followed?"

Thera, embarrassed that she had let her guard down, said nothing.

"You're not," added Ferguson. "But keep your head in the game, all right? We're just at the start of this."

ACT II

The face of things a frightful image bears,
And present death in various forms appears.

—Virgil, *The Aeneid* (Dryden translation)

1

In some alternate universe, Corrine Alston was perpetually ten minutes ahead of schedule. Her habitual punctuality impressed friends and influenced enemies. Her hair always looked perfectly groomed, and her stockings never ran.

But that was an alternate universe. In this one, Corrine was lucky if she managed to stay within fifteen minutes of the bulleted times her secretary prepared for her. As the President's personal counsel, Corrine found her days filled with appointments, phone conferences, lunch and dinner meetings, and—on occasion—real legal work. She was three weeks past-due for a haircut, and finding time to buy a new pair of panty hose could take a month.

"They're waiting," said her secretary, Teri Gatins, as Corrine rushed into her office for the ten a.m. conference call. Corrine's day had started with a phone conference at six; the half-filled cup of coffee she held in her hand was her breakfast.

"Thanks," said Corrine. She dropped her briefcase at the side of her desk, spun the chair around, and picked up the phone.

CIA Deputy Director of Operations Daniel Slott was already talking.

"It's a theory. I don't know if it's a good one," said Slott.

"What's that?" said Corrine.

"I was just explaining that we have a theory about what T Rex is up to in Bologna."

"Hey, Counselor. How's the weather at the White House?" said Bob Ferguson.

"They say it may snow," answered Corrine.

"Gee, wish I was there."

"Could you please recap the situation, Dan? What is the theory?" she asked.

"A gas or other agent being dispersed in a public square," said Slott. "T Rex's advance person took measurements of three piazzas near the center of Bologna."

"Dispersing gas? T Rex is supposed to be an assassin. That sounds more like a terrorist attack."

"Admittedly," answered Slott. "But it's not that out of line for him. T Rex likes to kill."

Besides Slott and Ferguson, the commander of the First Team's military force, Col. Charles Van Buren, was on the line, as was CIA Director Thomas Parnelles. Corrine had been appointed by the President to oversee Special Demands; while the members of the First Team still worked for either the CIA or the military, they answered to her as well. It was an awkward arrangement, intended by the President to give him tight control over the Special Operations force, while at the same time insulating him from it if something went wrong.

"Has this T Rex character used gas to kill someone before?" asked Colonel Van Buren.

"Everything but," said Slott. "He's used bombs, a mortar shell, a rifle, and at least twice a pistol from very close range."

Slott explained that the person they believed was T Rex's preparer or advance man—actually a woman who was using the name Arna Kerr—had taken measurements of three piazzas in the center of the old city. From that, one of their analysts had deduced that the attacks would take place there. Kerr's measurements were only necessary, said the analyst, if T Rex was planning to use a chemical gas; in that case, the killer would be considering how much gas to use to guarantee a kill. The size, wind pattern, and fact that the area was open argued strongly against an aerosol attack—in layman's terms, the sort of attack that would be made with biological weapons—but a quick-acting chemical gas, laid on thickly enough, would be deadly. The analyst thought that the fact that the assassination would look like a terrorist attack was intentional, since it would divert attention from the actual intent of the crime.

"We're looking at two weeks as the outside end of the time frame," said Slott, "because that's how long she rented the vehicles for. But in the three assassinations we've connected her with, T Rex has shown up much sooner—within forty-eight hours."

"This is a wrong turn," said Ferguson. "It doesn't fit with T Rex."

"If you have another theory, I'm all ears," said Slott.

"A bomb I could see. But gas? Too many things left to chance."

"He doesn't care how many people die, as long as his target is one of them," said Parnelles.

"Yeah, but he does care that the target dies. Gas is too iffy for that. Too many variables."

"Why else would she take the measurements then?" asked Slott.

"Maybe it's for a bomb; maybe he's going to use a sniper rifle; maybe T Rex just gives her a lot of things to do so she can't figure out what's up," said Ferguson. "We don't end up using half the intelligence you guys dig up for us."

While Slott defended the theory, Corrine considered the implications. If the attack was made in a public square, many people would be injured, if not killed.

"We're going to have to tell the Italians what's going on," said Corrine. "We're going to have to tell them what we have."

"That will ruin everything," said Parnelles.

"If they had information about 9-11 and didn't tell us, what would we think of them as allies?" Corrine said.

"We can stop T Rex," said Slott. "Right, Ferg?"

"If we figure out who he is."

"The President is going to have to make the call," said Corrine. "He has to have the final say here."

Fifteen minutes later, Corrine knocked on the door to the Oval Office and then went in, waiting while Pres. Jonathon McCarthy finished up a phone call with a congressman who was opposing Mc-Carthy's health-care reform package. The chief of staff, Fred Green-berg, stood near the desk, shifting his weight from foot to foot, his nervous energy a sharp contrast to the President's laid-back country-boy expression.

"Well," said the President finally, drawing out the word in the over-pronounced Southern style he liked to use when making a point. "I do hope you will consider my points, Congressman, just as seriously as I am going to consider yours. And you know I take them *very* seriously. . . . You have a good day yourself."

The President put the phone back on the hook.

"I've owned mules that weren't half as stubborn," he said.

"We're sunk," said Greenberg.

"Now don't go giving up the ship when we have only just spotted the iceberg," said McCarthy. "We still have a few moments to steer the rudder and close the compartment doors. Wouldn't you say so, Miss Alston?"

"On a difficult issue like this, it may take some time to win over votes," said Corrine. "Perhaps you should delay the vote."

"Spoken like a true lawyer, used to billing by the hour." McCarthy laughed. "You have something you need me to address?"

"Yes." Corrine glanced at Greenberg.

"I have to go answer a couple of e-mails," said the chief of staff. "I'll be right back."

When McCarthy and Corrine were alone, he folded his arms and leaned back in his chair.

"We are going to lose this one, I'm afraid," he told Corrine. "We just do not have the votes. But sometimes it's important to keep the horse in the race."

"Sometimes."

"What would you think of talking to Senator Segriff for me about this? He might be persuaded to come around. He is not an unreasonable man."

"Wouldn't it be better coming from you?"

"Sometimes a young filly can succeed where an old craggy nag will fail."

"So I'm a filly now, am I?"

McCarthy laughed and sat upright in his chair. "Deah, if I offended you, well then, I am just going to have to apologize. I assure you that I do not think you are a horse, young or otherwise."

"I hope not."

"Now what is so important that my chief of staff has to answer his e-mail personally, which I believe he has not done in six or seven months."

"Italy and Special Demands." Corrine gave him a brief summary of the phone conference.

"If the assassin is planning an attack in a public square, we have to notify the Italians," she told him. "We can't let an attack like that go off without warning them to take steps. If the situation were reversed, we'd want blood."

McCarthy tore off the top page of the notepad he had on his desk and rose. "I don't suppose Tom Parnelles likes the idea very much."

"He didn't voice his opinion."

"That would be the answer right there, I suspect." McCarthy crumpled the paper and tossed it into the basket.

"Ferguson—the lead op on the First Team—is worried that if we bring the Italians in on it, we'll tip off the assassin he's supposed to capture," said Corrine. "He argued against it."

"I'm sure Mr. Parnelles and Mr. Ferguson are on the same page on this," said McCarthy. "There is an argument to be made there."

"It's overweighed. Think of a hundred people dying in Minnesota or Omaha because the Italians wanted to capture a person they thought killed one of their intelligence officers. We wouldn't stand for it."

"No. We wouldn't. This would make the rendition flap look like a Sunday school debate over the devil's favorite lie."

Corrine nodded.

"The Director feels personally responsible for his officer's murder," continued the President. "Do you remember the incident, Corrine? No, actually you wouldn't, as it was just before you came on board," said McCarthy, answering his own question. "You hadn't joined the intelligence committee staff yet, had you? Well, Mr. Parnelles had just been appointed as chief of the CIA when his man died, and he took it almost as a personal insult. I believe the officer who was killed had had some association with him earlier as well. I believe he may have worked for him at one time, if memory serves."

"I think he feels responsible for his people," said Corrine. "I think that's natural."

"Yes, dear, that is natural, but you see, there are sometimes more important things to consider."

"Yes, sir."

"Tell the Italians. Find a way to do it while preserving our operation. And please, take care of this personally."

"Yes, Mr. President."

McCarthy drummed his fingers on his desk. "The wording on the Iran finding—have you finished it?"

"It's ready," she said, mentally changing gears. "We're not on the strongest grounds, Jonathon."

"Hopefully we won't need it. Secretary Steele continues to assure me that the Iranians are about to sign the treaty and give up their weapons, just as North Korea has done. It is a solution I much prefer. I just wish that the Secretary of State would get them to move with a little more *alacrity*."

Several weeks before, McCarthy had decided that the Iranian nuclear program had progressed to a point where it would have to be dealt with decisively. While his administration had been working behind the scenes to get the Iranians to abandon their program, Iran's Sunni neighbors, especially Saudi Arabia and Egypt, had concluded that they needed nuclear weapons to counterbalance their traditional Shiite enemies and had secretly begun to work on a bomb together. If they developed one, McCarthy believed, the odds of nuclear war in the Middle East or of terrorists obtaining the weapons would be astronomical.

The President had therefore decided to force the issue—he would offer aid to Iran and a full normalization of relations if they dropped the project. If they didn't, he would destroy the infrastructure that supported it.

Estimates by the CIA indicated that the program was still vulnerable to coordinated air strikes but would only remain so for a few more months; the President had set an internal deadline for an agreement at the end of the month, a week away. He'd asked Corrine to draw up a legal argument supporting a first strike. "Something a little more thoughtful than might makes right," he'd said. McCarthy greatly preferred a peaceful settlement, since an attack would bring very serious and not necessarily predictable repercussions; nonetheless, a nuclear arms race in the Middle East was an even worse choice.

"I can have the draft on your desk in an hour," Corrine said.

"No, no. I only want to make sure it's ready." Ever the poker player, McCarthy was thinking about using the finding as a way of forcing the Iranians to ante up—if they balked at Steele's proposal, he'd have the finding leaked to convince them he meant business.

And if that didn't work, then he'd have no alternative but to go ahead with the attack.

"Have you been following the situation in Iran?" McCarthy asked.

"Not as closely as I should," said Corrine. It was a defensive answer; she had actually been reading every report and briefing available.

"There continues to be resistance to the agreement, especially among the Revolutionary Guard. Talk of a coup."

"No one seems to think that's serious."

"Difficult to assess," said McCarthy.

He wasn't sure himself how seriously to take the rumors. Iran and its myriad political players remained largely an enigma.

"You'll have to excuse me, Miss Alston," he said, glancing at his watch. "It appears I am running late for my next appointment."

Already out of her chair, Corrine followed him to the door. The President reached for the handle, then paused.

"Your father was asking about you the other day, Corrine. He wanted to make sure you were getting your proper allotment of sleep. I told him you were, but I do not think he believed me."

"I'm getting plenty of sleep, Tom. He's just—you know Dad."

"Longer than you." McCarthy winked. "But perhaps we would do a better job of convincing him if the e-mails you sent to him did not bear time stamps indicating they were sent at three a.m. It weakens our case considerably, Counselor."

"Yes sir, Mr. President. I'll try to remember."

2

BOLOGNA, ITALY

Ferguson took a walk alone around the block after the conference call ended, working off some steam. The gas theory was a crock. Worse, they'd drifted into decision-by-committee territory; he wasn't supposed to do anything now until he heard from Corrine Alston.

Undoubtedly, she'd convince the President to notify the Italians, who would probably go apeshit and shut the whole town down. There'd be some cockeyed arrangement with the First Team acting as "consultants" or some such crap. T Rex would be smirking somewhere in the shadows.

Not only would he be tipped off here, but he'd realize that his operation had been compromised. If he was smart—and his track record suggested he was a genius—he'd tear it down and start from scratch. Arna Kerr would be out of work, and they'd spend years trying to find another lead.

Ferguson stopped into a café, and after a quick shot of espresso—for some reason the caffeine calmed him down—got back to work. The first thing to do was check out the university buildings Arna Kerr had gone to. They'd already planted video bugs in the foyers; he was interested in something else, something less obvious. He hoped he'd realize what it was when he saw it.

The art building was a large onetime mansion about a block off the Via Rizzoli. The place was being used as a temporary university building, but the choice was hardly haphazard. Though from the outside the building's dull brown blocks and gray cornices were overshadowed by the bright bricks of its neighbors, inside the place was as ornate as any palace. The walls of the entrance hallway were covered with marble; baroque-era statues flanked the thick red carpet that brought students and visitors inside. A large double stairway made of marble sat at the far end; its bronze banister was inlaid with gold. On the ceiling above, a bright faux sky featured cherubim amid its puffy clouds.

A security guard looked at Ferguson cross-eyed from a nearby archway as the op scouted around. Ferguson saw him and ambled over in his direction to ask, in English, if the man knew where Professore Pirello's classes were to be found. The guard told Ferguson in Italian that he was a security guard and not a member of the staff. Ferguson pretended not to understand and repeated the question. When he got roughly the same answer he thanked the guard profusely before walking past him into the main hallway.

Even in the corridor, the building's proportions gave it a regal feel. The walls had been recently restored and painted, their blue and gold pattern so vivid that it seemed to glow. The hall opened into another wide reception area, this one just as ornate as the one near the front entrance. A set of arched doorways led to a room decorated with late-Renaissance frescoes that ran all the way to the ceiling three stories above. Rather than a faux sky, the ceiling was covered in panels of what looked like gold leaf. It was actually a relatively new coat of paint, carefully applied within the lines of the original paper-thin panels; the genuine gold had been replaced sometime during the nineteenth century, when the owners had fallen on hard times.

Large carts of chairs were being wheeled into the room, and a crew was setting up a stage to the right. Ferguson wandered over and asked two of the workers what they were setting up for.

"They never tell us," said one of the men.

"Oh, I know what it's for," said another. "The genetics conference. Frankenstein will be here."

The man, an art student in his early twenties who moonlighted as a roustabout to support himself, began a diatribe about genetic mutation and man's inevitable decline. A large number of scientists from across the world were gathering to talk about using bacteria for man's good, said the student. It was clearly a disaster in the making.

"I thought this was an art school," said Ferguson.

The young man, himself an art student, sensed an ally, and gave Ferg a long diatribe in response, claiming that the school and the country were not serious about supporting its artists. His coworker rolled his eyes and went back to work.

"And the conference starts tonight?" asked Ferguson.

"There's a brochure on the bulletin board in the second-floor lounge," said the student. He saw his supervisor coming and decided to get back to work. "Read it, brother," he said, walking away. "You'll be surprised what they're up to. Frankenstein in a test tube."

3

When Jack Corrigan had first been offered the position with Special Demands, he'd seen it as a shortcut in his overall plan to advance to the upper levels of the intelligence establishment, where he hoped to become the boss of either the Defense Information Agency—his preference—or the CIA itself. He still thought Special Demands was a wise career move, but now realized it was not without its thorns.

Bob Ferguson being the main one.

"Ferguson can't accept *anything* I tell him," Corrigan complained when Lauren DiCapri briefed him when he returned to work. "Why would T Rex be going after a scientist?"

"Ferg didn't say he thought that was the target," said Lauren. "He just said this conference might be significant and we should get the list."

"And who's going to be paying T Rex? Greenpeace?" Corrigan scanned the information on the conference. The topic was bacteria in the food chain and how they could be bred to combat spoilage.

"No fricking way anyone here is going to be important enough to spend a million bucks on bumping off," Corrigan told Lauren, sliding the folder Lauren had given him back across the desk top. "I'm with Ciello. It's some sort of gas attack. Tell Ferguson this is a dead end."

"Ciello went ahead and did some background on the people attending the conference," said Lauren, pushing the papers back. "There's one person that's interesting. Check the last page."

Frowning, Corrigan leafed through the documents. The final page contained a single paragraph on a man named Artur Rostisla-witch. Until three years before, he had been a top scientist with the Russian Federal Research Administration, on loan to a quasi-private laboratory outside of Moscow known to be used by the government for research into germ warfare. There had been some sort of internal shake-up; supposedly Rostislawitch no longer conducted primary research.

"All right, so big deal," said Corrigan, handing the briefing paper back. "He's not working with them anymore. This says he's teaching."

"Ferg thinks that may be a cover," said Lauren. "He wants more information on him."

"You discussed this with Ferguson already?"

"Of course."

"What do you mean, 'of course'? You should have waited until I came in."

Lauren clamped her teeth together. Corrigan was efficient and generally reasonable, but he had a very strict interpretation of the chain of command. He was the *lead* desk officer; she was relief—which to him meant he was the boss, she was whale shit.

"Really, Lauren, you should have told me."

"The conference starts with a reception in two hours. I didn't know when you were getting in," she told him.

"You could have called me at home."

"Right," said Lauren. She took the briefing paper. "I have to get back to the desk."

4

BOLOGNA, ITALY

Artur Rostislawitch frowned at himself in the mirror, turning his chin slowly as he inspected the whiskers he'd just shaven. Even as a young man, he'd never had a particularly smooth face, but the worries of the past few years had dug deep lines around his chin, and pulled out his cheeks so that he looked like an emaciated walrus. That made it difficult to shave closely, and there were still a few lines of hair caught in the furrows. He turned on the water and refilled the basin, deciding to try again. He wanted to look good tonight, even though he wasn't meeting the Iranian until tomorrow.

What if someone believed the story the Iranian had told him to tell, and really did offer him a job—a real job doing research?

He fantasized about it, thinking he might actually be offered a job. He saw himself leaving the city and immediately setting up somewhere—Switzerland, maybe, or even Taiwan, slightly away from the mainstream but still in a legitimate position. It could still happen, he told himself as he lathered on the foam; a scientist with his knowledge was a valuable commodity.

But Rostislawitch knew the truth. He was fifty, and Russian, and even the people who didn't know the specifics of his past weren't likely to take a chance on a scientist whose résumé was nebulous—let alone knowingly hire a scientist who'd worked with weaponized bacteria. The public hysteria about genetic engineering would make him a positive liability to any big company that hired him, even as a janitor: he'd be proof positive that they were out to poison the food chain.

The world was an ironic place—very Russian, Rostislawitch thought. One's past channeled him into a difficult future.

Twenty-five years ago, Artur Rostislawitch had been the equivalent of a superstar in his field, a young prodigy who had found a way to easily induce mutations in a select group of bacteria. His work for the Defense Ministry had earned him not just an apartment in Moscow and a dacha on the Black Sea but his own research lab about fifty miles outside of the capital. Two years later, his work had progressed to the point where a special bunker had been built to contain it; completely underground, the facility had elaborate protocols and security equipment not so much to keep people out but the bacteria being developed there in. The only unfortunate thing about the facility was its location in northeastern Chechnya, a vile place in Rostislawitch's opinion, though the lack of any real possibility of culture or entertainment did help focus him on his work.

He'd celebrated his thirtieth birthday alone, toasting himself in his lab room with a large cake and a bottle of vodka. He'd felt a bit sorry for himself. His wife was at the dacha, but a pending visit by Gorbachev to the lab meant Rostislawitch couldn't get away long enough to visit her. He'd gotten pretty drunk that night—so drunk in fact that he had spent the next day in bed, trying to overcome his hangover.

Little did he know that that would be the highlight of his career.

The discoveries that had come so easily in his twenties had already started to thin out. The strands of bacteria that he had produced—members of the same family as those that cause botulism—proved insufficiently hardy; slight variations in temperature killed them, making them unsuitable for use in weapons. And since his work was designed to produce bacteria that could be used as weapons in a war against the U.S., this was a major problem.

Still, he persevered. He found a family of bacteria that seemed promising—B^{589-A}. It was uncharacteristically difficult to replicate, unfortunately, because of a quirk in its genetic structure. That took even longer to solve.

In the meantime, the Soviet Union ceased being the Soviet Union. Gorbachev was replaced by Yeltsin—a boob who had Rostislawitch's dacha and apartment taken away. Biological weapons, never as glamorous as nuclear bombs or energy rays, fell further out of favor.

The war in Chechnya was an utter disaster; at the end, Rostislawitch and his staff fled barely twelve hours ahead of a rebel assault. As a safety precaution, he had ordered that the bunker be blown up, along with all the stores of B^{589-A}. Tears came to his eyes as the ground reverberated with the first explosion; he watched as the earth rolled with the shock waves, dust rising like steam as the plastique did its work sixty feet below. By the time he boarded the canvas-topped UAZ jeep the military had sent to evacuate him, Rostislawitch was bawling like a baby.

For eight months, he did absolutely nothing. He and his wife had moved to St. Petersburg and lived with his brother and his family. Ironically, he looked on that period as now one of the happiest of his life. He and his wife had renewed not so much their marriage but their friendship; Olga went everywhere with him, to all of the ministries as he applied for funds to resume his research. She remained faithful and encouraging, supportive in a way that she'd had little chance to show in his years of success.

An image of her came to him now—Olga with his two nephews, minding them while his brother and sister-in-law went out to the store. The boys were three and four, a handful but in a good way. They called Rostislawitch "Uncle Baboon" because he could pretend to be one so well. Olga would hide her grin as they begged him to play.

It was only after Yeltsin died that Rostislawitch had found his way back to the research. The lab was a poor one, outside Saratov. The security was a joke, and the equipment was worse. He was lucky, however, to have two decent assistants, and slowly began re-creating his original research.

And then, five years ago, after a long, long struggle, they had made a breakthrough with $B^{589\text{-}A}$, creating a mutation that allowed the bacteria to breed five times as fast as other members of the family. This made it virtually impossible to stop. Anyone infected would begin to die within twelve hours; by the time the symptoms were seen, it would be far too late to treat.

Several problems remained to be solved before the bacteria could be actually used as a weapon, but they were mechanical things, in Rostislawitch's opinion. He stood on the brink of a great success, one that would revolutionize warfare.

And then the roof caved in.

One afternoon, Rostislawitch was summoned to Moscow without explanation. He was driven to the Kremlin, and surprised—stunned, really—to be brought into the presence of the Premier, Mikal Fradkov, the second most important man in the Russian government after the President. Rostislawitch felt flattered, and stood trembling. When Fradkov began to speak, Rostislawitch was so nervous that he didn't comprehend the Premier's few sentences.

Suddenly Rostislawitch realized that Fradkov was very angry.

"What kind of man are you?" Fradkov demanded.

Rostislawitch looked at him in amazement. "Just a Russian."

"A Russian who wishes to doom mankind."

Rostislawitch had long considered the consequences of his work; he knew very well that his creation was designed to kill indiscriminately and in great numbers. But he considered it nothing more than what a nuclear bomb would do. The Americans, he was sure, were working along much the same lines. Russia needed its own weapon as a defense.

Unsure what to say, Rostislawitch began to explain that he was only following orders.

"Whose orders? What member of the government told you to do this work? The minister of defense? When did you last meet with him?"

Only then did Rostislawitch realize that he had somehow gotten himself into the middle of a political fight. He'd become a pawn in a struggle between Fradkov and the army.

Fradkov did not lose many battles at this stage of his career, and he did not lose this one. Rostislawitch's work had played a minuscule role in the trial used by Fradkov and his allies to punish the defense minister, but it was enough to effectively end Rostislawitch's career.

Worse, Olga became ill shortly after her husband's "audience" with the Russian Premier. Sick with the flu, she was taken to the local hospital in Saratov, where they were living practically under house arrest. At the hospital, she caught a much worse infection—a strain of streptococcus resistant to antibiotics. She died within a week.

In a final irony, the strain was one Rostislawitch had considered but rejected for use as a weapon some twenty years before.

Fradkov's campaign against the defense minister complete, the lab's funding was restored. Rostislawitch's project, however, was given short shrift. Supposedly newer ideas—one involved the bubonic plague, so how could that be new?—were in vogue, and researchers familiar with them received top priority. Rostislawitch, tainted forever by his political troubles, was shunted to the side. He was forced to take a job teaching introductory biology at a nearby college to earn money. The director of the lab was a friend of his, and so allowed him lab access, but only during off-hours. He had continued his work with E. coli B^{589-A}, keeping the strain alive, though by now no one else seemed to be much interested in it.

Except for the hour or two he spent in the lab each day, Dr. Rostislawitch hated life. Sometimes he thought of killing himself; other times he thought of killing a large number of people. He fantasized about killing Fradkov especially, until an airplane accident deprived him of the pleasure.

Then came the Iranian, with his offer. The Iranian didn't know exactly what he was asking for; apparently he had heard of Rostislawitch's work through Chechnyan friends who were fools and dullards. But to give the devil his credit, the Iranian sent a man to speak to him who did know what he was looking for, and who was intelligent enough to know that Rostislawitch could supply it.

And now he was here.

A new beginning. More like an old ending, a final gesture of payback to a world that had treated him so poorly. He had no doubt the material would be used. He wanted it to be.

He wished that weren't true. He wished he could feel something, anything. Then he might have something to live for.

Shaving done, Rostislawitch retrieved his white shirt and began buttoning it slowly, rehearsing his English so that he could make his job pitch. For just one night, he decided, he would make himself believe that it wasn't a cover story, or a fantasy, that he really did hope to get a legitimate job to put his skills to use. For just one night, for his dead wife's sake, he would believe in himself and a future that did not involve destruction and terrible agony, let alone revenge.

5

WASHINGTON, D.C.

Even though the State Department had emphasized that the meeting was not only important but time sensitive, the Italian ambassador's secretary claimed the earliest he could meet with Corrine was one p.m., and then only for ten minutes.

"Typical with the Italians," said Undersecretary of State Gene Lashley as they drove up to the ambassador's residence in suburban Washington. "My bet is that he doesn't get out of bed until then."

"I see."

"Mention that we're planning a reception at the embassy with free booze and women, they'll be all over it," Lashley said sarcastically as the State Department limo stopped at the front door. "They have a different set of priorities."

Corrine kept her thoughts, not particularly charitable, to herself as she followed Lashley into the residence.

"*Buon giorno, signor ambasciatore,*" said an Italian, gliding across the tiled foyer as Lashley entered. "The ambassador is just finishing up his business."

The Italian's eyes found Corrine.

"Ms. Alston? *Si?* Such a beautiful woman to be working as counsel to the President," continued the aide, who swept his hand to the side and bowed slightly at the waist. "Beauty and intelligence—America is a wonderful country."

"The ambassador's aide, Luigi Prima," said Lashley.

"Pleased to meet you," said Corrine, holding out her hand to shake.

Prima took it and raised it to his lips as he bowed still lower, kissing it. "So wonderful to meet you."

"He's a bit over-the-top, even for the Italians," said Lashley after Prima showed them to a study to wait for the ambassador. "But I imagine you get a lot of that."

"A lot of what?"

"Men fawning over you?"

"I really don't."

Lashley didn't believe it. The President's counsel—the daughter of McCarthy's closest friend—was a beautiful woman, pretty much what you'd expect for someone whose mother had been a movie actress. Corrine might be wearing a dark blue suit, plain on anyone else, yet on her it could have been an evening gown.

"Undersecretary Lashley, good to see you, my friend," said the Italian ambassador as he entered the room. Corrine and Lashley rose. Ambassador Rossi was a short man with jet-black hair combed straight back on his head. Like his aide, he was dressed in a perfectly tailored suit and exuded a slight scent of cologne. His walk was a strut, his head and chest jutting forward; he strode with confidence and just the slightest hint that he was in a hurry.

"Ms. Alston, the President's counsel, so nice to meet you," he said, taking her hand.

"Thank you." Corrine was relieved that he simply shook her hand.

"Maybe you will join us for lunch?" said the ambassador.

"I'm afraid I don't have the time," Corrine told him.

"A pity." The ambassador turned toward the door. "Bring some coffee please," he said, though it appeared no one was there.

"The reason we've come, Mr. Ambassador—," started Corrine.

"Wait now; you'll have some coffee first."

"I really don't want to waste your time," she said. "I know you're very busy."

"Ah." He waved his hand and sat down. "I am not busy for a representative of the President. Sit. Stay."

"It's a very grave matter," said Corrine. She gave a brief outline of the possible plot the CIA had discovered, leaving out any information about the operation that had discovered it.

The ambassador's smile quickly turned to a frown.

"The President is greatly concerned," said Corrine. "He has sent several officers to the city to help in any way that they can. He realizes that their presence may be very politically sensitive."

"And what exactly was the nature of the operation that developed this information?" asked the ambassador. "It did not come out of the blue, I imagine."

"No," said Corrine. "It was standard intelligence gathering, but I'm not prepared to go into details about it at this time."

"I see." The ambassador's tone indicated otherwise.

"It is of a secondary nature, certainly compared to this," said Lashley.

"Another rendition?" The ambassador stared at Corrine. "That is why the President sends his personal lawyer?"

"I'm here because the President wanted to convey his deep concern," said Corrine. "To emphasize how seriously he takes the matter. It was not related to a rendition."

The ambassador smirked. "But, of course, if there is a legal concern, you will be in a position to handle it."

"Hopefully, it won't come to that."

"You are going to oversee the situation yourself?"

"I will keep an eye on it, yes. But the CIA has its own personnel who are certainly capable of proceeding on their own. The Deputy Director of Operations will be contacting your intelligence officials as soon as I tell him I've met with you."

"Very good. You will stay for lunch?"

"I'm afraid I can't."

Ambassador Rossi rose. "Then if you will excuse me, I must inform my government."

6

Ferguson took a quick swig from the cup, draining the *caffèllatte*, then launched himself out of the café just as Artur Rostislawitch passed by. The Russian wasn't difficult to spot; he wore a thick cloth coat, full-length and frayed at the bottom. He moved defensively, shoulders tucking and weaving as he went, as if he were afraid he was going to be knocked over by the pedestrians who passed.

Ferguson took out a cell phone as he walked, staying about a half block behind.

"You ready there, gorgeous?" he asked Thera. The cell phone was just a cover; he was using his radio, which was at his belt under his sweater. He had an earbud in his left ear and a mike pinned to his lapel.

"I'm ready, Ferg."

"We have two more blocks. Why don't you go ahead into the reception and pick him up inside?"

"All right."

Guns and Rankin were nearby, scanning the buildings and the crowd. They had no proof that Rostislawitch was the target, and now that he'd gotten a good look at him, Ferguson was inclined to think he wasn't. But T Rex was after someone, and for the moment this was the best candidate they had.

Rostislawitch had no idea he was being followed. On the contrary, he'd never felt so alone in his life—ignored, already a ghost. He kept his head tilted downward and his hands deep in his pockets as he approached the hall where the opening night of the conference was to be held.

Even during his younger years, Rostislawitch had not attended many scientific conferences. He wouldn't have been able to talk about his own work; it was too secret and would have been extremely controversial, to say the least. This suited him just fine—he was not particularly gregarious, nor did he like to travel. He spoke only Russian and English, which he had studied in school. Though he had a wide English vocabulary, his accent was so heavy that he had a great deal of trouble making himself understood. And few people he came in contact with outside of his homeland spoke Russian.

Light streamed into the street from the building. Rostislawitch reached into his coat pocket for his convention credentials, but there was no one at the door to check them. In fact, the only official he saw when he entered was a tall, thin woman taking coats. He exchanged his for a plastic medallion, then walked to the table on the right, where the credentials of some of the featured speakers were on display. Journal articles and in some cases academic texts were on small stands next to or above glossy photographs of the scholars. Brief résumés in bold, single-spaced text were taped beneath the pictures.

"An interesting array," said a short woman next to him.

Rostislawitch smiled, but kept his eyes on the write-up of Dr. Herman Blackwitch, an American who was working with techniques to retard spoilage of certain seed oils. The man had graduated from Stanford University, worked in Italy as well the U.S., and was now a consultant to a large (and unnamed) food packager.

Rostislawitch wondered if he could have had such a career for himself.

Then another thought occurred to him—the work might simply be a cover. Blackwitch might actually be working on an American biowar project.

Yes, most likely. People who thought the Americans weren't planning something along those lines were hopelessly naive.

Across the room, Thera was sizing Rostislawitch up. None of the academics were particularly good dressers, but he stood out in his awkwardness. His black double-breasted suit with its broad pinstripes was at least a decade behind the times, and probably hadn't been very stylish at the time, especially not on him. The rust-colored wool sweater he wore beneath it made him look as if he were the Tin Man after a night out in the rain.

A small bar had been set up near the hallway. Thera went over and asked for a vodka tonic. Now armed, she worked her way back across the room to Rostislawitch. She circled behind him, then came up near his side just as he turned. He bumped into her, spilling her drink across his jacket and the floor.

"Oh, I'm sorry," said Thera. "I didn't see you there and you turned so quickly."

Embarrassed, Rostislawitch started to apologize himself. When he realized he was speaking Russian and she was speaking English, he stopped and stood there, his face beet red.

"Thera Metaxes," Thera said, using a cover name to introduce herself. "Thera Metaxes. I'm a post-doc."

"Dr. Rostislawitch."

"You're Russian."

"Yes."

"That was vodka I was drinking."

Rostislawitch said nothing. The woman was pretty—a drawback for a scientist. She would have a hard time being taken seriously.

"Would you like to buy me a replacement?" asked Thera.

Rostislawitch felt his face grow hotter. "I don't have—" He stopped and cleared his throat. "I'm afraid I haven't much money."

"They're free," said Thera. She hooked her arm around his and led him toward the bar.

R ankin was sitting in the passenger seat of a car they'd rented, watching the feeds from the video bugs Ferguson had planted earlier. He had three windows open in the fifteen-inch screen; between them he had a complete view of the reception area.

Guns and Rankin had checked the building for bombs with a handheld sniffer an hour before. Security was practically nonexistent—not that you could really blame the academic types for thinking they were too boring to be attacked.

"How are we looking?" Ferguson asked over the radio. He'd gone up the street.

"Thera's with him at the bar," Rankin said.

"Hey, Ferg, check these two guys on the motorbikes coming up toward you," said Guns. "Moving kind of slow."

"All right. Stand by."

Rankin turned his attention back to the screen. Thera's radio was in her purse, turned off; to contact her they'd have to call her sat phone. They'd wired into the building's fire alarm; if anything looked suspicious Rankin could activate it by hitting a combination of keys on his computer.

"Why am I looking at these guys, Guns?" asked Ferguson.

"They were going real slow in front of the building."

"You mean they were driving responsibly? That's a hanging offense in Italy."

Guns laughed.

Something on the left-hand screen caught Rankin's eye. A man with a briefcase had entered the building. Rankin zoomed the image, watching as the man declined the coat attendant's offer to take the bag. The man looked furtively around the room, then went to the table where the résumés were displayed. He slipped the case down to the floor, then abruptly turned and began walking quickly toward the door.

"Shit." Rankin shot upright in the car seat, then struggled to get his fingers on the combination of keys to sound the fire alarm. As he did, he began to shout into his mike, "Ferg, Guns, guy with the beard coming out. Left a suitcase under the table. Thera, there's a bomb under the table at the front!" he added, forgetting she wasn't on the circuit. "Go! *Go, for Christ's sake!*"

7

A spider scurried across the hotel room desk just as Anghuyu "Atha" Jahan sat down to use the phone. The Iranian grabbed it by one of its long legs and held it up, watching as it wriggled. The creature, puzzled at its sudden capture, was desperate to get away.

"You're such a little thing," said Atha.

He took hold of another of the creature's legs, holding them apart. The spider bent its body over, trying to spin itself free.

When he was a boy, Atha enjoyed pulling the legs from spiders. Then one day his father caught him, and slapped him in the ear.

"These are God's creatures, hallowed be his name," Atha's father complained. "You should show compassion."

For several years, Atha avoided spiders and insects of all kinds. Finally—in a mosque, as it happened—he saw an imam squash one as they walked together. And from that moment Atha realized that was the way of the world.

The powerful squashed the less powerful. He did not have to look very far for examples. At the time, Saddam the Iraqi butcher was sending missiles into Iran, killing hundreds of innocents. Brave young men, including two of Atha's cousins, sacrificed themselves in suicidal charges to beat back the Iraqi army from their land.

All the while, the West stood by and encouraged the butcher, supplying the Butcher of Baghdad with missiles and intelligence. Later, they discarded him as callously as a farmer killing unwanted cats, snapping his neck after a show trial.

That was the way of the world.

Atha believed that his life started at that moment the imam squashed the spider. He had put his talents to great use, working with friends high up in the Revolutionary Guard and the government. Parsa Moshen, officially the education minister but unofficially the head of the Revolutionary Guard's overseas operations sector, was one of his closest mentors.

Not a friend. The minister did not have friends. Even Atha, who'd known him many years, remained fearful of him.

Atha's realization that the strong ruled the weak had paid off for both him and Iran. He had worked to make himself strong, as measured by money, and to make his country strong, as measured by weapons and other modern conveniences such as pharmaceuticals and aircraft parts. And now his greatest contribution to the country, as well as to his fortune, was just a day or two away.

By the grace of God, a large number of people—millions of people even, it was very possible—would die in the process. It was the way of the world.

Atha jerked his hands apart, maiming the spider. Its mangled body dropped to the floor, squirming, unable to stand.

As an act of mercy, he crushed it with his toe.

BOLOGNA, ITALY

Thera grabbed Rostislawitch's arm as soon as the alarm sounded.

"This way," she said, pushing him toward the hall.

"But the door."

"Come on," she insisted, tightening her grip.

Surprised by the woman's strength and persistence, Rostislawitch let himself be led down the hall as the fire alarm began to bleat. The others seemed momentarily stunned by the noise.

"Go; there's fire; get out," said Thera, yelling in Greek-accented Italian and then English. She reached the end of the hall and pushed

Rostislawitch with her into the reception room, pointing toward a door at the far side. "There, go," she told him.

"What's going on?" he said.

"Come on. There's a fire. I know the way out."

Rostislawitch wondered if this was the Iranian's doing—if he had decided on an unconventional way of meeting. He started through the door, then froze, seeing that it led to a set of steps down toward the basement.

"Not down there—go right! Right! Hurry," said Thera, nudging him again. She'd pulled the headset of her radio out and heard Rankin say there was a bomb inside the building.

"Which way?" asked Rostislawitch.

"The window there," she said. "It's on an alley. Come on!"

"I don't smell smoke."

"Come on!"

The man who'd taken the suitcase into the reception hall hurried toward a Fiat across the street. Ferguson trotted to catch up.

"Guns, you on the bike?" he asked as he drew closer to the man.

"Yeah."

"Black Fiat. I'll get the plate."

The fire alarm was ringing and people were starting to file out of the building, though not in much of a rush.

"Rankin, call in some sort of bomb alert to the police," said Ferguson.

"I already did."

"Where's Thera?"

"She's going out the back."

"I'm here, Ferg," said Thera.

"Get out; there's a bomb."

"No shit. We're in the alley."

Meanwhile, the man who had left the suitcase under the table had stopped at the trunk of his car. He popped it open and reached inside. Ferguson, thinking the man had spotted him, ducked into the nearby doorway and reached to his belt for his pistol. He watched as the man pulled another suitcase out of the car.

"Ferg, what's going on?" asked Guns. He was a few yards down the street, sitting on a motorcycle. Like many Italians, he hadn't bothered putting on his helmet.

"I'm not sure," answered Ferguson. "Let's see. Get ready to grab him."

The man closed the trunk and started back toward the art building. Ferguson kept his gun down and pressed against the door, staying in the shadows as the man passed a few feet away.

"Coming at you, Guns," Ferguson whispered.

"Yeah, I see him. What's he got? Another bomb?"

"Don't know." Ferguson trotted to the car, glanced at the empty interior, then knelt in front of the trunk. He picked the lock, lifting the lid cautiously; there was nothing inside except an undersized spare and some crumpled plastic grocery bags.

Ferguson pulled the small bomb sniffer out of his pocket. The "sniffer" would react to the chemicals used in plastic explosives, such as Semtex, by sounding a tone and lighting a red LED on the outer casing. The light stayed off.

Ferguson slammed the trunk closed.

"Guns, why don't you circle the block, get out of here," he said.

"What?"

"Just go. This may be some sort of trick to flush us out. That or Rankin got his underwear twisted again."

BOLOGNA, ITALY

The alleyway was dark, and Rostislawitch tripped over a small pile of boxes as he strode toward the street. Thera grabbed his back and steadied him, helping him out to the light. A fire truck was just turning up the block; they watched it veer left and right as the driver overcorrected, its bumper barely missing the cars parked on either side of the street.

"What's going on?" Rostislawitch asked.

"I don't know," said Thera.

"Did Atha send you?"

Thera considered saying yes, but was afraid he'd catch on if she bluffed. Better to play it straight, she thought.

"Who's Atha?" she asked.

"Who sent you?" demanded Rostislawitch.

"No one sent me. I'm from the University of Athens. I'm a post-doc student. I thought I might come here and see what chances I had of getting a job. I'm not sure whether I want to teach or just do pure research. It might be selling out."

"Oh, Athens." Despite her claim, Rostislawitch was now convinced that Thera was in fact working for the Iranian, probably checking him out before the meeting.

"You've been to Athens?" asked Thera.

"I've stopped in the airport a few times. Never in the city."

"A shame," Thera told him. "There's so much history there, in the countryside. The city itself is like any city, unless you have family. But the ruins, those are impressive."

"I see." Rostislawitch stepped back as another fire engine roared around the corner.

"Would you like to get something to eat?" asked Thera.

"Yes," said Rostislawitch. "I am a little hungry."

A mong the many lessons Ferguson's father had taught him was always to look as if you belonged where you didn't. A slight frown, a firm glare, and a determined stride were far more valuable than an identification card—though he could have produced a card showing he was a police investigator had anyone stopped him as he strode into the art building.

"Ferg, what are you doing?" Rankin asked over the radio.

Ferguson ignored him. Spotting the suitcase, he walked to it and pulled it from under the table.

"Ferg!"

Combination locks on either side of the suitcase held it shut. Ferguson placed his thumbs on them, then pushed the levers simultaneously. The loud clicks echoed against the high ceiling.

"Jesus, Ferg," said Rankin.

"I don't see the big guy here." Ferguson pushed the lid up. The suitcase was filled with pamphlets.

"You see this, Rankin?"

"Yeah, I see it, Ferg. What the fuck do you want me to say?"

"Something along the lines of, 'I screwed up big-time,' would do it."

"Like I'm supposed to have X-ray vision? The guy acted exactly as if he was planting a bomb. I didn't want Thera to get killed. I thought it was T Rex."

Ferguson straightened. A pair of firemen came through the door; one of them had an axe.

"*Dove il fuoco?*" they asked. "Where is the fire?"

"*Non so,*" said Ferguson. "I don't know."

The firemen rushed toward the hallway. Ferguson took out his small bug finder and scanned the room, looking for bugging devices. He smelled a setup—someone must be watching, and now knew they were there.

"Maybe you ought to get out of there, don't you think?" said Rankin.

"I'm already burned as it is," said Ferguson. He was in no mood to realize he'd made a pun, let alone laugh at it.

"The guy with the suitcases is coming in," said Rankin.

"Maybe I'll arrest him. I noticed a spelling mistake on the brochure."

10

BOLOGNA, ITALY

They spent the next few hours trying to figure out if they had been watched. Rankin was mad at Ferguson for saying he'd screwed up when really he'd done the most logical thing under the circumstances.

Ferguson was mad at himself for not having realized that it might be a trap. Guns, who'd cycled back around the city and was watching Thera, wasn't quite sure what either of them was angry about, and tried to ignore the sniping in his headset. The only person completely focused on her job was Thera, who'd bought Rostislawitch dinner and listened to him talk about how much he missed his wife. It was a touching story, heartrending in a way, and not the sort of thing she'd expected from a man who according to the Cube had spent his life working on efficient ways of killing large numbers of people with microscopic bugs.

When Rostislawitch went back to his hotel to go to bed, Thera planted a video bug outside his room, then went downstairs and tapped into the phone interface unit in the boiler room. Ferguson, meanwhile, rented a suite on the second floor that they could use to watch him if necessary. After checking the room, he went down to the lounge to check it out and wait for Thera. Afraid to drink because he was so tired, he ordered a bottle of Pellegrino and sat at a booth that gave him a good view of the doorway.

Had T Rex really snookered him, or was he just thinking too much? Did they even have the right target in the first place?

By their very nature, First Team missions tended not to move in a straight line; if figuring out who T Rex was and grabbing him was an easy job, someone else would have been assigned to do it. But difficulty wasn't an excuse, Ferguson thought; they'd botched it this afternoon, and it was his fault, not Rankin's.

Ferguson's body felt beat to piss, and his mind wasn't sharp. He told himself it was because he hadn't slept much and hadn't had much of a break between missions, but he couldn't shake the nagging suspicion that something else was going on.

Maybe the cancer was sucking energy out of him, draining him like a short circuit in a car battery. There was going to come a time when he couldn't do this job, where he'd be a second too late to react, and that would get not only him but the rest of the team killed.

Thera was the one in harm's way right now. If she died because he couldn't figure out what was going on, he couldn't live with that. He just couldn't.

"You just drink water?"

"The bubbles give me energy," he said, looking up into Thera's green eyes.

"You're Irish."

"And you're . . . something," said Ferguson.

"Greek."

"Your English is pretty good. How'd you know I was Irish?"

"Your accent gives you away. I spent a year studying in Dublin, and two in London. I thought you were English at first."

"Have a seat." She was getting better at lying, Ferguson thought. He almost would have believed her.

"I don't think so. Thanks."

"Your loss."

"Maybe." Thera went to the bar and ordered a White Russian.

"I'll pay for that," said Ferguson, getting up and walking toward the bar as the bartender brought Thera her drink.

"Thanks. I don't think so," she said.

"You sure?"

"You're cute, but—" Thera felt a pang of regret, as if she weren't just playacting.

"There's always a but," said Ferguson. He dropped a ten-euro note on the bar and walked out.

Twenty minutes later, the team assembled in a suite in the Hotel Vespucci across the street: technically Guns' room, reserved for him by Corrigan. Rankin, who'd had to park the car in a hotel garage several blocks away, was the last one in; he gave Ferguson a scowl and then went and sat at the far end of the sofa, glaring at him.

One of these days, Rankin thought, no shit, he was going to punch Ferguson in the mouth.

"Tough night," said Ferguson. "I think we all oughta get some sleep. If Rostislawitch is the target, I figure we can take six hours. If he's not, then it probably doesn't matter how long we sleep."

"That's it? That's what we're doing?" asked Rankin.

"If you have another idea, Skippy, I'm all ears," said Ferguson. "Fire away."

"I don't see why anyone would want to kill Rostislawitch," said Rankin.

"Maybe the Russians," suggested Thera.

"Why wait until he's out of the country then? No way. Corrigan's brief says he's teaching basic biology classes. That's not a real important job."

"How do you know?" asked Guns.

" 'Cause unlike you, Marine, I went to college."

"Relax," said Ferguson. "I agree, but he looks like the only guy at the conference who's halfway worth targeting. By who, I don't know."

"The Russians aren't going to hire out to kill him," said Rankin. "And they're not going to wait until he's out of the country."

"They killed Alexander Litvinenko in London," said Thera.

" 'Cause they couldn't lure him back to Russia." Rankin folded his arms.

"Skip's got a good point," said Ferguson. He leaned back in the seat, his head on the back cushion so that he was gazing at the ceiling. "Maybe I was wrong about this. Maybe the theory that he's going to hit a public square is right. Maybe it is some sort of gas attack. Maybe a bomb, I don't know. We're missing too many pieces of the puzzle right now. Back to square one. But get some sleep first."

Rankin snorted. That was as close to a full-blown apology as Ferguson ever made. "I'll take the watch," Rankin said.

"I got it, Skippy."

"You can't let it be, huh?" shot Rankin. "You can't just say you were an asshole and let it go."

Ferguson just grinned and said nothing.

11

WASHINGTON, D.C.

Corrine glanced at her watch. It was a little past 6 p.m.—just after midnight in Italy. She picked up the encrypted phone and called Ferguson.

"O'Brien's Real Italian Delicatessen," he said.

"I have the name of the Italian SISDE liaison who's on his way to Bologna," Corrine said. She'd learned that the best way to deal with Ferguson was to ignore his jokes. "He wants to meet first thing in the morning."

"Can't wait. I'll try to remember to shave first."

"What did Rostislawitch do tonight?"

"Not much. I'm not sure we got the right guy."

"The Italians have a theory. They think the target may be a drug company president who's supposed to be the dinner speaker Thursday. He's going through a messy divorce."

"Have to be pretty messy for T Rex to be involved."

"How about rich, too? The Italians say he's worth a half-billion dollars at least."

"Well, that might do it," said Ferguson, his voice enthusiastic for the first time since the conversation began. "You have information on that?"

"The Italians have it. Corrigan was going to have your analysts put together a report as well. He's in Switzerland right now. He's only flying in for the dinner, then leaving. They'll keep him away from the squares."

"*Piazzas*."

"Right."

"We're sure T Rex isn't a terrorist, right?"

"You tell me, Ferg. You've been working on this."

"No, I don't think so. He tries to make it look that way sometimes, but that's either to throw people off the trail or to make sure he gets his guy. He doesn't mind killing people."

"You OK, Ferg?"

"Fine. Why?"

"You sound . . . tired." Some weeks earlier, Corrine had discovered that Ferguson suffered from cancer. She felt sorry for him—sympathetic maybe, not sorry—but she wasn't sure exactly how to express it. Ferguson hadn't told anyone, and wouldn't—Parnelles would take him off the First Team if he found out that he had that kind of illness. "Tired or down."

Ferguson scoffed. "Thanks, Mom. I'll wear my peppy hat for our next phone call."

12

Contrary to Ferguson's expectations, the SISDE intelligence officer in charge of the Bologna "situation" was extremely businesslike, efficient to the point of seeming Prussian.

Italy had two different intelligence agencies that dealt with terror; SISDE answered to the interior minister, while SISMI was under the direction of the military. Their responsibilities overlapped, and they weren't known for playing nice together. Italian politics favored complex ambiguities, not to mention mud, muck, and mayhem; rather than being above the fray, SISDE and SISMI wallowed in it.

Most of Ferguson's admittedly limited experience with the Italian intelligence community was with SISMI, military intelligence; the last liaison he'd dealt with was a drunk. The relationship was less than functional, though the meetings were a lot of fun.

Marco Imperiati was 180 degrees in the other direction. Fifty years old, the SISDE officer was a short man; at five-four his face barely reached Ferguson's chest. But Imperiati had an intense look that made him seem considerably taller, and his voice made his underlings move quickly.

"You are late," he told Ferguson when they met at the police station, where a suite of rooms on the third floor had been commandeered. Imperiati's English had a British accent and a staccato rhythm.

"Got stuck in your traffic," said Ferguson. He glanced at the large paper map of the city on the office wall; it was dotted with arrows and pins indicating lookout posts.

"Why have these people chosen Bologna?" asked Imperiati.

"It's one man. We call him T Rex."

"Why Bologna?"

"I guess his target is here," said Ferguson. "Other than that, I have no idea."

"Tell me about him."

Ferguson repeated what he knew would have been in the briefing paper Slott forwarded to SISDE. Imperiati listened without expression, his eyes locked on Ferguson's. He didn't trust the American; in Imperiati's experience, the CIA always reserved some vital piece of information. And even if that was not the case here, he had no doubt that the Americans had a different agenda than he did. He suspected that they had known about the plot for weeks, if not months. Had they notified his government earlier, proper preparations could have been taken. Now he was playing catch-up, and it was very possible that he would not be able to prevent a catastrophe.

"So who is he?" said Imperiati finally.

"I wish I knew," said Ferguson.

"No theory."

"A very good assassin, but probably not as good as his reputation makes him seem." Ferguson walked over to the map, looking at it.

"You could say that about anyone."

"Pretty much. Present company excluded, of course."

The slightest hint of a grin appeared at the corner of Imperiati's mouth, where it died a quick and lonely death.

"His advance person checked these three squares out," Ferguson said, pointing. "And these buildings. We have a theory the genetic conference is involved, because it's being held in the art building. Maybe T Rex thinks his target will move through one of those squares. They may have tours organized—"

"We'll cancel them."

"Discreetly," said Ferguson.

"Of course."

"But it could just be a coincidence." Ferguson looked back at the map.

"Where is the advance person?"

"I understand she left yesterday." Ferguson wasn't lying, of course, though he did suggest that he hadn't been here. Imperiati didn't buy it.

"Had we been notified, I could have had her arrested. We would have interrogated her."

Ferguson nodded. Imperiati was surprised that he didn't offer an excuse. It impressed him, though only slightly. "And you have no idea who his target is?"

"We have a theory. Last night we did. Today I'm not so sure." Ferguson told him about the Russian, again saying little more than what Imperiati would already have been briefed on. "I understand you have a candidate?" Ferguson added when he was finished.

"Several." Imperiati told Ferguson about the drug executive Corrine had mentioned last night, then added that two Italian ministers were supposed to be in the city within the next few days. One was addressing the genetic conference; the other was visiting a new exhibit at a small museum near Porta San Donato.

"You think someone would pay close to a million dollars to kill an art minister?" Ferguson asked.

"Well, this is Italy. We do take art very seriously." Imperiati attempted a smile; it died about halfway to his lips. "But the fact that she is the niece of a Sicilian Mafioso involved in a power struggle may be relevant."

"True."

"We will cancel both visits at the last minute."

"If you do that, we're not going to catch T Rex."

"That is not my concern."

"If he's really been hired to kill one of those people, he won't stop just because the visit is canceled. If you have the minister, or a stand-in, come to the city, you'll still be able to catch him."

"Maybe. Or maybe he gets away. In the process, if there is a bomb, if there is a gas attack, even a gunfight, innocent people die. Innocent citizens. Those are the people whom I worry about."

Ferguson figured this wasn't the time or place to get into a philosophical discussion about who really was innocent in this day and age, so he let Imperiati's statement pass without comment.

13

While Ferguson met with the Italians, Thera and the others continued to watch Rostislawitch. Security at the conference had been tightened considerably; Thera had to show her forged pass, then wait as her name was checked against a master list of conference attendees. Fortunately, Corrigan had taken the precaution of having her name added overnight, as well as making sure that her credentials with the University of Athens were in order.

The back entrance Thera had gone out with Rostislawitch as well as the side doors, and all of the windows on the first floor, had been locked, with alarms attached, and a cell phone interrupter was now operating inside the building, making it impossible for anyone to call in or out, much less use a phone to trigger explosive devices. The team's radios were not affected, but since the Italians were using detection devices, the radios were reserved only for emergencies. Thera kept hers in her purse while she attended a panel discussion on the function of enzymes in bacteria mutation. She found the topic fascinating, though somewhat over her head. Corrigan had forwarded a collection of papers on microbiology, DNA manipulation, and bacteria for her to study, and she read them when the lectures got boring.

Rostislawitch saw her as the session broke up. She waved, then waited for him to come over.

"Old news," said Rostislawitch derisively. He'd read papers along similar lines nearly a decade before.

"Do you think?" asked Thera.

"Don't you?"

"Everything is interesting," she said.

"And tell me about your work."

"If you found this old, you would run away if I say anything in the least about it."

"Oh, I'm sure I wouldn't." Rostislawitch tried to think of something to say to encourage her—he'd been a fool to criticize the others' work, making himself look more important but at the same time scaring her off.

Of course she had no interest in him, so she couldn't be scared off. He was old enough to be her father.

"Lunch?" Thera suggested.

"My budget is very thin."

"So is mine. But I saw a shop nearby where they sell sandwiches and little pizza tarts. The prices look cheap."

"Let's go then," said Rostislawitch.

Y ou hear what they're talking about?" Rankin asked Guns. Thera and Rostislawitch were in a small stand-up café a few blocks from the art building. The place had a counter facing the window where people could stand and have a quick bite to eat. Rankin, sitting on a Vespa a few yards down the street, watched from the outside; Guns had gone in behind them, and was pretending to talk on his cell phone.

"Stuff about Russia. You got the outside covered?"

"What do you think I'm doing? Picking my nose?"

Guns laughed. "You're getting as funny as Ferg."

Rankin practically bit his tongue to keep from replying.

A panel truck turned down the street. He watched nervously as it made its way past the building. T Rex liked big bombs, and even if this wasn't the area he'd had scoped out, surely he could strike anywhere.

The one thing they had going for them was that he wasn't suicidal; he wouldn't drive the truck he planned to blow up. Then again, he could easily hire someone who was. Or get them involved unknowingly.

"Boom," said Ferguson, coming up behind Rankin.

He jumped.

"Shit, man. Cut it out."

"Wound a little tight, are we?" Ferguson turned and scanned the block, then took out a pack of cigarettes, as if he were asking for a smoke.

"I don't like this spot," said Rankin. "Thera's too vulnerable."

"Why'd you let her come here?"

"We checked it out beforehand," said Rankin. Ferguson always put him on the defensive. "We sniffed all the cars. No explosives."

"So why are you nervous?"

"I'm not nervous. I said it wasn't the best place."

"She's moving," said Guns.

Grateful for the interruption, Rankin started the bike.

14

BOLOGNA, ITALY

The assassin put down the field glasses. The shot was gone.

There was no point taking a risk. The aim, after all, was to retire after this hit: one last payoff would make things perfect. There was time.

The Americans had clearly tipped off the Italians; the place was ringed with security people. That in itself was not necessarily a problem, merely a challenge to be overcome. More than likely the preparer had been spotted somehow, but that could play in the assassin's favor: the preparer had been given many things to do to throw off the scent. Merely avoiding the plan suggested by those things would increase the chances of success tenfold. Improvisation, while something the assassin did not like, could be arranged.

Quickly, the assassin put the glasses back into the suitcase, then turned to the bed where he had put the RPG-7. The Russian rocket-propelled grenade launcher looked almost like a toy on the king-size bed.

"Another time," said the assassin, packing it away.

15

Rostislawitch checked his watch. He was supposed to meet the Iranian in five minutes; it would take at least ten to reach the Orologio, which was over near the Piazza Maggiore.

And yet he continued walking with the girl back in the direction of the conference. Was he bewitched by her? Or was he having second thoughts about the Iranian?

Rostislawitch wasn't sure.

He stopped abruptly. "I just remembered an appointment," he told her.

"An appointment?"

"Yes, I—I promised to see a friend of a colleague. It's a chore. Someone who has not been in good health and I am going to cheer her—him, I mean, I'm going to cheer him up. I hope you'll forgive me."

He berated himself—why had he said "her"? And then, why had he changed it? That only made it worse.

"Sure," said Thera. "See you later?"

For a moment—a slim moment—Rostislawitch thought of asking if she'd come with him: not to the meeting, but away, far away, to America maybe, or any place where he might find a way to start over. But it was a foolish idea, and it evaporated long before he heard her ask if she'd see him later.

"Yes," Rostislawitch replied. "Good-bye for now."

G oing back to the south," said Guns, who was watching Rostis-lawitch from a bicycle.

"All right. You see the Italian trail team?" Ferguson asked.

"In that blue car, right?"

"Yeah."

"They have anyone else?"

"Not that I've spotted," said Ferguson. "Rankin, you see any-body?"

"No."

"Ferg, what do you want me to do?" asked Thera, back on the radio circuit now that Rostislawitch had left.

"Go ahead back to the conference. See if you see anything suspicious. Guns, you shadow her. Rankin and I will follow Rostislawitch. Let's see who he's meeting."

"You sure the Italians can keep him safe if T Rex is around?" asked Thera.

"Not my concern." Ferguson turned and started walking down the Via Ugo Bassi, keeping Rostislawitch between himself and Rankin. "I want T Rex. I want him to take his shot or I won't have a chance of getting him."

"Ferg."

"You sound like you're worried about him, Thera. The stuff Rostislawitch works on can kill a few thousand people in the time it takes to sneeze. You know who his target was when he started working, right? Um, let's see. That would be during the Cold War. Gee, could it be the U.S.A.?"

She didn't answer.

"The Italians have another team on him," said Rankin. "Couple of guys in a brown Fiat."

Ferguson reached the corner and waited for the light. He saw the brown Fiat approaching. Up ahead, a pair of police cars were parked about two blocks from the piazza.

Rostislawitch came into view, walking quickly and holding a piece of paper in his hand. Ferguson guessed it was a map, since Rostislawitch kept looking at it.

"All right, I got him," Ferguson told Rankin, crossing the street just ahead of the Russian. "We'll let the Eyetralians get in close."

Rankin grunted in reply. Ferguson reached into his pocket, tapping the radio control so that it played music; he cranked the volume as Rostislawitch neared, just in case the scientist wondered why he was wearing earphones.

Rostislawitch walked by without noticing. He was more than ten minutes late now, and walking so quickly that he felt almost out of breath. Nearing the piazza, he saw a pair of police cars blocking the road. Suddenly he was filled with fear.

Were they looking for him?

It was a ridiculous thought, and yet he couldn't shake it. Despite all of his precautions, he was sure he was about to be caught.

Rostislawitch continued to walk. He lowered his gaze, focusing on the stones of the walkway. He turned left, moving toward the hotel. There were police everywhere around, some with dogs.

They weren't after him. There were too many officers, too much of a commotion—he saw a police van ahead, a kind of a command post with men inside.

It must be something for the tourists, something to convince them that it was safe.

Even if the police weren't here for him now, wouldn't they be eventually? If he dared to return to Russia, would they get him there?

She was a good girl, that Thera. She reminded him of his wife in a way. Then again, every woman he met, everyone who was nice to him anyway, reminded him of his wife.

Greed pushed him through the square and down past the fortresslike building toward the hotel. Greed not for money, but for revenge. They'd let his wife die. He had to get back at them somehow. That was why he was doing this. He hated everyone—the autocrats who ran Russia, the Americans who had forced Russia into poverty, the world that spat on a dying woman who could have been easily saved with the proper care.

Rostislawitch's heart nearly stopped as a policeman pointed at him and said loudly, "*Signore!*"

Rostislawitch froze.

"*No, signore,*" repeated the officer.

"*No parlo Italiano.*" Rostislawitch forced the words from his mouth.

"*Non parla Italiano?*" said the policeman, asking if he spoke Italian.

"No."

"We've closed this part of the street to foot traffic," said the man, still speaking Italian though there was no hope of Rostislawitch understanding. "You'll have to go over to the other side."

He pointed, and said the words more slowly.

"Cross?" said Rostislawitch in English.

"*Sì*," said the policeman. "Go there. Then you can cross. This way is blocked off."

Rostislawitch, trembling, retraced his steps and went to the other side. His chest felt as if it were going to explode, and he worried that he was going to have a heart attack. By the time he reached the side street in front of the hotel, he was panting.

The street had been turned into a pedestrian mall years before, though cars occasionally drove up to make deliveries or drop off passengers. The hotel entrance was marked by two small trees in fancy buckets; precisely clipped, the trees were like slightly oversized bonsais. Above them, a pair of video surveillance cameras stood guard, watching the nearby benches and the long planters that divided the walkway. Rostislawitch nodded at another policeman, then entered the hotel.

When Ferguson noticed that the Italians were staying outside, he decided to follow Rostislawitch and find out what he was up to. Ferguson sauntered into the hotel lobby, smiled at the clerk at his left, and walked through to the lounge, figuring he'd check that first. Sure enough, Rostislawitch was sitting in a booth at the far end, talking to someone Ferguson couldn't see. There were about a dozen people in the place, most of them having lunch. Ferguson walked through to the bar, tucked back around a corner to the left.

"Vermouth," Ferguson told the bartender, leaning across. As he did, he noticed a familiar face in the booth nearby: Nathaniel Hamilton, a British MI6 agent. Staring at him.

Ferguson smiled, then raised his glass in a half salute. Hamilton's frown deepened.

Which convinced Ferguson it would be a good idea to go over and say hello.

"So, how's Her Majesty's favorite public servant doing these days?" said Ferguson, slapping his glass down on the table and sliding into the booth.

"Keep your voice down," Hamilton told him. "Jesus, man. Have a brain."

Ferguson grinned, then sat back in the seat. "Who you following?"

"What makes you think I'm following anyone?"

Ferguson started to get up. Hamilton grabbed his arm.

"Tell me why you're here and I'll tell you what I'm doing," hissed the MI6 agent.

"Fair enough."

"Well?"

"You go first."

"No."

Once again, Ferguson started to get up. Hamilton had an unfortunate reputation for reneging on similar arrangements, and Ferguson wasn't about to trust him.

Once again, the MI6 agent took his arm. "Just sit down and stop making a show of yourself. You're always being a nuisance, Ferguson."

"Nuisance is my middle name," said Ferguson, sipping his drink.

16

BOLOGNA, ITALY

Rostislawitch shook his head.

"The agreement was money in the account. Then I will give you the location."

"I am just trying to make things more efficient," said Atha. "But you seem not to trust me."

"I take all the risk. You have all the benefit."

"Now, now, the offer is a fair one. You will be a rich man."

"Mr. Jahan—"

"No, no, call me Atha. It is my name since I was small."

The Iranian sat back in his seat. When the technical leader of the project had suggested he meet Rostislawitch at the conference in Bologna, Atha readily agreed; it was easy to move around Europe, and the Italians were not generally as watchful as the Germans or even the

French. But there had been a considerable increase in police activity in the city today, and he knew that as a foreigner he might very well be watched. While anyone listening in would think he and Rostislawitch were talking about coloring dyes for carpets—a simple code Atha had suggested in their earliest communication—it was a thin veneer.

"The offer is fair if you carry through with it," said Rostislawitch. "I have no guarantee."

Atha sighed. "If you were to come with me to Tehran, you would see how trustworthy we are."

"I'm not going to Tehran."

"Your dyes are very important to us, at the right price." Atha caught sight of the waiter and held up his glass. The waiter nodded, though in Italy that was not a guarantee that he would return before midnight. The only country with worse servers was Egypt, in Atha's opinion.

"Maybe you should have some lunch," he told Rostislawitch. "A full stomach calms the mind."

"My stomach is already full."

Rostislawitch glanced around the restaurant. There was a dark-skinned man at a table not far away—the Iranian's bodyguard, he guessed. As for the other two dozen or so people here, most seemed to be international businessmen discussing deals, just as Rostislawitch and the Iranian were doing.

But maybe not. Maybe the place was packed with spies. Rostislawitch had no way of knowing.

Was this the way he wanted to spend the rest of his life, looking over his shoulder? Rich, yes, but at what price?

What did it matter? His life was over anyway. Wasn't it?

The waiter arrived with Atha's iced tea.

"Do you want another vodka?" Atha asked Rostislawitch.

The Russian shook his head. They had to use English to communicate, the only language they had in common. Atha's Italian was good, though heavily accented. He felt his Spanish was better. His English, of course, was superb, a matter of great pride.

Atha sipped his drink for a short while, considering what to do. Much depended on his obtaining the material very quickly. What had begun some months before as a fantastical project now had assumed great importance; indeed, the minister demanded that the action Atha had arranged be launched within a few days. Atha was prepared to do so, but only if he got the material. Without it, he was ruined.

But he must act confident. It was the prerequisite for success in such situations. The lion could tremble on the inside, but his roar needed to be strong and shattering.

"You are having second thoughts. I understand," Atha told the scientist calmly. "It is a difficult task. And to become rich in one transaction—it seems almost too good to be true. As if the Prophet, all praise be to him, were to suddenly invite you to his home."

Rostislawitch said nothing.

"It's a tremendous thing," said Atha. "We will talk tomorrow. I will call you at your hotel."

"The money first," said Rostislawitch, looking up into Atha's eyes as he rose.

Atha sat back down. "I don't know if I can give you the money first."

"It's the only way I can do it."

"Perhaps an installment."

"No. All of it. In accounts only I can access."

Atha searched Rostislawitch's face. The Russian was greedy or he wouldn't be here, but exactly how greedy was he? Enough to run off without delivering?

Atha did not think he was. But avarice was a notoriously difficult vice to gauge. Rostislawitch showed no outward sign of it—no fancy watch, no chauffeur waiting at the curb. His suit was ill fitting and old. But that might only mean he liked to hoard his money. Only a saint could know a man's soul and sins, and Atha was not a saint.

Rostislawitch's face was pale, his eyes a little too wide-open. Atha saw desperation in his stare; he was a man pushed to the edge.

That was as close to an assurance as Atha was going to get.

"The material is available?"

"You'll have it as soon as I have the money."

"Good," said Atha. "I will call you tomorrow. I will arrange for the accounts to be opened and the money transferred." He reached into the pocket of his sport coat and took out an envelope. "A token for you. Some spending money for you, as a gesture of friendship, not as a payment."

Rostislawitch frowned, but then took the envelope and stuffed it into his pocket.

He was greedy enough to do business with, Atha decided, rising from the table. The rest would fall into place.

17

BOLOGNA, ITALY

"The man's name is Anghuyu Jahan. They call him Atha for short," Hamilton told Ferguson. "Though why I'm not sure. It was some sort of baby name that stuck."

"Who calls him that?"

"Anyone and everyone. Why are you here?"

"Vacation."

"Sod off, Ferguson."

"I've tried."

"Who is the Russian?"

"Rostislawitch something or other."

"Come now. We have a deal."

"Just like we had in Nigeria?"

"Am I going to hear about that the rest of my life? I was under orders."

That wasn't entirely true, but Ferguson let it pass.

"His name is Artur Rostislawitch. He's a biologist who knows a lot about making germs. Got into some sort of political trouble a few years ago, and now is underemployed."

"Germs? As in bacterial warfare?"

"That's what they say."

"Oh, Jesus."

Ferguson sipped his drink, trying to decide whether Hamilton's reaction was real or not. It was tough to tell with the Englishman—he was such a rotten actor that sometimes his genuine reactions seemed fake, and vice versa.

But now suddenly a plot to kill Rostislawitch made sense to Ferguson. The scientist was offering something up to the Iranians; they'd want to get rid of him as soon as the deal went through.

And they'd want someone good to do it. T Rex.

Hamilton saw Atha get up from his table.

"I am afraid you'll have to excuse me, Robert," he said. "Her Majesty does not pay me to sit around in bars drinking all day."

"What exactly does she pay you for?"

Hamilton smirked, then left the restaurant. It was only when the waiter approached that Ferguson realized Hamilton had left him with his bill.

18

BOLOGNA, ITALY

Rostislawitch turned the wrong way out of the hotel; when he finally realized it he had walked several blocks in the wrong direction, down Via Farini, and was lost. So when the police car pulled up next to him, he was relieved.

"Could you tell me how to get to Porta San Donato?" he said, pronouncing each English word as distinctly as possible. "I have a conference there. I'm late. The University of Bologna."

He wanted to say that he was a scientist, but the word in English had left him.

"*Dove il passaporto?*" asked the policeman.

"*Scusi?* Excuse me?"

"*Il passaporto,*" repeated the policeman. "Where is your identification."

"I—my passport?"

"*Sì. Il passaporto.*"

Rostislawitch patted his pocket, though he knew it wasn't there—he'd turned it in to the desk at the hotel. Panic surged through him. The policeman got out of the car.

"Sir, where is your passport? Are you a member of the European Union?"

The policeman was speaking in Italian, but the gist of what he was saying was clear enough. Unsure what to do, Rostislawitch reached for his wallet.

"That's not a passport."

"At my hotel," said Rostislawitch, using Russian and then English. "My passport is there."

"Into the car please," said the policeman, opening the door.

Rostislawitch hesitated. It had been quite a while since he had traveled outside of Russia. This couldn't be normal. Did they know why he was really here?

"*Signore, per favore,*" said the policeman. "In the automobile, please."

He did not have a gun on his belt. Rostislawitch might be able to get away.

But what would he do then?

"My hotel is on the Via Imerio," he said in English. "If you take me there, they can give you the passport. They locked it in their safe."

The policeman once more gestured toward the car. Seeing no other choice, Rostislawitch got in.

Ferguson got within ten yards of Rostislawitch while the police were questioning him. He saw Rankin on the other side of the street, ready to interfere.

"No, hang back," Ferguson told him over the radio. "I'll deal with this."

"What the hell's going on?" Rankin asked.

"This is what happens when you cooperate with the Italians," said Ferguson. "They screw everything up. Go grab some lunch. Check on Thera when you're done. I'll call you."

"You sure, Ferg?"

"Yeah. Better that there's no witnesses when I strangle Imperiati."

———

The SISDE officer was waiting for Ferguson in the upstairs squad room of the police station. In the few hours since Ferguson had left, the room had taken on the air of a television production room; there were several dozen screens, each clustered in a different area around the outside of the large room. Imperiati, sleeves rolled up but tie still tight to his collar, strolled back and forth among them. He was wearing a wireless headset.

"What have you done with Rostislawitch?" Ferguson demanded.

"Signor Rostislawitch lacks proper documentation. He is being questioned," said Imperiati blandly.

"Come on, Imperiati. We were working together."

"Partners, eh? And what do you call a partner who does not fully—*come si dice?*—disclose what he knows?"

"What didn't I tell you?"

"Signore Rostislawitch had laboratories in Chechnya. Is he a war criminal?"

"Not that I know of. No."

Imperiati turned the corner of his mouth upward in a wry smile. "Is he the target, or is he in a better position to be the murderer, signore?"

"He's the target," said Ferguson. "Maybe."

"And why would someone want to kill him?"

"I haven't figured it out yet."

"You have a theory, no?"

"No."

Imperiati shook his head.

"Listen, you told me yourself that you have two other likely targets," said Ferguson. "Why arrest him?"

"He has not been arrested. We are very careful about our legal procedures here in Italy, signore. It is within the police's rights to ask for identification. If a foreign citizen does not have a passport, he can be detained."

"When was the last time that happened? Nineteen thirty-nine?"

A uniformed police officer standing near the doorway signaled to Imperiati, who beckoned him over. Ferguson pulled out a chair and stared at the nearby surveillance screen.

Had T Rex been nearby when the police stopped Rostislawitch?

Ferguson wondered. They hadn't seen anyone on the street, but maybe he was in one of the buildings. Maybe the police arresting—or whatever Imperiati wanted to call it—Rostislawitch was a good idea. Maybe T Rex would be waiting outside, or feel anxious about getting the job over with. Maybe it would flush him out.

Lemonade out of lemons. More likely Rostislawitch would be killed right under the Italians' noses.

"Do you know a Nathaniel Hamilton?" Imperiati asked Ferguson when he returned.

"Sure. MI6. British agent."

"Why would he want to talk to me? Is he working with you?"

"Not with me. He has some interest in Rostislawitch as well."

"Why?"

"He wouldn't tell me," said Ferguson, rising. "I don't think he likes me."

Imperiati told the policeman to show Hamilton to his office.

"Where are you going?" Imperiati asked Ferguson as he started to follow him down the hall.

"I thought maybe you could use a translator."

"My English isn't good?"

"It's fine. Hamilton's is pretty sub par."

Imperiati frowned.

"I should have known you'd be here, torquing things up," said Hamilton, spotting Ferguson as he came up the stairs.

"Come on, Hamilton. That's your job."

"This way, Signor Hamilton," said Imperiati.

"I'm going to go grab a coffee," Ferguson told Imperiati. "Want anything? Coffee, maybe a little cannoli?"

"*No grazie.*"

"Your loss."

19

Under other circumstances, Rostislawitch might have demanded to call the Russian consulate. Having just left the Iranian, however, he thought it best to keep his mouth shut until he could figure out what exactly was going on.

The police had taken him to a small police station on the outskirts of the city, shown him to a room, and asked him to fill out an identity paper. As soon as he sat down at the desk and picked up the pencil, they left, and hadn't been back since.

He wondered if the Iranian had arranged this to intimidate him. It seemed unlikely; they already had an agreement.

Maybe it was nothing. Rostislawitch wanted it to be nothing—a desire he couldn't trust.

There were other Russians at the conference. He knew two of the scientists vaguely; the others he didn't recognize. Perhaps one was an intelligence agent, and had somehow learned what he was up to.

That was impossible. No, not impossible, but improbable.

Besides, the Russian intelligence agencies would *not* have the Italians arrest him.

The paper filled out, he got up and paced the room. If he got out of here, he would go back to his hotel, lock the door, and not leave until it was time for his train home.

He'd like to see the girl, Thera, with her curly black hair and darting green eyes. She might think of him as her father or a kindly uncle, but he'd like to see her anyway.

If he got out of here.

20

BOLOGNA, ITALY

"We've been looking at the photos you uploaded, Ferg," Corrigan told Ferguson as he sat in a café across the street from the police station. "He's not on any hot list we have."

"The name doesn't mean anything?"

"Supposedly a banker. Did some deals for Iran but nothing major that we know of. Nothing from MI6, but you know how that goes. I have Ciello working on it."

"Get back to me."

"Well yeah, but—"

Ferguson killed the connection and looked at his watch. It was now two in the afternoon—which made it 8 a.m. back in the States. He got up, went to the phone booth in the back, and after dumping in a few euros punched in the 800 number of his phone card, then Corrine Alston's cell.

"This is Corrine."

"This is Ferg."

"Bob—"

"Call my sat phone from a secure line."

"Bob—"

Someone had sat at the table near where Ferguson was, so he went outside and strolled down the street. A pair of police officers—plainclothes, but obvious—strolled by, and Ferguson started to wonder if maybe Imperiati had sent someone to watch him and listen in. Ordinarily he wasn't too paranoid about having a conversation in a public place—he knew from experience that it was easy to leave out enough details to keep most eavesdroppers confused. But now he went over to an idling tour bus and stood by it, waiting for Corrine to find his number and call back.

"I was beginning to think you forgot me," he told her when she finally did, about five minutes later.

"I do have other things to do."

"Drop them."

"I can't drop the President, Ferg."

"Too heavy, huh?"

"What's up?"

"The British have been watching an Iranian named Anghuyu Jahan. His nickname is Atha. He's bought things for the Iranians before. You're going to have to press Corrigan to find out exactly what. He had a meeting with our guy at lunch today. Could be he's looking for information about weaponized bacteria."

"Can you speak up? I'm having trouble hearing you. It sounds like you're next to a bus."

Ferguson laid out the situation for her, explaining that if the Russian was trying to set up some sort of deal with the Iranian, that might be a reason for him to be assassinated.

"What we need is information from MI6 on what the scoop is with the Iranian, why they're following him for starters."

"Is that related to T Rex?"

"No, but it's a heck of a lot more interesting," Ferguson told her. "I'll keep looking for T Rex. See what you can do about this."

"What about Rostislawitch?"

"Oh yeah, that reminds me. The Italians just picked Rostislawitch up on suspicion of failing to like red wine."

"They put him jail? I can't hear you."

"They're holding him."

"Do you want me to try and get him out?"

"No, it's not a big deal. I think the British are trying, because they think Atha's going to meet with him again and they want to be there. The British MI6 agent who's working the case is rather dull."

"Does MI6 know about T Rex?"

"Not from me, but the Italians may tell them. Then again, maybe not. Imperiati isn't dumb. Maybe he won't like Hamilton, either."

21

"If you hold him, they won't be able to meet. There won't be a transaction. Months of work will be lost." Hamilton pitched forward on the small metal chair, trying to drive his point home to the Italian. It was more like several days—the tip that Atha was traveling to Europe had been passed last week—but *months* sounded considerably more impressive.

"I don't want a catastrophe in Bologna," said Imperiati.

"This isn't about Bologna. It has nothing to do with Bologna. They came here because the conference gave Rostislawitch a pretext. It has nothing to do with him."

"The Americans had information that there will be a terrorist attack."

Hamilton snorted.

"They believe an assassin has been hired to kill someone here and in the process he will kill very many other people."

"The Americans don't know their arm from a tree trunk."

"Scusi?"

"The American CIA is not what it once was," said Harrison. "We'll leave it at that. Ferguson? You're best off ignoring anything he tells you."

"He seems competent enough."

"I could tell you stories, believe me."

One thing about Ferguson did impress Hamilton—he had an uncanny knack of getting people to think he was God, or at least his stand-in. Persuading the Italian might not take much, but Hamilton had seen him turn several accomplished Algerian double agents into putty. Women he might understand—the rogue was good-looking, after all. But men? He was nothing but a smart aleck.

"The decision on what to do with Signor Rostislawitch must be made by someone above me in rank," said Imperiati. "It is not my decision."

"Well, who is that then? How can I talk to him?"

"She—Gina Assisi. You would speak to her in Roma."

"Great," said Hamilton. He rose. "In the meantime, take my advice and ignore half of what Ferguson tells you."

"Only half?"

"The other half will be the opposite of truth. So if you switch it around, you'll be all right."

Imperiati found Ferguson in the squad room after he finished with Hamilton. The America CIA officer was examining some of the surveillance feeds.

"Anything interesting?" asked Imperiati.

"Everything's interesting," Ferguson told him. "It's just a question to what degree."

"And so is anything here interesting to the proper degree?"

"No. If T Rex has been watching Rostislawitch he's been very careful about doing so."

"Why do you call the assassin T Rex?"

"It was a code name he used on one of his cases."

"The one where he killed a CIA officer?"

"Yes, actually."

"My superiors spoke to your superiors. They wanted to impress on us the importance of capturing this man."

"Did they?"

Imperiati shrugged. "Everyone has matters of importance. Perhaps you would like lunch?"

"Why not?" said Ferguson.

The small trattoria two blocks away had been recommended by one of the local police detectives, partly for its discretion and partly for its minestrone. Imperiati savored both, getting a back booth and sorting through the soup as if he were looking for gems in a pan of stream sand. He poked the vegetables and beans and macaroni with his spoon, herding them to the center of the bowl, then scooped and slurped.

Ferguson stuck with the veal piccata. He liked his food both solid and stationary when he ate it.

"Signor Hamilton doesn't like you much," said Imperiati.

"Not much. But then I don't like him. He screwed up something I was working on in Algeria two years ago. Almost got me killed."

"And what was that?"

"You've worked on things you can't talk about, I'm sure."

"I'm sorry. My career has been very boring," added Imperiati. "I've never had action outside of the country."

Imperiati paused; *action* was not quite the correct word, but apparently it had served.

"So yes, very boring," he said, continuing. "But I like it that way. I can go home to my wife, my children. A boring father. But a successful one." Imperiati snared a piece of celery in the soup. "Now, the Americans and the British come to Italy, come to my city, and for them, boring is no good. They want adventure."

"Not me," said Ferguson. "I want T Rex."

"But to get him, you are willing to have some adventure, yes?"

"I'll take whatever comes."

"While I would prefer things to be boring."

They ate in silence for a while. Both men realized they had different agendas, and both had been told to pursue them at all costs.

"Did Hamilton tell you why he's here?" Ferguson asked.

"He is trying to stop a business transaction."

"I doubt that. More than likely he's not sure what's going on. Except for the obvious."

"The obvious?" asked Imperiati.

"Germ warfare expert talks to a country looking to replace nukes on its weapons of mass destruction menu. Pretty simple."

"Too simple maybe."

"Maybe," agreed Ferguson.

"And so your man is trying to kill him?"

"Maybe. If he's working for the Iranians."

"Do you see my difficulty?"

Before Ferguson could answer, Imperiati's cell phone rang.

"*Scusi*," he said. He took out the phone and walked a short distance away.

Ferguson guessed who it was and what they said from the frown on Imperiati's face.

"Signor Rostislawitch will be released," Imperiati told him when he came back to the table.

"Are you going to warn him?" Ferguson asked.

"I am not sure what use a warning would be," said the Italian. "We are to watch him. We may make a decision to arrest him if necessary. He will only leave the country if we wish it."

"And if MI6 wants it."

"Why do you think the British put pressure on us?"

"Because I know we didn't."

"A decision to arrest him would be made by my superiors," said Imperiati. "If it were my decision, he would be deported now."

"A boring solution," said Ferguson. He got up. "Time to get back to work, I'm afraid. Good luck with the soup."

22

CIA HEADQUARTERS, LANGLEY, VIRGINIA

Daniel Slott got up from his desk and began pacing around his office, holding the phone up to his ear and trying not to knock anything over with the long cord.

Corrine Alston was on the other end of the line, calling about the British and wondering why they hadn't told the CIA what they were up to.

While he would hesitate to call himself fond of Corrine Alston, Slott had come to respect her over the past year or so that they'd worked together. She labored under two great handicaps—her age and her good looks, both of which made people think she was an intellectual lightweight. But she handled things with tact and even finesse, managing not only to do her job as the President's "conscience" on Special Demands but in several instances actually helping the group accomplish its goals.

Still, though, she was an outsider, and even though she'd worked for the congressional intelligence committees, Corrine needed to be educated in some of the most basic intelligence "facts."

Including the one stating that one's allies were never to be trusted.

"We do work with MI6, and MI5, very closely," Slott told her. "We are allies. But believe me—*believe me*—they don't tell us everything they're doing. Just as we don't trust them. I mean tell them."

It was a Freudian slip, but it was definitely the truth. There was a great deal of rivalry between the U.S. and British intelligence services. Even on matters that they worked closely on—in Iraq and Afghanistan, for example—there were rivalries and jealousies and what the State Department people called "lack of candor." On both sides.

"What are they doing with the Iranian then?" Corrine asked.

"I have a call in—"

"What's your best guess?"

"I really don't like to guess."

"Make an exception."

Slott glanced down at the one-page Agency dossier on Anghuyu "Atha" Jahan. It claimed that he was a legitimate banker, and that while he had worked for the Iranian Interior Ministry some years before, he no longer had any formal connection with Iran's foreign service or any part of its government. This was supposedly because of conflicts with high-ranking members of the Revolutionary Guard, which controlled much of Iran's foreign services and spy network. Lately he had traveled to Africa, though the paper did not say why.

Obviously the dossier was not complete.

"If Ferguson thinks the Iranians are trying to get some sort of access to the Russian biological warfare program, he may be right," said Slott. "Rostislawitch would be a good point of contact. Maybe this is a preliminary recruitment. The British may know more."

"Will they tell us?"

"Maybe. I can't guarantee anything, Corrine. We don't control them. I have a few things going on with them now, including the guerillas in Indonesia, but I have to tell you, they can be damn tight about saying anything. They get—if things were reversed, I wouldn't be telling them anything about T Rex. Or as little as necessary. It was the same thing with the Italians. Really, we only went to them because you insisted."

"If the British aren't going to cooperate, maybe the President should talk to the Prime Minister."

"I didn't say they weren't going to cooperate." Slott put his finger into the phone cord, twisting it around. "I just said they haven't gotten back to me yet. Maybe they're checking with their people in the field."

"I'd like to talk to them myself."

"That's my job."

Suddenly angry, Slott set himself behind his desk, physically ready for battle.

"You're right," said Corrine, realizing she'd overstepped her bounds. "I'm sorry. Of course you're the one to talk to them."

"I'll let you know what's going on."

"I'm not trying to do your job, Dan. I'm just trying to do what the President wants me to."

"I understand," he said, reaching to disconnect.

23

BOLOGNA, ITALY

Thera spent two hours pretending to take notes in a session on the uses of bacteriophages, or viruses that infect bacteria, to alter DNA. She kept sneaking glances at the others in the room, trying to see if T Rex or one of his minions was there looking for Rostislawitch. But the sixty or so people seemed to be legitimate biologists, or at least were very good at keeping their eyes from glazing over.

Thera left the session early and walked through the hall, checking to see if anyone was hanging around. But she was the only person who was suspicious. A small table had been set up in the lobby with coffee and tea; Thera poured herself a cup of the latter, giving her an excuse to look around some more. As she poured herself some milk, two men came down the hall for coffee. One was in his fifties or early sixties, not rotund but far from svelte, his corduroy sport coat barely able to close over his midsection. The other man, taller, with a black goatee, wore a tight shirt with a mock turtleneck. He had Merrell Wilderness hiking boots with bright blue shoelaces on his feet, and a Bulova chronograph about two links too loose on his wrist.

"You seem very studious," the man said to Thera, speaking English with a German accent.

"Not really."

"American?"

"Greek."

He obviously thought Greek women were easy: his face lit up and he extended his hand.

"Gunther," he told her.

"Thera."

"You are teaching where?"

"I'm doing my post-doc," said Thera, repeating the cover story they had worked out for her.

"What was your thesis?"

"I'd be afraid to bore you," she told him.

"Not boring." He glanced at the older man who'd come out with him. The man smiled back.

"Thera Metaxes," Thera told the other man.

He introduced himself shyly. His English was not as good as his young colleague's—a fact he told her in German.

"My German, I guess, is not very good, either," answered Thera in German.

"But you do speak it."

"Not very well."

"Then you must come with us and we will help you improve it," said Gunther. "We are just sneaking out."

"I was going to meet a friend," Thera told him. "I may be late already." She glanced at her watch.

"Oh, the Russian."

"Who?" said Thera.

"I saw you this morning with a man," said Gunther. "I thought perhaps a colleague."

"That was just someone I've met here," said Thera. She couldn't tell exactly what Gunther's interest was—did he want to pick her up? Or was he interested in Rostislawitch?

Was this T Rex? He looked athletic, reasonably fit, and strong, though those weren't necessarily requirements.

"Someone you just met?" asked Gunther.

Thera forced a laugh. "He's not a boyfriend."

"You have no boyfriend?"

Thera tilted her head and gave him a closed-mouth smile.

"I'm late," she told him. "But maybe we can talk later."

"Your dissertation."

"Yours would be more interesting," she said, putting the tea down and walking out.

24

BOLOGNA, ITALY

Atha felt his chest constricting as the minister berated him. They were using an open phone, and while they were using words that had nothing to do with the material or the Russian, surely the minister's vehemence would be a tip-off to anyone listening. Atha was sure he would be arrested as soon as he hung up.

But the venom in the minister's voice was worse: "If the loan does not go through, your position will be terminated. The dock is ready to be built."

It wasn't a loan that they were talking about, and it wasn't Atha's job that was at stake.

The Iranian hung up the phone and walked out of the train station to his Mercedes. The driver was arguing with a policeman, who was in the process of giving him a ticket. Atha got in the back without saying anything.

He could not afford to be cheated. It would be one thing—a very bad thing, admittedly—to fail to get the material, but another thing entirely to give the money away and still not get it. He had to be sure.

Would the Russian be so foolish as to have the material with him?

Probably not. But if he did, that would be an easy solution to the problem of trust. Indeed, it would greatly add to Atha's profit.

It was a possibility that would have to be investigated.

And if Rostislawitch had no intention of turning over the material, if this was all a scam, what then?

Well, then he would simply be forced to cooperate. There was no other choice.

Perhaps he should simply take that option now.

No, too risky—the scientist might find a way to resist, at least long enough to upset the minister's plans, which in turn would go badly for Atha.

"Take the ticket from the policeman and let us go," Atha told his driver. "We have much work to do this afternoon."

25

BOLOGNA, ITALY

The crown jewel of the motley fleet of bicycles, mopeds, scooters, and motorcycles the team had rented was a Ducati Hypermotad 1100, a smallish street bike that could do 200 kilometers an hour without breaking a sweat. Ferguson retrieved it from a hotel lot near the police station and went out to the substation where Rostislawitch had been taken, getting there just as the Russian climbed into a police car to be driven back over to the conference.

Imperiati had ordered that Rostislawitch be given a full apology and an explanation about there being a terrorist alert in the city, implying that he'd been picked up in a case of mistaken identity. Ferguson wasn't sure how far that explanation would go; it didn't particularly matter to him, and he suspected that Imperiati wanted the Russian to know it was false. From the Italian's point of view, the best thing that could happen now would be for the Russian to leave.

Ferguson hoped he didn't leave Bologna, though he was prepared to follow the scientist if necessary. He was still Ferguson's best, albeit tenuous, link to T Rex. The Iranian connection gave Corrigan some new queries to push, and maybe there'd be something to shake out of the British. But for now the best approach seemed to be following Rostislawitch.

The police took the Russian out of the center city onto one of the roads that circled Bologna, giving their surveillance teams a little more time to get into position in the center city. Ferguson cranked the motorcycle, hunkering down toward the bright red gas tank as the wind whipped against his helmet. He sped ahead, wove through a trio of trucks, then slipped off the highway to let them catch up.

"Rankin, they're about five minutes away," Ferg said over the radio. He'd clipped his microphone to the padding at the bottom of the helmet near his mouth. "What's going on?"

"Nothing exciting. Police swept the block in front of the art building a half hour ago. I'm two blocks away. I just parked the bike."

"Anybody look suspicious?"

"Just me."

Ferguson laughed. Rankin had made a joke, made himself the butt of it—*and* it was almost funny.

There was hope for him yet.

"Listen, Thera wants to talk to you," said Rankin. "She's got a theory on some Germans, like one of them may be T Rex."

"Where is she?"

"She went to find out where their hotel was. She talked to Corrigan about getting some background on them."

"Are they in the Conference Center?"

"They went out for lunch. I've been looking for them around here, but I haven't seen them."

"I'll be there in a minute. Do me a favor and check with Guns over at Rosty's hotel. Make sure he's ready in case Rostislawitch decides to go over there at the last minute."

"I just talked to him. He's ready."

"Talk to him again."

Ferguson revved the bike and spurted back into traffic. He had a little trouble with the clutch, jerking slightly as he upshifted.

The police car was about a half mile ahead, its top clearly visible in the thickening traffic. By the time it turned back onto the city streets, Ferguson was only a few car lengths behind.

Ferguson assumed that Hamilton or one of his people was in a car not too far away, though he hadn't seen the MI6 officer. Of course, it would be just like Hamilton to drop Rostislawitch after making a big row about him.

Traffic had snarled near Porta San Vitale. The police car squeezed around a blocked intersection, moving westward along San Vitale and then up toward Zamboni.

"About three minutes," Ferguson said over the radio.

Rankin started walking up the block away from the building where the conference was being held, figuring that if T Rex was watching the place, he'd be easier to spot from behind after the police car came up. The fact that they were in the middle of a city made things difficult; there were plenty of buildings nearby where he could hide. A number were private buildings that a stranger might not have access to—but then a fifty- or hundred-euro bill might easily change that. The police had a pair of sharpshooters with binoculars on the roofs, but Rankin considered them next to useless—by the time they saw anything, it'd be too late.

Fortunately, his job wasn't to protect the Russian.

As Rankin crossed the block, he spotted the police car up ahead, stuck in traffic. As he glanced around, still in the roadway, a yellow panel van veered across the intersection, nearly hitting him. He jerked back, cursing.

"Yo, motherfucker," he yelled.

The truck angled into a space near the curb next to a hydrant. Rather than backing up and pulling in properly, the driver jumped from the cab.

Rankin's first thought was that the jerk wanted a piece of him.

Then he realized the man was running in the other direction.

Rostislawitch saw the traffic and decided his best bet was to get out of the car and walk the final two blocks to the art building.

"*Grazie, grazie, signore,*" he said. He reached for the handle at the back door, but the lock was arranged so that the door could only be opened from the outside.

"You want to get out here?" asked the policeman in the passenger seat. He used English, but Rostislawitch had a little trouble with the accent.

"Here? Yes," said the Russian finally. "I'll walk."

He wanted to get away from the police, away from everything, as quickly as he could.

The policeman hopped out of the car and opened the door.

"Once again, we apologize," said the policeman, standing stiffly to emphasize the formality of his statement. "If we can help you, you must only call."

"It's OK. OK," said Rostislawitch. He left the door open and began walking toward the building.

Ferguson swung the bike to the other side of the police car, then inched around it, moving in first gear. Rostislawitch began walking swiftly ahead in the direction of the building. Ferguson started looking for Rankin, who should have been nearby, when he caught sight of a woman on the corner opposite him. She was tall, about five-ten in flats, with windblown blond hair that came straight back from her forehead. She looked harried, her lips pale and parched, and she had a cell phone in her hand.

Ferguson knew the lips well. He'd kissed them several times, most memorably the night the woman had saved his life. Her name was Kiska Babev, and she was a member of the Russian Federal Security Service or Federal'naya Sluzhba Bezopasnosti, or FSB, the main successor to the KGB.

"Ferg!" shouted Rankin over the radio. "That yellow truck halfway down the block. I think it's a bomb!"

Kiska was looking at her cell phone. Rostislawitch was walking swiftly, approaching the truck.

Ferguson cranked the Ducati, shooting forward with a burst of speed. Five yards from Rostislawitch he leaned hard and sent the bike into a skid; he put a little too much weight on the side and flew off, tumbling into Rostislawitch as the Ducati slid across the cobblestones.

Ferguson draped his body over the Russian, intending to grab him and run. But before he could get up, the van exploded.

ACT III

His outward smiles conceal'd his inward smart.

—Virgil, *The Aeneid* (Dryden translation)

1

It was as if a twister had come at him sideways, throwing Rostislawitch down and then pummeling him with debris and grit, turning the day black. He couldn't breathe and he couldn't hear. A man had been dropped on him, a helmeted motorcyclist. Something had exploded—Rostislawitch felt the concussion and thought of Chechnya in the final days he'd spent there.

There was a humming sensation—not people singing, but a kind of vibration that came from inside him. He thought of his wife, of the little church where they had gone to marry in the days when worship was still officially outlawed, though the authorities looked the other way or even attended themselves. The sensation was the same as what he felt standing near the altar as the pipe organ played, the floor, the walls, vibrating with its sonorous tones.

Sweat poured from his body. Someone looked at him, stared into his eyes. They might be speaking, but he couldn't hear.

Was he dying? He didn't think so. He didn't wish it, even if it would be an escape. To wish for death was wrong.

The sky suddenly turned very blue. Rostislawitch thought of the girl at the conference, Thera. He'd like to see her again.

And the Iranian?

Maybe he had done this. Or was it perhaps the work of the Russian FSB, trying to eliminate him?

The humming stopped; Rostislawitch heard a scream and then the sound of a siren in the distance.

After the initial shock of the blast cleared, Rankin froze, unsure whether to chase after the man who'd left the van or go for Ferguson, who'd been back on the other side of the van, closer to the bomb. Then Rankin's instincts kicked in and he ran across the street, racing toward the prone figures curled against the side of a building. He started to touch Ferguson's body, bracing himself for blood and worse; instead, Ferguson rolled over to his stomach and then jumped, unsteady but intact, to his feet.

Rostislawitch was a few feet away, dazed and breathing heavily, but seemingly OK. The nearby cars had taken the brunt of the explosion; one was on fire.

Ferguson pointed at Rostislawitch. "Is he OK?" he asked, his voice faint.

Rankin thought Ferguson's helmet was muffling his voice. But as Rankin bent to check the Russian more closely he realized the explosion had temporarily damaged his hearing.

"He's breathing," said Rankin, straightening.

Ferguson pointed down the street. "Check and see if anyone's watching," he said.

"I saw a guy get out of the van."

"Shit."

"You sure you're all right?"

"What'd he look like?"

Rankin described the glimpse he'd gotten—a man, five-eight, with a blue jacket and a green ski cap.

"Which way?" asked Ferguson.

"That way."

"Go. I'll talk to the Italians. Go. *Go!*"

2

WASHINGTON, D.C.

Corrine Alston was in the middle of a meeting with lawyers from the FTC about the proposed language approving the merger of the two satellite radio companies when she got an alert on her Blackberry to call Daniel Slott. She stifled her angst, and waited a few seconds for the proceedings to reach a natural pause before excusing herself.

"Slott."

"This is Corrine Alston."

"There was an explosion in Bologna. Our people are OK."

"T Rex?"

"Not sure. Not a bad guess, though. We're still getting details. This was five minutes ago."

"Does the President know?"

"I thought you'd want to update him yourself."

"I will, thanks."

Simple courtesy, Corrine wondered, or was Slott trying to make sure he wasn't associated with a setback?

"I finally heard back from British MI6," added the CIA's Deputy Director. "They've promised to cooperate."

"Will they?"

"Maybe," said Slott. "They didn't have much else about Atha. Some humint said he was worth watching in Italy. Human intelligence. The source was vague. That's their story. I don't think they're lying, but it is thin."

"I'm calling the President right now," she told him, hanging up.

3

BOLOGNA, ITALY

Atha took a deep breath as the elevator opened, then walked out into the hallway of Rostislawitch's hotel. Unlike most large hotels, there were no signs to show which way the numbers ran; Atha had to check on the doors and then guess the right direction. The hotel's hallways were laid out in an intersecting H pattern, with an occasional dead end due to an oversized suite, and it took him five minutes to find the room. By then, sweat had begun dripping down his sleeves to the palms of his hands, and running down his back. When he found the door to Rostislawitch's room, the Iranian hesitated a moment, then knocked.

There was no answer. By now the scientist would be at the conference several blocks away. Atha knocked again, then reached into his pocket for the electronic room key.

The device was an emergency key card that could be used as a master key. The one downside was that, like any key card, it would leave an audit trail in the hotel system; depending on how the doors and locks were wired and what procedures the hotel followed, it could alert the main desk. Atha had posted his driver in the lobby as a lookout to warn him if they sent someone in his direction.

His talk with the minister had left Atha jittery, even fearful. He had never been under such pressure for a deal before. The rewards would be much greater—many times so—but the sharp beat of his heart made him think that even if he was successful, he had traded several years of his life for it.

Atha's hands were so wet with perspiration that the card slipped and fell to the floor. He quickly scooped the card back up, slid it into the slot and then out, and pushed the door open.

The room was small, and empty. The bed had been made. There was a small briefcase next to the desk and an old piece of luggage on the stand near the window. Atha reached into his pockets and pulled on some rubber gloves. Then he began pulling open the drawers.

There was nothing in them. He went to the minifridge below the desk, kneeling so he could look inside. Some orange drink, water, a few beers, and wine. Atha looked at each bottle carefully, making sure they were legitimate.

The problem was he didn't know how big the package with the material would be. Dr. Hamid, the expert who had helped Atha set up the project and who was now waiting for him to return with the material, had said the material could be contained in a relatively small vessel, and could be stored for several days at room temperature—one of the benefits of the design. But beyond that, his description was vague. The material, Hamid believed, could be carried in a liquid or in a gel. Since only Rostislawitch had seen it, any description was only a guess.

Atha rose and opened the suitcase. There were clothes, and two photographs—one of Rostislawitch with a woman, and another of just the woman herself. Atha assumed it was Rostislawitch's wife, who the scientist had mentioned had died some time ago. She was a small woman, with a ruddy, darkish face and brown hair. A handsome face, despite her years.

The Iranian continued hunting through the clothes, placing them on the bed carefully to make it easier for him to look. There was nothing in the bag but clothes. The socks at the bottom had small holes in the heels; the pants next to them were frayed at the bottom.

It was useless. Rostislawitch was a brilliant man, a scientist, a genius. He would not keep the material with him. That was a simple precaution.

Had he left it in Russia? He had promised to make it available within twenty-four hours.

So it *was* a ruse. A trap. Maybe Russian intelligence was behind the entire thing. Atha's own intelligence service had assured him Rostislawitch would be acting alone, but what did those fools know? They were guessing, telling him what they thought the minister wanted to hear.

Atha returned the clothes to the suitcase and smoothed out the bed. He started to leave, then remembered the briefcase.

He stared at its position against the desk, memorizing it. Then he picked it up and looked at it. Made of leather, it had a flap over the top secured by a simple lock; Atha pushed the center clasp; it sprang open, the case pitching down because of its weight. Papers and pens flew onto the floor. Once again, Atha began to sweat profusely, his hands trembling.

He put the briefcase on the bed and looked inside. There was one large book, in Russian; he couldn't tell what it was about, but it looked like some sort of reference or textbook. There was a spiral-bound notebook next to it. Atha pulled it out, looked at a few pages; it was completely blank. A folder in another compartment had loose-leaf paper filled with what looked like notes for a lecture.

Atha replaced them, then knelt to look at the papers. They were travel documents, some in Italian, some in Russian—printouts of Web reservations, he thought.

He was beginning to translate the Italian when his mobile phone rang. Atha jumped to his feet.

"What?" he said, pulling the phone from his pocket.

"Something is going on. There are sirens. Did you hear the thud? An explosion?"

"No. What's happening in the lobby?"

"Everyone's looking out the window, and going into the street."

"Keep watching. I'll be down shortly."

Atha snapped the phone off, and slipped it back into his pocket. Then he picked up the travel documents.

Rostislawitch had taken the train from Moscow to Munich, and from Munich to Italy.

But not to Bologna, at least not according to the ticket information. He'd gone to Naples.

Why go that far south, only to double back and return?

Perhaps he had made a mistake, buying the ticket to the farther city, then getting off beforehand. But surely a man without much money, which Rostislawitch was beyond doubt, would have turned in the unused portion.

He would not have bought it in the first place. That was the sort of mistake one did not make; even a man unfamiliar with Italy's geography would know to go no farther than Rome.

Atha went through the papers again. Was there a hotel reservation? What would Rostislawitch have done in Naples?

There were more papers indicating he'd taken another train from Naples, this time to Rome, and from there to Bologna. He'd had only fifteen minutes between trains in Naples, and five in Rome.

Fifteen minutes would not have been very long. But he must have used it to leave the material somewhere. Or to give it to someone.

Atha went back to the suitcase and searched it again, this time looking for a receipt or a key or some other clue that would tell him what Rostislawitch had done in Naples, or anywhere else along the route for that matter.

Atha couldn't remember the train station there. It was relatively big, he thought. How long would it take to get from one train to another, to find the right platform? Five minutes, at least, if you weren't familiar with it. Maybe more. Barely enough time to leave the station and get back.

Had someone been waiting there for Rostislawitch? The background information the minister had developed months before said the scientist had virtually no friends, and no foreign contacts; it was what made him such a likely target in the first place.

Hiring someone to take a package would not be difficult, but who would you trust? Naples was the sort of place where one could find people willing to do almost anything for a price, but there was always someone on the next corner willing to outbid you, then have your throat slit for a joke.

If the scientist handed the material off to someone, it could be anywhere. But if he had no accomplice, then it would have to be very close to the station.

Naples. Atha could go there himself: his backup plan for leaving Italy had been arranged around leaving from the port city, if flying out by air to Libya seemed too dangerous.

He was getting ahead of himself. The material might be at any stop along the way: the fact that the scientist bought the ticket did not mean that he had used it, or at least not all of the portions.

Still, a man on a tight budget would tend to economize where possible.

There should be a clue somewhere among Rostislawitch's things. An address or a key, a phone number.

Atha went through the drawers and then back into the suitcase quickly; he found nothing.

Maybe the scientist had it with him. Well, in that case, finding it would be easy—though not a job for Atha.

His phone rang again. He snapped to on.

"Yes, what?"

"There are police cars, sirens, soldiers on the street!" said the driver.

"Calm down," said Atha, though hardly calm himself. "Go outside. Move the car. Drive. I'll tell you where to pick me up. Go."

4

BOLOGNA, ITALY

By the time he arrived at the hospital, Rostislawitch had shaken off the daze of the explosion and the resulting chaos. He checked his arms and legs carefully, and knew he was all right. But the nurse who saw him as he was wheeled in couldn't understand what he said—his English had deserted him, and his Russian was very fast, fueled by adrenaline. She waved the gurney toward a warren of curtained rooms at the right. Two doctors came over, talking to him in Italian and then in unsteady English, but Rostislawitch failed to make them understand that he was fine. They flashed their small lights in his eyes, poked his chest, and ran their fingers around his forehead.

"Bones broken?" asked one in English, examining Rostislawitch's legs.

He understood the words and said in Russian that he was OK, but English remained stubbornly beyond his tongue. He had no choice but to turn his body over to them for a few moments, allowing himself to be twisted and pulled. When he didn't shriek, the doctors concluded that he was probably all right—but ordered X-rays and a CAT scan to be sure. Then they moved on to the next curtained cubicle.

Rostislawitch pushed himself upright on the bed. It had been a considerable time since he'd been in a hospital—not since Olga's final days.

He remembered the large wardroom, the smell of death disguised as medicine.

And Olga's face, staring up at him from a cowl of sheets, her life drained down into an invisible hole beneath the mattress, the last drops slowly seeping away.

That week he'd wanted the whole world to feel his grief.

And he still did. Take revenge against everyone.

Rostislawitch stared at the curtains in front of him, his eyes focused on the pattern of the folds, imperfect waving lines up and down. He had no choice but to go ahead with the Iranian. He'd kill him otherwise.

The curtain pulled open abruptly. A nurse appeared. Rostislawitch stared at her, confused, then saw there was someone behind her.

Thera, the girl from the conference.

Thera.

"Are you OK, Professor Rostislawitch? We heard—we thought—there was an announcement at the conference that you were dead."

Her eyes looked puffy, Rostislawitch thought.

Thera switched to Greek, speaking rapidly, telling Rostislawitch that she'd been very concerned and come immediately.

"I am fine," said Rostislawitch, in English. The first words seemed to break through a wall. The others were easier. "I am OK. How did you hear?"

Thera put her hand to her chest, explaining that the conference sessions had been temporarily postponed, and announcements made about the blast. His name had been mentioned.

She was lying, but for that moment her concern was real to her, and not one person out of a hundred could have detected any insincerity. She thought of what she would feel if her uncle had been hurt; he looked a little like Rostislawitch, though not as far out of shape.

"I was worried," she repeated. "Concerned."

Rostislawitch felt a surge of energy, then embarrassment over how he must look. "I am ready to leave," he said, starting to get up.

"Are you sure? They said you needed X-rays."

"X-rays?" He waved his hand, then pushed his feet over the side of the bed to the floor. "A good vodka. That is what I need."

5

Miraculously, no one had died when the bomb exploded, but the attack had unleashed a firestorm of political and media chaos, with officials and newspeople descending on the city. Imperiati managed to stay behind the scenes, passing off the public face of the emergency to a deputy interior minister whose specialty was public relations. But the SISDE officer had no way of shucking the real responsibility, and he seemed to have aged several years when Ferguson finally managed to get to the police station in answer to several calls. Ferguson expected him to blame the U.S. for the attack, but instead his first words were, "It could have been much worse."

Ferguson nodded.

"You were almost killed," said Imperiati. "I thought you did not care about the Russian."

"I don't. I was screwing around with the bike and lost control."

Imperiati processed the words, then raised an eyebrow. The American had an odd sense of humor.

"The police think this was a terror attack," said Ferguson.

"And you don't?"

"I think it'd be a pretty big coincidence," said Ferguson. "We know T Rex is looking to strike his victim here, and make it look like a terrorist attack. And you didn't encounter earlier intelligence of a group targeting the area."

"How do you know that?" said Imperiati defensively.

"Because you would have told me the other day if you did. Not necessarily in words," added Ferguson quickly. "But in the way you questioned me."

Ferguson was correct, but the Italian intelligence officer resisted telling him so. "I have to keep an open mind," he said.

"Sometimes that means resisting the obvious conclusions. T Rex has used a bomb like this before. Even though it wasn't at one of the places his people scouted out, it has to be him. I can get some forensic people here to help you. Real quiet."

"We have many experts. The work will be very thorough. The information your people have supplied has already been useful," added Imperiati. "We will continue to share information of mutual benefit."

Ferguson pulled the chair behind him out and sat down, studying Imperiati. He needed the Italian's help, but he was uncomfortable saying so. He remembered something his father had told him once: it's more difficult working with an ally than with an enemy.

When had he told him that?

Just before Moscow, where the Frenchman had screwed him, and Kiska had saved his life.

"There is something on your mind?" Imperiati asked.

"Yeah. Just before the bomb went off, I saw someone with a cell phone."

"A cell phone was used for a trigger." Imperiati knew this not because of any great forensic discovery but from simple police work—one of the first officers on the scene had found a portion of the bomb in a nearby yard.

Ferguson nodded as if he'd known, rather than merely suspected, this. The jammer in the art building wasn't strong enough to affect the block where the bombing took place.

"Can you describe the person with the phone?" said Imperiati.

"I can do better than that. I know who she is: Kiska Babev. She works for the Russian FSB."

"Is that your T Rex?"

"I don't know. I'm not sure why she would kill Rostislawitch."

Imperiati clapped his hands together. "But of course it makes sense. The MI6 agent, Harrison, follows an Iranian who meets with him. The Russians must be following, too—they want to eliminate him."

"Why wouldn't they get the Iranian then? Or just arrest our guy?

Killing him means they can't question him, find out who might be helping him, that sort of thing. Plus it can be messy. Collateral damage, as we've seen."

"He is in Italy. They cannot arrest him here."

"True. But we think T Rex is a freelancer," said Ferguson. He was still trying to work it out himself.

"You are sure about that? You told me—*che cosa hai detto?*—you said that you did not know who he might be. He could be anyone. Even yourself."

"I think we can rule me out." Ferguson rose. "If I get you information on Kiska Babev, background, aliases, can you find out where she is?"

"I would definitely appreciate the information," said Imperiati. "As far as finding her, I cannot guarantee. Of course we will want to find her, if she was there as you say. A witness if nothing else."

"That's right."

"I assume you're hoping I will share."

"I'd appreciate it."

The SISDE officer nodded. "We will do what we can."

"You'll have the information in ten minutes. At your e-mail address."

6

CIA BUILDING 24-442

Thomas Ciello lowered his head toward his computer, determined to ignore Debra Wu, though he knew she was standing in the doorway a few feet behind him.

"Thomas, I'm not going away," said Wu.

"I'm busy."

"Do you have the information Corrigan needs or not?" She turned her right hand over, glancing at her fingernails, which she'd just had done in a rose shade to match her lipstick.

"I'm getting it. Information doesn't just appear by magic, you know. I can't just blink my eyes and get it."

"Thomas, no one's going to blame you for getting it wrong," said Wu. "You have to just relax and move on."

"I didn't get it wrong!" Ciello jumped up from his machine. "I didn't say it was going to *be* a gas attack. I said possibility. *Pos-si-bil-i-ty.* Maybe. Could be. Not definite."

"Do you have the information on Kiska or not? Corrigan has to give it to the Italians *now*."

"I'm getting it."

"Cripes. All you have to do is pull it from the library."

"There's a lot more involved in intelligence analysis than calling up a file, Debra." Ciello flailed his arms. "I don't just pluck things out of the air."

"One of your little green men can't whisper it in your ear?"

Ciello sharpened his stare into a death gaze. The world was filled with skeptics, people so narrow-minded they couldn't see past their own lacquered fingernails.

"Just forward it to his queue, OK?" said Wu. "In five minutes."

"I'll do what I can," said Ciello, though she'd already swept out of the office.

The analyst turned back to his computer. He actually had the information that Corrigan needed, a simple outline of who Kiska Babev was—he'd gotten that when Ferguson's first text message came in. But Ciello knew that what the team really wanted was information proving or disproving that she was T Rex. And this was considerably more elusive.

Literally within minutes of the explosion that had sent Rostis-lawitch to the hospital, Ciello had begun looking for evidence that connected it to T Rex. The style precisely matched two previous T Rex assassinations, one in 2003 and the other barely twelve months ago. Details of those bombs were forwarded to the Italian investigators; several parallels had already been discovered, including the same detonation system, with the same wiring technique for the battery. At the same time, Ciello had noted that there was a distinct lack of parallels between bombings by "real" terrorists—most important, no uptick in monitored communications before the strike. The Italian investigators would have to collect considerably more information, of course, and would have several false leads—two separate groups had taken re-sponsibility for the attack—but Ciello was reasonably certain that the bomb had been the work of T Rex.

What was much more difficult, however, was discovering T Rex's identity. Ferguson's information about seeing Kiska Babev using a cell phone just before the bomb exploded was tantalizing, especially since the Italians had quickly concluded that the bomb was set off by phone. But as far as Ciello was concerned, it was merely a hint about a possi-ble direction his work should take.

Ciello had retrieved all of the Agency's information about Kiska Babev, trying to find evidence that she was T Rex. He'd begun by looking at what might be called the Agency's résumé on her, a brief dossier about where she'd gone to school, where her family was, and what her specialties seemed to be as a member of the FSB.

The information in these résumés tended to be somewhat sketchy and at times unreliable, depending on the individual. The Agency did not have access to most FSB officers' real résumés, and the information infrastructure in Russia—school and birth records, for example—was nowhere near as complete as in the West. Beyond that, the FSB, like the CIA and other intelligence agencies, often took steps to confuse anyone who happened to be watching, announcing divi-sions that didn't exist and purposely confusing work assignments and job titles. So Ciello's next job had been to assess how accurate this dossier was likely to be, and where the gaps were. He'd decided that it was at least in the ballpark; Babev appeared to be a colonel, relatively high up in the FSB structure, with an assignment that allowed her to travel despite her being based, apparently, in Moscow.

Besides the résumé, the Agency had a number of contact reports, mission briefings, and other documents containing information on dif-ferent foreign agents. Only rarely did the reports directly contain any-thing useful about the subject—Ferguson's, for example, were typically as terse as classified ads—but considerable information could be teased from them. Where the contact had been made, to take a simple exam-ple, not only revealed where the agent was assigned but often what part of the FSB he or she worked for and how high up the ranks he or she was. If there were enough reports, a pattern emerged showing the agent's specialties. And the lack of certain types of reports—nothing showing attempts at recruitment, to again give a simplistic example—could reveal a lot about an agent's function as well.

The portrait of Kiska Babev that had emerged was of a thirty-something overachiever—Ciello had three different sources for her birth date, all different—persevering against the traditionally male-dominated Russian intelligence structure. She seemed to have a specialty in science and had possibly started in the FSB's Science and Technical Service. Seven years before she had worked in what was charitably known as industrial espionage, with a cover as an administrative assistant to Aeroflot, the Russian airline company. After that, she had been in Chechnya, then Georgia; at some point she switched from recruiting scientists to spy to helping track down terrorists. Her face had been identified in a photo of onlookers at a thwarted Chechnyan terrorist attack on a Russian school in 2004; she seemed to be working undercover there, and had not received any notice in the admittedly brief write-ups about the incident.

It was in her anti-terror role that she had met Ferguson in Moscow. Ferguson was working undercover on a project to stop the clandestine flow of items that could be used for nuclear bombs and "dirty" radiological weapons. His exact reasons for being in Moscow were not included in his report, nor did he say much about Kiska Babev. But he had clearly had some interaction with her, since he not only listed her name but also made a notation that indicated she had assisted him.

Having studied everything the CIA knew about Kiska Babev, Ciello had then tried to find a match between her dossier and what was known about T Rex. The Agency had generic profiles for the different sorts of miscreants one might encounter in intelligence work; Kiska's background and personality did not mesh with what one would supposedly expect from an assassin. While Ciello considered the profiles little more than pop psychology, he nonetheless noted that there was no indication that Kiska had had any serious weapons or demolitions training. She had, however, been in Chechnya; one of T Rex's favorite methods of killing people involved car bombs, a technique employed there against the Russians.

Hard evidence of a connection was even more difficult to find. Ciello tried to place her at or near the scene of the assassinations, trying to match her description with the descriptions of possible suspects or even witnesses, trying to find any connection, no matter how thin, between her and the deaths.

The police reports on the murders contained very little useful information, beyond the evidence that the assassin was extremely thorough and professional. At first glance, there was little to connect any of the crimes to each other. The victims ranged from political figures, to businessmen with Mafia connections, to the CIA agent. It was the CIA, not a police agency, that had made the link, tracing wire transfers that moved through an Austrian account before and after each murder. Those transfers were used to identify several other murders, and a rough pattern had emerged. From there, they had found the advance person, and the message using T Rex as a name.

The accounts the money had passed through had been closed long ago. Apparently T Rex had developed a better way of getting his pay, because there had been at least one assassination connected with the advance person where the transfer wasn't detected. Most likely, said one of the analysts who had worked up the T Rex profile, he had adopted a system of multiple accounts and smaller transfers, but the efforts to discover them had not yielded any results.

Ciello had to go through channels to look for accounts in Kiska's name at the banks that had been used for the transfers—a request that, even for a high-priority operation like Special Demands, took some time to process and involved considerable paperwork and bureaucratic maneuvering, even with the banks that the agency had a "special relationship" with. Results would take several hours, if not days.

The CIA had a limited ability to track credit card transactions made by Russians in Europe. In theory it should have been easy to connect Kiska with a transaction in Bologna and then work backward from there. But scans of data from the Russian banks the Agency had access to, as well as Western banks known to be used by the FSB, failed to turn up transactions in Bologna.

He next began looking through databases of airline tickets, extending back ten years. The rolls were the result of voluntary antiterrorist projects, but the collection was useful for other purposes as well. Ciello, whose clearance gave him direct access to the databases, ran searches on Kiska Babev's name and known aliases, and came up with a dozen different hits or matches. He'd been examining them when Wu came in.

It took him a few moments to get past her interruption and re-member precisely where he was: correlating the flights with possible return trips to see if there was an alias that he didn't know about. His theory was that Kiska might use one name for inbound or outbound flights and another for the other leg of the trip. Finding a match be-tween a pair of flights would give him another name for the financial queries. It was a complex search, however, with a wide range of poten-tial variables, and after a few false matches—similar names that proved to belong to different people—Ciello had to concede that he wasn't getting anywhere. He went back to the flights themselves, trying to coordinate them with anything known about the assassinations. He found only one, but it was provocative: a trip to France a week before the American CIA agent Michael Dalton had been killed. She'd used her real name, with payment arranged through a Russian travel bureau known to be used by the FSB.

Tenuous, but definitely something. More than just the outline Wu had demanded.

Ciello typed up a quick summary and sent it to down to Corri-gan.

Corrigan fought back a yawn as he queued up the segment from the surveillance bugs for Ferguson. It wasn't that he was bored—the six-hour time difference between Italy and the States was killing him. He was in effect pulling two eight-hour shifts, with Lauren DiCapri filling the last. They needed another desk person, though finding someone with the proper training, clearances, and temperament—they had to get along with Ferguson—seemed impos-sible.

"You ready, Ferg?" Corrigan asked.

"Yeah, if I'm not keeping you awake."

"I'm sorry." Corrigan hit the key to upload the video snippet to the satellite. From there it was downloaded to Ferguson's secure laptop.

"Yeah, that's definitely Atha. How long was he in Rostislawitch's room?"

"Ten minutes. I have a little bit of audio, but it's muffled. The maid must have been in the room downstairs running the vacuum."

"Let me hear it."

"I can send you a transcript."

"Fine, but let me hear it first."

The audio was completely indistinguishable; only with the aid of a high-tech sound scrubber had they been able to get anything from it. But of course, Ferguson being Ferguson, he wanted to hear that for himself.

Corrigan sent the files, then put his hand over his mike and yawned again. As he did, his computer chirped, indicating he had something new in his priority e-mail queue.

It was the Russian report from Ciello. Corrigan opened it.

"So Atha goes into the room while Rostislawitch is away, probably to search it. He calls someone on the phone," said Ferguson. "Can we get the phone number?"

"Come on, Ferg. Be real."

"That's a no?"

"By the time we set something up with the NSA for that, forget it. He'll have a new phone by then. You'd have a better chance using a scanner to intercept his calls."

"All right. Did you send that brief to Imperiati?"

"I just got it now," said Corrigan, opening the file Ciello had sent.

"I asked for the brief hours ago."

"These things take time," said Corrigan. "And it was only a half hour."

"I told you to get it together at least an hour before I met with Imperiati."

"It takes time," said Corrigan. He skimmed through the summary, then saw that Ciello had done a lot more than put together a standard Agency report on an FSB officer.

A lot more.

"Hey, Ferg, Ciello has Kiska in France when Dalton gets killed." Ferguson didn't answer.

"Did you hear that, Ferg? He has her in France. Shit. It's the smoking gun. *She's got to be T Rex!*"

"Let me talk to him."

"To Ciello?"

"No, Dalton. I want to know what the weather's like up there."

Ciello was a master at teasing information out of the intelligence agency's databases and files, but when it came to making a simple phone connection on the in-house lines, he had a great deal of trouble. The procedure for using the encrypted line involved entering a department code as well as a personal code, which of course he could never remember without consulting the instruction manual he kept in his bottom desk drawer. This meant he had to find the key for the drawer; by the time he finally got Ferguson on the line, the op was beyond testy.

"I almost hung up on you, Ciello. Where have you been?"

"Um, here. I haven't left the building since yesterday. I slept on the floor. Corrigan says it's OK as long as I don't tell Mr. Slott. It kinda helps my back."

"Listen, Corrigan tells me you can connect Kiska Babev to Michael Dalton's murder."

"Um."

"What's *um* mean? Are you studying yoga or something?"

"Um, no. I have one flight record. He went to France a few days before."

"She. Kiska's a she."

"I knew that."

"That's all you have?"

"I'm working on more information. To get data—"

"You look at credit card information?"

"In the works. To get access to the records, first we have to make—"

"All right. Kiska has a second cousin in a mental institution in Romania."

"Um, sorry to hear that."

"Don't be. Her last name is Stronghauf or something along those lines—it's German. The mental hospital is right outside Baja Mare. There can't be too many institutions around. Find out the name, then give it to this guy whose phone number I'm going to give you, and he'll find the accounts for you. Or if you're really nice to him, he'll tell you how to get them yourself. Save you a couple of hours, if not days."

"Um—"

"There's that *um* again. You sure you're not practicing yoga?"

"The cousin isn't named in any of the reports."

"What a shock. Guy goes by the name of Fibber. Here's his number—"

"Is this outside, um—strictly speaking, am I breaking protocol? Because the privacy laws, see there's an internal counsel who's supposed to review requests, even when they involve overseas—"

"*U tebya cho ruki iz jopi rastut?*" said Ferguson.

"My hands are where they're supposed to be," said Ciello.

The Russian expression—literally "are your hands growing out your ass?"—was generally used to deride an inept boob.

"Well, then do what I'm telling you," answered Ferguson. "Use my name as soon as Fibber answers the phone. But don't 'um' him; he's not into that New Age crap."

"Corrigan always says we should totally obey the procedures because otherwise—"

"*Hooy tebe,*" said Ferguson, using a Russian expression that meant "don't mess with that," though it was rather more emphatically put. Then he dictated the phone number; the country code indicated it was in Nigeria.

"Run your request through channels as a backup," added Ferguson. "This way, no one will complain. You just don't mention that you already have the information."

"Oh."

"You're not as dumb as you sound, Ciello. I didn't know you knew Russian."

"Just curse words." He'd made a study of them several years before; they helped break the ice when dealing with Russian UFO experts about the so-called Siberian Series Sightings.

"*Otvai,*" said Ferguson.

"Piss off yourself."

Ferguson laughed. "Talk to you later."

7

Thera hesitated before getting out of the cab, scanning the block in front of the hotel for anything suspicious.

"Maybe I'll just go to bed," said Rostislawitch, getting out on the other side.

"How about dinner?" Thera asked. "Are you hungry?"

Rostislawitch looked across the roof of the taxi. She was beautiful and concerned, and despite the difference in their ages—despite the fact that he knew, knew, that she would not be interested in him sexually—he wanted badly to make love to her.

Even acknowledging the thought to himself felt awkward. And yet many older men had younger women. Many. Why was he different?

They were handsome, and rich. He was neither.

"Professor?"

"You should call me Artur," said Rostislawitch. "Artur is what friends call me. And I have never liked to be a professor. Research has been my true calling."

"I'm sorry. I keep forgetting."

"You deserve dinner for rescuing me. Let's have something nice. Yes," said Rostislawitch, suddenly sure of himself. "Come on. Let us see what we can find in the hotel restaurant. It is supposed to be very good."

Ferguson moved the binoculars slowly, scanning the street. There were two Italian surveillance teams on the roofs near the hotel, and one more on the top floor of the hotel itself. But no sign of Kiska, or the Iranian.

"Thera's on her way in," said Guns, who was on the street a few yards behind her.

"Got it," acknowledged Rankin, who was in the lobby.

Ferguson continued to scan the buildings after Thera and Rostislawitch went inside. He assumed that T Rex would know by now that he—or she—had missed. Would the assassin try to finish the job quickly, or wait until some of the heat died down? Ferguson could make a good argument either way.

But Kiska Babev as T Rex? That still didn't quite fit, despite what Ciello had found, and even though Ferguson had seen Kiska's alabaster face, her thick black lips, and the cell phone: a bomb detonator. Or maybe just a cell phone.

"They're going into the hotel restaurant," said Rankin over the radio. "Maître d' is talking to them, I assume telling them they're closed until seven. Going to the bar."

"Give her some space," said Ferguson.

"No shit."

Guns checked in; Ferguson told him to circle the block a few times and then head over to one of their safe rooms and grab a nap: he decided T Rex would undoubtedly need some time to reload as well as let the pressure die down. If he'd been thinking of striking right away, he would have gone to the hospital.

Or she.

Ferguson was thinking about whether he might take a rest as well when his sat phone began to buzz.

"Yeah?" he said, making the connection.

"No funny jokes this time?" asked Corrine Alston.

"Lost my sense of humor when I crashed the Ducati," said Ferguson. "Beautiful bike. Seat was a little uncomfortable, but I could live with that."

"Are you OK?"

"Corrigan didn't tell you?"

"No. Are you OK? What happened to you?"

"One of the spokes went through my liver," said Ferguson. He picked up the field glasses and went back to scanning the street.

"Ferguson, are you pulling my leg?"

"I'm fine, Counselor. What's on your mind?"

"I want to know what's going on. Is the Russian agent T Rex?"

"What Russian agent?"

"Corrigan said you guys are looking pretty hard at a Russian FSB colonel as T Rex."

"Corrigan wouldn't know a Russian FSB colonel from his mother-in-law," said Ferguson. Stinking Corrigan had a big mouth. "I saw a Russian op on the street just before the explosion. It doesn't mean she's T Rex."

"Where is she now?"

"We're working on it. The Italians are helping. Or we're helping the Italians, depending on your point of view."

"Do you think the Russian FSB wants to kill Rostislawitch?"

It was a possibility, but Ferguson didn't think it was likely—they would have had a much easier time bumping Rostislawitch off in Russia. If Kiska was T Rex, this was a freelance assignment on the side.

In that case, the last place she'd want to clip him would be in Russia; there'd be too much potential to link it to her.

"I really don't have enough information to get into theories right now," Ferguson told Corrine.

"You thought the Iranians wanted to kill him. Could that theory still hold? Does this mean he's given them something, or won't cooperate with them? What does it mean?"

A cab pulled up front of the hotel. A woman got out, a blonde.

Kiska Babev.

"Ferg?"

"The answer is 'D: all of the above,'" said Ferguson. "I'm going to have to get back to you."

8

Corrine hung up the phone. She was used to Ferguson's quick hang-ups by now and knew it was usually because he was working. Still, it was clear he was holding something back.

Of course he was. Ferguson never told the whole story about anything.

Her intercom buzzed. "The chief of staff just called. The President wants to move the two o'clock up to twelve fifteen and make it a working lunch," said her secretary, Teri Gatins. "I ordered you a Caesar salad. OK?"

Corrine glanced at her watch. "It's twelve thirty."

"He said he was running fifteen minutes late."

That was *so* Jonathon McCarthy, thought Corrine, getting up.

Secretary of State Jackson Steele ran his fingers through his curly white hair, pushing it back on his scalp. It was thick and so bright that it reminded people of the cotton his ancestors had once picked, and Steele sometimes wondered if the Lord had given it to him as a warning not to forget his humble beginnings.

"All I'm asking for is a week. Less. We're almost there. The Iranian ayatollahs have already signed off on the agreement. Give me a week and we'll have a full commitment. The bombs will be eliminated and inspections will begin."

"What sense does it make to let them have a biological weapon?" asked Defense Secretary Larry Stich. "It's potentially as devastating as a nuclear bomb. More so."

"I didn't say we should let them have it. I'm saying we should put off any overt action until the treaty is signed," said Steele.

"The Revolutionary Guard is threatening a coup if the treaty is signed," said Stich.

"That's not going to happen. They don't have the power. There's a reason their leader is only education minister. If he was truly powerful, he would be the Prime Minister, or at least defense."

Stich found the comment ironic—he didn't feel particularly powerful at the moment, given that he clearly was failing to carry the argument.

"If we move too forcefully, there's always the potential that word will get out," said Steele. "That could change the balance in Iran. We have to keep things calm until the treaty is signed. Observe, yes. Act, no."

"If the treaty is signed," said Stich. "In the meantime, they may get away."

"Ignoring a germ warfare program just to get this treaty signed seems like a very poor idea to me," McCarthy said. "A very poor idea."

There was a knock on the door.

"That will be either our food or Miss Alston," said McCarthy, rising. "I doubt it will be Tom Parnelles. He is worse about schedules than I am."

It proved to be both their food *and* Corrine Alston, who apologized for being late.

"Oh, you are not late, Miss Alston," said McCarthy, settling back into his chair as a steward set down a tray for him. "We were taking advantage of a hole in the Secretary of State's schedule to digest the situation vis-à-vis Iran."

"There's a joke in there somewhere, I'm sure," said Steele. "Probably at my expense."

"Well, I was about to call you a holy man," said McCarthy, winking at Corrine. His mirth was short-lived. "Am I to understand that you have an update from Italy?" he asked Corrine.

"Yes, sir, I do." Corrine explained quickly what she had been told, adding that their "people"—she never named the members of the First Team, of course—believed a Russian FSB agent might have been involved.

"The Russians are working with Iran?" said Steele.

"No. The thinking is that T Rex is freelancing. They're still trying to work out what's going on."

That point was reinforced by the CIA Director, who made his appearance a few minutes later. Thomas Parnelles told the others what Slott had learned from MI6—that the Iranian operative, Anghuyu "Atha" Jahan, was a supposed Iranian businessman who had arranged relatively minor deals in the past. One or two had been related to the nuclear program, though most involved getting around the economic boycott instituted because of the program. The Iranian seemed to be fairly close to the government's education minister, Parsa Moshen— who was also the head of the Revolutionary Guard.

"Moshen opposes the nuclear treaty," said Steele. "But his star is on the downside."

"Maybe not if he can start up a biological warfare program," said Parnelles. "This would give him a chip to come back with."

"So they buy a scientist?" asked Steele.

"More likely they're buying information from him," said Parnelles. "Techniques, DNA sequences. Otherwise, they would have no need to kill him. We think we know who the killer is—a Russian FSB agent, probably freelancing for Iran. She may not even know who she's working for. In any event, if they've authorized the murder, then the scientist has already given them what they want."

"Excuse me, Tom," said Corrine, "but our people—your people—aren't convinced that the Russian is T Rex. They're still looking for more data."

Parnelles, annoyed by the "our people—your people" faux pas, snapped back.

"Nonsense. The Russian is the killer. And we have to take her into custody."

"Why don't we just let the Italians handle that?" said Steele. "Have them apprehend her for this bombing, get her out of the way. You go on and follow these people, apprehend them after the treaty is signed."

"They'll be back in Iran by then." Parnelles had little confidence in the Italians. He was also annoyed with Corrine, for undercutting him.

And with Ferguson, since clearly that's where her information came from. Parnelles had reviewed the report from the desk man, Corrigan, himself; it looked pretty obvious.

"Given what we have discovered here," said McCarthy, "this assassin is a side issue. We can let the Italians deal with her for the time being."

"It's not a side issue." Parnelles struggled to keep his voice civil. "Jonathon, it's not a side issue. This agent—this woman—killed one of our best people. One of my people. We need to bring her to judgment. Killing a federal officer is a capital crime."

"I'll have no trouble pulling the switch on her personally," said McCarthy. "But I do not believe she is our first priority. Now that we know that there is a program to develop biological agents—germ warfare if you will—that is where our assets should be directed. We need more information about it. The First Team is in position to gather it. That is what they should be doing."

"They can do both," said Parnelles.

McCarthy looked over to Corrine.

"I agree," she said.

"But we shouldn't do anything that will disrupt the treaty," said Steele.

"Let's send the horse across that bridge when we come to it," said McCarthy. "Now everyone eat up, because I'm going to have to kick y'all out in a few minutes so I can meet with the head of the National Restaurant Association. I wouldn't want him thinking we're not doing our share to support our nation's restaurants."

9

BOLOGNA, ITALY

Ferguson ran down the stairs from the second-floor room, slowing to a brisk stroll as he reached the lobby. Kiska Babev was standing in the middle of the reception area, glancing around at the bright yellow sofas and blue sideless chairs as if she were looking for someone.

He did an exaggerated double take when she turned her head toward him.

"Of all the people in all the gin joints in all the world," Ferguson said, riffing on Bogart. "Kiska Babev."

"Robert Ferguson." It had been quite some time since Kiska had seen Ferguson, but she remembered him well. "How are you, Bob?"

"Good as ever. You?"

"Very good."

"They let you out of Moscow?"

"Once or twice a year," she told him.

"And you're in Bologna. Italy. Of all places." Ferguson twisted around examining his surroundings, as if he'd been dropped here. "What brings you to Bologna?"

"It's a lovely city."

"So is Moscow."

"I needed a little break."

"You needed a break? Work got to you?"

"You're the one who lives a dangerous life, Bobby," said Kiska. "What brings you to Bologna?"

"Renaissance art. I've always been fascinated by it."

Kiska smiled. She suspected that Ferguson was here for the same reason she was here—Artur Rostislawitch. But there was no sense asking; Ferguson was a consummate liar, better than she was.

A very attractive one, handsome and intriguing in his own way, but still a liar.

"Want to get a drink?" Ferguson asked. "Or are you busy?"

"I'm never too busy for an attractive younger man." Kiska rose. Best to find out what he was up to now. "Where would you like to go?"

"There's a bar through that hallway over there."

"I think perhaps another place. Quieter. Where we can find a corner alone."

"Even better."

Rankin wondered what the hell Ferguson was doing as he watched him walk out the front door with the blonde. She didn't seem his type—sophisticated rather than trashy, in her thirties, with a scar on her right cheek. It wasn't until they were out the door that Rankin realized she might be the Russian assassin, T Rex, the woman who had dialed in the explosion.

Was Ferguson out of his mind?

Rankin went upstairs to the room they were using to watch Rostislawitch, got out the laptop, and after punching in the security codes and sliding his thumb over the reader brought up the file.

It *was* Kiska Babev.

Christ.

Prosecco, *per piacere*," Kiska said to the waiter, ordering a bottle of the bubbly Italian wine.

"Italian. I'm impressed," said Ferguson.

"Don't be," said Kiska. "That's about all I know."

"Your English is even better than the last time we met."

"And your Russian?"

Ferguson told her in Russian that he would like to thank her by sleeping with her, the sooner the better.

"You are just as fresh as you always were, Bobby," she said. "But you must work on your accent."

"Now?"

"Later. I get so little chance to practice English these days."

The waiter brought the wine, opening it with a flourish, popping off the cap with a bottle opener.

"Cheers," said Kiska, holding up the glass.

"*La'chaim!*" said Ferguson, holding his up as well.

"Speaking Yiddish now?"

"Is that Yiddish or Hebrew?"

"Yiddish."

"You've been to Israel lately."

Puzzled, Kiska took a sip of her wine. "Why do you think that?"

"I thought maybe you were doing some side work with the Israelis," said Ferguson. The theory had just occurred to him—the Israelis, seeking to keep Rostislawitch from helping the Iranians, hired T Rex to kill him. It made sense, though he thought from her reaction he was wrong.

Unless, of course, she wasn't T Rex.

"The Israelis—I would think they would be very picky about

whom they worked with," said Kiska. "But you would know better than I."

"Mossad can be very professional. You might not even know you were working with them."

"But you, Bobby, you would know. You would know everything."

"I didn't know the man with the gun was at the end of the alley."

"I was happy to help." Kiska thought about that day as she sipped her wine. She could easily have let Ferguson go, let him get killed—it would not have hurt her in the least. On the contrary: as things turned out later, it would have been better.

But she had warned him, and instead of the *mafiya* thugs killing him, he killed them. They were slime and deserved to die, but that hadn't entered into her calculations, either.

No, it was as her section head had said later, accused her later: You were in love with the American. Not a lot, but a little. Just enough.

Just enough. Yes. And not love but infatuation. Mild. A kind of lust. Very different. And temporary, fortunately.

"So what were you doing on Via Bola," said Ferguson.

"Via Bola?"

"When the truck exploded. You were nearby."

"Was I?" Kiska put down her wine. "And how would you know that?"

"I saw you," said Ferguson.

"You were there?"

"More or less."

"I guess you could say the same for me."

"You should talk to the Italians about it."

"Why would I talk to the Italians, Bobby?"

"Maybe you saw something."

"Are you working with them?"

"We have some common interests."

"And would those include Artur Rostislawitch?"

"They're not interested in Rostislawitch. Why are you interested in him?"

She'd thrown the name out, trying to see what his reaction would be. She expected a diversion—but that was what an ordinary operative would try. Ferguson had always been much more subtle, accomplished beyond his age.

It was a great shame that he worked for the U.S. He would have made an excellent protégé. And lover. For a bit.

"We have an interest in all good Russian citizens," said Kiska, sipping the wine.

"That would leave him out, wouldn't it? Wasn't he involved in some political scandal?"

"Ah, he was a pawn. An unfortunate in the wrong place at the wrong time. This happens." Kiska drained her glass. "I'm on my way to talk to Dr. Rostislawitch right now. Would you like to come?"

It was a move right out of Ferguson's own playbook—push the confrontation as far as possible; make the other side withdraw.

"You've gotten better," Ferguson told her.

"Thank you." Kiska rose. "Coming?"

"Unfortunately, I have some other business to attend to. Maybe we can trade notes later."

"Gladly." She reached into her pocket and took out a business card, pushing it on the table. "Call my mobile. Or send an IM."

"Only for business?"

Kiska smiled, but said nothing else as she turned and left.

S ee if you can get a bug into his room."

"Ferg?" said Rankin.

"No, it's Santa Claus."

"I thought it was too risky to go into his room."

"Do it. Kiska Babev is on her way back over to the hotel. I want to hear what she says to him."

"You don't think she's on her way to kill him?"

"If she is, we'll have the whole thing on tape, right? Get a bug in there."

"Ferg, Thera's with him in the restaurant."

"Yeah, I know. Go bug the room."

"But—"

"Skippy. Just do what the hell I tell you, all right? I don't have time to bullshit."

The line went dead. Rankin snapped the phone off. One of these days he was going to slam Ferguson's head into a wall.

10

Somehow, he started talking about Olga. Rostislawitch couldn't help himself. The words just began pouring out, unbidden. Several times he asked the girl if he was boring her; she insisted he wasn't.

He thought she was fibbing, but he was grateful for it.

In truth, Thera wasn't lying at all. The scientist was genuinely fond of his wife. It fascinated Thera, his devotion, his love. How could someone who felt so deeply about another person develop a weapon that would kill thousands and thousands of people?

Thera could ask a similar question of herself. She was prepared to kill people if necessary. There was a disconnect between the job and who she was, a deep line that let her function and remain human at the same time.

Was it that way for him? Or did he simply not think about the implications of his work?

Thera couldn't ask those questions, of course. She tried to think of possible surrogates, considered steering the conversation to a topic like Bosnia or Chechnya, but there was no substitute that would really satisfy her curiosity. So mostly she just listened.

At seven, the dining room opened and they went in and sat down. Rostislawitch continued to talk, laying out much of his history as a young scientist. They both ordered spaghetti and sole in a vermouth sauce.

Suddenly everything began to remind Rostislawitch of his wife. He told Thera about a dinner he and Olga had had just like this on their first anniversary. He could taste the meal again, the memory was so vivid.

Thera excused herself between courses and went to the ladies room' so she could check in with the others.

"About time you checked in," said Rankin.

"I've been with Rostislawitch."

"T Rex is on her way over."

"What?"

"Kiska Babev." Rankin had had doubts about her before, but it suddenly seemed very obvious—and Thera was in danger. "She's going over to the restaurant right now."

"Where are you?"

"I'm putting a bug into Rostislawitch's room. Get the hell out of there."

"Is she coming to kill him?"

"Crap, Thera, just go."

"I can't."

"What do you mean you can't? She'll kill you, too."

Thera popped off the phone. She didn't have a weapon with her—she'd left it at the hotel when she knew she was going to the hospital; they had a metal detector at the door and she didn't want to risk getting stopped.

But she couldn't leave Rostislawitch to die.

What was Ferg thinking?

11

BOLOGNA, ITALY

Ferguson made sure that Kiska was on her way back to the hotel, then crossed the street and went into a small store specializing in knick-knacks for tourists who thought they were above the normal kitsch. There were fake statues and miniature artworks, pretend easels with Renaissance replicas. Ferguson walked swiftly through the place, pushing aside the curtain to the back room and walking in. The woman who owned the store began to yell, asking what he was up to, but he ignored her, continuing through the storeroom to a back hall that led to a bathroom and an exterior door. He slipped open the lock and went out, where he found his way barred on all sides by the walls of the neighboring buildings, including the hotel to the store's immediate left. He glanced upward, thinking at first that he would climb to the roof and go down. But he saw that one of the hotel's second-story windows was wide open. He pulled the small wooden bench over, tipped it onto its side, and used it to climb high enough on the wall so he could grip the ledge. Then Ferguson scrambled up and jumped into the room. He sprinted to the door, barely noticing that the room was unoccupied. The zigzag layout of the interior confused his ordinarily impeccable sense of direction, and when he turned into a stairwell he thought led to the basement he found he was wrong. He had to backtrack, racing up the stairs and around to a second doorway before finding the right one.

When they'd checked the building out the other day, the team had discovered that the basements were connected. The dimly lit passage between them was cluttered with boxes and cleaning supplies; Guns had carefully rearranged them to make it easier to get through. Unfortunately, someone had put another box on the floor in the interim; Ferguson tripped over it and flew headfirst into the side of the wall, tumbling into the shadows.

Something scurried nearby. Ferguson started to get up, then noticed a pair of red eyes staring at him from a few feet away.

Then something ran across his back.

Suppressing a yowl, he scrambled to his feet.

Rankin slapped the video bug to the base of the lighting sconce on the far side of the bed in Rostislawitch's room. He scanned the room quickly to make sure he hadn't missed anything, then left. Out in the hall, he ran to the elevator.

He punched the button. The indicator said it was on the twelfth floor. He was on the sixth.

Rankin pulled out his radio. "Ferg?"

No answer.

He pulled out his sat phone and called Thera back. She didn't answer, either.

Rankin felt a rush of anxiety, worried that Kiska or T Rex or whoever the hell she was would simply go into the restaurant and blow it up, killing Thera in the process.

Not to mention him.

He glanced up at the elevator's floor indicator. It was still on twelve. Cursing, he bolted for the stairs.

When Ferguson reached the landing at the rear of the hotel restaurant, he realized that his knee felt a little wet. He glanced down and saw that he'd landed in some water when he'd fallen; both legs were drenched nearly to his crotch. He'd fallen into a puddle in the basement without realizing it.

Clearly a faux pas in fashion-conscious Italy. He'd have to make it work for him.

He pulled the small Glock pistol he had at the back of his belt around so that it would be easier to grab when he was sitting; then he pushed through the door, walking swiftly through the kitchen of the restaurant and out into the bar area, where he swung onto a stool. He could see Thera and Rostislawitch in the other part of the room, to his left, but ignored them.

"*Ciao,*" he said to the bartender. "*Peroni, per favore.*"

The bartender nodded and put a beer glass to the spigot. He seemed to take an inordinate time to pour the beer, as if it were an arcane art in a country that greatly preferred wine.

But his timing was impeccable—the glass arrived just as Kiska entered the restaurant.

"Whoa!" yelled Ferguson, making the beer spill and jumping up as if it had gotten all over his pants.

"Bobby, what are you doing here?" asked Kiska, coming toward him.

"It's happy hour," Ferguson told her, grabbing a napkin and daubing his pants.

"Are you drinking or bathing?"

"Little of both," said Ferguson. "Care to join me?"

Rostislawitch turned back from the confusion at the bar. He was suddenly very tired, though he was only halfway through his meal.

"Would it be all right if I called it a night?" he asked Thera. "I don't feel like dessert."

"Are you OK?"

"Just tired."

"Sure," said Thera.

"I'm going to go up to my room." Rostislawitch reached into his wallet, carefully sorting through the bills.

"I'll pay my half," said Thera, putting her hand on his as he started to leave enough for both of them.

"No, no," said Rostislawitch.

Thera managed to convince him to let her cover the tip. She got up with him, and walked out, studiously avoiding looking at Ferguson and the woman with him.

"Good night," Rostislawitch said at the elevator. "I'll see you tomorrow."

Thera hesitated, worried that she was sending the scientist to his doom. But she had no choice. Impulsively, she stretched up and gave him a peck on the cheek.

Caught off-guard, Rostislawitch managed a smile, then got into the elevator.

12

BOLOGNA, ITALY

MI6 agent Nathaniel Hamilton stared at the leaves of the fake fig tree in the hotel suite. It was a very good fake, so close to real that even Hamilton, who spent much of his spare time gardening, hadn't been able to tell it was fake until he touched the undersides of the leaves. They'd even put real dirt in the planter. There were certain things the Italians were very adept at.

Blast forensics was another one, mostly because of their experience with the *mafiya*. They were not in the same class as the Israelis, of course, or even the British, but already the investigators had correctly identified the type of explosive and the general manner of the bomb's construction, linking the design to weapons used in Chechnya. This was no small matter; it would have been very easy to look for a link to organized crime, to either the Mafia or one of the Balkan gangs that had lately begun to foolishly try to move into the country.

The general population, of course, would immediately suspect Al Qaeda, though the bombing had none of its typical earmarks. The spokesman for the Italian police had carefully explained this at the televised press conference a few minutes before, but Hamilton had no doubt that the news stories would continue to speculate that terrorists had been involved—especially since at least one group had claimed responsibility for the blast.

Hamilton folded his arms. The Italians and their investigation into the truck bomb was not really of concern to him; it wasn't even clear that Rostislawitch was a target, after all. No, Hamilton's bloody problem was the Americans, or one in particular: Bob Ferguson, a royal pain in the arse, as the chaps back at the pub would put it.

The MI6 agent found Americans to be annoying as a general rule, but Ferguson took it to a high art. He had *some* ability as an operative, Hamilton had to admit, but surely Ferguson owed a great deal of his career to fortunate blunder and judicious bluster. Like all Americans, he refused to admit this to anyone, most especially himself, and was therefore exceedingly hard to stomach, let alone deal with.

But deal Hamilton must. The main office had just made this clear in a terse IM:

Cooperate with the Americans. Highest authority.

Highest authority, yes. No doubt this had been agreed over tea and scones at the American embassy in London. Or Scotch and rocks at the British embassy in Washington.

Hamilton sighed, then erased the message from his mobile.

Best to get it over with as soon as possible. He tapped the number he had been given into the phone. With any luck, he'd get voice mail.

13

Rankin reached the lobby just as Thera was turning away from the elevator. He froze for a half second, unsure what was going on, then tried to nonchalantly walk past her. But he was panting, out of breath from the long run.

"Hello," said Thera. "Don't I know you?"

"I'm not sure."

"Ferg's in the restaurant," she whispered.

"With Kiska?"

"He's with a woman. I didn't get a good look at her face."

"Where's Rostislawitch?"

"Went up to his room."

"Come on," said Rankin, backing toward the stairs. "We'll go upstairs. I put a bug in Rostislawitch's room."

"We can't leave Ferg alone with her, if she's T Rex," said Thera.

"I wouldn't worry about him. He's probably talking his way into her pants right now."

The conversation in the bar did concern pants, though they were Ferguson's, not Kiska's.

The Russian agent realized that Ferguson had shown up specifically to keep her from Rostislawitch. The Americans must be trying to woo him away; the attractive woman he'd been having dinner with was undoubtedly part of the plan.

If this had been the old days, during the Cold War, Kiska's task would be clear: she'd call in backup, grab Rostislawitch, and return him to the Soviet Union. But the Cold War had ended when she was in grade school, and Russia was no longer the Soviet Union. Citizens, even those with classified clearances and important specialties like Rostislawitch, were in theory free to do what they wanted, and had to be treated carefully, especially in a country with a scandal-hungry media.

Which meant she had to be subtle.

"You really surprise me, Bobby," she said, balling a beer-soaked napkin into her hand. "I didn't think you did these sorts of cheap escapades."

"Yeah, I'm a klutz sometimes."

"I'll see you around."

Ferguson caught her hand. "Sure you won't stay for a drink?"

She looked down at his pants. "I'm afraid of where it might go."

Ferguson smirked, then watched her leave. He pulled out his sat phone, pretending to call while turning on the radio.

"Rankin, *dove vai?*"

"What?"

"Where'd you go?"

"Thera and me are in the second-floor room. Rostislawitch is upstairs in his room."

"Kiska just left the bar. She may be going up there."

"We're watching."

"Where are the Italians?"

"They have two people in the car down the street, one guy on a roof watching the front of the building. Other guys knocked off. They're not coming in, right?"

"Imperiati says they have to keep their distance. He's not a suspect in the bombing."

"Ferg, what's going on?" asked Thera. "Is she going to try again?"

"You're assuming she's T Rex."

"Well, is she?"

"I don't know. I don't think so. I don't have it all together. I'll be up in a minute."

He had just flipped down the phone's antenna when a call came through. It was Corrigan.

Ferguson glanced down the bar; the bartender was still at the far end, serving whiskeys to two Americans trying to look younger than they really were.

"Hey, Wrong Way," Ferguson said to Corrigan. "What's happening?"

"Wrong Way what?"

"You never heard of that? Pilot who flew the wrong way?"

"Listen, Ferg, I need an update. Mr. Parnelles wants to know what's going on. He's pretty hot."

"Hey, I like the old guy myself, Corrigan, but I don't think he's much to look at."

"Stop busting my chops, Ferg. He's really leaning on me. He wants a report."

Ferguson laughed. Corrigan had no clue what real pressure was like—*especially* from Parnelles.

"That's all you called about?"

"The MI6 guy is trying to get ahold of you. He called your backup number. Message says he's been told to cooperate with you. Doesn't sound real overjoyed about it."

"That makes two of us."

"Wait; don't hang up. Tell me what to tell Parnelles."

Ferguson glanced down at his slacks. "Tell him my pants are wet."

"What?"

"Did Ciello get that credit card information on Kiska?"

"That may take days, Ferg. You know the legal red tape."

The bartender came over, pointing at Ferguson's empty beer glass. Ferguson nodded. The man pushed the sodden napkins off the bar into a wastebasket, then went to get him a refill.

"Why do you want him to dig into that for? Don't you think the Russian is T Rex?"

"No."

"Who else could it be? She was in France when Dalton was killed. The Italians say the bomb is similar to ones used in Chechnya. Kiska worked in Chechnya. Bingo."

"Completely settled, Corrigan. You're a genius."

Ferguson took the new beer from the bartender and took a swig; it shot immediately to his head. Then he realized it wasn't the beer at all. He'd forgotten to take his pills that morning. No wonder he was speeding—missing a dose of the replacement hormones had the odd effect of boosting his energy level temporarily.

The doctors, of course, didn't believe him; in theory it should do the opposite. But he knew a rush when he felt one.

He reached into his pocket for his pillbox and slipped the little pills onto the bar counter next to the glass.

"I'll get after Ciello," Corrigan was saying. "In the meantime, what can I tell Parnelles?"

"Tell him she wouldn't sleep with me, but I still have hopes."

"Ferg, come on. Be serious."

The bartender was hovering nearby. "Talk to you later, Wrong Way," said Ferguson, hanging up.

"What are those?" asked the bartender, pointing at Ferguson's pills.

"Viagra," said Ferguson, popping them into his mouth.

"I thought Viagra was blue."

"This is the placebo edition."

ooks like Kiska called a cab," Rankin said, watching the feed from the video bug on the laptop in the second-floor suite. He had the screen split; the left side showed the lobby, the right side Rostisla-witch's room upstairs.

"You sure she didn't sneak a booby trap up there?" said Thera. She was pacing near the door.

"I would have seen her. Chill, would you? You're making me nervous."

There was a double knock on the door, followed by a buzz at the lock. Ferguson walked in.

"So?"

"Kiska is getting a taxi. Shouldn't we be following her?" asked Rankin.

"Nah. She's not T Rex." Ferguson went to the minibar and took out a water.

"You sure, Ferg?" asked Thera.

"Pretty sure. How are you?"

"I'm OK. If she's not T Rex, why did you go into the bar?" Rankin asked.

Ferguson shrugged. He was willing to bet his life that Kiska wasn't T Rex, but not Thera's. He let his eyes linger for a moment, memorizing how she looked: jeans and a sweater, no makeup, hair pulled back, consciously trying to look plain so she'd fit in easier undercover. But she couldn't hide how beautiful she was.

What would he trade if he could change the circumstances? Money? He had plenty of that.

That was the first thing people thought of—money. Oh, the brothers would laugh at him, wouldn't they? An abject lesson. Stand before the throne of Saint Peter, they'd say, and talk of money. See where it gets you, Mr. Ferguson.

Would Saint Peter have a throne? Or even a gate? And why was it Saint Peter, anyway? Why wasn't it James or John?

"What are you thinking, Ferg?" asked Thera.

"I'm trying to think why someone would pay so much money to kill Rostislawitch. I can't come up with an answer. He's just not worth the expense."

"I thought you said the Iranians would do it."

"Why bother? Who's he going to tell?"

"I think it's pretty obvious," said Rankin. "The Russians are going to kill him because he's double-crossing them and dealing with the Iranians."

"Then why not just arrest him in Russia?" said Thera.

"There's probably some reason they can't that we don't know," said Rankin.

"Maybe." Thera straightened. She caught Ferguson staring at her, giving her a look as if she'd done something wrong.

"Hey, look at this," said Rankin, pointing at the laptop screen.

Two young women in short dresses were in the corridor in front of Rostislawitch's room. They knocked on the door.

"What's going on?" Thera asked.

"Hookers, I'll bet," said Rankin.

"They're going to kill him," said Thera.

"Maybe," said Ferguson.

"Jesus—we can't let them."

"Yeah, we can," said Ferguson.

"Ferg!"

He put his hand on her shoulder. "Relax and watch the screen."

14

Rostislawitch lay facedown on the bed, unable to sleep even though he felt very tired. All he could think of was Thera's kiss on his cheek.

What had she meant by that?

Nothing, surely. It was the sort of innocent gesture that women sometimes made, young women especially, free with their emotions. It didn't mean anything but *I'll see you later, thanks for dinner, you're a nice old guy even if you bore me.*

It didn't have to mean that. If he went through with the deal with the Iranian, he would have plenty of money. Money was the great equalizer; he'd seen young women attracted to older men because of it all his life.

But Thera wasn't like that. She wasn't swayed by money. She was a scientist—young, not sure of herself or her work, but ambitious no doubt, or she wouldn't be here. If he were to offer her a job, praise her work, that would be the way to seduce her, not telling her they would run away together and live on a desert isle.

A knock on the door jerked him upright.

"Yes?"

"Professore?"

Thera? Rostislawitch got up and went over to the door. "Who is it?" he asked.

"Professore?"

It didn't sound like her. And yet his desire was so great that he had to see. He opened the door, letting it catch against the clasp.

Not Thera. Two girls.

"What do you want?" he said in English.

The women did not understand. "Atha sent us," they told him in Georgian-accented Russian.

Atha, the fool: these must be whores.

Rostislawitch started to close the door.

"Wait, wait, *professore*," said the girl closest to the crack. "If you don't let us in, we won't get paid."

"Please," said the other. "Take pity on us. We are Russian like you."

"You sound Georgian."

"My mother was from Moscow."

Rostislawitch closed the door. Before he could turn away, the girls were banging on it, and crying.

"Please, please, *professore*. You don't have to do anything. Just let us in so we can say we were there. Please. We won't get paid."

"Go away."

Something bumped against the door. One of the girls began to moan; the other sobbed loudly.

Rostislawitch opened it again, but kept the clamp in place. The girl he'd spoken to was now sitting on the floor, her back against the door, crying.

"Why is she crying?" he asked the other girl, who was kneeling next to her.

"She needs the money for her boy," said the other woman. "I need the money, too. Please. You don't know how difficult it is for Russian girls in this country. Please let us in."

Sighing, Rostislawitch pushed the door closed, then opened it.

"Get in before someone sees you," he told them.

The woman who had been sobbing rose, rubbing her eyes with her arm as she came in. Her companion followed.

"It is just that your friend promised to pay us well, but only if you had a good time," she told him.

"Is he watching?"

"He's sure to be nearby somewhere."

"Well, get in," he said, though they were already inside. "Not *there*."

The girl who was crying had thrown herself spread-eagle on the king-size bed. Her friend ran her hand on Rostislawitch's shoulder.

"We can make you feel very good," she said.

Rostislawitch pushed her hand away. "Stop or I will throw you out."

"Don't yell." She took a step back. "I am Francesca. That is Rosa."

"Francesca. Rosa. Those aren't Russian names. Or Georgian."

"They're the only names we use for this business."

"What are you doing in Italy? You should go back home."

"To do what? To be poor cleaning ladies?"

"Why did Atha send you?"

"To have a good time." The girl's collarbone poked out from the top of her dress. Her midsection was pinched—Rostislawitch would not be surprised if either of them hadn't eaten properly in months.

"Are you drug addicts?" he asked.

"Drugs?" Francesca shook her head. "No drugs. We have no drugs for you."

"No. Do you take them?"

"Professore."

Rosa slipped off the bed and came around to confront him. She had a tattoo of a green rose on the side of her neck, and a small snake on the top of her left breast. She was not overly endowed, but her boobs seemed as if they would burst out of the material. She told him in Italian that he had a lot of nerve talking about drugs when it was clear that he was such a dead dick he needed friends to find him whores. Rostislawitch understood none of it, though her anger was clear enough.

"Rosa, Rosa. Relax," said Francesca. "Just relax."

"I didn't mean to insult you," Rostislawitch said. "Here. We'll get something to eat. Call for room service." He pushed over the menu.

"Are you sure you don't want to relax?" said Francesca, once more touching his sleeve.

"No, thank you." Rostislawitch pushed her away again, more gently this time.

He was tempted. How could a man not be tempted?

But no. He would not have sex with a whore, Russian or otherwise.

"Professore? Can I use your bathroom?" asked Francesca.

"Go right ahead."

Rosa had retreated to the chair, where she sat cross-legged, her dress showing much of her thighs. She was pouting.

"How long have you been in Italy?" Rostislawitch asked.

"Too long," said Rosa.

"You are high on something, aren't you?" said Rostislawitch.

"If I was high, I would be jumping around. Am I jumping around, *professore?*"

He shook his head, but he wasn't convinced.

"You should let us give you a good time. Your friend will be mad," she told him.

"He's not my friend." Rostislawitch sat on the edge of the bed. "He's a business acquaintance."

"All the more reason," said Rosa. "You do your business; we do ours." Her face brightened as Francesca returned to the room. "Perhaps you would like to watch?"

Rostislawitch didn't understand.

"Francesca, come here," said Rosa in Italian. She stood up and kissed her.

Francesca resisted at first. Rosa ran her hands across the other girl's back, down to her butt. She cupped both cheeks, raising the dress with fingers before slipping them into Francesca's panties. Francesca began kissing back. The two girls pushed into each other, their breasts rubbing. Rosa slipped downward, pulling Francesca's underwear down and nuzzling into her crotch.

Rostislawitch stared, mesmerized.

"Stop," he said finally. "Stop."

But they didn't. Francesca slipped her hands to the back of Rosa's dress, unzipping it. Then Francesca hooked her fingers around the top and pushed it down. Rosa let her arms fall and the dress slipped down, revealing a pink lace push-up bra. In a moment this, too, was unhooked, and Francesca began licking the other girl's nipples.

Rostislawitch tried to push them apart. Rosa reached for his hands, grabbing at him to join them.

"No," he told her. "No."

"*Professore,* come on. Live a little."

Rostislawitch pulled back. Rosa fell onto Francesca and they collapsed giggling onto the bed.

The scientist felt completely out of place. As a young man at university, he'd seen clandestine nudie shows and been turned on by them, but somehow now either his age or the setting had the opposite effect. He felt as if he'd walked in on the middle of an argument between two friends rather than a sex act.

The two women were now completely naked.

"I'm going to the bathroom," he told them finally. "And when I come out I hope that you will be gone. Tell Atha that I appreciate—thank him for his generosity."

"Join us, *professore*," said Francesca, looking up from the bed.

Rostislawitch felt a last twinge of temptation, the slightest urge to be caressed. If he closed his eyes, he might be able to convince himself that they were not hookers bought by an Iranian who was trying to make a deal.

But who would they be? Not Olga, certainly. And not the girl, Thera, who had been so kind to him.

If she were here, he would make love to her. He'd been a fool not to invite her upstairs.

"*Professore*," said the woman.

Perhaps it was a trap, Rostislawitch thought. Maybe Atha thought he could blackmail him.

"When I come out, I hope you will be gone," said Rostislawitch, going to the bathroom and locking the door.

15

BOLOGNA, ITALY

"Hell of a show," said Rankin, watching.

Thera crossed her arms. She felt embarrassed for Rostislawitch, and angry that he had let the girls in in the first place.

Ferguson, meanwhile, sat in the overstuffed chair opposite the couch, considering what the girls had said about having been sent by Atha. If the Iranian was behind the botched assassination, why would he now send two whores up to Rostislawitch's room? To throw him off the trail? To keep him in the room? Clearly the girls weren't assassins themselves, since they were unarmed. Unless they intended to kill the scientist by giving him a heart attack.

Ferguson got up and went into the bedroom, where a small carry-on bag held some of their backup equipment. He took a new SIM card for his local cell phone; after installing it, he dialed the number Hamilton had left and got the British MI6 agent's voice mail.

"So we're having fun," Ferguson said. "What are you doing? Call me back at this number."

Ferguson grabbed a new pair of pants to change, but was interrupted when his sat phone began to ring.

It was Parnelles.

"Hey, General."

"What's going on, Robert? Corrigan tells me you were with T Rex in a bar. Did you grab her?"

"Corrigan's wrong. I wasn't with T Rex. I was with Kiska Babev."

"Robert, I've seen Corrigan's report. There's good evidence there."

"One possible coincidence. Some parallels. We're still working on it."

"If she's not T Rex, who is?"

"I'm not sure yet. It may be me for all I know." Ferguson laughed.

"This isn't something to joke about," said Parnelles sharply. "This is good information about the Iranians," he continued, softening his tone. "It's good. You should develop it. But I want you to get T Rex. That has to remain a priority."

"I don't think Kiska Babev is T Rex. And even if she was, at this point I can't just haul her back. She's not going to come easily."

"Don't let that be a problem. You know how to take care of this."

"You want me to shoot her?"

Parnelles cleared his throat. Ferguson could picture him, sitting at his desk, his face tinged slightly red. His brows would be low on his forehead, a look of disappointment on his face.

Was that how they did it in the old days? The Deputy Director of Operations, or maybe someone even lower on the chain of command, would call his dad and say, *Take care of this guy?*

Ferguson didn't like to think of his father as a killer, though he knew that his father had killed people.

Less than Ferg had.

"Robert, I'm counting on you to do the right thing," said Parnelles finally.

"I try."

Parnelles hung up. Ferguson turned off the phone and once again grabbed the fresh pair of jeans, but Rankin was calling him from the other room.

"They're going through his stuff," said Rankin, pointing at the computer screen as he came out.

"Turn up the volume," said Ferguson, squatting down to get a better view of what was going on. One of the girls, naked, was standing by the bathroom, talking softly. The other was going through Rostislawitch's wallet.

"She's got something," said Rankin.

"We don't need the play-by-play," said Thera.

They watched as Rosa examined a small piece of paper in the wallet. She opened the desk drawer and took out a pad, copying something from it.

"Zoom this," Ferguson told Rankin.

Rankin had already started to try. He selected the area of the screen and then the zoom tool, but the girl's naked back blocked the view.

"Has to have something to do with what the Russian wants to sell the Iranian," said Rankin. "That's got to be it."

"Yeah. Did you scan that room for bugs when you went in?"

"Yeah. It was clean. Why?"

"Just wondering who I have to share this with." Ferguson sat back down, considering what to do.

Were the girls working for the Iranian, as they said? It would be clever of Hamilton to tell them they were, a kind of misdirection play while he had them look for information.

Ferguson would have to trail them to find out.

"All right, here's what we're gonna do," Ferguson told them. "Thera, you're going to get some sleep. Use the other room. But go to sleep. We're going to need you later. Rankin, you watch Rostislawitch. If you need backup, call Imperiati's people. Here's his number."

"I got it already."

"What are you going to do?" Thera asked.

"Change my pants," said Ferguson.

16

Hamilton's phone beeped, telling him he had a message. He waited until the Iranian had parked his car before dialing in to find out who it was.

Ferguson finally had gotten back to him, cheeky as ever. He hit the redial.

"Well, Mr. Ferguson, I'm told I should cooperate with you fully," Hamilton said when Ferguson answered.

"Always a pleasure to be working with our allies," said Ferguson. He seemed a bit winded, and there was a clicking sort of mechanical sound in the background, gears moving.

"Whatever are you doing?" asked Hamilton. "Working out?"

"Riding my bike."

"In this cold?"

"It's not that cold."

Crazy Yanks. All of them.

Hamilton watched Atha leave the parking garage and walk in the direction of the Moroccan restaurant. It was no surprise; he'd gone there the night before as well. Yesterday Hamilton had gone in and watched from the bar. Tonight he thought he'd stay in the car; the smell of the food sometimes bothered his stomach.

"So do you have anything new?"

"Nothing at all."

"Maybe we should get together and trade notes," said Ferguson.

"I don't really see the point," said Hamilton, switching off his motor. Maybe he would go in after all. "I am in the middle of something and—"

There was a knock on his car window. Startled, Hamilton turned and saw Ferguson grinning at him.

"What the hell are you doing?" asked Hamilton, lowering the window.

"Following those two women getting out of the cab over there," Ferguson said. "My bet is they're going to see Atha."

"Bloody hell."

"You have that place bugged, or should we go inside?"

A tha saw the waiter giving the two girls a hard time. He raised his hand. Francesca saw it and pointed. Reluctantly, the waiter let them through.

"Here, a receipt, just as you predicted," said Rosa, unfolding a piece of paper on the table. "Left baggage."

"Excellent."

More than excellent, he thought—better than he could have wished for. But he warned himself not to get too optimistic.

"Is it at the bus station?" said Francesca. "We can go and get it if you want?"

"No, that's fine," said Atha. "How about a drink? Some wine?"

"How about our money?" said Francesca. She held out her hand.

"Oh, ladies, don't be so quick. The night is young."

"That's extra," said Francesca.

Rosa ran her fingers across the back of his neck. "But we are willing to negotiate."

Y es, we have these sorts of things," said Hamilton, holding up the tiny bug. "Probably made in China."

"I think you can get a better deal out of Thailand," said Ferguson, taking out a receiving unit disguised as an MP3 player. "Drop it on the floor as you pass."

"Why should I drop it?"

"Because I'm picking up the bar tab."

"In that case, I will be right back."

Hamilton got up and made his way toward the restrooms, choosing a course that would take him near the Iranian. By now the two hookers were hanging all over him. Atha seemed oblivious to the disapproving glare of his neighbors, let alone Hamilton. The MI6 agent let the small bug slip from his fingertips. It bounced on the floor, coming to rest under Atha's chair. It was tiny, as small as a fly. But the thing that impressed Hamilton—and horrified him, if truth be told—was the fact that Ferguson treated it as a throwaway device. It would be crushed underfoot within an hour, and he didn't care. It was all very incredibly wasteful. How could you compete with people with those sorts of resources to burn?

By the time Hamilton got back to the table, the waiter had deposited a bucket of ice and a bottle of Asti. Ferguson was listening to the conversation at the other end of the room, sipping the wine.

"Italian pseudo-Champagne?" asked Hamilton.

"What did you want?"

"Cognac at the very least." He held up his hand and tried catching the waiter's attention. "So?"

"He's telling them about Paradise."

"No doubt."

Ferguson took one of the earphones out and held it toward him.

"That's quite all right," said Hamilton.

"Afraid you'll get cooties?" Ferguson let the small earphone dangle while he sipped his wine. "So tell me about our friend Atha. How long have you been following him?"

"I really did tell you everything earlier, I'm afraid. I wish I could get a bloody drink."

Ferguson raised his right hand, pointing toward the ceiling. Within moments, the waiter appeared.

"A cognac for my friend. Something nice," Ferguson said in Italian.

"Hmmmph," said Hamilton.

"Refresh my memory. How long have you been watching Atha?"

"I suppose for many months. Not myself. I have better things to do with my time."

"Because you're an important man," said Ferguson.

"I have other ways of wasting my time."

"You just got on the case?"

"That's right. I was working in Africa and then this came along."

Hamilton told Ferguson about Anghuyu "Atha" Jahan's background, giving a more detailed version than he had earlier. Atha had been born in 1969 to a family that had once been fairly prominent in

Iranian politics, but had fallen out of favor with the shah and in effect been banished to the city of Mashhad in the far eastern portion of the country. The problems with the shah helped the family when he was overthrown; though they were hardly part of an inner circle, they were well-off enough to send Atha to school in Great Britain. He studied engineering and finance; in the nineties he had helped arrange loans for the construction of docks and oil pipelines. The British believed that he had profited greatly from the loans; in any event, by 2004 he was traveling through Europe, where his main task was arranging for the purchase and shipment of prescription drugs through gray-market channels. He bought some equipment for the nuclear program as well, though nothing major; Hamilton had been told he was a "pinch hitter," filling in for more prominent deal makers. But he was also close to the Revolutionary Guard and the Iranian education minister.

"Unclear whether he was working for the government or as a freelancer," said Hamilton. "Immaterial really. And then he had a falling-out with someone, and returned home for two years."

"And suddenly he's back." Ferguson turned his gaze toward Atha's table; the two girls were playing with Atha's hair.

"And my assignment was to find out why. The Russian is obviously the answer."

"When did he first make contact with him?"

Hamilton's cognac finally arrived. He swirled it in his glass, then took the slightest of sips.

"My superiors do not tell me everything. I am not sure. I was only given the assignment recently."

"When you were in Africa."

"That's right."

"You heard about him there?"

"Wouldn't have known him from the odd lion, I'm afraid."

"What else are you supposed to do?"

"At this point, simply gather whatever else I can. And share with you, I suppose."

"What about Rostislawitch?"

"What about him?"

"Are you trying to eliminate him?"

"Why would I do that?"

"To keep him from working for the Iranians."

"I'm not with that section." Hamilton took another sip from his cognac. "Who tried to kill him?"

"I think the bomb earlier today was aimed at him," said Ferguson.

"I heard some group already took credit."

"Some people are always taking credit for others' work."

Hamilton assumed—correctly—that Ferguson was making an oblique reference to his own behavior, but he laughed nonetheless.

"Blowing up an entire block would not be a very effective way of killing one man. And if that was the intention, they missed."

"True."

Ferguson noticed that Atha was getting up from his table.

"Looks like your man is about to show himself a good time."

Ferguson started to get up, intending to go outside and trail Atha's car. Hamilton stopped him.

"Your turn," said the MI6 agent.

"How's that?"

"I would like to know a bit more about the Russian."

"He's a scientist who's worked in germ warfare. I think the Iranians are trying to recruit him."

"That much I already know. Come on, Ferguson. I've given you background. I'm trying to cooperate. Is he working for the government? Is Rostislawitch involved in a network? Is he just giving information? Is he going over to them? Tell me."

"I'm not sure yet."

Ferguson sat back down as Atha and the girls began making their way toward the door.

"The Iranian is small fish," said Hamilton. "If the Russians are trying to export biological weapons, that's a major problem."

"Could be." Once again Ferguson started to leave, and once again Hamilton grabbed his arm.

"What are you doing?"

"Following Atha. You can help."

"I rather think you're the one helping," answered Hamilton.

"Good. Pay the bill. I'll call you when he gets to wherever it is he's going."

17

Rostislawitch remained in the bathroom of his hotel room, sitting on the floor for more than an hour after he heard the girls leave. He realized he was being silly, even foolish, but he could not manage to get to his feet.

He stared at the bottom of the mirror above the vanity, where the very top of his head was reflected. Once thick and black, his hair was now a thinning splatter of gray and black, the gray looking like speckles of paint scattered by someone working on a ceiling as he passed by.

As Rostislawitch stared at the mirror, it occurred to him that it was not the head of an old man. Not a young man, certainly. But the hair was not that of a man *entirely* past his prime.

Rostislawitch got to his feet, bringing his face into view. He leaned over the sink to get a closer look.

A worn face in need of a shave, and a good night's sleep. A tired man.

But not one who was spent. Not at all.

Yet he acted as if he were dead. This whole scheme, this whole plan—it wasn't so much to make money as to get revenge on the world for taking his wife, a last act before going to the grave himself.

Which he would have done, stepped in front of a train or found some pills. He'd never consciously admitted it to himself, but as he stared now into his eyes he knew it was true, knew that would have been the next step—not taking the train to Turin, not flying to India and disappearing as he had planned. The next step would have been to shrivel into nothingness.

He didn't want that. He wasn't ready for death.

He could take Atha's money and do a great deal with it. He could live a life of leisure, with a new identity.

Or he could simply go back to Russia, forget about the Iranian and his whores.

Assuming he got rid of the material. If it were found by someone, the results would be catastrophic.

The baggage ticket. It was in his wallet. If it was stolen, he'd never get the bag back without telling the attendant what was in it. That was as good as signing an arrest warrant.

Rostislawitch undid the lock and pulled open the door, rushing to the bureau where he'd left his wallet and watch earlier. He grabbed open the trifold, surprised that the whores had left it.

His two credit cards were in their pockets. His money—rubles at the back, euros in front—still there.

And the baggage ticket, folded neatly in half. Still there.

Still there.

Rostislawitch put the wallet down. What he needed to do was to sleep, to rest. In the morning he would have more energy. In the morning he would be able to think more clearly about his future, about what he should do.

And in the morning he would see the girl, Thera. She probably didn't like him romantically; he couldn't flatter himself. But the fact that she took an interest, the fact that she might look up to him as an older scientist—that was something worthwhile.

He would think about that in the morning.

Rostislawitch took off his pants and shirt and climbed into bed. It smelled of the whores' perfume.

Perhaps he should have made love to them after all. It would have been a story to tell friends years from now.

He could still tell it, though he would be the butt of the joke.

Why not? A good story was a good story, Rostislawitch mused, closing his eyes and drifting off.

18

"Guns, what are you doing?"

"Ferg?"

"No, it's your fairy godfather calling to tell you that you just won the lottery."

Ferguson was standing next to a post in the Bologna train station, watching Atha as he counted his change at a newsstand. It had taken more than twelve rings to wake Guns; Ferguson had begun to worry that something had happened to him.

"I'm sorry, Ferg. I was pretty deep in sleep."

"Listen, I need you to get up and get dressed. Rankin's on his way over to pick you up. You guys are catching a train to Naples. I think."

"Uh, OK."

"You're going to have to move. The train is leaving in thirty minutes. I'm going to buy you tickets now."

"Sure."

"You're not going to fall back to sleep, are you?" Ferguson asked. "You sound pretty tired."

"I'm with you, Ferg. I'm with you."

Twenty minutes later, Ferguson spotted Rankin and Guns walking in the side entrance to the train station. He circled behind them, then picked up his pace to catch up.

"Hey," he said in a stage whisper as they paused near the sign showing the departing trains and their tracks.

"What's going on?" Rankin asked.

"I don't think we're being watched," said Ferguson, looking up at the board as he spoke. "But I couldn't sweep the place. The train is on track four. Hamilton is on board, in the second car. I got you guys first-class tickets."

"Hey, thanks, Ferg," said Guns.

"Don't mention it. It's all they had. The train is packed from Rome south. You're going to Naples." Ferguson pointed up at the board, as if he were helping them, then let the tickets fall from his hand. Guns stooped to pick them up, then pretended to hand them back to Ferguson but palmed them instead.

"You're getting good at that, Guns," Ferguson told him. "Next I want to see you pull a quarter out of your nose."

"I'm working on it."

"So what's the deal with Hamilton?" asked Rankin. "We trust him or what?"

"As far as you can throw him," said Ferguson. "He's following Atha, and we're following Atha, so we might just as well do it together. I don't know how much he's holding back. Maybe nothing. Whatever the hookers copied out of Rostislawitch's wallet got the Iranian excited," Ferguson said. "He missed sleeping with them to make sure he could catch this train."

"What whores?" asked Guns.

"You snooze you lose," Ferguson told him. "Go; your train is leaving in about five minutes."

"Ferg, are you and Thera going to be OK by yourselves?" Rankin asked. "T Rex will take another shot for sure."

"We'll be all right. After he gets the luggage, steal it from him."

"What's in it?"

"If I knew, you wouldn't have to grab it from him, would you?" said Ferguson. "Probably work papers and computer disks. It may just be clothes. If you can get it without Atha figuring out we're on to him, that would be great. If not, that's the way it goes. If things start getting too tight, you can call the Italians in."

"Guns and I can handle it without them."

"Just think what I would do, and try not to do the opposite."

"Screw yourself, Ferg."

————

Aboard the train, Atha stretched his feet and shifted against the window, trying to get comfortable. He planned to sleep on the train—he'd have little time to do so later if the material was in the left luggage area, as the luggage check-in rooms were called.

If it wasn't there, then he'd have to grab a flight back to Bologna and continue working on the scientist. There'd be little time to sleep then, either.

The girls had claimed Rostislawitch had been quite randy. Obviously, sex was his weakness; Atha should have realized that from the start.

But what man wasn't vulnerable to a ripe breast thrust in his face? Even Atha had succumbed.

Seat taken?"

Hamilton looked up at a tall, wiry man, an American, standing in the aisle.

Surely one of Ferguson's people, Hamilton thought, though he looked more like a soldier than a spy. CIA agents tended to look like down-at-the-heels salesmen, Ferguson being a notable exception.

"Please, sit," said Hamilton.

"Jack Young," said Guns, holding his hand out. "People call me Guns."

"I see," said Hamilton, concluding that here was a man who had made his fetish work for him.

"You're Hamilton?"

"Please. Have a seat." Hamilton glanced around the coach. It was empty except for an older couple near the door, though the ticket seller had predicted it would be full by the time they pulled into Naples.

"Ferg talked to you?" asked Guns.

"Oh yes."

"You think Atha is going all the way to Naples?"

"That's where his ticket is for," said Hamilton. "I would not take a bet either way."

"Rankin is a few seats behind him. That's my partner."

"Jolly good."

They sat together silently for a while, Hamilton wishing the man would get up and go to another car. Finally Hamilton took out his mobile phone.

"I have to make a phone call," he told Guns. "And I rather value my privacy."

"Sure." Guns got up slowly, then walked to the front of the car, pausing at the vestibule before passing to the next coach.

Hamilton was already working on a text message:

Cooperating as told. New opera more interesting. Request permission stay with it. Yanks will take old show on road.

Would the desk recognize that "new opera" meant the Russian scientist? Or even that the Iranian was the "old show"? They could be intolerably dense at times.

He'd just have to hope they would. The text message was encrypted, but he'd learned years ago not to put too much stock in such things, and spoke in riddles whenever possible.

Years ago, indeed. Hamilton turned his head to the window. The Italian countryside was so dark he could see only his face and the interior of the coach.

I'm quite ready to retire, he told himself, noticing the furrows in his brow. After this, I'm done. Done.

19

BOLOGNA, ITALY

Ferguson stood in the doorway, watching Thera sleep. She was curled up around her pillow, her arms covering her face as if shielding her from the light.

He was tempted to climb in with her.

His lust was going to wear him out.

"Up and at 'em, beautiful; the day is ready to dawn," he said, clapping his hands. "Come on, Thera; let's get going."

"*Ugggh.*"

"Want me to make you some of that lousy coffee?" Ferguson said, squatting down at the side of the bed.

"What time is it?"

"Just about four a.m. Come on. Get up; take a shower. I want to grab about two hours of sleep before Rosty is on the move."

"I thought it was Guns' turn," said Thera, still not fully awake.

"Guns and Rankin are following the Iranian. Come on, up, up, up." He rose and started for the door. "Nice jammies by the way."

"Screw you," muttered Thera. She was wearing a T-shirt and sweatpants, and knew she looked like hell.

The coffee was indeed terrible, so bad that Thera stooped to putting in two packets of sugar and even a bit of powdered milk in an attempt to make it palatable. She sipped it, then took a quick shower, not bothering to wash her hair. Ferguson was waiting when she was done, standing so near the door she bumped into him. Thera felt herself flush.

"I'm giving myself two hours," he told her. "But if Rostislawitch gets moving before then, you wake me up, you hear? You don't go anywhere without backup. All right?"

"Sure."

"Don't 'sure' me. 'Yes. I will wake you up or I will forfeit my first, second, and third child to you.' Got it?"

"Yes."

"Good. Don't forget, I sleep in the nude, so if you have to come in for something, be prepared."

"Ha, ha."

Ferguson smirked and then disappeared into the bedroom. Thera knew from experience that he did not sleep in the nude, and in fact sometimes kept his shoes on in case he had to get up quickly. But that was Ferg—busting and semi-flirting, dead serious about his job but little else.

Thera took her coffee and went over to the desk, where the laptop display showed the feed from the video bug Rankin had planted the previous evening. Rostislawitch was sleeping, arms and legs spread-eagle beneath the covers.

She checked her watch. It was a little past four, ten p.m. back in the States. Unsure when Ferguson had last checked in with the Cube, she called herself.

Lauren DiCapri greeted her with a complaint about some of the video bugs they'd planted two days ago; their batteries had run down and the units were no longer feeding images to their boosters.

"We'll take care of it when we can," Thera told her.

"We can't see what's going on."

"You don't have to."

"I don't mean now."

"Neither do I," said Thera, annoyed by Lauren's tone. For some reason the desk people tended to act like the ops worked for them, rather than the other way around.

"Where's Ferg?"

"He's sleeping," said Thera.

"What's up with him and the Russian agent? Is he sleeping with her?"

"What do you mean?"

"Everyone here knows she's T Rex, but he won't admit it."

"Do you have anything useful to say?"

"You don't have to defend him," said Lauren.

"I'm not."

"OK, Thera. I'm uploading the new keys for the phone encryptions. Use them if you have to use pay phones."

Thera got up from the desk and stalked over to the coffeepot. She splashed some of the coffee onto the table, then burned her fingers as she daubed at it with a napkin.

Aside from her snarky tone, Lauren did have a point. Why *didn't* Ferg think Kiska Babev was the assassin? He hadn't really explained.

He rarely explained anything, did he? Pretty much he did what he pleased—including sleeping with people he was spying on, like T Rex's advance "man."

God damn him.

Thera finished cleaning the table and went back to the desk. She'd been gone so long that the screen saver had popped on.

She set the coffee down and tapped one of the arrow keys. She had to enter a password and use the thumbprint authentication before the screen would clear.

When she did, she saw that the light was on in Rostislawitch's room. He was no longer in his bed.

Thera backed the feed up, hoping to see him going into the bathroom, which was just out of range of the camera. Instead, she saw him get up, take his shoes and coat, and go out of the room.

"Ferg! We have a problem!" she yelled, switching the feed to look at the other bugs.

20

NAPLES, ITALY

Atha made his way from the train platform through the station, letting the businesspeople and students rush past him. It wasn't quite five—the train had been about a half hour late—and the station was not entirely awake yet. He walked past a row of gated stores, then found the left luggage room; the sign said that it didn't open until eight.

There was no sense waiting at the station. Atha decided he would find some place for breakfast, then conduct a little business by phone. There were many arrangements to be made.

Atha didn't think it likely that he'd be followed, but he decided to take a turn around the station just in case. Glancing at the departures board, he realized an Italian military policeman near the ticket counter was staring at him. Atha's skin was not noticeably darker than that of many native Neapolitans, but somehow the policeman seemed to have identified him as a foreigner. He had his thumbs in his belt, ready to pounce.

Under other circumstances Atha might have confronted the man, but now he decided his best course was to simply leave without creating a fuss. He spent a few more moments checking the board and consulting his watch, pretending to mentally calculate his time between trains.

Then he moved to his right, making sure to keep his gaze well away from the policeman.

It seemed to work. Atha reached the row of closed stores before turning sharply right, aiming toward the side exit to the station. No one bothered him, and he thought he had escaped notice when two carabinieri suddenly appeared at the side of the archway that led to the exit.

"*Mi scusi, signore. Dove va?*" asked the shorter of the two men. His tone was polite, and the accent northern rather than Neapolitan. His hand rested on the butt of a submachine gun slung over his shoulder.

"Where am I going? I was hoping to find a place for breakfast. My train doesn't leave for several hours," replied Atha in Italian.

"May we see your ticket?"

"I haven't bought it yet," Atha told him. "I thought I'd get something to eat first."

"You are going where?" asked the taller policeman.

"Salerno," said Atha, sharpening his tone in response to the man's own gruffness. "Why?"

"Let us see some identification," said the first man, still conciliatory.

"But of course."

Atha reached into his pocket and took out his diplomatic passport. The carabinieri examined it, leafing through the pages and then coming back to the cover where his picture was posted. They pretended not to be impressed by the diplomatic stamp, though in theory it meant he should have special treatment—or at least lip service in that direction.

"There is a train to Palmero in fifteen minutes," said the taller man.

"True. But then I would arrive too early. And Palmero—it is not Naples, is it? I would expect to get a better breakfast here."

The man chortled, then took Atha's passport from his partner to check it himself.

"I wonder where a good place to eat breakfast would be," said Atha. "A place with fine coffee but not too expensive."

"Nowhere in Naples," said the shorter man good-naturedly. Then the two carabinieri began debating the various merits of a handful of small shops in the immediate area.

What the hell are they doing?" Rankin said, griping behind a bottle of orange drink as he stood near the newsstand, as far as he could tell the only place open in the station besides the ticket window.

"The police don't trust Arabs," said Hamilton, next to him. "Even though they make up half the city's population."

"He's Iranian. That's not Arab."

"Even worse."

"You sure your driver's outside?" asked Rankin.

"Americans take very little on faith, do they?"

"One of us oughta get out there, in case the police stop us, too."

"They won't stop us," said Hamilton. "But very well. I'll go."

Rankin put his hand out. "I'll go."

"The driver won't recognize you."

"I'll figure it out."

Hamilton closed his eyes and turned his head downward. It was a gesture of disappointment he had learned from his first master in grade school—appropriate, Hamilton thought, given that he was working with Americans.

"If we're going to work together, you're going to have to trust me," he said softly.

"Yeah," said Rankin, heading toward the door. He gave Guns a slight nod. They'd worked out the plan on the train: Guns would stay in the station, watching the left baggage area, while Rankin and Hamilton followed Atha wherever he went.

Hamilton took out his mobile phone to call Jared Lloyd, the operative waiting in the car. He described the American, telling Lloyd to pick him up and wait.

"He's quite a crank, with a nasty disposition," added Hamilton. "Never fear—if he gets on our nerves too much, we'll throw him in the bay."

21

"I'm really sorry, Ferg. I spilled the coffee and I wasn't paying attention," said Thera as she reran the video captures. "It was only for a
minute or two. I'm sorry."

"Don't worry about it," said Ferguson. He hunched over the
screen, their shoulders touching. Rostislawitch had gotten out of bed,
pulled on his shoes, taken his coat, and left in less than ninety seconds.
The video bugs caught him in the hall, and then the lobby going out.

"He must have been lying in bed awake for a while," said Ferguson.

"There were no calls or anything. Maybe he has an appointment
to meet someone for breakfast."

"Maybe." Ferguson scratched at the stubble on his chin. "All
right. Take the radio and some bugs. You check the little cafés and
whatnot to the north; I'll go south. Take the red moped. It goes with
your face."

"I'm sorry, Ferg. I know I screwed up."

"It's all right. I doubt he went far. Don't worry."

"I'm really sorry."

"Hey, relax. It's really not that big a deal. We all slip sometimes.
OK?"

She nodded, but somehow his compassion made her feel even
worse.

Rostislawitch pulled his coat closed against the wind, continuing
down the narrow street. He'd slept for several hours, but in his
restlessness he felt as if he hadn't gotten any sleep at all. He was filled
with a nervous energy, unsettled and anxious.

He was almost glad to feel it, though. It was a positive thing, a rumbling of forces he hadn't felt in years. It was as if he'd been going through the world with a thick wool blanket over his head, secured there with coils of heavy rope. Now the rope had loosened, and he could see bits of daylight coming through the folds. Maybe, if he kept fighting, he would lose the blanket entirely.

The weather had been relatively warm in Bologna, at least to someone like Rostislawitch used to Russian winters. But this morning the wind was biting and there was a cold, near-freezing mist. Rostislawitch decided he would find a place to warm up for a while, a place where he could sit and think. The first place that presented itself was a church.

A small group of parishioners had gathered for the five a.m. mass. Rostislawitch walked inside and sat at a pew at the back of the chapel where the mass was held, not wanting to intrude. His ancestors had been Russian Orthodox, and despite the Communists' prohibition against religions, Rostislawitch had been raised in that tradition and even married in an Orthodox church. But between habit and science, his belief in God had dwindled; he looked at religion now as mostly a quaint relic of a time when people needed to blame the supernatural for things they could not control in their lives. He had not been in a church in many years.

The Roman Catholic mass seemed plain, almost stripped-down, compared to the Russian Orthodox celebrations Rostislawitch remembered. He watched as the priest moved swiftly about the altar, consecrating the bread and wine into the body and blood of Jesus Christ. This part of the mass was common between the two branches of Catholicism, the central mystery that the brother faiths shared. Rostislawitch leaned back in the pew, considering how the two branches had become estranged. It was the story of mankind entirely—from the Bible's Babel to the present day, small differences becoming a wedge, members of the same family then drifting away, until only the animosities were what was remembered.

How could you kill a brother?

That was what his work with the bacteria was aimed at doing. He could rationalize and say that he was trying to prevent deaths, trying to develop a weapon that would guarantee that others would not strike Russia. But at its core his work was aimed at killing many people indiscriminately, no matter what justifications he gave.

And if it was difficult to defend his work for the government, how much harder then was it to defend what he had planned to do— give the material to Atha?

There was no defense. Rostislawitch wanted to kill people, and expected it to be used.

That was the simple truth. He had come to hate his fellow man. And himself.

It was a terrible, horrible plan, fully intentional, a great sin.

That was what he had gotten up early to do? To seal the deal? To become a murderer?

Tears ran down his cheeks.

Rostislawitch heard rustling nearby. He looked up into the brown face of a young nun, standing in the pew in front of his.

"Signore, are you well?" she asked in Italian.

Not quite sure what she was saying, but realizing she was concerned for him, Rosislawitch smiled and stood up.

"Are you OK?" the nun asked in English.

"Thank you, Sister, yes," said Rostislawitch. "I was thinking about my wife."

"Is she ill?"

"Dead."

The nun's face knitted into a concerned frown. "She is with God then," she said, patting his hand. "I will pray for her."

"Thank you."

The nun nodded, then turned back toward the altar to pray. The mass was over, and the congregation had dispersed. Rostislawitch bowed his head, as if in prayer, then sidled out of the pew and began walking around the church, contemplating the saints on their pedestals, considering what he must do.

22

The strong coffee helped Atha think, and by the time he had finished breakfast he had concocted a plan for getting whatever was in the locker with a minimum of exposure. It was still very early, but the vendors had begun setting up their wares on the streets near the station, and Atha had no trouble finding a good price on a piece of cheap luggage. More difficult was finding a street person whom he could provisionally trust. They were all thieves, of course, hardly a handicap under the circumstances; the difficulty was to find one who might be counted on to return the bag—or whatever was in the locker—to him for a sum approaching what they had agreed on. Atha finally settled on a man in his early twenties who walked with a limp; in the worst case he should be able to chase him down.

Atha gave the man a small advance and told him to meet him near the train station at precisely nine a.m., then went to a small *osteria* or restaurant to make some phone calls. His first was to the minister, who had left several messages on his voice mail demanding to know what was going on. Atha called and told him that he was in Naples and not to worry; they would soon have the material as planned.

"Why are you in Naples?" demanded the minister. "Where is the Russian?"

"The Russian is not important," said Atha. "The material is here."

"Everything is waiting. You are a day late already."

"These things take time. When I obtained—"

"That's immaterial. We must move quickly. The timetable is not our own."

The barely suppressed rage in the minister's voice made Atha tremble.

"I will need to make some new arrangements concerning my transportation. I had originally arranged for a merchant ship—"

"The arrangements will be made," said the minister. "You are behind schedule."

"Actually, Minister, I said that—"

"Do not argue. Just get it done!"

Atha pulled the phone from his head as the receiver was slammed down on the other end.

Still on the phone?" Rankin asked Hamilton.

"Bloody hell, he hasn't left, has he?"

Rankin folded his arms. "I could have bugged the damn place and we'd know what he's saying."

"We're not taking risks, Yank. This is my show, remember?"

Rankin pushed back against the seat. Ferguson might be a jerk, but he sure as hell knew what he was doing, unlike this British bozo.

"He's off the phone," said the driver. "Coming out."

Rankin pulled his baseball cap lower on his head, shielding his face as the car pulled out of its space. The Iranian walked out of the store and turned right, heading in the direction of the train station. Traffic had picked up considerably, and within half a block they had lost sight of him.

"Shit," said Rankin, banging on the dashboard.

"Calm down," said Hamilton. "We know where he's going."

"Do we?" snapped Rankin.

Someone up ahead began honking their horn. The road ahead, barely two lanes wide, had four cars abreast, all trying to get into an intersection that seemed jammed as well. Traffic came to a complete halt.

Rankin grabbed the door latch.

"What are you doing?" asked Hamilton.

"I'll follow him. Keep your phone line free."

"Americans," muttered Hamilton as Rankin slammed the door.

The cars were packed so tightly that it was difficult to get through. Rankin finally decided that the only way he could get to the side was to climb on bumpers, which elicited curses and even more horn blowing.

When he reached the sidewalk, he had to duck around a fully loaded garbage Dumpster that smelled as if it hadn't been emptied since the Second World War.

He pulled the radio's earbud up from beneath his shirt collar. "Hey, Guns, you there?"

"Yeah, I'm here, man."

"Atha's coming your way."

"I'm ready."

"I'm on foot. Hamilton's stuck in traffic with Jared."

"OK. You get something to eat?"

"No."

"I'm sitting in a pastry shop. I can get you something. They have these very nice cheese danish things. Don't know what they're called, but they're killer."

"No thanks."

"Hey, I see him."

"All right. Don't get too close."

Rankin began trotting, ducking around a pair of businessmen who were themselves ducking a vendor selling umbrellas. When Rankin reached the main entrance, a nine-year-old boy stepped in front of him and asked if he wanted his shoes shined. At that moment, someone bumped into Rankin on the right. As he started to duck out of the way, a third man attempted to take Rankin's wallet.

Rankin plunged his elbow into the first man's stomach, then swung his left hand out and grabbed the man trying to take his wallet, throwing him to the ground. The first man took a swing at Rankin, who managed to push him off. Rankin reached for the Beretta at the back of his belt, then stopped, a policeman running through the door of the station.

"Get the hell away from me," Rankin told the would-be pick-pockets. "Go!"

But instead of running off, the first man made a run at him, plunging his head into Rankin's midsection. Rankin smacked the side of the man's head with his fist, then punched him in the gut with his other hand. The man crumbled to the ground, out of breath.

The policeman had paused to figure out what was going on. Now he sprang into action, blowing a whistle and unholstering his weapon.

Rankin looked for a way to sneak away without having to deal with the authorities, but a police motorcycle had managed to find a way through the traffic jam behind him and was riding up on the sidewalk. He stepped back, watching as the pickpockets began pleading that they were the victims, calling Rankin a brute and saying that he was the one who should be arrested. A plainclothes detective approached Rankin, and asked in Italian what he had seen happen.

"I'm sorry, I don't speak Italian," said Rankin.

"Non parla Italiano?"

"I only speak English."

"I see. Wait *un momento*, please."

"I have to get a train."

"Un momento, please," repeated the man, gesturing to someone on the now-crowded steps. "A moment."

"How come this kind of stuff *never* happens to Ferg?" Rankin muttered to himself.

23

BOLOGNA, ITALY

Ferguson was having his own problems in Bologna.

Neither he nor Thera had been able to find where Rostislawitch had gone. He wasn't in any of the small cafés and coffee bars within ten blocks of the hotel, nor had he gone over to the conference building early. Ferguson finally conceded to himself that they'd lost Rostislawitch, at least temporarily; he planted some fresh video bugs and booster units, then met Thera in a hotel restaurant near the art building.

"I'm sorry, Ferg. I'm really sorry," she told him as he sat down. "I'm really sorry."

"He'll turn up. I've lost people before."

"I checked the hotel. He's still registered. I left him a message on his voice mail, saying he should call me."

"Great."

The waiter came over. Ferguson ordered a *caffèllatte*, then sat back in his seat, watching the people pass outside.

"The old guy really likes you, doesn't he?" said Ferguson.

"He's not that old."

"So you like the mature type, huh?"

The waiter appeared with Ferguson's coffee.

"He seems very nice," said Thera.

"Sure, for a guy who's perfecting ways to mass murder people," said Ferguson, stirring his coffee.

"I didn't say he was perfect."

"Unlike me, huh?"

Thera flushed. "You're always fooling around," she said angrily.

The air drained abruptly from Ferguson's lungs, as if he'd been punched in the stomach without any warning.

Oh, Christ, he realized, she loves me.

He tried to think of something to say, something to tell her—he wanted to say how he felt, but to temper it with reality, with their jobs and what was happening to him, the cancer, everything—but before he could think of what to say a face loomed in the crowd passing by the window.

"Rostislawitch," hissed Thera. "He's going to the conference."

"Get over there," said Ferg. "I'm right behind you."

"Ferg—"

"Yeah, yeah, yeah. Go."

24

Guns spotted Atha coming into the train station, walking briskly with a shiny black carry-on bag rolling at his side. Taking out his fake MP3 player, Guns tuned to the channel for the bug he'd planted near the luggage area. Then he drifted toward the men's room near the baggage check-in counter, listening as Atha walked up to the attendant and asked to check his bag. Guns thought it must be part of an exchange, but the suitcase didn't contain wads of cash; the clerk opened it and found only a pair of sweaters.

Atha took his receipt, then left, walking up in the direction of the train platforms.

Guns checked around, trying to catch anyone who might be trailing Atha, then slowly started in that direction himself.

"Rankin, what's going on?" he asked, switching his "player" back over to the radio circuit.

"I have a problem. Stay away."

"Huh?"

"Pickpockets tried to roll me. I'm with the police. I'm going to have to give up my cover."

"Are you kidding?"

"I don't sound like I'm making a joke, do I?"

Rankin said something Guns couldn't make out to a policeman.

Guns wanted to ask Rankin what he thought was going on—why would Atha check a bag rather than retrieve one? But obviously Rankin was in no position to answer.

Probably he'd be just as baffled as Guns was.

Ferg would know—he always knew. He had some sixth sense about things that none of them quite shared.

Atha, meanwhile, went into a small store that sold mineral water, bought himself a bottle, then walked across to a magazine kiosk, where he got a copy of the newspaper, then went and sat down on a bench at the far side of the station. He dug into his pocket for the luggage receipt, then took out the slip of paper with the numbers the prostitute had copied for him.

The luggage ticket was a simple piece of white paper, with the word *scontrino*—ticket—stamped above a black line where the clerk wrote the letter and number of the locker or bin where he had placed the bag.

Rostislawitch's number was only one digit different from his—4 rather than 8—and Atha considered simply altering the number with a pen. But he decided to stick with his original plan and, after satisfying himself that the carabinieri were no longer watching him, walked back toward the exit. There he saw the policemen in the process of arresting a pair of pickpockets; rather than walking close by, Atha went out the side. Avoiding the police entirely, he circled around the block until he came to the Hotel Naples. There he walked through the lobby to the business center. Within a few moments he had a photocopy of the baggage ticket. A pencil eraser lifted the original claim number; he made another copy, put in the right number, and then used the center's paper cutter to fashion a *scontrino di bagaglio* that looked so much like the original that after folding it and putting it into his pocket he had to pull out the prostitute's note to make sure he had the right one.

The war against pickpockets and other scammers at the Naples train station had been going on for over a hundred years. The policemen detaining Rankin were therefore somewhat resigned to the fact that there would be many battles, and knew they would have to husband their resources for the long haul. The repeated protests of the American finally convinced them that he would never do as a witness, and thus they released him, even as they pushed the miscreants into a car for a ride to the station, where their names would be recorded and their photos taken. It was of some consolation, the policemen thought, that the criminals had chosen a victim willing to fight back; both of the would-be pickpockets looked considerably worse for wear, and were likely to take at least a few days off nursing their wounds.

Rankin went inside and grabbed a table at one of the small food kiosks. Guns had followed the Iranian into the hotel, where Atha had created a new luggage ticket, then turned him over to the two British MI6 agents so he could go and rent some scooters in case they needed more transportation.

In a dark mood, Rankin sipped his coffee and waited for Atha to return to the station. The incident with the pickpockets had thrown Rankin off. Until then, he'd thought he had everything under control.

His cell phone rang.

"All right, Yank. Atha just gave something to a ratty-looking man who walks with a limp," said Hamilton.

"When he comes out with the bag, brush into him, then call for the police," Rankin told Hamilton. "I'll come up behind you and grab the bag. Worst case, the police will end up with it, and we can examine it at the station."

"We don't want the Naples police involved in this," said Hamilton. "They're too corrupt. It will be better to grab him on the street. We'll be closer to the car."

"The traffic sucks."

"Relax, Stephen. I've done this sort of thing before."

Rankin ground his teeth together.

A man with a limp and a tattered sweater headed toward the luggage check. Rankin started toward him, then spotted Atha only a few feet behind him. He put his cell phone back to his ear.

"Hamilton, Atha's right behind this guy. He's going with him to the luggage check."

"Very good, very good. I'm just coming in the door."

Rankin stayed back, expecting Hamilton to close in. But the British agent stayed back as well. The video bug showed the Iranian getting a bag and then standing nearby as the other man got a similar bag. In seconds, they were both outside the luggage area, moving in opposite directions.

"I have Atha," said Hamilton. "Take his accomplice. Don't cause a stir."

Rankin followed the man as he wheeled his bag toward the ticket counter. Rail-thin, with a beard several days old, the Italian dragged his right foot as he walked, his shoe's metal heel scraping on the floor. Rankin had no trouble closing the distance between them, standing with only one person between him and the man. It was tempting to grab the suitcase and simply run off, but there were so many policemen around that he was sure to create a commotion. The man took the suitcase with him to the ticket window.

The man was exchanging a ticket, or at least trying to. They were arguing about something—Rankin's Italian wasn't good enough to let him know about what.

It had to do with an exchange. The man was trying to get money for an unused train ticket.

Rankin thought about what he was seeing—an unkempt, possibly homeless man, trying to come up with cash. He wasn't the sort of person that would be a regular Iranian agent.

But that fit: Atha had hired prostitutes in Bologna, using them to do jobs he couldn't do himself.

The person behind Rankin prodded him. A window had just opened up.

"I made a mistake," Rankin told her. "You go."

He moved away, standing to the side as the man who'd taken the bag came away from the counter, his ticket still in his hand.

"Where's it to?" asked Rankin.

"*Che?*" said the man.

"The ticket." Rankin pointed. "I'll buy it from you."

The man eyed him suspiciously. The man didn't seem to speak English, so Rankin decided to make do with the universal language—money.

"Fifty euros," said Rankin.

"*Cento,*" said the man immediately.

"Screw you. The ticket's worthless to you," said Rankin, turning away. He wasn't sure how long to play it; he took two steps, then turned back around.

"Throw in the bag and you've got a deal," said Rankin, pointing.

The man didn't understand.

"The bag. Luggage."

The man squinted, still unsure what he meant.

"*Ecco,*" said Rankin, touching the bag. "Here. This."

"*Cento? Si,*" said the man.

His quick agreement told Rankin everything he needed to know—the bag was worthless—but he paid the man anyway.

Hamilton closed in behind Atha. He was tempted to grab the bag and toss it to Jared in the car. But if he did that, he'd be tipping Atha off to the fact that they were on to him, and the Iranian would undoubtedly flee. Hamilton's assignment was to delineate whatever network Atha was part of; if he grabbed the bag or even Atha now, he would in fact fail to fulfill his objectives.

So he let Atha go, following him down the street to a cab. Guns, nearby on the rented Vespa, zoomed in close to follow while Hamilton got in with Jared.

They followed the taxi to the port area, a long pilgrimage over crowded streets through colorless clouds of carbon monoxide and the relentless rant of Neapolitan curses. Hamilton liked Italy, but not this part of it—garbage strewn and smoggy—even the air smelled rancid, the stench of dead fish and factories wafting in the breeze.

"Take a right there," Hamilton told Jared. "It's shorter."

"We'll get stuck at the cross street."

"Take the right. It's shorter."

Jared turned at the last minute, tires screeching. For two blocks, it appeared as if Hamilton was correct; there was no traffic on the narrow road. But the deep potholes made it hard to go too fast, and midway down the third street they found themselves once more embedded in traffic.

"You might do better by walking," said Jared.

"Guns is with him," said Hamilton. "There's no need to go crazy."

Guns watched from a block away as Atha's cab stopped in front of a row of dilapidated brick buildings near the docks south of the city's main port area. Instead of going into one of the houses across the street, Atha crossed to the waterside, climbing up a set of concrete steps and disappearing down the side. Guns drove down the block far enough to see Atha clambering down a wooden ladder to a narrow dock and over to a small fishing boat. A burly man came out from the wheelhouse to help him board. The Iranian held on to the suitcase he was carrying for dear life, refusing to give it to the other man even though his balance was precarious. Finally, he managed to tumble onto the deck. The other man laughed, and they both went inside.

Hamilton and Jared drove up a few minutes later. Rankin, on the scooter Guns had left for him, rode up almost on their tail.

"About time you got here, Yank," said Hamilton, as if he'd been waiting for Rankin all morning.

"Why didn't you grab the suitcase?" Rankin asked.

"Because my job is to investigate the man, not what he's carrying."

"He's got plans for a bacteria that'll kill people in there."

"That's Ferguson's theory."

"More than just Ferg's."

"Listen, Mr. Rankin, I'm in charge here."

"Bullshit. If you didn't want to grab the suitcase, you should have told me that at the station. Ferg said I shouldn't trust you."

"Ferguson is not one to talk on the issue of trust. There's no harm done. He's down in the boat."

"He's going to sail the fucking boat out of the harbor."

Rankin looked down at the water. The fishing boat was tied up by itself, but there was a small marina about fifty yards away.

"I think it might be a meeting," said Guns. "Or maybe they're waiting for somebody."

"One of us is going to have to go down there and bug the boat," said Rankin.

"Are you daft?" said Hamilton. "They'll see you."

"He's got a point, Skip," said Guns. "We might just as well go grab the suitcase ourselves, like we're robbers."

"No!" said Hamilton.

"Then we're going to have to get the Italians involved," said Rankin. "It's the only way we'll find out what he took from the locker."

"Guns' idea might work," said Lloyd. "You and I could stay back and follow them afterwards."

Hamilton was about to object when they heard the tug's engines turn over and pop to life with a deep rumble. All four men looked at one another; then Rankin reached to his belt and took out his Beretta.

"Back me up, Guns," he said, starting for the stairs. He reached them just in time to see the burly man Guns had spotted earlier casting off the line. "Stop!" Rankin yelled. "Stop!"

He fired a round just in case the man didn't speak English. The man dove back to the wheelhouse. Rankin began clambering down the steps. He was almost to the wood dock at the bottom when the Italian reemerged from the cabin, a Skorpion submachine gun in his hands.

Guns, at the top of the steps, screamed a warning, but it was drowned out by the rattle of the small Czech weapon blasting through its twenty-bullet magazine.

25

CIA BUILDING 24-442

Ferguson's tip about Kiska having a cousin with a German last name in a mental hospital somewhere in Romania—and the suggestion that she used the cousin's identity for her credit card accounts—wasn't the most stellar piece of intelligence Ciello had ever received. But the analyst persevered.

His first problem was the fact that he did not speak Romanian. That was easily overcome; when the Agency Romanian language expert proved unavailable, Ciello stole a page from Ferguson's book and went for outside help, in this case a UFO expert he knew who lived in Craiova and had recently published a moving though overly assonant sonnet sequence on UFO abductions there. Craiova was a long way from Baia Mare—opposite ends of the country, in fact—but his fellow UFO buff had his own network of informants, and within an hour or so had obtained a list of all of the patients at the two mental institutions near Baia Mare.

The fact that there were two, not one, gave Ciello a bit more work to do; he ended up with five possible names of women who might be related to Kiska Babev. A preliminary search of the names turned up nothing, but this wasn't surprising. Ciello sent his formal requests for information on possible bank and credit card accounts over the CIA system; he got an automated response informing him that he would have the results "as soon as humanly possible"—an odd comment, he thought, given that it was generated by computer.

Then he called Ferguson's friend in Nigeria.

"Ah, you called. Very good. Just about lunchtime here," said the man. His English had a slightly exotic accent. "Mr. Ferg promised you call before lunch."

"I have five names I need to check out for bank accounts."

"Five? Mr. Ferg said only one. Five—that was not what he said."

"Well, five is just five ones put together," said Ciello, not sure what other explanation he could give.

"But it is more than one. This is the key point."

"Well, shit happens."

The man thought the expression was uproariously funny, and began laughing so hard that Ciello had to hold his phone away from his ear.

"Shit happens. Yes. Yes. I think this all the time. Shit does happen. A-ha."

"Can I give you the names?"

"My friend, today, for you, because you are the friend to my friend, and because it is lunchtime, I am going to save you very much work. You will look the names up yourself. Today only—because you are friend to Mr. Ferguson."

"Great," said Ciello.

"One name, five names, a hundred names. Today you do what you want. Because, my friend, shit happens."

"Sure does."

The man gave Ciello a Web site and an access code; all would be revealed when he signed on.

"Look in an hour. If not there, then, no information can be found."

"An hour?"

"Give or take. Lunch comes first. Shit happens, no?"

Fibber was still laughing when Ciello hung up the phone.

26

The Czech-produced Skorpion was more a machine pistol than a sub-machine gun; its light weight and poor balance made it hard for a novice to handle, especially one who was trying to shoot with one hand while on the run. The bullets had the intended effect, however: they sent Rankin diving for cover. Since the narrow wooden dock offered none, he dove into the water, barely escaping the spray of 7.65mm bullets. As the water roiled, he pushed himself away, doing his best to stay underwater until finally his lungs felt like they were about to burst. When he surfaced, he realized that the rumble he'd felt nearby had come not from the bullets but from the propellers pushing the boat from the dock. The fishing boat was already some thirty yards away; Rankin took a few strokes after it but saw it was hopeless. He turned back and found Guns and the others gaping at him from the railing above the dock.

"Why the hell didn't you shoot back?" Rankin yelled. "Crap. He's getting away."

Guns—who had not only shot back but hit the gunman while Rankin was underwater—said nothing. Hamilton shook his head.

Rankin climbed up on a dilapidated tire and pulled himself out of the water. He'd lost his pistol when he jumped in; he gave a cursory look around the dock though he knew it was hopeless, then climbed up the ladder to the stairs and the street.

"You should have grabbed the bag on the street when you had the chance," Rankin told Hamilton.

"Don't tell me what I should or shouldn't have done, Yank," answered Hamilton.

Cursing, Rankin went through his pockets. He still had his radio and headset, plus his sat phone and his wallet.

Guns, meanwhile, took a photo of the boat with his small camera, then pulled out his phone to talk to Corrigan back in the Cube.

"We're going to need the Italian coast guard," he told him. "Atha got away with whatever the Russian scientist sold him. They're in a fishing boat; it's not that big, fifty-something feet. It didn't have a name. I'll upload a photo."

"Screw the coast guard," said Rankin, pointing toward the marina. "Let's grab our own boat."

"We can't steal a boat," said Hamilton.

"One more word out of you and I'll throw you off the side," said Rankin. "Than you'll smell as bad as I do."

27

THE TYRRHENIAN SEA, OFF NAPLES, ITALY

Atha dragged the injured sailor to the cabin, trying to be as gentle as possible. He'd been struck twice, once in the chest and once in the stomach; blood covered both sides of his sweatshirt, and a trail led back to the stern of the boat. Atha tried to put him into the bunk, but the man was too heavy for him to lift, and he decided the sailor was better off on the floor.

"I'm going to get something for a bandage," Atha told the man.

The man grunted in response. Foam slipped from his mouth, blood and spit mixing together. The sailor grabbed at Atha's arm, wrapping his own around it.

"I'll be back. I need to get you a bandage," said the Iranian, pushing the hand away. The man fell back against the deck.

Up on the bridge of the small boat, the captain was staring at the sea ahead, both hands on the large wheel.

"Are they following us?" Atha asked.

The man did not respond.

"Are there bandages somewhere? A first-aid kit?"

Again, the captain said nothing. Atha spotted a box marked by a white cross next to the fire extinguisher; he grabbed it off the bulkhead and went back to the cabin where he had left the wounded sailor. Opening the box, Atha saw a few pads of gauze, far too small to staunch the flow of blood. He took one anyway, then went down on his knee and tried to find the man's wound. As he did, he realized the man had stopped breathing. Blood was no longer spurting from the wounds. Atha touched the man's face; it felt like wet putty, slick with the man's sweat and the spray from the water. For a moment, he thought of trying artificial respiration, even though he knew it would be useless. Then he pushed down the sailor's eyelids, said a quick prayer, as much for himself as for the dead man.

Rising, Atha realized he was covered with blood. He went to the head, a small, crowded restroom that barely fit a tiny sink and toilet. The soap in the sink was gray, covered with oil; he dug his fingernails through it, revolted by the grime but determined to cleanse the blood away. The faucet produced only a slight trickle. Atha washed his hands and arms as best he could, but even after ten solid minutes there were still red streaks up and down his arms. Bits of blood had coagulated on his fingernails and in the ridges of his hands. He picked at them for a while longer, then gave up.

Out on the deck, he retrieved the small submachine gun and looked to make sure that no one was following them. There were at least a dozen boats between them and the shoreline, but none were particularly close.

He wasn't sure who the men were who had tried to stop them. He guessed Italian secret service agents, though they hadn't identified themselves. It was also possible they were confederates of the man he'd hired to retrieve and swap the bags. In any event, he'd have to assume they were the former, which meant the Italian coast guard and navy would soon be looking for them.

Where the men had come from was another good question. Most likely they'd been following him from the train station, though he hadn't seen anyone. That was his fault—once he had the bag he'd simply moved as quickly as possible, not taking his usual precautions because he wanted to get to the boat.

Atha took the gun inside, reloading it before going to see the captain.

"I think we are all right," Atha told him. "How long?"

The captain didn't acknowledge him. Atha was tempted to hold the gun at his head and demand an answer, but he realized that would serve little purpose.

"Your man is with Allah, blessed be his name," said Atha, laying his hand gently on the captain's shoulder.

The captain said nothing. He was an Iranian by birth and spoke Farsi fluently, but he had lived in Italy since he was seven and felt more Italian than Iranian. He was brooding on the fact that it would now be difficult for him to return to Naples for several weeks. He made a good living by smuggling items for the local Mafia and other "businessmen," but everyone had a certain territory, and he would not be able to operate from another port. Atha, though he paid well, employed him very rarely, and had just cost him a great deal of money. Not to mention the problem of disposing of his deckhand.

Atha left him to his business. He went back to the cabin where the sailor had died, kneeling over Rostislawitch's suitcase. In his haste as the shooting began, he had neglected to zip it shut. Instead of closing it now, he opened it again, reexamining the contents—twelve flat, sealed glass cases, no larger than a child's yo-yo. They looked like flattened jelly jars or the bottoms of the glass honey pots he remembered from childhood.

The brown, jellylike liquid inside might very well be honey for all he knew. It might very well be a scam.

Or perhaps the Italian secret service had made a substitution.

There was nothing he could do about that now. He had to trust that Allah, all praise due to him, had a plan.

Atha zipped the suitcase, grabbed the rest of the bullets for the machine pistol, and went on deck to keep watch.

28

Ferguson twisted around as he walked, scanning the second-story windows on the small block, trying to make sure the knot of scientists ahead weren't being followed by anyone other than the pair of undercover Italian policemen Imperiati had assigned.

Ferguson didn't see anyone, but that didn't make him feel any more comfortable. Rostislawitch and Thera—Rostislawitch really, with Thera agreeing—had decided to skip the first morning session and join a small group of scientists for brunch at a restaurant three blocks from the art building. Ferguson hadn't had time to check out the place beforehand. He trailed along now as the group found the door and tromped up the steps to the second-floor dining room, exchanging jokes in the pidgin English they all shared.

Ferguson walked past the stairs that led up to the restaurant, continuing to the end of the block and crossing over. He stayed under the arched promenade, pretending to window-shop while glancing around. Finally convinced that there was no one watching, he doubled back toward the restaurant. He slipped two video bugs in to cover the street, then went upstairs.

The room was shaped like an L, with tables lined up together along a narrow passage to the deeper part of the room. Ferguson glanced at the maître d', then saw Kiska Babev sitting by herself about halfway down the long row.

"That's my date," Ferguson told the maître d', walking over to her.

"*Ciao*, baby," said Ferguson, pulling out the chair. The maître d' rushed to push it in for him.

"You're late," she said.

"I wanted to make sure we weren't followed. Don't want people talking." He turned to the waiter, who had just appeared at his elbow. "House red."

"A little early for wine, Bobby."

"I like to get a head start on the day."

Kiska had persuaded one of the scientists in the group to suggest the place for breakfast, and to try to bring Rostislawitch along. The man didn't know she was an FSB agent—he thought she was with the Science Ministry, her cover—but was happy to oblige when she assured him that she would sign for the tab. She needed to confer with the scientist about a grant offer from a drug company, she explained, but wanted to do so discreetly.

"I knew you would be here," Kiska told Ferguson. "Because I knew that Dr. Rostislawitch would be. Why did you tell Signor Imperiati that I was involved in the bombing yesterday?"

"That's not what I said."

"It's what he heard."

"His English isn't that good."

"His English is better than mine."

"Nah. His accent is all wrong."

Kiska found it difficult to control her anger at the accusation. "You caused a great deal of trouble for me," she said. "I suspect I am still under suspicion. All because of a lie you told for fun, I suppose."

"Who says it's a lie?"

Kiska reached across the table and slapped his cheek. Though he saw it coming, it still stung.

"I am not playing your American wise-guy games anymore, Bobby."

"You're making people stare."

"I don't care if they stare," she said, switching to Russian.

"Well if you don't care, I don't care," answered Ferguson, also in Russian.

The waiter, Ferguson's wine on his tray, approached cautiously. Ferguson gave him a smile that said, *Women, what can you expect?* The Italian put the glass down, raised an eyebrow in sympathy, and retreated.

"Why are you in Bologna?" Kiska demanded, still speaking Russian.

"We went through this yesterday."

"I will tell you, Bobby, I do not like being accused of being a terrorist," she said. "I do not like this charge being made to my embassy."

"All I told him was that you were a possible witness. Which you were."

Kiska was not sure how much of that to believe, but she needed to move past her own anger, or she would never find out what the Americans were doing, or what was really going on here.

"I will tell you in truth why I am here," she said. "And I expect truth from you in return."

"I'm as truthful as they come."

"Artur Rostislawitch works in a sensitive area regarding bacteria that can be used as weapons."

"Against international law?"

"There is nothing preventing his research, as you very well know," said Kiska. "Your scientists work on similar projects. He has had access to very sensitive materials. His career—he has suffered professional setbacks which are none of my concern. Politics. In any event, it is conceivable that he is disgruntled, which I believe you know."

"Doesn't look like the happiest guy in the world," said Ferguson, shooting him a glance.

Someone had just told a joke and Rostislawitch was laughing.

"Then again, you never know," said Ferguson.

"Some days ago—just before he came to Bologna in fact—one of the safety indicators at a lab where he worked was tampered with. There are some who believe he took material, a culture of bacteria that might be used as a weapon."

"There's a question about it?" said Ferguson.

"There are many questions. Nothing may have been taken; he may not have been the one." Kiska paused. She did not like the ambiguity herself. "The material was something that he worked on himself. It is an old culture, from a program that is no longer sanctioned. He comes here, and you are watching him. Why, I wonder. Has my friend switched from tracking down nuclear material for his government to recruiting Russian scientists? Usually that is a job for an academic, or perhaps a lower-level officer. But then there is a bomb, and though my friend is near it when it explodes, I am blamed. So what is going on, I wonder. What is going on, Bobby?"

"If you keep talking loud enough, Rostislawitch will hear you and you can ask him yourself."

"I intend to. Why are you in Italy?"

"I'm trying to catch the person who wants to kill Rostislawitch."

Kiska could not entirely cover her surprise. "Who is it?"

"Some people think it's you."

"I told you, no games."

"I'm being honest."

The waiter started to approach, but one glance from Kiska sent him scurrying back to the kitchen.

"Why would I kill him?"

"Maybe to keep whatever it is he took from coming to me," said Ferguson. "Except I wasn't the one buying it."

Needing a moment to process everything he had said, Kiska changed the subject.

"The girl you have cozying up to him—she wouldn't have taken it?"

"She doesn't look like the double-crossing type, does she?"

Kiska leaned back in her seat. "If you are not buying the material from Rostislawitch, who is?"

Ferguson shrugged. "I haven't heard that anything is for sale."

"Why would someone want to kill him? It must be related to material, or his research."

"You know better than me. I'd love to find a motive. Then I'd find out who it was. I don't really care about the scientist." Ferguson leaned ever so slightly over the table. "I care about the murderer."

"Why?"

"He killed one of my people."

Kiska's anger had dissipated. There was something about Ferguson that made him difficult to stay mad at. More likely it was her own flaw, some hard-to-map chink in her personality that wanted to forgive handsome men their sins.

A deadly flaw, she thought.

"And you don't know who the murderer is?" Kiska asked.

Ferguson shook his head.

"Waiter, we're ready," Kiska said, using English as she raised her hand to summon him.

"I don't have a menu," said Ferguson.

"Have the lamb omelet," she told him. "It's very good."

"Lamb omelet?"

"It's very good."

Kiska ordered for both of them. Ferguson, meanwhile, tried to decide if what Kiska was telling him was actually true. It was certainly alarming, but the FSB wasn't known for volunteering information like that. Even in their earlier encounter, Kiska had never been this forthcoming.

But what possible angle could she be playing? Get him to do something that would lead her to the scientist?

Maybe Rostislawitch wasn't her target at all—maybe the First Team and its infrastructure was: give them a lead and see how they reacted.

Was he overthinking it?

"So you know that someone is trying to kill him, but you do not know who," said Kiska. "Where did you get such information?"

"It's complicated," said Ferguson.

"Then you may have the wrong target."

"I may." Ferguson took a tiny sip of wine. "So tell me about the material that's missing. What was it?"

"It's a bacteria, a type of E. coli. That's all I know."

"E. coli is the stuff in our stomachs."

"Some is. There are many, many varieties. Some harm us; some don't."

"And this one does. Why?"

"I honestly don't know. That is not my specialty." She waved her hand. "I'm told that the material may have been the subject of a weapons program at one time in the distant past, but that it was decided to be too . . . inappropriate. Difficult to use."

"Why?"

"Bobby, you look for answers that even I do not have access to. You haven't changed."

"Who would he sell to?" asked Ferguson.

"If not you?"

"If not me."

"I see someone from Bundesnachrichtendienst, covered as a commerce attaché. Clumsy, for the Germans."

"BND is so unimaginative," said Ferguson.

Bundesnachrichtendienst—BND—was the German intelligence service.

"I assume there are others," said Kiska, who had put her assistant in Moscow to work vetting the names of the scientists enrolled at the conference. "I don't get out of Moscow that much."

"A shame."

Kiska looked over in the scientist's direction. She couldn't see him from where she was sitting, but she imagined that he would be smiling, happy—perhaps he had already completed the deal and was on his way to becoming rich.

Or maybe not. She had been on cases where a string of circumstances led to great suspicions, all of which later proved unfounded.

But Ferguson's presence told her there was something real. How much of what he said was a lie she couldn't tell. In the past, Ferguson had not so much lied as left things out. He was certainly doing that here, but what details was he omitting besides the information on how they had tracked the killer? Did he actually know who it was? Was Rostislawitch even the target?

"We're watching the scientist's accounts," Kiska said.

"Probably he has one you don't know about."

"It's possible."

"We could compare notes."

"Give me the list that you have and I will tell you if it's correct," said Kiska.

"Nice try," said Ferguson. "I don't think we have any, actually."

"That I don't believe."

"We're not as omniscient as you think."

"I don't think you're omniscient, Bobby," she said, looking into his eyes. "I've worked with you before."

"Touché," said Ferguson, raising his glass.

"I'm going to talk to him after lunch. I don't want you to interfere."

"Fine with me."

Ferguson's face was still red where she had struck him. Kiska reached across the table and touched his cheek. "I didn't mean to hurt you."

"I've been slapped before. You expect that from Russian women."

"Always with a joke."

She ran the side of her finger down his cheek. He was a very dangerous man, but a handsome one. She nearly said something she would have regretted, but fortunately the waiter approached with their meals.

Thera excused herself from the table and walked in the direction of the ladies' room. As she did, she saw Ferguson sitting with the Russian FSB agent, who was running her hand down his cheek.

He just couldn't resist, could he, Thera thought to herself, pretending not to see.

29

THE TYRRHENIAN SEA, OFF NAPLES, ITALY

Rankin, Guns, and the Brits didn't steal the boat. Renting—albeit at an exorbitant rate—was easier and faster.

The fishing boat Atha had boarded was an old vessel, weighed down by rust and caked crud. Their boat was much newer—a large cabin cruiser about half the size of the other craft and, while not the speediest vessel on the water, capable of 30 knots.

Corrigan told Rankin that the Naples harbor patrol—actually part of the police force—was sending its three launches out. The Italian Guardia Costiera—the coast guard—had a patrol boat about eight miles to the south and another to the north; both were on their way as well.

"You think that the Italians can really help?" said Hamilton derisively. "You're really a novice at this, aren't you? At least Ferguson knows where to butter his toast."

"Ferg ain't here," said Rankin, moving toward the bow.

Guns, standing against the rail with his binoculars, pointed toward a boat in the distance.

"That it, you think?"

Rankin took the glasses. Shaped like a small tug, the boat had a large stack directly behind the small wheelhouse. There was a boom at the back.

"Yeah, I think so," he agreed, handing the binoculars back.

"You gonna apologize?"

"For what?"

Guns looked at him for a second, then raised the glasses to his face.

"I'm not Ferg," Rankin said. "I'm not perfect."

"Ferg ain't perfect, either." Guns put down the glasses. "I shot the son of a bitch while you were in the water."

"Oh." Rankin realized, belatedly, that Guns hadn't been criticizing him; he was angry because Rankin had yelled at him for not firing at the gunman. He should have realized that, and would have, had he not been obsessed with measuring himself against Ferguson. It wasn't his fault that the Iranian had gotten away, even though he was blaming himself.

"Hey, listen, I got a little hot back there," said Rankin. "I'm sorry. I know you probably did your best."

"Yeah. None of us are Ferg," added Guns.

"A good thing," muttered Rankin.

Rankin had the captain cut the motor when they were about a mile from the fishing boat. No one seemed to be on deck. The boat was moving at about 4 knots due south; it had obviously slowed down at some point, but its pace now remained steady.

"Maybe the Iranian was wounded as well," suggested Hamilton as they took turns examining the boat through Guns' binoculars.

"Maybe."

Rankin took out his sat phone. "Corrigan, where is that coast guard boat? You know?"

"To your southeast. It's still a good half hour away."

"Thanks." He turned to Guns. "What do you think? Wait for the Italians?"

"If he's got papers in the suitcase, he could be destroying them," said Guns. "There's smoke coming out of the smokestack."

"We don't want to wait for the Italians," said Hamilton. "We don't want them involved."

"Why not?" said Rankin.

"Because the more people involved, the more things go to hell."

You can say that again, thought Rankin.

"We can take the rigid-hulled boat over and find out what's going on," said Guns. "The only thing is, we only have one gun, right?"

He looked at Hamilton. Neither of the MI6 agents was armed.

"Figures," said Rankin.

"I say we go," responded Hamilton.

"Thanks." Rankin turned to Guns. "I'll take the point if you want."

"No, it's OK. I'm a better shot."

Rankin didn't think so, but he let it pass.

Hamilton had Jared Lloyd stay behind. The three men climbed into the cruiser's small rigid-hulled inflatable and sped over to the fishing boat, which was still moving at a slow but steady pace. Rankin took the boat up against the port side of the fishing craft; Guns leapt aboard and moved swiftly toward the smokestack, ducking behind it as he tried to peer through the open doorway in front of it. As Rankin started to follow Hamilton out of the boat, he saw an emergency kit at the side. He opened it, and took the flare gun, figuring it was better than nothing.

The door to the rear of the fishing boat's small superstructure was open. Guns and Rankin crouched on either side as Hamilton moved around toward the front. Neither man could see what was going on.

The Beretta felt tiny in Guns' hand. In a perfect world, he'd have something considerably bigger—a shotgun would have been nice.

"Stay behind me," he whispered to Rankin as he stepped into the gray space. He had both hands on the Beretta, his finger pressed against the trigger—anything that appeared was getting blasted.

The space was divided by a narrow corridor, with a cabin on each side and the bridge at the front. Guns moved to the left, ducking into the first space, trying to stay out of the direct line of fire from the front and search the cabin at the same time. It held lockers and a pair of benches, bolted to the floor, an assortment of gear and boxes piled randomly at both sides. It took him several seconds to scan them all, to make sure that the lines he saw were straight and unmoving.

"Come on," hissed Rankin, who'd checked a similar space on the opposite side. Rather than waiting for Guns, he moved forward, through a small hallway, then ran forward, looking for the bridge.

Guns ran to keep up. He saw Rankin run forward, shouting something. Guns plunged into the space after him, throwing himself to the right, sure that they would both come under a hail of bullets.

But the vessel's bridge was empty, the wheel tied by a rope into position.

"Shit," said Rankin.

Guns moved his Beretta around the space twice, using it to direct his gaze. Then he went back to the cabins they'd bypassed. A figure lay on the deck in the cabin at the port side. Guns slid over to him on his knee, weapon ready; the man was dead.

"Guns!"

"Dead guy," said Guns, back on his feet.

The door to the other cabin was locked. Guns heard someone talking inside, the voices still muffled.

"Come out," he yelled. "Hands high."

There was no answer.

Guns put his hand on the lever that worked the door. "*Viennee quee*," he said, phonetically sounding the Italian words for "come here."

No one stirred.

Rankin stepped between Guns and the door. "Let's try this," he said. Then without explaining he put his foot on the door lever and kicked it open, firing a flare into the cabin.

The small missile ignited with a low *thwapp*, and the room burst yellow and red. The scent of burning metal filled the corridor, and dusty smoke began curling upward. Guns started to push around Rankin to get in, but the fire flared; he heard the sound of a dull explosion, as if they were miles, not feet, away.

Rankin pulled the fire extinguisher off the nearby wall and began shooting the canister's contents while he was still in the corridor. He pushed the nozzle inside the cabin, spraying blindly but choking the fire.

The cabin appeared to be an office; above the desk was a radio, which must have been what they heard. The place was empty.

"I need air," Guns said, coughing. He grabbed Rankin, pulling him with him through the boat to the deck.

Hamilton looked down on them from the roof of the superstructure.

"No one?" he asked.

Guns managed to shake his head, still catching his breath.

"Bloody hell," said the Englishman, taking out his sat phone.

ACT IV

The gods are just, and will revenge our cause.

—Virgil, *The Aeneid* (Dryden translation)

1

Practically since the day he graduated from college, Jonathon Mc-Carthy liked to start his mornings by sitting at his kitchen table, sipping coffee and reading the newspaper. He had continued that routine as a senator, and saw no reason to drop the habit as President.

The fact that his kitchen was not exactly what one would call "cozy" never entered into his consideration. And while staff members had often volunteered to start their day early enough to fix a proper breakfast, McCarthy had gently turned them down—and issued standing orders directing that no member of the domestic staff arrive at the White House, kitchen included, before six a.m. The Secret Service delivered his newspapers and a special briefing booklet at five, leaving it on the small wooden counter at the center of the room; the agent would flip on the coffeemaker and retreat. McCarthy typically arrived a few minutes later—except on the odd mornings he decided to sleep in, when he would make his appearance promptly at 5:30.

Rarely did McCarthy allow his sessions with the Fourth Estate's work product to be interrupted, and rarer still were the times he invited someone to join him.

But today was one of those occasions.

"Are you sure now, dear, that you won't have a bit of sugar in your coffee?" he asked Corrine Alston as he fussed over the pot. "You know that I make this *very* strong in the morning."

"No, Mr. President. It will help perk me up."

"I thought maybe my charming presence would be enough for that." McCarthy's wry voice echoed against the high ceiling. He set down her cup and took his seat. "Give me the bad news, please. No varnish, miss."

Corrine told the President what the First Team had discovered—it appeared that material from a Russian biological warfare program had been obtained by the Iranian agent. The Italians, called in to assist, were asking questions about exactly what was going on. So far, Daniel Slott had given them very vague answers.

"I'm sure the Secretary of State will appreciate that," said McCarthy. He wasn't being sarcastic—the Italians were not known for keeping secrets, and Steele would undoubtedly feel that any news about this would scuttle the nuclear treaty.

Then again, perhaps it deserved to be scuttled. McCarthy sipped his coffee pensively.

"The Russian agent who told us about the material," said McCarthy. "This is the same woman who has been identified as the assassin, T Rex?"

"Our man there doesn't think that's right. He doesn't think she's T Rex at all."

"Why not?"

"He says the evidence doesn't add up."

"If she is, she might be saying something like this to throw him off the scent," said the President. "The fox leaving an old sock for a hound in the tree on the other side of the hollow."

"The Iranian did get something from the locker in Naples," said Corrine.

McCarthy sorted through the newspapers on the table. The executive news summary in the binder included all of the important articles, but he liked to go through the papers anyway; it was part old-fashioned gesture, and part a way of seeing what other people thought was important.

"That puts this briefing in a different light," said McCarthy, retrieving the latest assessment on the Iran situation from the State Department.

"I've read it."

The assessment included an intercept from the National Security Agency of a speech by Parsa Moshen being circulated among high-ranking Revolutionary Guard members. In the speech, Moshen promised "a radical new weapon to devastate the West" and promised that it would be used if the treaty was signed. "After a demonstration of our power," Moshen added, "we will resume our rightful place in society. Or we will struggle on alone."

"We'd best get the bacteria back," said McCarthy dryly, his understatement eloquently underlining his order's urgency.

2

THE MEDITERRANEAN SEA

The captain had not wanted to go into the water, but after Atha heard the radio calls from the coast guard and saw the mast of a vessel he knew must be following them, he managed to persuade the man that it would be their only chance of escape. Once they were in the water, the reason for the captain's reluctance became obvious—he was a terrible swimmer, and could barely stay afloat. Thus Atha had been forced to inflate the rafts much sooner than he had planned; as he clambered into his he thought he saw the boat that had been following them looming on the horizon. But that had proven to be a false alarm; aided by the wind and current, they were able to paddle to the rendezvous without being seen.

A small boat met them after they had been in the water for only a half hour. The tiny craft doglegged north before circling to the southwest, its roundabout route taking it away from the two Italian patrol vessels stopping and searching boats in the area.

Partly because of all this maneuvering, the ride to the cargo ship took nearly six hours. It would have been uncomfortable in any event, but a storm was moving in, and the waters became increasingly choppier. Atha found himself leaning over the side for the last two hours. When he was finally brought aboard the ship, with his precious luggage double-wrapped in two giant trash bags, he went right to his cabin.

He was lying in the bunk when he remembered that he had not

called the Russian scientist as he'd promised. He debated whether this was necessary at all—now that he had the material, he didn't believe he would need ever to speak to Rostislawitch. But never was a long time; it was conceivable that there would be some business need in the future.

In which case he should make the payment. It was not a minor sum, and he would much prefer keeping it in his pocket, even though he had not intended to.

Perhaps he should call just to keep Rostislawitch in the dark. Or had the scientist been the one to tip off the authorities?

Atha debated back and forth what to do. Perhaps he could get information from the scientist about who was following him. Perhaps he would only be giving information to them. Finally, he decided to call the scientist and see what he might retrieve from a conversation. He got up and turned on his satellite phone. But the phone, damaged by the sea's salt water, refused to work.

There was a knock on his cabin door.

"What?" grumbled Atha.

The sailor on the other side of the door knocked again.

"What is it?" Atha demanded, pulling open the door.

The man in the corridor handed him a note. Belatedly Atha realized that the man did not speak Farsi; except for the captain, the crew was Filipino.

The note was from the captain, telling Atha that he had just heard from the helicopter; it was ahead of schedule and would arrive in a half hour.

Atha put his shoes back on, then went back up to the bridge, taking the suitcase with him. It was not very heavy—an odd thing, he thought; to be capable of so much damage it ought to weigh much more.

The storm that had been approaching earlier was now almost upon them, and the waves swelled in front of the ship, and raindrops were beginning to pelt the glass at the front of the bridge.

"Is this weather safe for a helicopter?" Atha asked.

"I couldn't say." The captain shrugged. "I'm not a pilot. But I will give you a life jacket if you wish."

"I'd prefer a parachute," said Atha.

The captain thought he was making a joke, and laughed.

3

As soon as the fishing boat was thoroughly searched and secured, the Italian coast guard's patrol ship rejoined the rest of the searchers, criss-crossing the nearby waters for another vessel that Atha might have escaped to. Unfortunately, there were many possibilities, and even with the assistance of an airplane, within a few hours it was clear that there was no chance of finding him. Police officials in towns and cities all along the southwestern coast of Italy, and on nearby Sicily, were all alerted, but neither Rankin nor Guns had much hope that Atha would be found.

The Italians thought they were looking for a man who might be responsible for the Bologna bombing. With the bomb still getting serious media attention—it had been dubbed the "immaculate bomb" because no one was killed—they pressed on with the search. The navy compiled a list of ships that were heading to either the eastern Mediterranean or northern Africa. About four dozen had been within a hundred miles of the fishing boat, and all were designated to be searched. Three were beyond the reach of the Italian coast guard: a ferry to Tunisia and two small cargo vessels bound for Libya. Calling from aboard the Italian coast-guard cutter, Rankin asked Corrigan to enlist the U.S. Navy to help.

"These ships were all pretty far from the fishing boat," said Corrigan.

"Sure, but there was probably a little boat involved," said Rankin. "Something too small to be tracked easily. Maybe two or three."

Corrigan told him that a navy Orion patrol plane was already en route, and that a guided missile destroyer might be able to help. In the meantime, he'd try to find a helicopter that could be put at their disposal, either to aid the search or to get them to a ship if the Iranian was found.

Guns, meanwhile, had gone up on deck. A storm was kicking up; raindrops from the approaching clouds were spraying against his face.

"They're trying to get an Orion patrol plane out from Sigonella on Sicily," said Rankin, joining him.

"That's good."

"What are you doing out here? It's raining."

"I know. Think that will make it easier for him? Or harder?"

"Got me."

"Easier, I think," said Guns.

"You looking at something?"

"Just thinking."

Rankin started to go back inside.

"What do you figure is wrong with Ferg?" Guns asked.

"What do you mean, what's wrong with him?"

"He's always taking pills. You notice that?"

Rankin shrugged. "Look like aspirin or something."

"Too small."

"Go pills, maybe."

Go pills were amphetamines and modafinil, a narcolepsy drug sometimes issued by the military for pilots and others who had to stay up at night.

"Nah. He takes them in the morning."

"Why? You think he's doped up?"

"I think he's sick."

"Don't get obsessed with him," said Rankin. "Ferg's Ferg. Just another guy. Just like you and me."

"You're one to talk," said Guns. But his companion had already gone back into the ship.

4

Kiska waited until Rostislawitch was in the main hall of the art building, surrounded by people. She walked directly up to him, gently nudging a Danish scientist out of her way.

"Dr. Rostislawitch. I would like to speak to you, sir," she said in stiff Russian.

Rostislawitch, caught off-guard, didn't even ask why. He followed Kiska as she walked out of the building and across the street, her heels clicking loudly on the pavement. The FSB colonel continued to a small coffee bar and walked to the back, where a small room was set aside for regular patrons. She nodded at the owner as she passed. The man smiled; she'd promised him a hundred euros to keep others out for the few minutes her conversation would take.

"What is this about?" asked Rostislawitch as she pulled out a chair.

"In a moment." Kiska opened her purse and took out a small radio finder, which would tell her if the place had been bugged. She didn't actually care if Ferguson overheard the conversation, but she did want to know if he was listening in.

Apparently not; there were no signals.

"What are you doing?" Rostislawitch asked again.

Kiska left her device on the table between them.

"Doctor, you are employed by the Karamov Institute, are you not?"

Rostislawitch's last hope that he had been singled out by mistake vanished.

"I am on the payroll, yes."

"You are an important member of the Institute."

"I have very few duties these days."

"Doctor, there are circumstances where it does not pay to be modest. I am well aware of your abilities. As are many others."

"Then you are aware that my abilities are not being put to use, except in the most mundane manner."

"That is not my concern, and is probably a matter of opinion," said Kiska. The scientist's arrogance shocked her. He was, she believed, contemplating treason, but had the gall to pretend, at least to himself, that he was not at fault because he was bored. "A few days ago, one of the locks in a sensitive area was tampered with."

"Was anything taken?"

"The investigation continues. You were among the people who knew of the area, and the combination to the lock."

"If I opened it, there would be a record," said Rostislawitch. "There are many safeguards in the lab."

"You know which area I'm talking about?"

"I can guess," said the scientist, doing his best to backtrack.

"I see. What area is that?"

Rostislawitch hesitated, unsure whether a wrong answer would simply make it obvious that he was trying to divert attention from himself. He knew there would be no record of him going in or out; without a record, there would be no proof. He knew also that he would not have been the only one who had been in the lab.

"We are talking about either the monkeys, or the critical storage area," he said, deciding to combine the right and wrong answers. "There are digital code locks in both areas. I have been to both regularly."

"Several other areas do as well," said Kiska. She had not thought she could get a confession from Rostislawitch—there was, in fact, considerable doubt as to whether anything had even been taken, as she'd admitted to Ferguson. But now she sensed that she had the scientist under her control; she would press him as far as possible. "Why mention those?"

"Because those are the only important areas where I have access."

"The clinic is not important? The medicine area."

"I have access there," Rostislawitch said. "But no, I don't think it would be that important. Not unless they have resumed the experiments—which they told me they would do without me."

"Why did you come to Bologna?"

"I'm here at a conference. As you know."

"Who have you met here?"

Rostislawitch rose. "I don't have to answer these questions. We're not living in the old days."

"Sit down, Dr. Rostislawitch. You may not care much about your position, but I am sure you would feel terrible if your brother lost his. And if Irena Grinberg and her husband were similarly unable to find work."

"Don't threaten me."

"If you interpret that as a threat, that's your business."

"What is it that you want?" he asked, still standing. A day ago, she might have been able to browbeat him, but today he felt strong, able to resist.

Kiska rose. She was several inches taller than the scientist, and she leaned forward across the table, emphasizing her physical advantage.

"Who have you spoken to here?" asked Kiska.

"I've spoken to many people at the conference."

Kiska shook her head. "Don't be coy, Doctor. You must not do anything that would endanger others."

"Blackmail will get you nowhere."

"The others I'm speaking about are the people who would be hurt by the material you took."

"I didn't take any material."

Kiska stared into his face. She saw guilt there, fear—he had taken something; she was sure of it.

"Doctor, the lives of many people could be in your hands. Do you trust the Americans?"

"I do not trust the Americans at all."

"The girl you took to dinner the other night is an American."

"She's Greek."

Kiska frowned. It was sad to see how easily a man could be fooled by a woman who took an interest in him.

"Check her more carefully," Kiska suggested.

"I don't have to check her," said Rostislawitch. He knew this was the sort of trick the FSB played to make him suspect everyone. That was how these spies succeeded, by making one paranoid. The KGB had done it; whatever agency succeeded the FSB would do it. It was in their blood.

"There was an explosion the other day, while you walked on the street," said Kiska.

"Yes?"

"The Americans believe you were the target. I myself was nearby—I had just arrived from Moscow. Who do you think was trying to kill you?"

"Me? It was a terrorist attack. They weren't aiming at me."

"Are you sure?"

Rostislawitch clamped his teeth together, afraid that anything he said would give him away. He made his face angry; he had a right to be angry, he thought, and bitter.

Despite the scientist's bluster, Kiska knew she had rattled him. While she lacked the evidence she would need to arrest him, Kiska felt it was now only a matter of time before he did something to give himself away. He might even do it voluntarily, if she could play him right.

"I can help you," said Kiska, softening her tone gradually. "I can get you home. Repair things."

"There's nothing to repair. If you have any real weight with the Institute," added the scientist, "then make them give me my rightful job back. Make them use me the way I should be used, instead of as a babysitter. Tell them it is foolish to allow me to go to a conference, and then hound me there."

And with that, he stalked from the room.

Ferguson waited until Kiska and Rostislawitch had been gone for a half hour before going into the café. By that time the room had been reopened, and the table he wanted near the wall was occupied.

In any other country, he might have waited for the two men sitting there to leave. But drinking coffee in Italy could be an all-day affair, and he couldn't spend that much time waiting. Thera was back at the conference, her only backup the Italian security people.

Fortunately, he had come prepared.

"*Scusare,*" he said to the men, standing next to the table. He purposely used the wrong form of the word before switching to English.

"Excuse me. I'm from the U.S. and I'm a little lost. Hey, what was that?" he added, turning as if he'd just spotted something out of the corner of his eye.

As he spun, he released something on the table.

"*Ratto!*" yelled one of the men as the mouse Ferguson had dropped scurried around the silverware.

The other man jumped to his feet, sending his chair flying.

"Grab it," said the first.

Within moments, the place was in a tumult: half the patrons were trying to grab the poor mouse; the other half were trying to get away.

Ferguson calmly righted the chair that had been knocked over, sat down, and reached under the table for the small digital recorder he'd left behind earlier. He ripped off the tape holding it and took the small device, barely bigger than a portable USB memory card, and walked calmly out of the restaurant.

He felt a little bad about the mouse. But given that the pet store around the corner had advertised it beneath a sign that said: "Feed your snake real food tonight," he reasoned that he had at least given it a fighting chance for survival.

5

THE MEDITERRANEAN SEA

Atha pushed the hood of the rain slicker as far down over his face as it would go. The rain was really pouring now, crashing across the bow of the ship in what looked like solid sheets. The vessel rocked up and down with the waves, pitching to its sides as the sea knifed against its bow, pummeling the ship. The wind was so loud that he couldn't hear the helicopter, though he knew from the spotlight that it was nearly overhead.

The Iranian had been winched up to a helicopter several times before when he was younger, so when he had worked out this plan he did not think it would be very difficult. But he had not counted on this rain and the heaving sea; simply standing on the deck made his stomach feel queasy.

A black streak of rain lashed across the ship. Atha stared at it a moment, then realized it was the rope from the helicopter that was to winch him aboard. A sling that looked more like a rubber inner tube for a bicycle than a harness hung at the bottom; it crashed against a large vent on the foredeck and got hooked there. Atha ran to it, dragging his suitcase as he went.

Before he could finish hooking himself into the sling it started upward. He barely managed to keep hold of the suitcase as he was tugged toward the chopper. Though he'd tied it to a life jacket and wrapped it in garbage bags to make sure it remained waterproof and would float, in this storm he doubted he would see it again if it slipped from his grasp. He clenched his fingers around it as the rope twisted. The wash from the rotors and the spray of the water drenched him, soaking him to his bones despite the heavy rain gear he wore.

At last he reached the doorway of the helicopter. A crewman grabbed at Atha's bag, but he refused to give it up; he was dragged inside by it, rolling back toward the doorway as the chopper bucked in the wind. Another man grabbed hold of Atha and wrestled him against the bulkhead, where he managed to get out of the harness. He lay on the floor as the door was shut and the chopper began gaining altitude.

Thanking God for his delivery, Atha got up and sat on the narrow bench at the side of the cabin. I'm safe, he thought to himself. As if to rebuff him, the helicopter pitched sharply to the right, throwing him against the two other men. For the first time since he'd come aboard, Atha looked into their faces and realized that they, too, were scared, perhaps even more than he was.

"There will be a bonus on our safe landing," he promised. When that failed to cheer them, he added, "We are doing Allah's work, all praise be to him. He would not let us die before our mission is complete."

The crewmen exchanged a doubtful look before nodding.

6

Nathaniel Hamilton stepped off the small plane at the Bologna airport and hurried into the tunnel toward the terminal. Having effectively ceded the search for the Iranian to the Italians and the Americans—Jared Lloyd was in theory "liaisoning," but Hamilton had few illusions about who was really in charge—he was at least temporarily reduced to getting whatever he could from the other end of the equation, the Russian scientist.

London, of course, had no clue what should be done next. In one breath, Hamilton's supervisor said he would pummel the Americans for stepping into the middle of their operation. In the next, he said how lucky they were for following a hunch and he would damn well make sure they got credit for it.

Hamilton had been around long enough to realize that, his boss's opinions notwithstanding, the mission had so far been neither a great success nor a terrible failure. The Americans were worried about whatever Rostislawitch had handed over, but in Hamilton's opinion the network Atha belonged to was much more important. Was Rostislawitch part of a network of scientists in Russia willing to supply state secrets to Atha? What were the Iranians' real plans?

The first thing Hamilton did when he got to Bologna was take a room at the Stasi, a boutique hotel just at the edge of center city. It was an expensive place; his boss would surely have a fit when he saw the bill. But Hamilton wanted a place with a bed that wasn't made out of melted-down cannons.

Once he'd checked in, Hamilton took a taxi to the bus station. He walked in the front door and then promptly out the side, walking down the block to an alley, where he turned right and walked to the door of a small building wedged between two larger and much older structures. A sign on the faded wood proclaimed that the place had been condemned; the sign was at least two years old. Hamilton took a look around, then unlocked the door and stepped inside.

There was no light or electricity; he had to use a small pocket flashlight to find the strongbox he'd come for.

A touch of paranoia took hold as he knelt to the box. But it quickly passed. He put his key into the lock and opened the lid, then reached in and took what he needed—keys, credit cards, SIM cards for his phone, and finally the guns: a PK pistol and a six-shot dummy cell phone.

"Now, then," he said to himself as he rose, the pistol and fake phone tucked into his pockets, "let us see what sort of mood the estimable Mr. Ferguson is in this evening."

Truth be told, Ferguson was in the mood for a long nap. He'd followed Rostislawitch back to his hotel, where the scientist was apparently in the process of taking a very long shower. Unfortunately, the battery in the video bug Rankin had installed the day before had run down, and Ferguson had to rely on the backup audio near the door. It was difficult to hear much except for the shower.

For the moment, Ferguson was on his own. He'd sent Thera to move some of their cars around so they wouldn't be towed or ticketed; after that, she was supposed to rest. She wasn't due back until seven, when she was to meet Rostislawitch for dinner in the lobby.

The Italians, British, and Russians all knew pieces of what was going on, but as far as Ferguson could tell, they didn't know as much as the team did. The Italians didn't know about the bacteria that had *possibly* been taken; they thought the Iranian was a witness or participant in the bombing. The British didn't know what Kiska had told Ferguson about the material, though they knew that Atha had met with the scientist. The Russians didn't know about Atha, since Kiska hadn't gotten to town until after the meeting.

What did they know that Ferguson didn't?

Plenty, maybe.

What didn't he know that was important?

Number one, who T Rex was.

Not Kiska. But the problem with eliminating her was that left no one else as a possible candidate. By now the Agency had checked the bona fides of every scientist at the convention without coming up with a match; the Italians had conducted their own check of the backgrounds of the caterers and the others hired for the event. This had resulted in a few surprises—including the arrest of a man wanted for heroin smuggling and the detention of a number of suspected illegal immigrants but no likely candidate for T Rex.

Meanwhile, the Italian investigation into the bombing was moving ahead at a snail's pace. The plastique explosive had been isolated but its chemical "tag"—a kind of fingerprint that would indicate where it had been manufactured—had not yet been identified. The truck that had blown up had been stolen from a town about five kilometers away; the police had no leads in the theft.

So if it wasn't Kiska, who was it?

Ferguson took the laptop into the bathroom with him so he could watch the feed from the video bugs covering the hall outside Rostislawitch's door and listen to the audio bug while he shaved. Rostislawitch had finally finished his shower and was now talking to himself, complaining about Kiska.

Ferguson didn't want it to be her because she'd saved his life. Was that really it?

If she was T Rex, he'd have to take her, and of course she wasn't going to just come with him, and then Parnelles's wish would come true. He'd have his pound of flesh, and maybe some problems with the Italians, but those problems he wouldn't mind.

But maybe Rostislawitch wasn't the real target; maybe the car bomb was "just" a car bomb, or even a feint to throw them off the trail. Imperiati's other target was due tonight, the keynote speaker at the dinner Rostislawitch and Thera were going to.

Ferguson listened as the Russian turned on his television. A middle-aged woman came down the hallway near his room, stopped, and went back to her room. She emerged with a sweater a few moments later. Ferguson watched her, planning what he would do if she was T Rex.

But she wasn't. She got in the elevator at the end of the hall and descended to the lobby.

———

At 6 p.m., Ferguson called the Cube for an update. It was the first time in recorded history that he had checked in precisely at the time he was supposed to, at least according to Lauren DiCapri.

"If I'd known it was an occasion, I'd've worn a tie," he told her.

"What are you wearing now?"

"Nothing but a smile. Tell me what's going on."

Lauren's update consisted largely of two facts: Rankin and Guns still had no idea where the Iranian had gone, and Parnelles and Slott were both angry with the world.

"You especially," she added. "They can't figure out why you won't admit Kiska Babev is T Rex."

"If I did admit that, what then?" said Ferguson. "You think she'll just fly home with me?"

"Knowing you, sure."

"Listen, is Ciello around?" asked Ferguson.

"As a matter of fact, he wants to talk to you. First, though, the Brits are also kind of mad at us. Hamilton had some sort of hissy fit, claiming that Rankin and Guns screwed up his surveillance."

"I'm sure that's bullshit."

"No doubt. But he's on his way back to Bologna."

"It's a free country, I guess. You giving me Ciello, or what?"

A slight hush descended over the line as she made the connection. There was a low tone, followed by Thomas Ceillo's slightly hyper soprano.

"Ciello here."

"So how's the *razvaluha*?"

"I don't have a jalopy, Ferg. I take the bus."

"Just joking, Ciello. What's going on?"

"That Fibber guy. Good stuff. Too much stuff. But very good stuff."

"Yeah. You didn't give him your Social Security or your bank account number, did you?"

"No, why?"

"Just checking. What do you have?"

Kiska did, in fact, use her cousin's identity for several credit cards and bank accounts. Ciello had not finished unraveling everything, but he had managed to figure out the pattern Kiska used, alternating credit cards and then getting new accounts.

"There's still a lot I have to dig out. But one thing I thought you'd like to know. Well, two things."

"Give me three if you want."

"One, she was in Peru last August. The Vice President was killed. The murder hasn't been, um, pinned to T-Rex, but it does have some similarities. Because, you know, he's important."

"That's it?"

"Number two, she was in the Czech Republic right before coming to Bologna. The local police raided a warehouse where plastic explosives were stored."

"Was the FSB involved?"

"I don't know. Not in the news story, but of course they might not be mentioned. I sent a text message to our embassy there. They haven't gotten back to me. Anyway, the point is, some of the explosives were missing afterwards."

"Good work, Thomas," Ferguson said, though neither item was all that useful. "Keep at it."

"I will. Say, Ferg?"

"Yeah?"

"Does this Fibber really have an uncle who inherited ten million dollars but can't collect it?"

7

BOLOGNA, ITALY

Thera examined her face in the mirror. Her eyes were drooping, her cheeks pinched.

She wished she could go to bed, sleep for three days, then get up and take a walk around Bologna without looking over her shoulder. She wished it were spring, not the start of winter. She wished she could

simply look at the art and enjoy the food without worrying that someone with a gun or a bomb was nearby.

She wished she could make love to Ferg, and not think about the
consequences.

Did she?

Yes, certainly. Though the way he acted about sex, the way he so
casually used it as a tool, it was a good thing making love to him was
just a fantasy.

Thera ducked her face to the sink. A little makeup and she'd be
back on her game.

Several blocks away, Rostislawitch was examining his own face in
the mirror, having just finished shaving. In the back of his
mind, he was replaying his meeting with the Russian FSB agent, the
blond she-wolf who'd tried to intimidate him in the back room of the
café.

Before their meeting, he'd decided he would have nothing more
to do with Atha. Now he was angry, insulted that he had been suspected of treason—even though, of course, the charge was correct.

More important, he wasn't sure what to do.

Replaying the meeting, he realized that the woman hadn't identified herself or who she worked for, but she didn't have to. Her arrogance was as clear a sign that she was with the FSB as if she had worn
a badge on her tight-fitting blouse. Like the KGB before it, the Russian Federal Security Service was used to bullying people, making demands instead of requests, insisting on getting its way. Its agents
assumed the rest of the world would bow down to it in all matters,
large and small. They were a law to themselves.

Loathe them, yes. But be careful. They would not simply fade away.

The question was not how much they knew about what he had
planned to do, but what they *thought* they knew. If they had actually
decided that he took the material, the worst thing Rostislawitch could
do at this point was simply go home as he had planned. They would
have no compunctions about arresting him. If they lacked evidence—
and he was sure they did; he had taken every precaution—they would
simply manufacture it.

Rostislawitch opened the drain and let the water run out of the sink, then wiped his face with a towel. If the choice was between running away and returning to a trap, the obvious thing to do was run away.

And his brother? Or the Grinbergs?

It was probable that the FSB would carry out the she-wolf's threats. They would be somewhat careful about it—there were *some* differences between Putin's Russia and Stalin's, after all. But most likely the Grinbergs would lose their jobs.

A shame. They had stood by him through all of his troubles. Irena Grinberg had been Olga's best friend, and had suffered greatly when she died.

He could give them Atha's money. Little by little, small payments. That would more than balance things out.

As he dressed, Rostislawitch remembered his visit to the church, and what he had felt there. At that moment, it had seemed like a turning point, a revelation that pushed him in an unchangeable direction. But now, barely a few hours later, its force had faded. He was wavering again, unsure what to do.

Rostislawitch glanced at his watch. Atha hadn't called, despite his promises yesterday.

Just as well. The FSB would find a way to listen in.

The one thing that bothered Rostislawitch was Kiska Babev's accusation about the girl, Thera. Was she an American agent? He dismissed it, and yet . . . could it be true?

Rostislawitch pulled on his pants. It was an old trick, wasn't it? Using an older man's vanity against him. The Russian FSB, the American CIA, they were all the same.

As soon as he came off the elevator, Thera could tell that something had changed since she'd seen Rostislawitch last. It wasn't just his meeting with the Russian intelligence agent. He'd been subdued after that, quieter; now there was something aggressive in his eyes, something harder. He'd made a decision about something.

Very likely Kiska had pushed him into making the deal with the Iranians, the exact opposite of what she intended. He acted aloof, as if he didn't care about Thera or anyone else, as if he'd hardened himself to do something he didn't really believe in.

She tried not to let her own knowledge of it show, keeping her voice upbeat, and slightly naive.

"Do you think the speaker will be interesting?" she asked as they walked outside. "More funding for research?"

"All of the drug companies are thieves," answered Rostislawitch. At the corner, he went to the curb and put his hand up for a taxi, even though they were only two blocks from the art building.

"I thought we were walking?" said Thera.

"I don't feel like going to the dinner."

"Oh," she said.

"I've made a reservation at a restaurant. The concierge recommended it. Come."

Thera hesitated. "Don't you think—"

"I'll go myself," said Rostislawitch as a cab pulled up.

Thera waited another moment, letting Rostislawitch start to pull the door closed before grabbing it.

"OK," she said, sliding into the car beside him. "I suppose the talk would have been boring anyway."

Ferguson was on a bicycle up the block when the scientist called for a taxi. He waited for them to pass, then turned up the radio volume, listening as Thera jabbered with the doctor, trusting that she would provide enough information for him to catch up if the traffic cleared and he lost them.

You're in a strange mood this evening," Thera told Rostislawitch in the taxi.

The scientist grunted. He wasn't sure what her reluctance to changed plans meant: it could be read as an honest desire to attend the event, in which case she wasn't a CIA agent. But on the other hand, it might be because she had compatriots waiting for her there, and was afraid to cross them up.

"Why is a young girl like you interested in me?" said Rostislawitch abruptly.

Thera turned to the scientist. "I am not a young girl," she said. "And what do you mean by *interested*?"

"You have a boyfriend?"

"Oh." Thera turned, facing the front of the cab. "Dr. . . . Artur . . ."

Thera stopped. This wasn't acting anymore, was it? Partly it was, and partly it wasn't. She did honestly feel concern for him. It wasn't all she felt, but it *was* there.

Ferguson, had he been in a parallel situation, would have come up with some sort of glib line, pushed the sex angle, and ended up kissing the woman. But that wasn't Thera.

"I do feel . . . *strongly* . . . toward you," said Thera, stumbling over the word *strongly*. "I wouldn't call it . . . I don't know what it is. It's really not boyfriend-girlfriend. You're so much . . . smarter than me," she said, substituting *smarter* for *older*.

She turned to him. Rostislawitch looked as if she had hit him in the stomach.

"I don't want to mislead you," continued Thera. She put her hand on his. He started to pull away, but she grabbed his hand. "I—love is not something I think about much," she said quickly. "I admire you. I do care—when I heard you were hurt my heart seemed to stop."

"But it's not sex," said Rostislawitch.

"No," she said. "I don't think so."

Rostislawitch pulled his right hand from hers and scratched his ear. Her response confused him even more. It wasn't what he wanted to hear. And yet it was not what a spy would say.

So perhaps he could trust her at least. Somewhat. Maybe.

"I don't want to hurt you," she said. "I feel that we can talk—when you talk I like to listen."

Rostislawitch smiled, in spite of himself. It was something his wife used to tell him, when he asked why she didn't answer him sometimes. He patted Thera's hand, even as he reminded himself to stay on his guard—she had proven nothing.

"Is that OK?" Thera asked. "Is it all right? Do you still want to have dinner?"

"I am very hungry," he said. "And I was told that this restaurant is very good. Of course we will eat."

8

The Italians were clearly among those who confused quantity with quality when it came to security. Not only had they blanketed the art building with soldiers, but they had carabinieri police officers surrounding the building. In addition, Nathaniel Hamilton counted at least five members of the Italian SISDE—the civilian intelligence force under the interior minister—as well as a SISMI or military intelligence agent. Admittedly, the latter seemed most interested in keeping an eye on his civilian counterparts, probably looking for details that could be used to blast them in an upcoming parliamentary debate.

The one person Hamilton didn't see was the Russian scientist.

Or Ferguson, but that was a plus.

The security measures complicated Hamilton's plans. Not only had he found it necessary to enlist the aid of the embassy to get tickets to the event, but he had had to appear before Marco Imperiati and personally state why he wanted to be there. The Italian intelligence officer had proceeded to give him a lecture about the importance of allies working together toward common goals.

"That is why I am here," Hamilton had protested, but for some reason that had failed to impress Imperiati. Exasperated, Hamilton finally asked if Ferguson was working with him closely; with a straight face, Imperiati replied that of course he was.

"Uncharacteristically for the Americans," the Italian SISDE officer added.

"I wouldn't trust him," said Hamilton.

"He says the same of you."

Hamilton stewed. He'd adopted a cover as a technology officer for Her Majesty's government, and in order to keep the cover semi-intact, he mingled with some of the British scientists at the affair. He smiled when Professor Barclay, a sixty-year-old Oxford don with breath that could choke a pig, ambled next to him and asked how he thought the affair was going.

"Very pleasant," lied Hamilton.

"You read biology, then?" asked the professor.

"I was a physics man myself," answered Hamilton. "Cambridge. But I find this all jolly interesting. An exciting frontier."

"Quite."

In actual fact, Hamilton had majored in the Romantic poets at Cambridge, but that was hardly the response a science officer would give.

"I do hope you're sitting at our table," added Barclay.

"With pleasure, of course," said Hamilton. He glanced toward the bar, making a mental note to fortify himself with a double Scotch before going in for the meal.

O utside the building, in a portico roped off for smokers, Kiska Babev was expressing her own frustration that Rostislawitch had not arrived. Unlike the British MI6 agent, however, Kiska at least knew where the scientist was—she'd just received a cell phone call from the agent she'd assigned to tail Rostislawitch.

"The Greek female is with him. I can't tell where they are going."

"Find out what they are up to. If they are leaving the city, let me know immediately."

"I don't think that's what they're doing. The airport is in the other—"

Kiska pushed the cell phone closed, cutting off the conversation in midsentence as a pair of policemen appeared.

"No cell phones," said the taller man, speaking in English.

"Not even outside?"

"No."

"I promise not to use it again," said Kiska. It wasn't a difficult promise to make—the Italians were using jammers that severely limited the places where the phones could be used. Inside was impossible, and outside was almost as bad.

"You must give it to us," insisted the police officer.

"Why? Do you think a cell phone is that dangerous?"

"Please," insisted the man.

"Very well," she said finally, retrieving it from her purse. "Will I get it back?"

"Absolutely, at the end of the night."

Kiska started to hand it over, then stopped. "Are you going to give me a receipt for it?"

"Of course," said the policeman.

"Well, where is the receipt?"

The men looked at each other.

"I will get it for you," volunteered the short man.

Kiska played with her phone while she waited, opening and closing it idly. Suddenly the back popped off and the battery dropped to the ground. As the man with her bent to retrieve it, Kiska slipped her finger against the small chip at the back of the battery compartment. Pressing firmly, she activated a circuit in the cell phone that rendered the phone inert. It could no longer remember its own number, let alone be used to make or receive a call.

This wouldn't be a problem for her. She had two more in her purse, retrieved from a stash in the ladies' room that she'd planted ahead of time to avoid complications at the door.

"*Eccolo,*" said the policeman. "Here you are."

"*Grazie,*" she said, letting her fingers linger on his as she took the battery. "This must be boring even for you."

"Eh." He shrugged. "There are distractions."

Kiska smiled. The man's companion pushed his way back outside through the crowd, a small piece of paper in his hand.

"Thank you," she said, taking the receipt and handing over the phone.

"If you need to make a call before the end of the night, just see us," said the taller policeman. "We'll help. There are only a few places where the signal will work."

"Thank you," she told him, making sure her eyes lingered just enough so that he would be greatly disappointed when she didn't turn up.

9

"Describe the technique for inducing transduction utilizing lambda."

Thera put down her fork.

"Artur, why are you asking me questions that any first-year biology student could answer?"

"I don't think a first-year student could handle the technique. They might not even know what a phalange is."

"Why are you quizzing me?"

Rostislawitch looked down at his plate. As he did, the waiter came up and refilled his glass with wine.

"Artur, what's wrong? You have been acting oddly all evening."

Rostislawitch shook his head. He put his fork in a piece of meat, then laid it against the plate. He sipped some wine, even though he thought he'd had too much to drink already.

"What's bothering you? Are you upset because I'm not interested in you as a boyfriend? Or is it something else?"

"I have to go back to the room," he said finally. "I'm not feeling well. Let's get the check."

Thera knew that the questions he'd been asking were intended to vet her. While she thought she'd handled them fairly well, she wasn't entirely positive. She waited while Rostislawitch paid the check, then held his arm while they walked outside and waited for a taxi.

"What happened to you?" she said. "Was it that woman who met you this afternoon? What was it she wanted?"

"I told you, it had to do with work. A minor matter."

"It has you upset. Does it have to do with me?"

A cab pulled around the corner. Thera would have let it pass by—she sensed she was on the verge of getting some sort of answer from him—but Rostislawitch raised his hand and flagged it down. Inside the car, he laid his head back on the seat and complained that he was tired. Then he said something to her in Russian.

"I don't understand," she said.

"You don't speak Russian," he said in English.

"I'm sorry."

"You're a good girl." Rostislawitch patted her hand.

"Professor, you've acted very strange all night. You started out asking about love; then you quiz me on procedures. Now you're sick."

"Just tired."

Rostislawitch sat back up. He'd been a fool to believe the she-wolf. The girl was honest and young . . . and just a friend. Perhaps that was what he was truly disappointed about. But it was OK. It was truly OK.

"I will feel better tomorrow," he told her. "I promise. I want to be your friend. I do want to be your friend."

"You are my friend."

"You're very kind. You're the only one that's looked out for me here. We are friends." Rostislawitch leaned toward the driver. "Her hotel is right up there," he said. *"Ecco."*

"I can go with you," Thera said.

"I'm just going to bed. Good night, sweet one," he said awkwardly as the taxi pulled to the curb. "I will feel better tomorrow."

What'd you slip into his drink?" Ferguson asked Thera over the radio as he followed the cab back to Rostislawitch's hotel.

"Nothing. He's acting really weird, Ferg."

"Kiska put pressure on him. He's afraid of getting caught."

"He was quizzing me."

"Maybe she told him you're a spy."

"That bitch."

Ferguson laughed.

"What's he going to do?" asked Thera.

"Push Atha to make the deal so he can escape to wherever he's thinking of escaping to."

"No, I don't think he's going to do that."

"Bet you ten bucks," said Ferguson, pedaling slowly past the hotel as Rostislawitch got out of the taxi and went inside.

There were no messages on his room's voice mail. Atha hadn't called. Maybe the FSB she-wolf had been to see him as well.

Rostislawitch paced back and forth in his room. He felt as if he was losing his mind. His thoughts flew wildly, back and forth, from one form of doom to another.

He'd acted like a fool with Thera. One moment he trusted her; the next he treated her as if she were the enemy. He'd started asking her those ridiculous examination questions, as if she were facing him in an oral exam at the end of the semester.

Poor girl. He didn't deserve even her friendship.

Rostislawitch took his wallet from his pant pocket and opened it. The check for the suitcase was folded against his euros. He took the check, crumpled it, and tossed it in the garbage.

He was done with it, done with everything.

He paced across the room, back and forth, his head racing.

They'd open the locker eventually. The attendant had said something about items having to be claimed after seven days.

They'd open it, and what would they find? A few odd-looking jars with strange jelly in them. It would look like mold. They'd throw the jars out.

Or maybe the police would be called—maybe the police were the ones who were in charge of abandoned luggage. What would happen then?

A science experiment. Into the garbage.

Or to a lab for analysis.

Nothing could connect him to the bag. But how much evidence would the FSB need? They'd show his picture to the clerk at the left baggage area and get him to nod.

Or worse: some fool would open the containers, not knowing what they were. The material would get on their skin, and eventually into the digestive tract. From there, an epidemic would start.

Statistically, it would take more than one person. One person, statistically, would not produce the critical mass needed for a truly devastating epidemic.

If you trusted the statistics. If you didn't consider a single death, or a handful, significant.

Rostislawitch paced some more. He could go there and get rid of the bag. It was the safest thing to do. And the right thing.

Unless the she-wolf was following him. Then it would be foolish.

He would have to make sure he wasn't followed. Rostislawitch put the check back into his wallet, took his coat, and headed for the door.

10

OUTSIDE OF TUNIS, TUNISIA

The Russian-made Mil Mi-8 was a versatile helicopter, though like most helicopters, it was not particularly well suited for flying through thunderstorms. To add to the discomfort, internal fuel tanks had been added to the walls of the cabin area, tripling its range but greatly reducing space. Atha and the two crewmen shared a small bench for the entire ride; standing up, they could take two steps before reaching the forward bulkhead separating the crew space from the cockpit.

The bathroom was a small pail that hung on a hook on the wall. When you were done, one man opened the cabin door and you emptied the contents into the slipstream. Emptying the waste successfully required a certain amount of body English.

When they finally arrived at the airport, Atha was so glad to be there that if it weren't for the fact that it was still raining he would have dropped to the ground and kissed the cement. His legs literally trembled the entire way to the terminal building. The suitcase with the scientist's material rolled along behind him, bumping through the puddles and skipping over the curb.

His journey was hardly complete—a chartered plane was due to take him on to Libya, where he would catch yet a third plane to fly on to the camp in the Sudan. But those rides would be in airplanes. Atha vowed he would never fly in a helicopter again.

Though Tunis was an Islamic country, it was not particularly friendly toward Iran. If the military officials at the airport had thought he was anything other than an ordinary smuggler, they would have been loathe to take his bribes. But as far as they knew, he was only transporting embargoed oil equipment and software. His generous landing "fee" was supplemented by an agreement to purchase twice as much fuel as the helicopter could hold, even with its expanded tanks; the difference went directly into the pocket of the colonel responsible for the airport.

Having arranged to pay the fees in advance, Atha was surprised to find a customs agent waiting to see him in the small terminal. The man insisted that Atha would have to come into the small office to speak with him privately, even though there was no one else in the building.

"Perhaps you should talk to Colonel Nawf," suggested Atha. "I believe we've already made our arrangements."

"I will have to see your passport," said the man.

Atha started to take it from his pocket, then stopped. It didn't look like a trap—there was definitely no one else in the building, and there had been no trucks or troops nearby. But giving the man his passport was the same as telling him who he was, and he didn't want to do that if at all possible.

Of course it could be arranged. It was just a matter of handing over more money—something he hated to do on principle.

"I have paid a considerable sum for the arrangements here," said Atha.

"I'm afraid I don't know anything about that."

"Is there some permit that I've forgotten? Is that what the problem is?"

The customs agent smiled. "Ah. Now you are beginning to understand."

"And how much does the permit cost?"

"Five hundred euros."

Atha did not have that much cash with him; there had been no time to get money in Naples.

"Would you take a check?" he asked.

"A check?" The man jerked his head back. Then he started to laugh. "A check?"

"Just joking," said Atha, reaching inside his jacket.

"A very funny joke," said the man.

He started to laugh, then saw the pistol in Atha's hand.

"Here you go. Five hundred euros," said Atha, putting the bullet through the man's forehead. "Don't bother with a receipt," he added, stepping around the man and the gathering pool of blood as he went to find his airplane.

11

BOLOGNA, ITALY

Ferguson had barely gotten himself settled in the suite below Rostislawitch when the scientist grabbed his things to go back out. Hurriedly securing the laptop, Ferguson headed down the steps, trotting through the lobby and reaching the revolving doors just as the Russian started outside.

"Oops, sorry, you go first," said Ferguson, awkwardly bumping against him. He gave his English a British accent. "Never can work these things out."

Rostislawitch frowned at Ferguson as he came through the doors.

"Sorry, mate," said Ferguson, waving and then trotting off up the street.

Rostislawitch shook his head, then watched warily as Ferguson disappeared around the corner. He looked up and down the block, trying to spot the FSB she-wolf or her minions. Finally a cab appeared and he got in. Not trusting that it had appeared randomly, he had the driver take him to the train station; there he caught another cab, this time back to the Americana, one of the larger hotels in the city's business

section. Another cab was just letting off a passenger when Rostislawitch arrived; he hopped in.

"I want to go to Firenze," he said, using the Italian name for Florence.

The driver started to protest. Florence was about 110 kilometers
away; the trip there and back could take three hours or more.

Rostislawitch dropped ten hundred-euro notes—all of the cash
Atha had slipped him at their meeting—onto the front seat of the car.

"Wouldn't that cover the fare?"

It would indeed. The driver was even agreeable to cutting through
alleys and taking sudden U-turns to make sure they weren't followed.

Two hours later, the driver dropped Rostislawitch off in the Piazza della Stazione, near the Florence train station. He walked around
the circle, once again checking for anyone who might be following
him, then went in and got a ticket for Naples. He found the platform,
then stood back after the train's arrival was announced, waiting until
the last possible minute before getting aboard.

The tracking bug Ferguson had surreptitiously placed on Rostislawitch's back when he "bumped" into him at the hotel doorway
made the Russian easy to track, and Ferguson was able to figure out
what he was up to pretty quickly. But having gotten so close to him
meant Ferguson didn't want to be seen again. This wasn't a problem
on the motorbike; he got to the station ahead of the scientist and
watched from inside as he walked around in front. But he had to guess
what the Russian was doing, and Ferguson wasn't completely sure that
he was correct until Rostislawitch got onto the train.

The scientist was being much more careful now that he knew
Kiska was watching him. But he was an amateur: he assumed that anyone following him would be literally following him, waiting for him to
make the first move. He never suspected that Ferguson had gotten
onto the train as soon as it pulled in, and was already in the car behind
him.

Nor was Ferguson entirely confident that the scientist wasn't being followed. True, no one seemed to have been following the taxi, but
a Russian op had been down the street when Rostislawitch's journey

from the hotel began. The man appeared to have lost Rostislawitch the second time he switched cabs, but Ferguson was still wary; it was possible that he, too, had used a tracking device and was nearby.

Ferguson took out his sat phone and called Imperiati. The Italian intelligence officer answered his phone in a crabby mood, and didn't laugh when Ferguson asked if anyone had died at the conference yet.

"Not so far."

"Drug guy still eating?"

"He gave his speech and left a half hour ago. No incidents."

"Very good," said Ferguson. He had never considered the drug company president to be a real target.

"Are you on a train?"

"Had to leave town for a few hours. I'll be back. I think."

"The Russian FSB agent was asking about you. She said you couldn't be taken at face value."

"I can't. What else did she say?"

"She was asking about an Iranian she thinks may be a terrorist. She offered to trade information."

"Did you take her up on it?"

"I'm considering it."

"I'd go for it if I were you. I'd be interested in how she found out."

"She told me she has sources at all of the hotels," said Imperiati.

"Did she tell you his name?"

"She was not willing to give details unless I reciprocated. I told her I didn't have any to give. Then I mentioned how I was hoping to live a boring life."

"That's not going to fly with her," said Ferguson. "She likes excitement even more than I do."

Ferguson asked if there was anything new on the investigation into the bombing; Imperiati, sounding somewhat distracted and tired, answered that there wasn't. Ferguson signed off, then called Thera to see what she was doing.

"Getting some beauty rest?" he asked, after it took several rings for her to answer.

"Not really." It sounded like a lie; her voice was sleepy and distant.

"Well, go ahead and get some. Not that you need it."

"Where are you?"

"Rosty got on the train like I thought he would. We oughta be in Naples in three hours or so."

"What's going to happen then?"

"He'll freak because the bag is gone," said Ferguson. "After that, I don't know. He has to go back to Bologna at some point. He left everything there."

"I should be there."

"Where?"

"Naples."

"It's kind of an ugly city, especially near the train station."

"What if he does something crazy?"

"Like?"

"Maybe he'll kill himself."

Ferguson hadn't really considered that possibility.

You have to be a hard-ass, his father once told him. He meant it as a reproach—he was telling his son that the young man didn't really have it in him to be a CIA officer. He wanted too much to save the world and trust people and do the right thing; he couldn't just stand back and let people suffer, let them die. Which you had to do.

"What are you thinking, Ferg?" Thera asked.

"That you really do need some sleep," he told her. "Stay in Bologna. We're going to need you at full steam tomorrow. OK?"

She didn't answer.

"*OK*, Thera?"

"Yeah. You're right. I am tired."

"G'night, ladies, g'night. G'night, g'night, g'night," he told her, killing the line.

12

It had been several years since Guns had participated in an armed ship boarding, and then it was simply an exercise. But the adrenaline and weapons were plenty familiar. He climbed down from the destroyer to the rigid-hulled boat, taking a place behind the team leader as the craft revved its outboard and slipped into a dark patch between the destroyer and the search beams playing on the cargo ship it had just stopped. The rain had passed, but the waves were still choppy and swells reached well over the hull of the tiny boat.

Guns and Rankin had come aboard the USS *Porter*, DDG 78, just an hour before, flying to the ship in the southern Mediterranean aboard an Italian helicopter. The *Porter* had been tasked to stop the last remaining vessel that Atha might have escaped to, assuming he had not found a way to sneak past the Italian coast guard and get back on land near Naples or Sicily.

Though the *Porter* was a destroyer, her firepower would have likely given her the advantage over a confrontation with a World War II cruiser. The ship had recently been deployed in an effort to stop pirates and gunrunners near the east African coast, and her specially trained SITT team—the letters stood for Shipboard Integrated Tactical Team—was well practiced at boarding and searching for contraband, human or otherwise.

The chief petty officer directing the team was a graybeard who claimed not to remember exactly how old he was; he'd groaned as he pulled on his bulletproof vest and the rest of his gear aboard ship. But there was a definite spring in his step as they pulled next to the cargo vessel: he lunged for the rope ladder at the ship's side, climbing up behind the point man.

Guns went up third, the strap for the shotgun he was carrying hooked through his arm so that he could wield the weapon quickly. The boarding party was met by a nervous-looking man standing in a tiny pool of light on the foredeck of the cargo craft. He told them in Spanish that they were welcome aboard and that the captain was waiting for them on the bridge.

"I'll bet we're welcome," said the chief as the rest of his men came up.

Guns didn't like the fact that the crewman was nervous. He glanced around the deck area nearby, trying to spot other men who might be waiting to ambush them. Such an attack would be foolish—it would take the destroyer only a few moments to sink the ship—but counting on someone else's ability to reason things out was an easy way to get killed.

With the SITT team aboard the vessel, the chief, Guns, and two other sailors made their way up to meet the captain. The captain protested mildly—the vessel was in international waters; there was no reason for an inspection—but then volunteered that since they had nothing to hide they would be happy to accommodate their friends from the U.S. Navy, and even inquired if they would like some tea. The chief politely declined the invitation and asked to examine the ship's log and papers.

Guns didn't bother looking at the papers, knowing they were unlikely to show that the boat had picked up a passenger. Instead, he walked around the bridge, silently sizing up the two sailors who were with the captain. The men seemed nervous. The mate at the ship's wheel kept jerking his shoulders upward, his hands still tight on the wheel though the boat had come to a full stop.

The chief explained to the captain that they had come because the Italians were searching for a man who had made a terrorist attack and was believed to have escaped Italy by boat. The ship's captain said this was a terrible thing, but of course not something he would be involved in. They had seen no small boat, let alone a terrorist.

The outcome of their talk was preordained, since there was no way the SITT team was leaving without having thoroughly searched the ship. But the chief played diplomat; cajoling a ship's captain into a state of semi-cooperation made his job considerably easier, if not necessarily safer.

Guns, meanwhile, went back down the ladder to the compartments below, thinking about what he had seen so far aboard the ship. The most obvious fact—Ferguson always said start with the obvious—was that the crew and the captain were of different nationalities. The crewmen were Filipino, while the captain had said he was Egyptian. That implied a certain distance between them, a possible weakness that Ferguson would have been quick to exploit.

Guns approached one of the crewmen, asking in Spanish if the ship had picked up someone at sea.

At first, the man pretended not to understand. When Guns repeated the question, the man told him no, they hadn't made a stop since Marseilles. Guns then asked if he was married, trying to make small talk—stalling really, while he thought of some way to determine if the sailor was lying. But the man told him that he was sorry, but he was busy and the person he should speak to was the captain.

Ferguson might have gotten the same results, Guns thought as he walked down the corridor. But he would have gone about it differently—small talk first, and . . . *and* he would have been much more leading when he struck up the conversation.

What happened to the guy you picked up? I can't find him anywhere. . . .

That was the vintage Ferguson question, leading and personable at the same time.

Guns tried it with the next crew member he met, but all he got in response was a blank stare. He tried describing Atha, but the man just shook his head. Part of the problem, Guns thought, was the difference between the Spanish spoken in the Philippines and Mexican Spanish, which was what he spoke. But he also wasn't quite able to seem as smooth as Ferguson. Guns wasn't as sure of himself, talking to people. He needed more of a pretext than Ferg did.

Guns walked on, moving out to the narrow deck area behind the ship's superstructure. There was a small boat tied there, a rigid-hulled vessel similar to the one the navy team had used to board. There was no way of telling if the boat had been out recently, or at least none that Guns could tell, but examining it gave him an idea. Back inside the ship's corridors, he accosted the first man he saw, telling him that he'd noticed some of the ropes on the boat were loose and suggesting they be fixed before the rough seas caused the craft to go overboard. He went out with the man, and helped him secure the ropes.

"Guess you guys didn't tie it tightly enough this afternoon," said Guns.

"The boatswain is an ass," said the man. "He doesn't know his job."

That was as much of a confirmation that Guns could get that the boat had been used, despite more suggestions and hints. The search didn't turn up anything, either, and after more than an hour of looking through the ship the navy sailors returned to the destroyer.

While Guns had been over at the cargo vessel, Rankin had been in a satellite phone conference with Corrigan and two intelligence officers aboard the USS *Anzio*, an Aegis-equipped U.S. Navy cruiser that had joined the search. The *Anzio* had picked up a long-distance helicopter contact near the Tunisia coast; the helo had been on a flight vector that could have meant it came from the cargo vessel Guns had just searched. It had also been flying through the teeth of the storm just a few hours ago. Not necessarily suspicious, but worth checking, Rankin thought.

"Corrigan, see what you can find out about Tunisia and tracking down helicopters there," Rankin told him after the intel officers got off the line. "While I go see if can talk some of these navy guys into finding a way for us to get there."

13

NAPLES, ITALY

Rostislawitch had assumed that the left baggage office would be open around the clock. When he arrived at the station and found it closed, he stood and stared at the gate for so long that a policeman approached and asked what was wrong. Rostislawitch told him he'd left a bag and wanted to retrieve it—had to retrieve it, in fact—but the officer told him to come back in the morning when the office opened.

The scientist next went to the stationmaster's office, which was also closed; he couldn't find anyone to help him at the information kiosk, either.

He didn't want to spend money on a hotel, but the police made him nervous. Finally he decided to buy a ticket for the next local train, which was due to leave Naples for Campobasso at four. He would get on the train, get off at its next stop, then come back; at that point it would be after seven and the station would be too busy for anyone to bother him.

The only complication came when he tried to buy the ticket. He had only a five-euro note left in his wallet; the fare was eight-twenty.

He didn't want to use his credit card, assuming that it would be easy for the FSB she-wolf to trace.

The clerk glared at him. Rostislawitch excused himself and walked away. He had made himself even more conspicuous, and wasn't surprised when another policeman came up to him and asked what he was doing.

"I have to retrieve a bag," he explained in English.

"Well, go home. You can't wait here."

"But it's a train station."

"And where is your ticket?"

Rostislawitch dug into his pocket for his return-trip ticket to Florence. The police officer wasn't impressed.

"The train to Florence does not leave until after lunch."

"No," said Rostislawitch. "It leaves in the morning."

The policeman showed him the ticket. Rostislawitch had bought an off-peak ticket, which meant that the officer was correct.

"Whenever it leaves, you can't wait here," said the policeman.

Rostislawitch strongly suspected that he was being given a hard time because he was a foreigner, but there seemed nothing he could do. He didn't want to roam the streets; he'd heard stories about how dangerous Naples could be. He decided that his earlier plan was his only solution. He would buy a ticket, and if necessary explain later, saying that he had come for the day to see the sights.

He'd stop in Rome as well.

In that case, it would be smarter to take money from his ATM account—there would be no record of his comings and goings. He went to the cash machine, took out twenty euros, then went back to the ticket window.

Ferguson had avoided the police's scrutiny by heading outside and skulking in the shadows of the building with an assortment of rats, human and otherwise. Because of this, he didn't realized Rostislawitch was boarding another train until it was almost too late. Ferguson managed to get inside just as the coach was leaving. He ran for it, but the platform ended about ten feet too soon.

Ferguson jumped to the track and began following the train. Like most European engines, the power came from overhead wires, so there was no danger of his hitting a third rail. But like many local trains in Italy, this one had an engine at both end of the trains, which made it considerably harder to hop on.

Ferguson was nearly out of breath when he finally got his hand on one of the large bumpers at the lip of the engine. He couldn't find a grip, and tried curling himself around it, but instead he was dragged along, half-hopping, unable to get enough leverage to pull himself onto the narrow fender protecting the wheels. He finally grabbed the couple assembly to his left, pitched himself forward, and managed to wedge the tips of his shoes into the small space between the bumper and the cab. The toehold gave him a moment to rest, but the train's shocks squeezed the compartment down against his toes, and he had trouble extricating his left shoe in one piece. Finally he got it out and climbed up on the coupler, gripping the window ledge and wiper assembly as he made his way over the cab.

The power car's cab was empty, but the door to get in was at the side of the train, and Ferguson decided it would be easier to get in through one of the connecting vestibules. He crawled past the pantographs, one hand holding on to the metal rail along the roof and his legs leaning off the side. By now the train was moving at a good clip, and in the darkness he couldn't be sure exactly where the car's roof ended. Finally, he came to the end of the coach and saw that the cars were joined by a cowling whose rubber seam was too tight to squeeze through.

Ferguson worked his way back to the power car and climbed down the side near the cab. Steel handrails flanked the door, but stopped about halfway up, a good five or six feet from the roof. He tried slithering down headfirst, but he couldn't hook his legs around anything secure enough to get down without dropping. Finally he managed to grip a piece of the insulation behind the driver's compartment and lowered himself down to the railing, his feet wedged precariously against the slick metal. After that, the six-inch ledge at the bottom of the door seemed as wide as Montana.

Picking the lock on the door would have been a simple matter if he had big enough tools—a pair of screwdrivers would have done it in thirty seconds—but the only large tool he had with him was his pocketknife. He pried the lock with the screwdriver blade, but he couldn't get it deep enough to get all of the internal gates to trip. Finally he realized he could fashion a crude lock spring from the plastic key card to his hotel room; he cut a sliver from the card, and together with the blade got the door to unlock.

By this time, the train was more than halfway to the next station. Ferguson took off his jacket and unrolled a small watch cap from the pocket, changing his appearance as much as possible. Then he started a quick walk-through to locate Rostislawitch.

The scientist wasn't in the next car or the one after that. Ferguson spotted the conductor asleep near the rear of the fourth car; he walked by as quietly and quickly as possible, continuing his search. Except for the conductor, this car was empty as well.

Rostislawitch was sleeping in the first car, hunched against the window. Ferguson retreated to the vestibule.

Ten minutes later, the train pulled into Campobasso. Ferguson got off, then trotted across the platform so he could see into the car where Rostislawitch was. The scientist didn't stir, so Ferguson ran back to the train—just in time to see Rostislawitch hurrying out.

Not wanting to be seen, Ferguson turned his body away but stuck his foot and knee in the door, which squeezed hard before reopening. As Rostislawitch ambled past, the door started to close again; this time Ferguson sacrificed his other leg to delay the train.

The conductor appeared in the door of the coach.

"Wrong train," Ferguson said, getting off. "I thought we were going to Naples."

Thirty minutes later, Ferguson was standing outside the station, watching as Rostislawitch dozed on a bench at the middle of the platform. Ferguson's sat phone rang; it was Thera.

"Where are you?" she asked.

"I'm in Campobasso. Lovely place."

"Why are you there?"

"I'm not sure. Rostislawitch came here. I don't know why."

"Do you want me to meet you there?"

"Where are *you*?"

"At the Naples airport."

"What the hell are you doing in Naples? I told you to get some rest."

"I sleep better on planes."

"Go over to the train station and stake out the left luggage area. There's a train back to Naples in about a half hour. If you don't hear from me, assume we got on it."

"How's Rostislawitch?"

"Looks a lot better than I do at the moment," Ferguson told her.

14

MISRATAH, LIBYA

The plane that flew Atha from Tunis to Libya was an Embraer EMB 120 Brasilia, a small charter transport that was generally used to fly oil workers to various locations around northern Africa. The seats were hardly plush, but the Iranian managed to get some sleep anyway, angling his feet into the aisle and leaning against the side of the plane. He was the only one aboard the aircraft except for the pilot and copilot. He did not know either man; the minister had vouched for them, which made Atha somewhat wary, but neither of them spoke to him once the plane took off.

They landed several hours later in Misratah, a coastal city in Libya about two hundred kilometers east of Tripoli. Atha had had occasion to use this airport before, and knew he would not be held up for an additional "fee" or surprised near the hangar by a government official with his hand out.

When the plane stopped moving, the copilot came into the cabin and opened the door. The sun had not yet risen; all Atha could see outside was darkness. The copilot reached his hand out to block the way just as Atha was about to step through. The boarding ladder had not yet been rolled into place.

The ladder was set at the side of what looked like a 1950s pickup; the driver brought it against the fuselage carefully, gently nudging the aircraft as he got it into position.

Waiting at the base of the stairs was a tall, skinny Arab dressed in a dusty brown flight suit. The man gave Atha a bright smile and bowed as he left the ladder.

"Commander Atha," said the man in Arabic. "I hope your flight was enjoyable."

Enjoyable was not the word Atha would have chosen, but he grunted in assent.

"Good morning, Ahmed. Are we all ready?"

"As soon as you called I had the plane fueled."

"You've been waiting here all this time?"

"I wanted to be ready. You said you could not predict when you would arrive."

Atha nodded. Ahmed had worked with him many times in the past; while he was not Iranian—his family came from Syria—he was trustworthy and conscientious to a fault.

Ahmed's airplane was a Fuji FA-200, a four-passenger, one-engine aircraft that had two things to recommend it: it was extremely dependable, and it could land and take off from short runways. Ahmed had made a few alterations to the craft, including installing state-of-the-art avionics and tweaking the engine for a little more horsepower, but structurally it was little different from when it had left the factory in Japan more than thirty years before.

Atha strapped the suitcase into the seat directly behind his, then turned around to fasten his seat belt. He checked his watch, then remembered that he had planned to call Rostislawitch.

"Something wrong, Atha?" asked the pilot.

"I was going to make a phone call. Never mind."

"If you have to make a call—"

"No, it's all right."

"Here's my phone." Ahmed reached to the dash of the light plane and took his satellite phone from its holster.

"No," said Atha, "I'd rather not use your phone."

"There is a landline in the hangar," said the pilot.

Rostislawitch might be helpful in the future. In any event, keeping him on the hook for another day or so was probably a good idea. There was always a possibility that Dr. Hamid would need to speak to him.

Atha was starting to get used to the idea of not paying him, however.

"Where in the hangar is the phone?" asked Atha, undoing his belt.

15

BOLOGNA, ITALY

Having failed to find the Russian scientist at the reception, Nathaniel Hamilton turned to the tarts, hoping they might shed some light on where Rostislawitch was. It was even possible, Hamilton thought, that the scientist had sought them out once more.

Finding the women proved more difficult than Hamilton thought it would be; there were several locations in town where the ladies gathered, each with its own set of regulars and, it seemed, different classes of clientele. Hamilton had only his memory of their faces and the noms de sex he had overheard thanks to Ferguson's bug—Francesca and Rosa. The names were hardly unique in the city, but eventually, thanks to a liberal sprinkling of incentives, Hamilton found a woman who looked a great deal like Rosa as she walked back from an assignation at a tourist hotel.

The MI6 agent saw fear in her eyes when he pulled his car along-side her. That was not an asset at this stage, and he immediately worked to assuage it, telling her that he knew it was late, but that she had been recommended by a friend, an Iranian friend named Atha. She was still wary, and so Hamilton told her that he was not looking for sex—true enough, though she didn't believe it. He wanted to talk about a scientist she had been with, and he would gladly do so at a safe, public place where she wouldn't feel threatened. And, of course, he would pay hand-somely.

"Never talk about the customers," she said, starting to pull away, "first rule of business."

"It may be a rule better broken," said Hamilton, easing the car forward to keep pace with her. "You can see that I am not a policeman."

"You're British; I can tell from your accent."

"There. So have breakfast with me. I'll buy you breakfast and we'll talk. Quietly, with no one else to know. The money's good." He revealed the two hundred-euro notes in his hand. "Not bad for a few minutes of companionship."

The woman hesitated, but was still not sold.

"There are things about the Iranian you should know," Hamilton told her. "They may save your life. And some of these things you would not want the police to know, at least not in connection with you."

Fear shot back into her eyes. *Now* it was an asset, reinforcing her instinct for survival.

"I'll add another two hundred. You'll be able to go away from the city for a few days," said Hamilton. "When you come back, Atha will be entirely forgotten."

Rosa had sensed that the Iranian was a very bad man—he'd paid far too much for what he wanted them to do—and a feeling of doom swept over her. Hamilton offered a way of pushing off the peril. She opened the car door.

They ate at a place that fancied itself an American-style diner, ensconced in a corner of Bologna that Hamilton had never visited. Brightly colored fenders from American cars hung on the steel wall above the long counter. Across from it sat bright turquoise booths with plush seats and Formica tabletops. Each featured an old-fashioned jukebox near the window, where the menu rather than songs was displayed. The decoration was garish, but not entirely American; large bottles of olive oil and trees of garlic were hung between the car fenders, and the dessert display was dominated by cannoli shells. The air smelled more of garlic and basil than cheap hot dogs, and the waiter didn't chew gum.

Rosa ordered only coffee; Hamilton went for a full American-style breakfast. She listened quietly as he told her that Atha had been involved in the car bombing two days before.

Rosa's eyes grew wide. Was the scientist involved?

Hamilton told her he wasn't sure.

"This involves several international agencies," he said breezily. "Your help would be greatly appreciated."

"I don't know anything."

"Of course not. But if I can locate the scientist quickly, then perhaps the entire matter can be wrapped up."

"How can you be investigating this if you are English?"

"Would you rather be talking to the police?" asked Hamilton, taking the euro notes from his pocket and pretending to examine them.

Speaking haltingly, Rosa told him all she knew of the scientist, where his hotel room was, and how they had found the ticket.

As she spoke, Hamilton finally realized that the scientist must have gone to Naples to retrieve the bag Atha had already obtained. He paid Rosa off, called Rostislawitch's hotel room just to be sure he wasn't there, then made his way out to the airport.

16

"I'm here," said Ferguson, answering the sat phone.

"Ferg, it's Lauren DiCapri."

"I was expecting Attila the Hun," said Ferguson. He spotted the light from the Naples-bound train in the distance, and began jogging toward the ticket machine.

"We think Atha called Rostislawitch's phone a little while ago."

"Think?" Ferguson started to take his credit card out to pay for the ticket, then realized the train was a lot closer than he'd thought. No way was he climbing aboard this one from the back—he turned and began sprinting for the stairs leading to the platform.

"We don't have a voice sample to match it, but he said he was Atha. He said he wasn't feeling well and would talk to him tomorrow sometime. The thing is, we traced the call to Libya."

"Good."

"Not good. Rankin and Guns are on their way to Tunis. That's where the helicopter—"

"Tell them to divert."

"OK. I thought you'd want—"

"It's all right," said Ferguson, taking the steps two at a time. "Listen, I'll call you back. I have to make this train."

Downstairs on the platform, Artur Rostislawitch waited for the train to pull in. He hadn't decided what to do with the material once he got it. Disposing of it properly was not a simple matter. Short of bringing it to a proper disposal station, which couldn't be done for obvious reasons, the best solution was to burn the material in a very hot fire. But the fire had to be very hot, like that generated by an iron-smelting plant. He wasn't sure where he could find one, or how he would talk his way in.

The train doors opened. Rostislawitch stepped inside. The train was about three-quarters full with early-morning commuters bound for the city, and he had to go to the middle of the car to find an open seat. He found a spot next to a pretty-looking woman wearing too much perfume. He attempted a smile; she gave him a frown in return.

When Rostislawitch looked up, he found the conductor staring at him expectantly. He reached into his pocket for his ticket and handed it to the man, who turned it over, then shook his head.

"It's not stamped," said the conductor. Rostislawitch had forgotten to validate the ticket at the entrance to the platform.

"I must have forgotten," Rostislawitch muttered in Russian.

The conductor, of course, didn't understand.

"*Turista*," said Rostislawitch. "*Io sono turista.*"

"Whether you are a tourist or not, you must validate your ticket," said the conductor. "Do you speak English?"

"I can speak English."

"You must validate your ticket," explained the conductor. "How can you be a tourist at this hour?"

"I was to visit a friend, but arrived too early, then realized—"

"Enough," said the conductor. "Next time, make sure to stamp the ticket at the yellow box."

Thera looked at the arrival board, then walked back toward the café diagonally across from the left luggage area. The shop had just opened, and the cup of Cafe Americano—espresso with enough extra water to make a cup's worth—was piping hot. She sat down, fanning it with a napkin. According to her watch, she had ten minutes before Rostislawitch's train would get there.

Her sat phone rang. Thera grabbed it from her purse.

"You're kind of obvious there," said Ferguson.

"Where are you?"

"On the train."

She jerked her head around. He didn't know where she was; he was just guessing.

"Ferg, where are you really?"

"I'm on the train to Naples, in the next car from Rostislawitch. We'll be there in five minutes. He's going to have to hang out for a while; the left baggage place doesn't open until eight. Plant a couple of bugs so we can watch, and meet me at the south door. OK?"

"The bugs are already in place."

"So get the hell out of the station."

"I wasn't going to let him see me."

"By the south door."

"OK."

17

OVER THE MEDITERRANEAN

Rankin and Guns were about five minutes from touching down in Tunis when Lauren DiCapri called Rankin and told him about the phone call Atha had made. There was no possibility of diverting at this point; Misratah was several hundred miles away. The navy lieutenant piloting the Seahawk helicopter told Rankin he'd have to not only refuel, but ask permission from his commander to fly them there.

"You'll get permission," Rankin told him. "That won't be a problem."

"How long is it going to take us to get there?" Guns asked.

"Top speed, once we're in the air, two or three hours."

"It'd be better if it were faster," said Rankin.

"It'd be better if this were a jet," said the pilot. "But it's not."

18

Rostislawitch tried consciously to slow himself down as he walked from the train to the luggage office, but he was brimming with nervous energy. He walked directly to the left luggage area even though he knew it would be closed. Then he paced for a few minutes, and went back toward the platforms. He remembered that he hadn't had anything to eat, and decided to get some breakfast, not because he was hungry but to have something to do. He left the station, walking along the edge of the sidewalk as he surveyed the neighborhood around the station. The city was now wide-awake: trucks jostled to find an opening in the traffic; businessmen walked with a determined pace to their offices; sidewalk vendors growled at beggars as they set up their wares.

The thing that Rostislawitch noticed most was the smell—the scent of garbage mixed with diesel and the sea. Naples was a dirty city, dirtier than Moscow, which even Rostislawitch thought was a filthy place.

He found a large café near the intersection two blocks from the train station and went inside. Sitting at a table near the window, he ordered a *sfogliatella*—a breakfast pastry—and coffee, using English. He stared out of the window, stirring his coffee mindlessly, still trying to puzzle out how to get rid of the material.

What would the consequences be if he dropped it in the ocean?

So long as the containers remained sealed, there would be no problem; even without the heavy tape he had wrapped around them and the carrying container, the canisters were waterproof. The problem would come if someone found the containers later. Anyone opening the vials while the bacteria was still active would be infected and die within a few days. Once they were infected, they would infect other people; there would be at least a small outbreak.

What happened after that would depend largely on how long it took the health authorities to recognize what was going on. In a worst-case scenario, a hundred million people could be killed—though an accidental exposure of the nature Rostislawitch was contemplating more likely would only affect a hundred or a thousand before the authorities could take measures to stop it.

Could they? Dealing with epidemics was not his forte, but he knew from the research data that the outbreak was likely to be misdiagnosed at the very beginning. Two or three days' delay in instituting quarantines and changing procedures at hospitals would have an exponential impact down the line.

Why had he not let such thoughts stop him earlier? What sort of man had he allowed himself to become?

A foolish, vain, hateful man. One he hated as well.

And one who deserved to be punished. He should turn himself in to the FSB she-wolf, let her lock him away in whatever modern gulag the state was using now. He didn't deserve to live.

Rostislawitch rubbed his face, still chilled by his stay in the suburban station.

He was not beyond redemption. That was the true message of the epiphany in the church the morning before—he was not beyond redemption. He had to persevere, stop wavering. He would dispose of the material, go back to Bologna, return to Russia.

And then?

Put his talents to work somewhere that could make better use of them. He could work in western Europe, or at least try.

And talk to Thera, every now and then. Other new friends as well.

He put his mind back to the problem at hand: how to dispose of the material.

There must be a city incinerator. He would find it, then bribe his way in.

Still having breakfast," Ferguson told Thera. "Anybody watching us?"

"Not that I see."

Ferguson turned the corner. A man in an old Italian army jacket was sitting on the sidewalk panhandling.

Ferguson sized him up. "How much for your coat?" he asked in Italian.

"*Scusi?*"

"I'll tell you what. I'll swap. This one doesn't have enough pockets."

"I like my coat."

"Fifty euros, plus mine."

The beggar bolted to his feet. Ferguson retrieved everything from his pockets, placing them in the jacket, which was just a little tight at the shoulders. When he pulled on his stocking cap, he looked like a regular Naples bum.

"Like my new look?" he asked Thera, walking back near the restaurant.

"God, I can smell you from here. You smell like a dog pound."

"Your glasses are dumb."

"Thank you." Thera had put on a pair of glasses and tied her hair back to help change her look. "Listen, Ferg. I've been thinking. Maybe I should meet him right after he comes out. He'll be vulnerable, look-ing for help. That's when I should talk to him."

"No, it won't work that way."

"The FSB is on to him. His only option is to come with us. We can help him."

"He's not quite ready yet, Thera. And he won't be then, either. Trust me. You walk up to him and blow your cover, he'll just freak. It'll be the final straw. Do it my way, OK? Then we'll be able to help him."

"All right."

Ferguson knew they weren't really going to help Rostislawitch. They might pump his brain for everything he knew about the Russian biological warfare program, but after that he was expendable. Worse. He'd stolen a weapons system—an experimental one, maybe, but one that was at least as dangerous as a nuke. The U.S. would not only turn down a request for asylum; they might very well hand him over with whatever evidence he gave them. They'd done the same thing to two men in the nuclear weapons case that had almost cost Ferguson his life.

But of course that wasn't what Thera wanted to hear.

"Keep an eye out for T Rex," he told her.

"She's not here, Ferg. She's back in Bologna."

"(A), T-Rex is not Kiska, and (B) she may show up here, too. They were following him in Bologna."

"You really don't think she's the killer, huh?"

"Nope."

"We'll see."

Inside the restaurant, Rostislawitch checked his watch and got up from his table.

"We're in business," Ferguson said. "Lay back."

It was now exactly eight a.m. Rostislawitch walked swiftly from the restaurant, taking long, quick strides, practically running. He would get the bag, go to an ATM machine for cash, then find a cab and ride to the incinerator. Bribe his way in. They could ask questions, but he would pretend not to understand. He could even show them the material if they wanted—it would look like pudding gone bad.

His heart raced as he walked. He was excited, in a strange way happy, glad to be taking action, even jubilant. He'd managed to tear the great weight that had covered him these past several years away. He was back to being himself.

Rostislawitch waited at the curb, looking for an opening in the traffic. Finally he decided to plunge ahead. Staring across the street, he stepped out and began walking swiftly. Cars continued to fly past, somehow missing him.

The drivers were even less considerate for Ferguson, whose appearance made him look like a native. He trotted across the avenue, hopping up onto the curb just as a red Fiat whipped within a few inches of his backside.

There was a line of people with bags at the luggage area, waiting to check them. Rostislawitch got in line, then decided to go and get money and come back. Out of the corner of his eye, he noticed a ratty-looking man watching him. The man seemed to be trying to get his courage up to ask for some money.

That was me, the scientist thought to himself. One step from the gutter.

Rostislawitch went to the bank machine and put in his card. Another record for the FSB people to question him about.

But it would make sense. His mind was working now. A tourist trip to Naples; he'd wanted to see what it was like. He'd come early to the city, gotten something to eat, then realized the place was far more expensive than he thought. A typical tourist.

He'd worry about the details of the story later. He'd get rid of the material; everything else would fall into place once it was gone.

Rostislawitch took three hundred euros from his account. It was nearly all he had left. Hopefully it would be enough to bribe a laborer in a garbage plant.

Toss the suitcase in the back of a garbage truck as it went in and he was done, free. That might be even easier.

"You have your ticket?" asked the clerk at the left luggage counter.

Rostislawitch's fingers began to tremble as he handed the ticket over. The man looked at it, nodded, then went to retrieve the bag from the locker in the next room. The bones in Rostislawitch's chest began to press against his lungs as he waited.

"Here," said the man, returning. He held up a green upholstered carry-on.

Rostislawitch's throat constricted. "That's not mine," he managed, speaking in English.

"No?"

"Mine is black. Just plain black." He glanced to his left and his right. Two people were behind him, waiting to check bags. "This isn't mine," he insisted.

The man looked again at the ticket, still in his hand. He frowned, then went back into the luggage room. Rostislawitch felt very hot. The back of his neck buzzed and his ears felt as if they were covered with an itchy wool.

"This is the right number," said the attendant, returning. He spoke Italian with a strong local accent, but Rostislawitch understood what he was saying—it was obvious from his gestures.

"Then there was a mistake. *Problema.* It's not mine. *Non il mio.* Mine was black. It had—it had thermos carriers."

"Thermos carriers?"

The attendant did not understand. Rostislawitch searched for some way of describing the contents without actually doing so.

There was no way.

"It had—an experiment I'm conducting," he blurted in English.

"I'm sorry, sir—"

"Let me look," said Rostislawitch, starting past the desk.

"You're not allowed back here," said the man, putting out his hand to stop him.

"I just want to look for my bag. It's very important. It's very—it's critical."

Rostislawitch pushed past the man and turned the corner into the room with the luggage. There were rows of lockers, and larger bags collected along the wall. The door to the locker where his bag had been was open. He put his hand inside, even though he could easily see that it was empty. He ran his fingers around the space, rattling the side of the empty box.

Rostislawitch grabbed at the locker doors near it, but they were all locked. Spotting the bags against the wall, he slid down to his knees near one that looked like his. Pulling it out, he laid it on the floor and unzipped it—nothing but clothes.

"You're not allowed here," said a policeman behind him.

"I've lost my luggage. It's very important that I get it back," said Rostislawitch in Russian.

The policeman did not understand. "Can you speak English?" he asked.

"English, yes. I've lost my bag. I need it."

"This may be true, but you're not allowed here," said the cop.

"Please. I have to find my bag."

Rostislawitch grabbed another case. It didn't look that much like his, but he had to do something—he had to find his bag.

The policeman took his shoulder. "You are not allowed here. Come."

"My bag. There must have been a mistake."

The clerk came over with his key and began opening the lockers nearby. Rostislawitch watched, trembling. None of the suitcases nearby looked like his.

"I need my bag," he said, when the clerk held out his hands, indicating he had no idea where it had gone.

"You can file a claim," said the policeman.

"It must be here."

The cop took hold of Rostislawitch's arm. Two more police officers had appeared at the doorway.

"I'm being very patient," said the policeman in Italian. "Because I know what it is like to lose a bag. But if it's lost, it's lost. Come on now."

Rostislawitch couldn't think. He only half-understood what the policeman had said, but the prods were emphatic, and he started to go out. Then he stopped, looked back, started again. He was torn between rage and logic—the bag must be here.

"Come on, sir," said another policeman. "Come on."

The scientist walked out of the room, his head pounding. The clerk shoved some papers in his hand.

"Make the report, sir," said the man. "Here is a pen. Just make the report. If the luggage turns up—sometimes this happens—we will be able to give it to you. If not, a claim. They are good about paying."

"You all right?" asked the policeman who'd been with him in the room. He was speaking English again; Rostislawitch could understand every word.

"I need a drink of water," said the scientist.

"There's a store right over there."

"Yes."

Rostislawitch started away. The FSB she-wolf must have taken the bag. She'd probably followed him here from Moscow.

What was he going to do?

He walked into the store and bought a bottle of water.

He could use something much stronger.

A few yards from the water store, Ferguson sat head down on the floor, watching as Rostislawitch sorted through his change. Ferguson rocked forward, then ambled in Rostislawitch's direction.

"I wonder if you have a coin for a smoke?" he asked in Italian.

Rostislawitch thought the disheveled man looked vaguely familiar but couldn't place him. He told him in Russian to get lost.

"You're Russian?" said Ferguson, answering in Russian as well. He pulled his head back, as if he didn't trust the man, then looked all around the station, as if they might be overheard.

"You understand me?" said Rostislawitch. He glanced left and right—was this one of the she-bitch's agents?

Unlikely, thought the scientist. He smelled to high heaven.

"Be careful, friend," said Ferguson quickly in Russian. "There are thieves all over, watching for Russians. They take their bags. Sell them."

Ferguson turned and began walking away.

"What?" said Rostislawitch.

Ferguson pretended not to hear.

"Hey, you, what do you know?" Rostislawitch practically shouted.

"I know a lot," mumbled Ferguson, just loud enough for Rostislawitch to hear.

"Tell me about this."

People nearby were staring.

"First I get something to eat," said Ferguson. "Not here."

Rostislawitch was unsure whether to trust the man. He looked as if he'd lived on the streets for some time, and his Russian was authentic, from Moscow. But his face wasn't Russian; it didn't have the Slavic thickness that Rostislawitch expected.

"Where do you come from?" Rostislawitch asked.

"Around."

"Where in Russia?"

Ferguson shrugged.

"Where in Moscow?" demanded the scientist.

"When I was young, Moscow."

"Why are you in Naples?"

"Hmmmm," said Ferguson, nodding.

"That's not an answer."

Ferguson started away.

"All right. I'll buy you something to eat," said Rostislawitch. "Where?"

"Outside the station. Some place where they can't hear."

"Who?"

"The KGB. They're everywhere."

"Yes," said Rostislawitch, not sure if the man was crazy or very sane.

19

Thomas Ciello put his fingers to his temples and squeezed, trying to relieve his headache. He'd been staring at the computer for so long that his neck and shoulders seemed to have welded themselves into a permanent forward slope. He tried twisting in his chair to loosen his muscles, but even the chair seemed frozen solid. Finally he pushed backward with his feet and rose slowly. Every joint in his body creaked.

"Argh," he moaned. He hadn't worked this hard or this long without a break since he set out to solve the August 2004 Alabama Black Triangle UFO sighting.

"Are you all right?"

Corrigan was standing in the doorway. This was a momentous occasion, thought Ciello—Corrigan never visited the research offices.

"I'm just a little tense," said Ciello. He bent over at his trunk, trying to stretch out his back. His fingers stopped a good foot above his toes.

"OK," said Corrigan, backing away. "When you get a chance, give me an update."

"Wait!" yelled Ciello. He started to unfold himself, but his back was locked. He couldn't move.

"Yes?" asked Corrigan.

"I—Kiska Babev is on her way to Naples."

"Excuse me?"

"Kiska Babev, the FSB agent. I've been tracking her credit card accounts. She bought a plane ticket to Naples a couple of hours ago. Air One. She got it right before for the flight. It's an hour flight. She may be there by now."

Corrigan stepped into the room. Ciello was still bent over at the waist. It seemed a little odd, but then again, intelligence analysts were supposed to be odd.

"You're sure about that?"

"I tracked all her bank accounts down. It hasn't been easy. I talked to this guy Ferguson knows and—"

"Put it in a report. I have to go to tell Ferg."

"OK." Ciello tried again to straighten, but couldn't. "You think you could help me get unfolded here?" he asked, but Corrigan was already gone.

20

THE SUDAN DESERT

The small airplane was flying low to avoid being picked up on radar. It was so low, in fact, that Atha thought several times they would hit a dune. He grabbed hold of the handle at the side of the windshield strut, gripping it tightly.

As usual, Ahmed was amused. He would tuck the plane up slightly, then back down, staying close to the contours of the earth. The desert was not quite the empty wasteland it looked on many maps. On the contrary, to Ahmed it teemed with life—desperate refugees escaping from Darfur or the Sudan or Chad, militiamen seeking justice or simply enemies, smugglers taking a convenient route. He loved the desert, especially when the radar detector tracked a radar somewhere above. It was impossible to tell what the signal had come from; military flights from Libya and Chad and occasionally NATO fighters crisscrossed the area. All were to be avoided at the pain of death; it was a challenge Ahmed relished.

Ahmed strained against his seat belt as he pushed his small plane forward, tracking through the highlands of northeast Sudan. If a jet were to appear above, he knew precisely what he would do, how he would turn and twist to get away, slinking into the crevices of the mountains ahead.

And then, like a photo suddenly coming into focus, they were there: Ahmed rose over a ridge and the camp spread out below, its buildings clustered around a tiny spring-fed pond in a scar-faced canyon.

Atha took a deep breath as Ahmed legged the plane onto the narrow, dusty landing strip. A great deal of work was about to reach fruition.

The Fuji FA-200 bumped hard on the strip. Ahmed came in a few knots too fast and had trouble braking; he needed the entire strip to stop. Behind him, a crowd of people swarmed the plane, hoping its occupant was in a good mood as he usually was when he returned from a long trip; he was known to throw candy to children and, on rare occasions, coins.

They would be disappointed today. Atha had not had a chance to pick up any sweets. They would gladly forgive him, however, for in many ways he was their savior.

He was also planning to be their executioner, though that part they didn't know.

Except for the large pond that supplied a modicum of water even during the dry months, Atha's camp was similar to the larger camps that dotted North Darfur, Sudan, and Chad farther south. Like those, it consisted of huts at irregular though relatively spacious intervals. The walls of the huts were generally made of rushes or other stalks of vegetation, trucked in from many miles away. The tops of these houses were plastic or nylon sheets.

With roughly five thousand people, Atha's camp was smaller than many of the refugee camps to the south, even those in Chad, which tended to be less imposing than the cities of death in the deserts of West and North Darfur. It had two small permanent structures, made of thick stone and lashed vegetation, their metal roofs covered by plastic sheets so they appeared less conspicuous. But the major difference was the people—compared to the people in the other camps, Atha's were far better fed, in far better health. For this was a necessary part of the plan: one could not start an epidemic with people who were already sick.

An old Jeep circled around the crowd. A young man in a baggy white tunic and pants stepped out of the Jeep, waving at the people before walking to the plane. Though not yet thirty, the young man was a doctor and a scientist, a man who knew nearly as much about bacteria as Rostislawitch did. Dr. Navid Hamid had, in fact, been a pupil of Rostislawitch's for a brief time in Moscow, though Hamid doubted he remembered him and Atha had thought it best to conceal that fact from the Russian when he had made his arrangements.

"Atha, you have made it back," said Dr. Hamid.

"By the grace of Allah, all glory to him," said Atha, reaching into the back of the plane for the bag.

"This is it?"

"Yes, Doctor. This is it." Atha handed over the bag. "How soon?"

"I can't be sure. Perhaps thirty-six hours to have enough to infect the camp—if everything we were told is correct, and if these samples have held up to transport."

"That was the entire reason for obtaining them," said Atha.

"As I say, if everything we were told is correct. Thirty-six hours."

"Go. The minister will want it done even quicker."

The doctor nodded, then went back to the Jeep. Atha turned and looked at the crowd around him. At least three hundred people were close by, and others were coming as well. Children, women, fathers. Most were members of the Massalit tribe, ethnic Africans from farther south, but there was a good number of Arab Africans as well. Without any exception that Atha knew of, they were Sunnis, though had they been Shiites like him he still would have felt no pity for their fates. The poor were puppets for the powerful; the only relief was to escape poverty. It was the lesson he had taught the spider in the hotel the other day.

"Your passage has been arranged," he told them in Arabic, speaking in a loud voice. "In a day, perhaps two, your journey will begin. Prepare."

There was silence. Even though it was the camp's common tongue, most of the ethnic Africans did not understand Arabic, or at best were far from fluent. But then suddenly one person held up his hand and yelled, "God is great!" and a giant roar of approval went up from the crowd.

21

Thera watched as Ferguson walked with Rostislawitch out of the station, toward a restaurant Ferguson had chosen because it had good acoustics for their bugs. The scientist looked dazed, still unsure of what was going on.

Ferguson looked like a paranoid street person.

Thera began following them. She'd bought a cheap shawl and covered her face and head and the top of her torso so she looked like a devout Muslim. With her face covered and Rostislawitch preoccupied, it was a simple but effective disguise, and she was able to get within a few yards without worrying about being recognized.

Because of the screening at the airport, Thera had left her weapons in Bologna, so she'd borrowed Ferguson's hideaway, a tiny CZ-92 Pocket Automatic barely five inches long. The gun felt almost like a toy in her pocket.

A car veered around the corner, heading toward the side street Ferguson and Rostislawitch had just turned down. The window began to open.

"Get down! Get down!" Thera yelled, throwing off her shawl. She pulled the CZ from her pocket and fired in the direction of the car, just as a submachine gun appeared in the window and began shooting.

ACT V

He whom you seek am I; by tempests toss'd,
And sav'd from shipwreck on your Libyan coast;
Presenting, gracious queen, before your throne,
A prince that owes his life to you alone.

—Virgil, *The Aeneid* (Dryden translation)

1

An infinitesimal moment of time passed, the space of a spark passing across an electrode. This shell of a moment contained a universe of action and thought, all possibilities to follow. Standing at its rim, Bob Ferguson saw them all—himself, the car, the submachine gun, Rostislawitch.

Ferguson's impulse was to push Rostislawitch down, to take cover. But that would have been a mistake; that would have been what the shooter wanted. Instead, Ferguson chose the unexpected.

How much of this was actual thought and how much reflex would have been impossible to say. But in the half second that followed, Ferguson twisted around and grabbed Rostislawitch by the arm, hooking his shoulder and arm into his. Then he threw himself not forward or to the ground but upward, in the direction of the passing car.

He landed on the trunk, dragging Rostislawitch with him. Ferguson threw his hand out, gripping the far side of the car as it sped down the road.

As strong as he was, Ferguson could not hold himself on the trunk of the moving vehicle, let alone support the added weight of Rostislawitch. They slid off the car after a few yards, rolling across the street into the gutter. Ferguson pushed Rostislawitch with him, forward, trying to move in the direction the vehicle had been going. He got another three or four yards before an explosion rent the air behind him.

Fire pitched upward from the side of the street where they'd been walking. Ferguson looked back and saw a sheet of red covering the block.

He had only one thought: where was Thera?

Rostislawitch, head spinning, felt himself being dragged back to his feet. He'd closed his eyes when the shooting started, clamped them closed as he flew through the air. Now he struggled to reopen them. He was pulled back, dragged toward heat.

"What are we doing?" he screamed in Russian.

His eyes sprang open and his vision returned; the bum whom he'd met in the station had him over his shoulder, carrying him into the fire.

"No!" he yelled, struggling to break free.

"We have to save someone," answered Ferguson. "Come on. It's Thera. *Thera.*"

Rostislawitch stopped fighting, but he was even more deeply confused. He felt as if he were in a dream, the world spinning so bizarrely that everything he knew was mashed together into the same physical place: Thera; his wife, Olga; Atha; and this bum; the streets of Moscow when he was a young man; Chechnya the inferno; Naples.

The flames receded, funneling back into a basement near where they'd been walking when the car came by. Ferguson pulled Rostislawitch with him.

"Thera!" Ferguson called. "Thera, where are you? Thera!"

The explosion had broken a water main below the street. Water hissed upward, a cloud of vapor rising from the grate next to the building like a geyser. Black smoke from several boxes of garbage and a nearby car that had caught fire curled across the narrow roadway, clawing at the buildings on either side.

Thera Majed rose from behind the car where she'd crouched. She hadn't realized what was going on until she saw Ferguson throwing himself into space. When the flames erupted she threw herself down, thinking it was too late, not for her but for him. She was sure she'd never see Ferg again, except in pieces, broken on the pavement.

And there he was, coming through the fire, carrying Rostislawitch with him, calling for her. She threw herself at him and he caught her, and for a long moment neither one thought of anything but the other: they wrapped their arms around each other; they held their hearts close against each other's chest. Then, like all moments, it disintegrated; they were back in the world.

"Are you all right?" Thera asked.

"I'm good."

"Your sat phone is ringing."

Ferguson hadn't realized it. He pulled it from his pocket. Corrigan had called, leaving a message. The sat phone was notifying him of it.

"Kiska Babev is on her way to Naples," said Corrigan. "She may be there already."

Thanks, thought Ferguson, sliding the antenna back down. He turned to Rostislawitch, standing only a foot away, not sure whether to believe Thera was really there. "Come on," Ferguson told the Russian scientist. "We'll find a place where it's safe, and explain."

2

MISRATAH, LIBYA

The airport at Misratah was primarily a military base, with its parking areas dominated by fixed-wing Aero L-39 Albatross fighter-trainers. But there was very little in terms of intra-service rapport between the U.S. and Libya. Rankin made a vain attempt at soliciting the base commander's help, telling him that he was sure that Atha's aircraft had landed here and that any cooperation would be remembered in the future. But his promise was too nebulous for the commander, who valued tangible and immediate rewards; he recommended that Rankin speak to the men in the control tower but added that personally he doubted there would be anyone there who could help.

Guns worked the opposite direction, walking over to the fixed base operator's shack and trying to strike up a conversation with the men there. He was wondering about airplanes that might have been fueled recently, he told them, because he was trying to find someone who'd flown out a few hours before. But there was too much of a language barrier—none of the men who fueled or worked on the planes spoke enough English to understand his questions, even with twenty-euro notes as an incentive.

The office manager understood, but claimed there had been no aircraft in or out in several days. She did this with her arms folded and one eye on the television in the corner of her small office inside the hangar. An Italian soap opera was playing on the television, the sound turned down while a translation of the dialogue into Arabic ran across the bottom. Guns turned and watched the program for a few minutes while he tried to think of another tactic.

A short, bald man with a beard pushed a broom into the office. The woman scolded him in Arabic, telling him he was late, but the man paid no attention. He swept the dust into a small pile near the door, then went back out into the hangar area.

"So, uh, who else can I talk to?" Guns asked the office manager when the program went to commercials. "I'm really looking for information and willing to pay."

The woman shrugged. Guns wrote a local telephone number down for her—untraceable, the number would be answered by Corrigan—and said that if she thought of anything, she could call. He left one of his twenties next to the note and left.

He wondered what Ferguson would do next as he walked toward the hangar door. Maybe see something that he wasn't seeing. Guns tried absorbing everything in front of him, staring, glancing—if there was something significant here, it just wasn't registering.

"I know what you're after," said the man with the broom, pausing over his work near the doorway.

Guns stopped, surprised not so much by what the man said as the fact that he was speaking perfect English.

"You want information about Ahmed." The man glanced around. "Flies out of here all the time in his little putt-putt plane."

"How do you know?"

"Ah, I don't know nothin'."

The man went back to sweeping. Before Guns could ask another question, the office manager's voice rang across the large building, once more scolding the sweeper in Arabic. The man pushed his broom toward a corner.

"He is a retard," she told Guns, walking toward him. The English pejorative flew from her mouth in three syllables: "ree-tuh-ard." "Not right in the head. Don't worry about him."

"I could see that," said Guns.

Outside, Guns walked as slowly as he could toward the helicopter, parked a hundred yards away. Rankin had already gotten back.

"They're probably all on the take," said Rankin, agitated, standing near the nose of the Seahawk. "Control tower guy lied to my face. He claimed he hadn't had a plane in or out for days, except for the military patrols. He does that in almost perfect English, then he pretends he doesn't understand when I ask if knows of any Iranians who fly in and out of here. How about you?"

"I'm not sure," said Guns. "But there's a guy in the offices there who might talk to us, if we could figure out a way to get his boss out of the picture. She's kind of a nasty-edged woman."

"Ferguson would go make love to her," said Rankin.

Guns laughed. He probably would—or at least flirt. "Well, that won't work for us."

"Are they together?" Rankin asked.

"There's an office inside. She's watching a soap opera. He's cleaning up."

"I'll tell you what. I'll go talk to her. You come around after me and see what the guy has to say."

The man with the broom had been watching them from across the cement apron, and Guns didn't have to do very much to get him to talk.

"They think I'm a dope," the man told Guns while Rankin went inside. "I'm not right in the head, but I'm not a dope."

"I'm looking for an Iranian," said Guns.

"That would be Atha," said the man. "He is always with Ahmed. Ahmed the pilot and his little plane."

"Yeah. That's right."

"I can tell you everything. Everything."

"And what do you want?"

"Get me out of here. I know you're American and I know you're a spy. Get me back to America."

"We could probably do that," said Guns, in his most casual voice.

"I'll be in your helicopter in half an hour."

"What's your name?"

"Just call me Paul."

P aul" showed up at the Seahawk five minutes after Guns and Rankin climbed in. Rankin thought Paul looked like a burned-out hippie, and the brief story he told of his background more or less confirmed the assessment: he'd wandered through Africa for nearly two decades, for fun and enlightenment.

"Done some good drugs," he admitted. "Got tossed in jail in Morocco for a while. Not a great place."

"So tell us about Ahmed," said Guns.

"You guys are going to get me back to the States?"

Rankin looked at Guns. He hadn't heard about the deal.

"Yeah, we'll get you there," said Guns. "I just have to work it out. But I will."

"I think I can trust you," said Paul. He turned to Rankin. "Not you." He turned back to Guns. "But you're OK."

Guns asked again about Ahmed, the pilot Paul had mentioned by the hangar.

"Flies a little Fuji FA-200. Tiny little plane. Putt-putt-putt-putt-putt. Fills up with his av fuel, comes back almost bone-dry. Goes south. Doesn't take much water."

"Why would he take a lot of water?" asked Guns.

"That's the desert, man. The desert. People are dying down there. No water. So he's going someplace with water. Dig?"

"Are you sure he's goes south?" said Rankin.

Paul snickered. "You don't trust me."

"No," said Rankin.

"Honesty. Ha. Overrated."

"How *do* you know he's going south?" asked Guns.

"Flight vector," said Paul. "I watch. Some days with glasses. You don't waste fuel in the desert. You go somewhere, you go. You know, I could fly that plane if he let me. I don't have a license, but I can fly. I could fly this plane."

"This is a helicopter," said Guns.

"I could still fly it."

"I think we can find our own pilot," said Rankin.

"Hey, I can find you pilots. I can get you lots of pilots."

"Yeah?" said Guns, thinking one might know Ahmed. Paul didn't seem like the most reliable source.

"Lots of pilots, man," said Paul. "Say, you got something to drink? Stronger than water, I mean."

3

The day his wife died, Rostislawitch had walked through town in a state of shock, his body numb with disbelief. He did this even though he had known for a while it was coming—his need for her was so strong that he had denied the reality of her passing until the sheet was drawn over her head. At that moment, confusion was drawn over him, and his soul was plunged into despair, from which he'd only just awoken.

He felt that way again, sitting in the abandoned factory building several blocks from the train station. He couldn't believe what the girl, Thera, was telling him.

He could believe some of it, but not all of it, not the part about her being an American spy, a CIA officer, even though the FSB she-wolf had said it, even though he had quizzed Thera surreptitiously about it before. She seemed too young, too innocent, to be so deceptive.

"I didn't mean to hurt you," Thera told him. "But someone had to get close to you to protect you."

Rostislawitch thought this might all be an elaborate trick, an operation they would call it, to get him to come over to their side. Maybe things were still the way they were during the Cold War, when Russians and the West were locked in a battle of spy versus spy. They'd get medals for bringing him in, and he would get a small flat in Texas somewhere, never heard of again until the she-wolf Kiska Babev hunted him down and took his carcass back for her own medal.

"Someone is trying to kill you. This is twice Ferg has saved you," Thera told him.

"When was the first?" Rostislawitch asked.

"In Bologna. The car bomb."

"That was a terrorist."

"No, that was an assassin. He likes bombs, and he likes to make his hits look as if they're the work of other people."

"No one saved me," said Rostislawitch, remembering. "Someone flew into me as the bomb exploded."

Ferguson interrupted, walking over from his lookout post near the door.

"The person that's trying to kill you is good. Very good," he said. "He—or she—killed a CIA officer two years ago. That's why we went to Bologna. Not because of whatever it was you stole, or because we want you to defect or anything like that. Because you're the target of someone we want. We want to catch him. Or her."

"Him or her?" asked Rostislawitch.

"We thought it was a he," Ferguson said. "We seem to have been wrong about that."

"Who is it?"

"I don't know."

"We're pretty sure it's Kiska Babev," said Thera. "The Russian FSB agent who interviewed you."

Rostislawitch remembered their meeting, the look in her eyes. She was definitely a killer, heartless.

"But now that we're here," continued Ferguson, "we can't help but be interested in what you gave the Iranians."

"I didn't give them anything."

"You weren't paid?"

"They stole it from my locker. You saw me. You were there. In your disguise."

Ferguson caught Thera's eye and signaled with his head for her to go back by the door and keep lookout. He'd posted video bugs, but it would take considerably more than that to make him feel comfortable now.

"Tell me about what they took," Ferguson asked the scientist in Russian. "How dangerous is it?"

Rostislawitch took a deep breath. He couldn't decide what to do, whether to trust the Americans or not. He watched Thera walking to the door. He longed to trust her, but how could he, when she had so obviously lied?

"If I drank what they took, would I die?" Ferguson asked.

"You wouldn't drink it," said Rostislawitch. "The taste." He shook his head. "You would never drink it. Or eat it. Not in that form."

"So how is it spread?"

"If I talk to you, my friends in Russia—they'll never be left alone."

"If the material is used by the Iranians, hundreds of people may die," said Ferguson.

"You're wrong," said Rostislawitch. "It could be thousands, even millions. Maybe millions if they know their business."

"Then talk to me. You don't want their deaths on your soul."

Rostislawitch stared at Thera, silent.

"Help us," she said, looking back into the room. "You're not a murderer, Artur. Help us."

Sobbing, Rostislawitch began to explain the different ways the bacteria could be used.

4

NAPLES, ITALY

This is what came of improvisation.

Hamilton folded his arms, watching as the firemen played their hose on the burned-out building. Augusto Leterri, one of the Naples police lieutenants in charge of the investigation, stood beside him, talking on his cell phone to a superior.

Ferguson was one lucky son of a bitch, Hamilton thought. Always somehow at the right spot at the right time, riding the right twist of fate.

He kicked at a brick from the building, which had partially collapsed about twenty minutes after the explosion. The problem was, there hadn't been enough time for the gas to fill the basement space. Another half hour, and the explosion would have claimed the entire block. That was the way he liked it: complete and utter obliteration, destruction on a grand scale. One could use a gun—certainly he had—or even a knife or poison, but where was the art in that? Where was the statement of annihilation? Where was the assurance of success?

No, the gas explosion, with the extra diversion of the hired gunner—that was the way it should have happened. And it would have, had they walked down one of the three other blocks where the trap had been set. This just happened to be the last, happened to have a geography that favored luck.

Luck. Always the deciding factor when you improvised.

"I'm sorry for the interruption," said the detective. "That was my boss. As I was saying, I doubt this was the work of terrorists."

"Why?" asked Hamilton.

"The inspector has already found part of the gas pipe broken," said the detective. "If there were a bomb, there would be more residue. We will look more carefully, because you never know. But from the way the witnesses described it, *phooosh.*"

He made the sound of a fire, raising his hands up from his belly to illustrate.

"But we will look into your theory of terrorists," added the policeman.

"I would," said the MI6 agent. There was nothing like an intelligent man, Hamilton thought; he could be so easily fooled.

Of course, it was possible that when they discovered that the gas pipes had been broken in buildings along three other nearby streets, in effect surrounding the train station, they would conclude that it was too much of a coincidence to be accidental. Then they would think of Hamilton's theory. Or maybe they would find a witness who mentioned the men in the car, and the gun. That would set them in another direction entirely.

Most likely, though, they wouldn't. The Naples police had a great deal to do.

The detective reached into his pocket for a business card. "You should call me if you get any other tips," he told Hamilton. "We take terrorism very seriously. We are glad to cooperate."

"I will," said Hamilton. "If you'll excuse me, I should go and check in with my embassy, just to let them know that I've done my job."

5

Thomas Parnelles slid the yellow pencil between his fingers, then turned it around, spinning it across his hand as if he were a magician and it was his wand. Quick fingers and sleight of hand were great assets in the spy game, he'd been told as a young man, though as far as he could remember he'd never actually used either of those skills in the field.

Magic—now that was something altogether different. That he had used many times. Or at least attempted to.

The pencil fell from Parnelles's hand and skittered across the desk, toward the tiny digital recorder that was replaying what the Russian scientist had told Ferguson less than a half hour before.

Corrine Alston grabbed the pencil as it fell off the side of the desk.

The player stopped.

"That's it?" she asked Dan Slott. The CIA's Deputy Director of Operations looked at Jack Corrigan, the First Team's deskman. He nodded.

"Atha may be back in Iran by now," said Corrine.

"He wouldn't have gotten there yet," said Corrigan. "The plane that Rankin says he took has only about an eight-hundred-mile radius. They'd have to stop and refuel."

"The part about him going south bothers me," said Parnelles. "Iran has spread money around for camps in the Darfur area, allegedly for relief. It might be a cover for a base."

"If this material is as dangerous as it seems, they might not want to work on in it in Iran," said Slott. "We are looking at the satellite data, and we've got a Global Hawk unmanned spy plane en route."

"A laboratory hidden in a relief camp will be difficult to detect by satellite," said Parnelles.

"Colonel Van Buren and the 777th Special Forces Group is being positioned to respond if necessary," said Slott.

"I think it's premature to consider an assault," said Corrine.

"From what we know of the bacteria, it can be prepared to be used relatively easily," said Parnelles. "They could launch an attack in a relatively short time."

"They'd be inviting massive retaliation," said Corrine. "A full-scale invasion."

"If we could figure out what was going on," said Slott.

"It would reverse the entire course of their foreign policy over the past year and a half," answered Corrine. "Everything they've been aiming to do—they've made major concessions on funding Hezbollah. Even without the nuclear treaty. This doesn't fit in."

"It does if you're Parsa Moshen and your power is slipping," said Parnelles. "The best thing that could happen would be an attack by the U.S. The Revolutionary Guard would become the most important force in the country once more. Even if you were invaded. You look at Al Qaeda in Afghanistan, in Iraq, and you say, 'If they could do it, we can do it.'"

"That's dangerous thinking," said Corrine.

"Exactly," said the CIA Director, slipping back in his chair.

MISRATAH, LIBYA

The pilots Paul told Guns and Rankin about could generally be found in a hotel overlooking the sea in Qasar Ahmed, the town next to Misratah on the Mediterranean; it was a Western-style hotel, which meant it had a bar and served alcohol.

"Very early," Paul told them as they rode the elevator up to the bar, which was located on the roof. "We may not find anyone."

"We have time," said Guns.

The bar consisted of a small, air-conditioned room and a much larger open patio, shielded from the sun by a large piece of striped canvas. The material flapped in the breeze, pulling hard against the ropes that held it down against the metal poles. Rankin and Guns followed as Paul led them to the far corner, commandeering a table that had an unrestricted view of the sea.

"Be back," said Paul, jumping up a moment after sitting.

"What do you think?" Rankin asked. "You think he's completely nuts?"

"I don't know," said Guns. "He definitely lost a few brain cells along the way."

"I hate hippies."

"My mom was kind of a hippy. For a while. When she was young."

"She doesn't count."

A waiter appeared. "You want?" he asked, his accent and tone making it clear that while he knew some English, he was far from fluent.

Then again, his English was miles ahead of their Arabic.

"Juice," said Rankin. "Apple juice."

"That'd be good," said Guns.

The waiter didn't understand him.

"Apple juice," said Guns. "Yes."

"OK. Juice. OK," said the waiter.

Rankin stared at the light green water rippling toward the horizon. There were dozens and dozens of ships and countless boats bobbing on it.

"Atha could go in any of those boats; we'll never find him," he told Guns.

"Why are you always so grouchy?"

"What do you mean, grouchy?"

"Yeah, you're always like, why are we doing this, or this won't work, or whatever."

"I'll try to be more cheerful for you."

"Be cheerful for yourself. Think positive."

Guns looked up and saw Paul coming through the door from the enclosed bar area. Another man, gray hair tied in a ponytail at the back of his head, followed him. He wore aviator frame sunglasses and a thick leather jacket despite the heat.

"This is George Burns," said Paul, introducing the man with a wink to let them know it wasn't the pilot's real name. "George, my friends Guns and Rankin."

"Hey." George Burns sat down. He was Caucasian, though deeply tanned, and wore American-style work boots and Levi's. But his shirt was the sort a native Libyan might wear, a loosely fitting tunic that fell below his waist. He reeked of alcohol.

"These are the spies," Paul told him. "They're looking for Ahmed and Anghuyu Jahan—Atha."

"I know where Atha is," said George Burns.

"Where?" asked Rankin.

"I'll take you there. But it'll cost you."

"You're lying," said Rankin.

"No more than you."

"How much do you want?" asked Guns.

"Fifty grand. American. Small bills."

"You're out of your fuckin' mind," said Rankin, getting up.

"A thousand," said Guns, tapping his partner.

"What is this, good cop, bad cop?" George Burns leaned back. "A thousand won't even pay for my fuel. Fifty grand is a good price."

Still standing, Rankin pushed his chair back with his leg and folded his arms. The guy seemed like all bluff. "Five thousand," he told him.

"No way. You guys don't realize what you're getting into."

"Tell us," said Rankin.

"I ain't worried about you."

The waiter came over with a bottle of Jack Daniel's and four glasses.

"Where's our apple juice?" Rankin asked.

"They don't serve juice," said Paul.

"Get us water then. Water?"

George Burns smiled. He took the bottle and poured himself four fingers' worth of the sour mash Tennessee whiskey into his tumbler. Paul asked for the water in Arabic, then put about a shot's worth of Jack into his own glass.

"Used to be this stuff was potent," said George Burns, holding up the glass so he could gaze at the liquid. "Now it's only eighty proof. Iced tea. Everything fades."

He drank the glass in a gulp.

"We can get you ten thousand," said Rankin.

"Fifty. Before I fly."

"Can't do it."

"Oh, well." George Burns picked the bottle back up and poured another four fingers' worth into his glass.

"Maybe we could get you twenty-five," said Guns. "But it would have to go into a bank account. We don't carry cash."

"We could figure out a bank account," said George Burns. "That we could do. But it would have to be fifty."

"You have no idea where he went," said Rankin.

George Burns turned toward him, stared for thirty seconds without saying anything, then looked back at Guns. "Put the money in my account, and we take off."

"You're going to fly?" said Rankin.

"I'm not walking. That's a real desert out there, Jack. A real desert."

"You don't have to fly us," said Guns. "Just tell us where it is."

"No. I take you there. I don't want any fighters on my tail, either. No paratroopers, nobody but you."

"My partner comes with me."

George Burns made a face, but didn't object. "We fly over their place once, come back. You mark the location with a GPS or whatever you want. Nothing else happens until I'm back, safe on the ground. *Capisce?*"

"Just tell us where it is," said Rankin.

"I take you there or no deal."

"You don't know where it is, do you?" said Rankin.

"You'd better tell your friend his attitude is about to bump the price another ten grand."

"We're not doing fifty," said Rankin. "Not even if you really do know where it is."

Guns got up and walked away from the table. Frowning, Rankin went with him.

"I think we gotta take a shot," said Guns.

"No effin' way," said Rankin.

"A flight of the Global Hawk probably costs twice that."

"I don't think he really knows," said Rankin. "He's a drunk."

"Corrigan can figure out some way to put the money in an account and then get it back if it's a bust, don't you think?"

"How do they get us back?"

"I trust him for that. Ferg would do it."

Rankin looked across the patio. George Burns had just downed his second glass of whiskey.

"Talk to Corrigan," Rankin told Guns. "Let me stop this guy from drinking anything else before he gets too loaded to talk, let alone fly."

7

NAPLES, ITALY

Ferguson watched from the doorway as the three Fiats drove slowly up the street and stopped near the entrance to the factory. Two men got out of the first car and walked forward, scanning the area.

Ferguson waited until they had passed, then slipped out the door, his Glock pistol in hand.

"You find anything, let me know," he said to them.

The man sitting in the passenger seat of the second car rolled down his window.

"You Ferguson?"

"Captain Helfers?"

"Yes, sir."

"You know where the Ramada is?"

"No, sir, but the cars have Magellan units."

"Program it in. Once we go, we don't stop. All right? Nobody stops. Tell them."

"Yes, sir."

Ferguson went back into the building. Rostislawitch was still sitting on the cement floor, legs folded yoga-style.

"Come on, Rosty, time to hit the road," Ferguson told him.

The scientist didn't move. He was very tired, and still in shock.

"We have to go in case our friends come back," said Ferguson. "We're only a couple of blocks away. This isn't safe."

Ferguson slipped the gun into the front of his belt. "Thing is, Rosty, T Rex has taken two shots at you and missed both times. I'm sure he's missed opportunities before, but I don't know what the odds would be on your surviving shot number three."

"Artur, it's the only way," said Thera, kneeling next to him. "Come with us now. At least you'll be safe."

Rostislawitch turned his head and looked into her eyes. It was possible, still possible, that they had staged everything for his benefit.

"I know it's hard to trust us," said Thera, putting her hand on his shoulder. "But come with us now. We can get you cleaned up, get you something to eat. Then you can decide."

Rostislawitch rose. He'd already decided. He had to trust them. He just had to. Whatever doubts remained.

Ferguson was already out the door. The civilian-clothed Marines were now at either end of the block, scanning up and down. He opened the door to Captain Helfers's sedan, then waited as Rostislawitch and Thera emerged from the building.

"You're in the middle," Ferguson told the scientist as Thera ran around the other side. After Rostislawitch was inside the car, Ferguson took a last look down the block, then got in and slammed the door. "Go; let's go," he said. "Just go."

"I'm not supposed to ask any questions," said Helfers as the cars sped down the block and turned toward the highway.

"Which is good because I'm not going to give any answers," said Ferguson.

"But I just—"

"No buts. You ask me no questions, I tell you no lies." He patted the Marine captain on the shoulder. "Tell the car behind us to get out in front at the next turn."

"You sure?"

Ferguson just laughed. Helfers, who was in touch with the others via radio, passed along the instruction.

They'd gone two miles on the highway when Ferguson leaned forward again. "Take a right and get down that exit," he told the driver. "Wait until the last second."

"But you said—"

"Right here. Don't tell the other cars."

Helfers started to protest.

"Relax, Captain. I've done this before." Ferguson turned and watched the road, making sure they weren't being followed.

"Looks clear, Ferg," said Thera, who'd been watching herself.

"Yeah. But that street looked clear when they tried shooting us up, too." Ferguson leaned into the front. "Straight. Then two more blocks, you take a left. We're not going to the hotel."

"Where then?" asked Helfers.

Ferguson shook his head. "When we get there, I'll let you know."

Ferguson's directions took them out of the city and down along the coastline five miles, to a small motel overlooking the sea. He'd considered taking Rostislawitch to the American air base, where he could provide much better security, but decided it might spook him worse. The scientist was still unsure whether he was doing the right thing or not.

Ferguson jumped out of the car as soon as they pulled up. He went inside and rented two rooms, checking and scanning them himself before letting Thera, Rostislawitch, and the two Marines in.

"Actually, we should get back to the base," said Helfers.

"Sorry, Captain, you're with us for a while."

"Can we call our men at least and tell them we're OK?"

"Corrigan will take care of that," Ferguson told him. "Don't worry. No one's going to accuse you of going AWOL. Park the cars over there," he added, pointing across the lot. "Away from our rooms, but where we can see them."

The two rooms Ferguson had taken were on the top floor of the two-story motel. Built in the 1970s, the hotel was similar to many American motels, with the rooms opening directly onto an exterior balcony or walkway. They had a good view of the highway and surrounding area, and while there was only one entrance from the road, there were trails down the hillside that would make it easy to escape by foot.

The motel did not, however, have room service, and Ferguson was still not comfortable enough to let anyone go for food, even though there was a place just down the highway. The truth was, the attack on the street had caught him off-guard. If Kiska had orchestrated it—and Corrigan's belated warning that she was in town certainly made that seem likely—then Ferguson not only had been wrong about her but had everything lined up in his head out of whack.

The two men in the car who had fired at them looked to be local street thugs, not very good with guns, or maybe not paid enough to make sure they hit what they were theoretically aiming at. But turning on the gas in the building beforehand—he realized now that he had smelled it, which perhaps accounted for the split second of alertness that he did manage—that was a T Rex move. The assassin must have known that they were in Naples, and at the train station. He—or she—had then calculated that they would go somewhere nearby. The plan had to have been made at least a half hour before they were actually on the street, and the order to go must have been given by someone watching them. Someone Ferguson hadn't seen.

Ferguson knew he wasn't omniscient. Even the best ops got blindsided occasionally; his father had. In truth, Ferguson knew he'd probably been caught off-guard like this dozens and dozens of times on every mission.

He still didn't like it.

Then again, the master assassin was slipping, as well. Was the legend overblown, as most legends were, or was Rostislawitch merely very lucky?

Maybe a little of both.

Thera had Rostislawitch sit in the chair near the desk. She pulled up his pant leg and examined the line of cuts on his shin. They weren't serious. She went into the bathroom and wet a washcloth to clean them.

"Artur, how are you feeling?" Ferguson asked Rostislawitch in Russian.

"Fine."

"She doesn't speak Russian very well," Ferguson said. "Would you mind if we used English?"

"She's a beautiful woman," said Rostislawitch, still using Russian.

"Yeah, she is," said Ferguson.

"Is she your lover?"

"I wish." Ferguson smiled. "English?"

Rostislawitch nodded.

"We have some people tracking Atha, but to be honest, he's pretty clever," said Ferguson. "If you help us, I have a way that we might be able to find him. If we do that, we can get the bacteria back before it does any harm."

"How?"

"From what I've seen of Atha's background, he's not an expert on biological warfare."

"He knows nothing."

"What if we told him that what he took is missing a key ingredient? Then we offer to supply it to him."

"It doesn't work that way," said Rostislawitch. "The bacteria—it makes an infection, like any disease; once it's in your system, it is the same as having food poisoning."

"That's not my point," said Ferguson. He looked out the window, watching the parking lot. Helfers and the other Marine were watching from the other room.

"There has to be something you could tell him," said Thera. "What if you planned to modify the bacteria in some way before they were used?"

"A specialist would know."

"Atha is not a specialist," said Thera.

"He'll have specialists with him. He is working with scientists, at least one. They had questions only a scientist would know to ask."

"Well, you have to try something," said Thera. She rose abruptly, angry with him: not because he had been planning to sell the bacteria to Atha or even because he had been foolish enough to let the Iranian take it, but because he was giving up.

"She's prettier when she's mad," said Ferguson in Russian.

"I know this is part of an act," answered Rostislawitch.

"It's no act," said Ferguson.

"What are you saying?" asked Thera. "I don't speak Russian. Use English."

"I told your friend you're both acting."

"I'm not acting, Artur. You said yourself, a lot of people could die." She tossed the washcloth into the bathroom, then turned to Ferguson. "I need air."

He didn't want to let her go outside, but the look on her face made it clear she was determined. If it was an act it was a good one, because it fooled him, too.

"Be real careful," Ferguson told her. "Here, swap guns."

His fingers lingered on hers for a moment as he took the small Czech hideaway. But that was the only luxury he allowed himself, and Thera quickly left.

"A game," said Rostislawitch in Russian. "Good cop, bad cop."

"No. She's the good cop. I'm just a prick."

Rostislawitch looked at the younger man's grin. He'd saved Rostislawitch's life, so at least as far as he was concerned, Ferguson wasn't a prick.

"You were the one on the motorcycle, yes?"

"The red Ducati," said Ferguson. "Nice bike."

Rostislawitch saw it again, the man hurtling at him. The explosion had come a few seconds later.

Twice Ferguson had saved his life. Once might be a coincidence or perhaps staged, but twice was not.

And given these second chances to live, what should he do with them? Let Atha go, let him kill untold others?

"Maybe I could tell them something that an expert would find believable. It would depend on how far they've gotten. But I don't know if I can get to Atha. He didn't always respond right away."

"He will if he thinks he has to."

"He's very clever. He may realize it is a lie."

"Got to give it a shot, no?"

Artur nodded. "Let us try."

8

The area around the Naples train station was filled with police and emergency vehicles by the time Kiska Babev arrived. She joined the line of commuters going into the station. She spoke almost no Italian, and the local Neapolitan dialect was lost to her, but through English she managed to puzzle out that there had been some sort of gas explosion nearby. But that explanation didn't quite fit with the increased security at the train station, where a policeman insisted on going through Kiska's purse and briefcase before allowing her inside. She asked him what was going on, but he pretended not to understand English and then shooed her inside.

The Russian FSB agent had put a watch on Rostislawitch's bank accounts and was alerted to both of his cash withdrawals within a few minutes of their being made. While the first one had alerted her to the fact that he was here, it was the second one that troubled her. The cash would be enough to buy a train or airplane ticket to dozens of places, and while he'd have to show ID to get out of the country, the cash would allow him to avoid using his credit card, which they were also monitoring.

She'd searched the airport without finding him, but had to wait until a backup officer arrived from Rome to take her place before coming here. There had been two dozen flights between the time the second withdrawal was made and when she had arrived; the number of trains was three times that. There were simply too many places for them to check.

The delay between the withdrawals suggested a change in plans following a meeting of some sort. Maybe he'd decided to go to Iran. If so, she might never find him.

Few, if any, of the travelers in the station seemed bothered by the extra security outside. Kiska walked through the concourse swiftly, wanting a feel for the layout of the place before actually searching more carefully. She walked over to the platform area, scanning the knots of waiting people. Once or twice she thought she saw the scientist, but closer examination proved she was wrong. She made her way to waiting areas, then began drifting through the shops when her pager buzzed.

She walked over to the far side of the station, making sure she had no one around her, and called her Moscow office.

"This is Colonel Babev. Antov?"

"Colonel, the scientist has just sent a text message using his private account."

"From where?"

"We're trying to trace it now. I have the message for you."

"Tell me."

"It is in English, addressed to the same account as the one last week saying he would be in Bologna. But this is very explicit: 'You have taken the suitcase. I was afraid you were not honest. As a precaution, I kept the phalange virus necessary to convert the DNA. The price is now twice, and two European Union passports, clean. I will be in Tripoli at the Alfonse Hotel this evening. I estimate that the virus will survive for another twenty-four hours. For technical references, check these sites.' And then there is a list of Web sites. Our consultants have not yet gone through them. They involve DNA in some way."

"The phalange is a type of virus that is used to introduce specific mutations," she told her lieutenant. "Get me a reservation at that hotel. Get me people—I want Stefan in Tripoli. Have him bring a team, Petra or—who was the girl from St. Petersburg?"

"Neda—on such short notice, Colonel, I think it would be impossible to get her. She's working with Demidas."

"Then tell Stefan to put together the best people he can find. In Libya, things are much more open. And ample weapons."

"I understand, Colonel."

"Get me a flight there. A ticket for Kiril as well. He's at the Naples airport now. Make them separate flights if possible. How long will it take you to trace the computer?"

"Another hour, maybe longer."

"Was it in Naples?"

"We're not sure."

It would be easier to take him in Tripoli, Kiska thought. But he might be prepared as well. Surprise him here and be done with it.

"Call me directly when you find it," she said.

"Yes, Colonel. I will."

9

NORTHEASTERN SUDAN

Atha, tired from his travel, slept late. He rose just in time for the noonday prayers, then took a long walk around the camp. The buses and trucks he had hired were arriving from the Sudan. By nightfall, there would be seventy-three, enough to transport five thousand people. The buses would then drive three, four, five hundred miles, to Al Jaw in Libya; Dunquiah in Sudan; Aswân, Abu Simbel, Al Kharijab, in Egypt; to Chad and Darfur. From there, their passengers would fly to France, Italy, Denmark, Egypt, Great Britain, the U.S. Within a week, many would be in hospitals, a few in the grave.

The West would be at the start of an epidemic of a sort unseen since the Black Plague of Medieval times.

It was a beautiful thought.

And he would be rich, and finally truly powerful. An even more beautiful thought.

Most of the refugees in the camp were busy bidding one another good-bye and getting their things together for the journey. Atha nodded at the families as he passed. They smiled at him; a few even lowered their heads in silent tribute to his status as their savior.

When he returned from his walk, Atha found Dr. Hamid was squatting on the floor of the lab in front of a sealed glass work area. He was wearing gloves and a special protective suit, though not a hood.

"Doctor?"

"Please stay near the door. Do not touch anything," said Hamid. "I will be with you in a moment."

The bacterial colonies that Rostislawitch had provided had bloomed and then crashed before their arrival; only a few thousand had survived the transport. Had these been ordinary bacteria and the conditions here perfect, those few thousand would have been more than enough to seed thousands of new colonies. But the hybridization of the bacteria and Dr. Hamid's relatively primitive lab complicated matters. The colonies were growing only about half as fast as his models suggested they would.

"It is slower than we hoped," said the scientist finally. "But it will do."

He turned around and faced Atha. "I should be ready to give the first doses this evening. We'll have to start slower than planned—just four hundred people. By tomorrow evening, we will be ready for the rest."

Atha nodded. The delay meant that some of the transports would sit here overnight, but otherwise it was a trivial matter, not worth bothering the minister about. In all but a few cases, the airplanes waiting for them were chartered, and would wait indefinitely. For the others, new tickets would not be a problem. The travel documents, visas, medical certificates, had been prepared weeks ago.

"From now on, you should take proper precautions in here," said Dr. Hamid. "A full suit. You must decontaminate carefully, wash very thoroughly. Remember, the material is very dangerous."

"I thought you said as long as I wash I am all right."

"If the bacteria gets into your mouth, it will enter your digestive tract. From that point, there is no stopping it."

"I will be careful," said Atha, deciding that he would simply not visit the laboratory again.

"Once we are ready, I would advise you not to eat or drink anything, either. Bottled water that you yourself handle, nothing else. The juice should be an incredible medium for the bacteria to grow, and I do not doubt that infection will be very easy. Remember, it is more potent than common E. coli. There waste is the main means of transmission. Here any fluid, even sweat, may make the transmission. A swimming pool, food, a washcloth, can become a medium of transfer. The bacteria is extremely virile. The professor was quite a genius."

"I have no doubt," said Atha.

"We should leave as soon as the distribution is complete," said the scientist. "The longer we stay, the greater the risk of infection."

Atha nodded. The final phase of the plan called for them to travel to northern Iran, where Navid would prepare additional cultures for storage and possible future use. Atha would look after his financial affairs, and take a vacation, assuming the minister did not have other plans.

The Revolutionary Guards were not universally appreciated in Iran, and Atha realized that the minister's overt power play might elicit a strong response. Atha was unsure exactly what the minister was planning, whether it would be a real coup or simply a putsch behind the scenes. Either way, Atha would be prepared, with money in several overseas accounts as well as Iranian banks.

Assuming the minister paid. Like anyone with power, he was not entirely to be trusted.

Atha took his leave of Dr. Hamid and went back to the hut that served as his quarters. He turned on his laptop computer to see that the minister had forwarded the payment to his accounts.

The money had not yet gone through.

Atha rose from his desk. He tried not to jump to conclusions—there must be an explanation.

And if there wasn't?

Then he would send his hordes to Tehran rather than Europe and America. There the devastation would be considerably greater, as the sanitary conditions in the poorest areas were terrible.

Atha sat back down, calming himself. It must be an error, he decided. He considered whether it would be wiser to talk to the minister by phone or to send him an instant message. Messaging him had the advantage of letting Atha craft what he would say. But the phone would bring an instant response.

Could he hold his temper on the phone? Perhaps not.

Still debating, Atha signed into the message service. There were several unread messages—including one that claimed to be from Dark Bear: Rostislawitch's code name.

An old one, Atha thought, scrolling through the others in queue. But then he realized that it had been sent only a few minutes before.

Most likely he's wondering what happened to me, thought Atha, selecting it to read:

You have taken the suitcse. I was afraid you were not honest. As a precaution, I kept the phalange vrs necessary to convert DNA. The price is now twice, and two EU psprts. In Tripoli at the Alfonse Hotel this evening. I est virus will survive for another 24 hs. . . .

The message was so long it spilled into two screens. A second text message added Web sites explaining the science.

Atha jumped out of his chair to get Dr. Hamid.

10

NAPLES, ITALY

As soon as the text message was sent, Ferguson had Corrigan send two more cars of Marines to the computer café.

"Go to the navy base. Get over to Tripoli," Ferguson told Thera as he pushed her into the car after Rostislawitch. "Wait for me."

"What about you?"

"I have an errand to run here."

"Ferg—"

"I'll see you in Tripoli." He hesitated, then leaned forward and gave her a kiss on the cheek. Then he banged on the top of the car. "Get going; go," he said, backing away.

The narrow street went straight up the side of a hill so steep that much of the sidewalk had been laid as steps. A worn metal pipe rail protected the street side. A good number of the storefronts had been converted into cheap apartments; the rest sold mostly secondhand items: books, clothing, even used plumbing. Above the stores were more apartments, their inhabitants a mixture of poor immigrants and young people who styled themselves bohemians and frequented the basement cafés that lined the block and the nearby avenue.

Ferguson crossed the street and forced the door on one of the buildings, trotting upstairs to the top floor. Seeing that there was no door up to the roof, he opened the window on the landing and found a fire escape ladder; it ran up as well as down. In a few seconds, he was walking across the roof's sticky tar to the front of the building, where he had a good view of most of the block.

Someone had brought a beach chair up. It was weather-beaten, but it was better than sitting on the tar. Ferguson carried it to the edge of the roof and sat down, feeling a little like he was at a baseball game.

Not the Sox. No one ever got a quiet seat like this at Fenway.

He peered over the side, watching the street. He shouldn't have kissed Thera, he thought. It was a distraction and a mistake.

But now that he had, what was he going to do next? What was he going to tell her? That he loved her?

The truth was, he played the rogue so much that being honest felt strange. He wasn't even sure how to phrase it.

I love you.

He didn't need anything else.

What he couldn't say was, *I have cancer. Maybe I'm going to die.*

Maybe not. The doctor seems pretty positive. Most people with thyroid cancer live.

Of course, usually it was caught a bit sooner. Usually it didn't come back. You could read the statistics any way you wanted.

Ferguson remembered he'd forgotten to take his pills that morning.

He reached into his pocket for his pillbox. A cab was just driving up the street. He slipped down near the edge of the roof, lying flat. A woman got out of the taxi, a blonde.

Kiska.

Ferguson rose and began trotting back to the fire escape.

Kiska brushed past the attendant and walked through the long, narrow room, surveying the patrons at the computers lined against both walls. Rostislawitch wasn't among them.

An alcove sat at the very end of the room. Kiska leaned forward, poking her head across its threshold and spotting a staircase. The steps were blocked off by a folding gate, the kind used to protect toddlers and infants from a fall.

She walked to it and pulled it out of her way.

"Signora! *Scusi*," said the attendant. "Ma'am, excuse me. You cannot go up there."

Kiska was already on the stairs, which turned after five steps. She heard something scraping above, then a yap—a little dog appeared at the top when Kiska turned the corner. It was kept there by a gate similar to the one below. The room was a kitchen—one that didn't appear to have been cleaned in months.

"Nice puppy," she said, looking around.

"Signora!" The attendant had followed her up the stairs. "There are no computers up there. It is my apartment. Please."

The attendant was a young man in his early twenties who looked the perfect computer geek; Kiska sized him up in an instant and decided she would have no trouble tossing him down the steps.

"I'm looking for someone," she said, and she pushed aside the fence holding the dog in. Freed, the animal scampered past her, and past the swooping grab of its master.

"*Madonna*," said the man, adding more serious curses as he followed the dog.

Kiska walked into the kitchen, turned the corner, and surveyed the apartment's two rooms. Clearly Rostislawitch wasn't here.

By this time, Ferguson had come down from the roof and crossed the street. He was just opening the door to the Internet café when he was met by a speeding ball of fur, which propelled itself through the open space and out into the street. The attendant, cursing at him for letting the animal escape, tried to pass as well. But the store was so narrow that there was room in the aisle for only one person at a time; he bounced into Ferguson, who threw him out of his way.

"Kiska!" yelled Ferguson. "We have to talk."

He drew the Glock from his belt, holding it behind his back.

"*Jesus!*" yelled the attendant, scrambling to his feet and running outside. One of the three people in the café using the computers threw himself to the floor; the other two, not entirely sure what was going on, stared at Ferguson as he walked past.

Upstairs, Kiska heard Ferguson yelling. As much as she liked the

American, his interference tended to be annoying, and she didn't care to discuss anything with him right now.

"Kiska!" Ferguson yelled as he reached the archway. He glanced back at the people in the store, staring at him in unbelief. "Good time to run," he told them. "Remember to save your work."

He waited until they were in the street, then put two hands on the Glock and threw himself across the space in front to the stairs, rolling over and expecting to be ambushed.

Nothing.

Jumping to his feet, Ferguson yelled for Kiska again, then took the steps two at a time, right shoulder against the wall, gun ready to fire.

"Kiska, we really have to talk," he said in Russian. "Tell me what you know about dinosaurs. T Rex, in particular."

The landing was clear. He started up, knowing she had to be close.

"T Rex, Kiska. How familiar are you with T Rex?"

Ferguson paused at the entrance to the kitchen. He couldn't hear anything, but from the layout he gathered that the rest of the apartment was around the bend in the wall. He tiptoed toward it, then saw a small metal toaster on the counter back near the door. Retreating, he grabbed the toaster, holding the gun toward the passage to the rest of the apartment.

"I have some questions about where you were at certain times. One of those has to do with a CIA officer named Dalton. If it weren't for him, honestly, I could blow this all off. You know, bigger fish to fry."

He put the toaster down and slid it across the floor. The other rooms were reflected on its side.

"Kiska? Would it be easier if I spoke English?"

He saw something moving in the reflection. Ferguson threw himself on the floor, rolling across the space, gun up, ready—and aimed right at a curtain at the far side of the apartment, fluttering in the breeze.

He ran to it and looked down. There was a fire escape that led to an alley, no trace of Kiska.

Ferguson climbed out, then jumped down into the alley. It took a second before he saw the low fence that led to the street behind the building. He ran to it and hopped over, just in time to see a blonde getting into a cab a block and a half away.

It was too far to tell for sure if it was Kiska, but Ferguson had no doubt it was. He watched as the car drove off.

"Just as well," he muttered to himself. "Just as well."

11

NORTHEASTERN SUDAN

"I'm just not sure," said Dr. Hamid, looking up from the computer. "These Web pages Rostislawitch referred you to give the general procedure for using a type of virus to modify bacteria. The procedure is common, but that's not a guarantee. It may be a bluff. It may not. He doesn't give real information about the virus or the bacteria. I have no way of telling."

"Examine the bacteria then," said Atha. "See if they are dangerous."

"They are a type of E. coli. It is in the family that he was working on, according to the papers that we have. But to know whether it is specifically the type that he developed as a weapon—I would need much more information. It's very active, and its genetic structure is unique. But the only way for me to really tell would be to infect someone and see what happens. And that could take several days."

"If he does have a virus, will we be able to change these germs?" Atha suddenly saw his fortune evaporating.

And then his life.

The minister still had not answered his query. Another problem. But this had precedence.

"I think we can follow the procedure, if it is straightforward," said Dr. Hamid. "But we were set up here to replicate the bacteria, which is relatively easy. Beyond that—"

"Yes, I know. No guarantees."

Atha needed to think. He stepped outside of the hut, wanting to walk, to move. Some of the refugees, anxious to be moving on, had gathered nearby. They saw him, and began cheering.

Atha put up his hand in acknowledgement. If he didn't let them leave soon, they'd probably riot.

It might very well be just a bluff. Rostislawitch was probably angry that he had been cheated and was fighting back.

He couldn't afford to take a chance, though, could he? Traveling to Tripoli, as annoying as it might be, was possible—Ahmed had the plane fueled and ready to go.

Dr. Hamid had turned off the computer and stepped outside the cottage. He was looking forward to the end of this. He'd been in the Sudan for nearly three months getting ready.

"I will go to Tripoli," said Atha. "Prepare some of the drinks with the bacteria, and get people ready to leave. Because it may just be a trick."

"Yes, that makes sense."

"Good. I'll call as soon as I know something."

12

OVER THE LIBYAN DESERT, APPROACHING SUDAN

As far as Rankin could tell, George Burns had only one thing in common with his namesake—he liked to smoke big, thick cigars. And he liked to smoke them in his plane, which stank up the entire aircraft.

Which was saying something, because the airplane was comparatively large—a 1960s-vintage two-engine Hawker Siddely 748 that in its prime regularly carried forty-eight passengers. The plane had seen use as both a passenger and a cargo aircraft, ferrying people first around India and then around Africa. George Burns had bought it from a somewhat shady government official in Senegal, overhauled the engines, replaced the avionics, and given it a fresh coat of paint.

Rankin sat in the copilot's seat. Guns made do with a jump seat immediately behind the pilot.

"Not much of a view," said Rankin as they flew over the desert.

George Burns didn't answer. He occasionally reached for the throttle lever between the seats, and every so often would glance at his global positioning map. But otherwise he stared straight ahead at the mountains that marked the edge of the desert.

"You don't really know where it is, do you?" asked Rankin. "You just have a general idea."

George Burns took his cigar out of his mouth, examined the ash—two inches long—then put it back.

Rankin saw a shadow on the desert floor to the west. It was from an airplane, and for a moment he thought it was their shadow, cast in an odd direction. Then he realized that it was too small, and shaped wrong. He spotted the plane a few feet above the shadow, moving across the earth as if it were part of a toy display.

"Hey, another airplane," he said, pointing.

George Burns turned and looked, staring as the aircraft moved past. It was no more than a mile and a half away.

"We're getting closer," he said, and then he didn't say anything else.

13

KALAMATA, GREECE

Col. Charles Van Buren jogged up the ladder into the command center of the 777th's MC-17, a Globemaster III combat cargo aircraft specially equipped to support the Special Forces Group. Van Buren and his men had just arrived from Aviano, Italy, relocating here so they could strike into Africa if needed. Additional support units, including tankers, C-130s, and Osprey aircraft, were being scrambled to assist.

"Mr. Ferguson for you, sir," said the communications specialist, holding up the phone.

Van Buren took the phone and sat down at the console. "Ferg, what's going?"

"Hey, Van. Corrigan give you the background yet?"

"We're looking for an Iranian with Russian biological warfare material. Maybe he's in Libya, maybe the Sudan. They're looking. That's what I know."

"Rankin and Guns have a lead on a possible camp. They hired a pilot to take them out there. He's real paranoid, so he may be right. If they find something, I say you hit it. But if Atha were smart, he'd be already back in Iran."

"Are you going to follow him?"

"Actually, I'm trying to get him to come to me," Ferguson said. He explained that he had convinced the Russian scientist to set a trap in Tripoli. "I could use some muscle there, three or four guys who can blend in."

They worked out the details.

"You doing all right, Ferg? You sound a little tired," said Van Buren when they were done.

"Yeah, I'm cool. Listen, be ready for anything on this. The professor says this stuff will tear your insides out and make you happy to die. You guys go in, you wear space suits, all right? MOPP NBCs, no fooling around."

"My guys are checking them out right now, Ferg. Talk to you later."

14

When Dr. Hamid first heard the airplane in the distance, he thought Atha had turned back for some reason. But after listening for a few more moments, Hamid realized the drone was of something larger. His first thought was that it was a relief plane, though they rarely passed this way. Then he thought it might be a flight from Chad, which had propeller-driven SF 260 trainers converted to attack craft, which its air force used against "insurgents"—which in actual practice meant defenseless civilians in camps like theirs.

"Be ready with the missiles," he told the Palestinian. Then Hamid went and put the bacteria into a safe where it would survive a bombing attack.

The Palestinian had already assembled his missile teams by the time the aircraft appeared. It was a two-engine plane that he did not recognize—not a fighter, he thought, but not a relief craft, either. It flew at about a thousand feet over the jagged ridge to the west; in his experience, no plane would fly that low unless it meant to land or strafe.

"Observe," he told the men over the radio. There were two teams, each with an American-made Stinger heat-seeking missile. Shoulder-launched, the weapons had been given nearly two decades before to freedom fighters in Afghanistan, then sold after the war on the black market. Though old, they were nonetheless potent; a low-flying, slow plane like this was an easy target.

The airplane passed overhead without turning to land. Just as the Palestinian was going to order the group on the east to fire, it turned back.

"Observe," he told his men again. "Be ready."

15

Rankin used binoculars to get a look at the camp. There was a landing strip, but no plane. The puzzling thing was the buses—it looked as if it were a school parking lot.

"Looks more like a camping ground than a refugee camp," said Rankin as George Burns circled back. "You sure that's it?"

George Burns didn't say anything. His cigar had burned down to a nub, the ash nearly at his lips, but it didn't seem to bother him.

Guns leaned close to the window over Rankin's shoulder, taking pictures with his small digital camera.

"What's with the buses?" Guns asked George Burns.

"Don't know." The pilot spoke in short bursts, keeping the cigar riveted to his lips. "Never saw them before. Only been over twice."

Burns pulled back on the wheel. He'd come down low so they could take pictures, but now he wasn't feeling too good about it. Even for fifty thousand dollars, there was only so much risk he was willing to take.

"There's no lab or anything down there," said Rankin. "If the Iranian came here, he didn't stay. Where can you go from here?"

"Shit!" yelled George Burns, spitting the cigar from his mouth.

Rankin thought he'd burned himself, then saw there was a red light flashing at the left side of the pilot's panel. He heard something like a waterfall behind him.

Protective flares. Someone had fired a missile.

"Fuck," said George Burns again, and a sharp shudder gripped the plane.

The missile hit the right engine, blowing it apart and starting a fire in the wing. If it weren't for the fire, George Burns would have been able to save the plane; the Siddely was a durable aircraft, and he'd flown it on one engine more than a half-dozen times. But the fire spread through the wing, and within seconds he began losing control.

"Buckle yourselves in," he said, searching for someplace to land. The camp was located on the far side of a narrow range of low mountains; beyond them to the northeast was open desert. George Burns held the plane up as long as he could, trying to get past the ridge to a point where he could glide into the sand.

His right wing began tipping upward; he struggled to hold it, then felt the controls start to give way—the lines that worked the controls had broken and he was losing the hydraulic fluid. Cursing, he jabbed at the pedals and tried pulling back on the control column, desperately trying to position the body of the plane to take most of the shock when it hit the ground. They were low—two hundred feet—but going too fast to land comfortably, even if they'd had a strip beneath them. He struggled to stay airborne as long as possible, let more speed bleed off, get his wings back level—he needed them level so they wouldn't tip, would just slide in, skim across the desert as he'd done twice before; third time was the charm, they said. . . .

The tip of the left wing hit the ground, jerking the right side of the plane forward as the belly slammed into the sand. The plane skidded sideways, sliding down a rough hill and then tobogganing up and across into a flatter plain of sand. Dirt and smoke flew everywhere; parts of the plane fell off and others disintegrated; the spine of the aircraft snapped in two.

But as crash landings went, it wasn't that bad. The plane remained relatively intact, and most of the heavy impact—and damage—was behind the flight deck. All things considered, George Burns had done an admirable job landing.

Unfortunately, Burns was not in a position to appreciate it. Thrown forward, his head had hit the dash; he died of a cerebral hemorrhage before Rankin and Guns managed to undo their seat belts.

"You all right?" Guns asked.

"I think I busted my arm."

Rankin blinked his eyes. He saw two of everything in front of him.

"I think we're on fire," said Guns. He stood, unsteadily, and turned to go out the door immediately behind the flight deck. But there was black smoke everywhere.

"This way," said Rankin, crawling through the windshield, which had blown out during the landing. Guns, coughing, stopped to unhook George Burns, then pulled him out behind him.

Rankin groaned as he fell onto the dirt. He was still seeing double. Stunned, he tried to pull his sat phone out of his pocket to tell the Cube where they were, but his arm wouldn't move. He stood up, dazed, blinking his eyes to get his vision back to normal.

Pushed out by Guns, George Burns rolled onto the dirt near him. Rankin could tell by the way he landed that George Burns was dead. He got to his feet as Guns jumped down.

"You all right?" Rankin asked.

"More or less. How's your arm?"

"Hurts." Rankin's eyes focused as he looked at his forearm. It was black and slightly swollen. He'd broken bones before and this had that kind of feel, though a little more intense. Inside, the bone had been displaced slightly—not enough for a compound fracture that would pierce the skin, but more than enough to cause a great deal of pain.

"Whoever shot at us will probably come looking for us," said Guns.

"Yeah. Pull the phone out of my pocket. Tell Corrigan we're OK. He probably started having a cow as soon as the GPS locator stopped moving," said Rankin, looking around to see if there was any cover.

16

CIA HEADQUARTERS, LANGLEY, VIRGINIA

Thomas Parnelles looked at the blinking red light on his phone console, hesitating before picking it up.

"Parnelles," he said, pushing down the button.

"MI6 is going ballistic," Slott said, without any other introduction or greeting. "Everyone but the janitor has called me. Their field guy is raising a major stink."

"That's not surprising."

"I need their help in Indonesia. I can't afford to just blow them off."

"Give them the usual company line," said Parnelles.

"That's not working. I need to throw them a bone."

"What bone do we have?"

"Bring them in on the operation. It was theirs to begin with. We should have cooperated with them from the start. Anyone other than Ferg would have done so as a matter of course."

Parnelles leaned back in his seat, gazing at one of the photographs on the wall, which showed him and Ferguson's father in their salad days. Slott was probably right when he said that anyone else would have opted to work with the MI6 agent, regardless of personal differences, but on the other hand, second-guessing the judgment of the man on the scene was not good policy. Especially when it was someone like Ferguson.

Parnelles had been guilty of it himself, urging Ferguson to concentrate on T-Rex rather than the Iranian, and he'd been wrong. Very wrong.

He should not have gotten involved. He should have stayed aloof, as he normally did. Even if it was an important mission, even if he did know Robert, even if Robert was so close to him he felt like a son—he should not have gotten involved.

And he shouldn't now.

"I see no reason to get MI6 involved in this. There's no room for them," Parnelles told Slott.

"It *was* their operation."

"*Was* being the operative word. Didn't Hamilton screw them up in the first place? Wouldn't they have been able to grab Atha?"

"That may be a matter of opinion," said Slott. "MI6's perspective is that they didn't know there was a possibility that material was missing. We didn't know, either—Ferg only found out after Atha got away."

While Parnelles thought Slott was playing devil's advocate a little too strenuously, it was also true that grabbing Atha could have caused problems as well. Had they done so, this phone call could easily have been about the diplomatic repercussions. Given the circumstances as they now seemed, he'd have preferred that—but would he have said that earlier?

"Can't you just tell Ferguson to take Hamilton along for the ride?" said Slott.

"Why should I tell him that? He works for you."

"Let's face it, Tom, he only listens to you."

"I'm not sure he listens to anyone," said Parnelles.

"If MI6 doesn't cooperate, then the Indonesia operation falls apart. We're back to square one. The rebels will overthrow the government within six months, and Al Qaeda moves in the next day," said Slott. "All Ferguson has to do is let Hamilton sit in a hotel room in Tripoli so the British can take some credit, for cryin' out loud. That's not much."

"We're assuming his plan is going to work."

"And if it doesn't, what's the harm with having this Brit there? Hell, MI6 can even share the blame."

Indonesia was important; the Agency was trying to thwart a coup there.

Parnelles looked at the photo again.

This was *exactly* the sort of thing he hated when he was in the field—being told what to do because of politics.

"I'll see what I can do," Parnelles told Slott, hanging up.

17

NEAR THE LIBYA-SUDAN BORDER

Guns spotted the truck coming down off the ridge when it was only a mile away. The rocks he and Rankin were hiding in were a half mile southwest of the aircraft; there were just enough to keep them from being seen.

Their first plan was to wait and watch. They'd left George Burns near the plane, facedown, then dragged the dirt so that it looked as if he'd crawled out on his own before dying. It was possible whoever was checking them out would think he was the only one in the plane and leave. If not, Guns and Rankin could wait in the rocks and ambush them up close. Both men had their pistols and several replacement magazines of ammo.

The plan itself was a good one—but too passive for either Guns or Rankin to stick with for very long

"There's only four of them," said Guns, peering from the side of the rocks as the truck circled around the plane. "I only see two rifles."

"Gotta figure the others have weapons of some kind," said Rankin.

"Yeah. They go in the plane, we got 'em. Come up from behind."

"Maybe," said Rankin. "Depends where they park the truck. If they leave it on the side, it'll be shorter."

"You OK with your arm?"

"It's my left arm. I'm fine."

He'd rigged a simple sling to help keep his arm against his body. If he didn't think about it too much—or look at it—the pain was bearable. Rankin checked his Beretta. Even with one hand, he'd have preferred his Uzi, but it was back in Bologna.

The truck stopped near George Burns's body. Rankin waited until two of the men began poking around the nose of the plane.

"Crawl until we're ten yards from the plane, or until they see us," he said. "I'll yell."

Neither man actually crawled; it was more like a three- and four-point scamper across the hot sand. When they were about forty yards from the plane, one of the men walked toward the tail section, looking in their direction. Rankin raised his gun to fire, but Guns beat him; the man fell as the shot cracked the air. Guns dropped to his knee, training his pistol on the left side of the plane. Rankin kept running, trying to cut down the distance between him and the men with the truck.

A man jumped from the cab and fired a pistol at him; Rankin fired back, but missed badly. Rankin started to sprawl in the sand to avoid the return fire; as he threw himself down he remembered his broken arm and tried to land on his shoulder to deflect some of the impact. But it was too late. The shock ran through his entire body, as if his bones had been pierced by hot steel nails.

Guns didn't have an angle on the man behind the truck. He moved to his right, starting to flank the aircraft, when he spotted one of the other men coming out from behind the left engine and wing. The man saw him at almost the exact same moment, but Guns was faster with the pistol than he was with the rifle, and a pair of bullets in his stomach laid him down.

Rankin's pain was so intense that he couldn't see or hear the bullets flying around him. He felt as if someone were squeezing his entire upper body; the pain radiated so fiercely that he couldn't even have said where he was injured.

When it finally lifted, it was as if he'd caught his breath. He saw the man huddled behind the truck, shooting at Guns. Rankin fired a shot just close enough to get him to duck back.

"Guns, you OK?" Rankin yelled.

"Yeah."

"Can you sweep around and get behind this guy?"

"I'll try," shouted Guns. "There's another one somewhere. Watch out for him."

"Yeah," said Rankin. He saw the shooter moving behind the truck and fired, this time hitting the vehicle close to the man's head. The man threw himself to the ground.

Guns, meanwhile, ran to the man who'd fallen near the tail of the airplane and grabbed the AK-47 he'd dropped. He was starting to move around the wing when he heard a loud cracking noise; he dove into the sand as the fourth man began shooting from inside the burned-out plane through a passenger window.

By the time Guns got himself turned back around and in a position to fire, the man had pulled back from the window. The Marine tucked the Beretta into his belt, and with the AK-47 ready he crawled toward the nose of the plane, expecting that the man would try to get out. Then Guns got a better idea—he jumped up and dashed to the side of the aircraft, flattening his body hard against it. He felt the fuselage shake and heard someone moving around, pulling himself through the windshield as Guns and Rankin had earlier.

A barrel appeared near the edge of the aircraft; Guns waited until he saw flesh and then fired, almost point-blank, into the cheek of the gunman. The bullets shattered the man's cheekbone with enough force to throw his turban headgear into the air; he fell to the side and Guns jumped forward, firing into the pulp that had been the man's face.

Rankin was having a harder time with his gunman. They were less than thirty yards from each other, and together had fired a dozen shots, but so far neither had hit the other. The pain of Rankin's broken arm kept him off-balance, his world tilting hard left. His right arm couldn't seem to keep the pistol's recoil from raising the barrel. Finally he stretched down on the ground, trying to regain his breath and clear his head.

His opponent, meanwhile, had his own problems. One of Rankin's first shots had broken the back windshield on the truck and sent bits of glass into his opponent's face. None had gotten into his eyes, but the blood streaming down his forehead made it hard to see. Unlike the others, the man was an ethnic African with no particular wish to die in jihad. Nearly out of bullets, he decided his best bet was to try to run away. He backed away from the truck, then saw something moving near the nose of the airplane.

Rankin, holding his gun out in front of him, saw the man raise his arm to fire.

"Guns!" Rankin yelled, squeezing off three, four, five shots.

The African fell. Rankin collapsed.

"Where'd he get you?" Guns asked a few minutes later.

"Didn't," said Rankin. "I don't think. But man, this arm is killing me."

Guns found a first-aid kit in the plane. They fashioned a splint to keep the arm and bone inside straight, lessening the chance of the break worsening. The strongest thing for pain in the kit was a bottle of aspirin.

"Not even worth it," said Rankin. But he took four anyway.

"Try this," said Guns, emerging from the aircraft with a full bottle of Jack Daniel's. George Burns had stashed it beneath his seat in the cockpit.

Rankin refused at first, then decided he might as well. He took a strong pull, then winced.

"This stuff'll kill me if the fracture doesn't," he said, before taking another swig.

18

Corrine Alston was working on a new draft of the finding authorizing action against Iran when her encrypted phone buzzed with a call from Parnelles. She picked it up, hoping to hear that she didn't have to bother finishing the finding.

"Corrine, this is Thomas Parnelles. I need a favor."

"What kind?"

"MI6 is giving us hell, and I'd like Ferguson to make nice to their agent, Hamilton. He doesn't have to kiss him, just answer one or two of his phone calls."

"Why aren't you going to tell him yourself?"

"Ordinarily, I don't talk to Robert in the middle of an operation," said Parnelles coldly. "That would be your job."

Corrine knew that Parnelles could easily talk to Ferguson himself if he wanted to; she was fairly certain that he had on other missions. Of course, a call from her had a different weight than a call from him.

It also meant he would not be connected to an order that Ferguson was bound not to like.

"If I talk to him," she told Parnelles, "I'll tell him this was your idea."

"You can tell him what you want. If you do mention me, say that I told you I owe him an apology."

19

Thera handed Rostislawitch the folded surgical pants and shirt when the navy C-2A Greyhound transport aircraft was fifteen minutes from the airport.

"You can put them on over your clothes if they fit," she told him. "We have to be ready when we land."

The scientist nodded.

"You don't have to come if you don't want to," she told him. "We'll fly you to the States. You'll be safe."

Ferguson had told Rostislawitch the same thing. But he knew that Atha was more likely to fall for the plan if he was there. He was the bait in the trap—the peanut butter his mother used to put on the spring so they could catch the mouse eating their larder.

Thera helped him pull the green pants over his shoes. An ambulance would meet them at the airport and they would pretend to transport a sick patient into the city. Just in case the Iranian had spies at the airport, they planned to actually go to the hospital, where a car would meet them to take them to the hotel—not the Alfonse, where the message had directed Atha to meet him, but the Americano, two blocks away. The Marines would go straight there, and be waiting when they arrived.

Thera pulled a blue pair of hospital clothes over her jeans and blouse, then tied her hair at the back with a rubber band. The navy had loaned her a pair of handguns; she wore one in a holster beneath her top, and would keep the other in the stretcher with their "patient," one of the Greyhound's crewmen.

The pilot announced that they were about to begin their final approach. Thera strapped herself in. Rostislawitch sat next to her.

"I hope you don't mind," the scientist told her. "But I don't like airplanes when they land."

"They have to land sometime."

"True," he said. Then he closed his eyes and gripped her hand.

It was cold and wet, and made Thera worry even more that he might not be able to stand the stress of meeting with Atha.

The sound of the plane grew as they pulled down onto the runway. They bounced slightly; Rostislawitch tightened his grip. Then the ride smoothed out and the brakes caught.

"We have a long way to taxi," warned the pilot from the front.

Thera took out her phone to call Corrigan and tell him they were on the ground in Libya. She could tell something was wrong from his voice. For a moment, she thought it was Ferg. He'd gone to the airport to take a commercial flight, wanting to check out Tripoli on his own.

At least that was what he told her. Ferguson was never good at sharing mission details, and hadn't entirely explained why he was going alone. Thera suspected it had something to do with T Rex.

Please, God, don't let him be dead.

"Rankin and Guns crashed not too far from the Libya-Sudan border," Corrigan told her. "They're OK. Van's setting up a mission to get them. They found a camp nearby—we think it's Atha's base. They're going to raid it at the same time."

"They're all right?"

"Yeah, they're OK."

"Where's Ferg?"

"His flight left Naples on time. He should get in about an hour or so after you get to the hotel."

"All right."

"Stay in touch, right?"

"You sound like my dad, Corrigan," she told him, hanging up.

20

Technically, one wasn't supposed to use a satellite phone while on board an airliner. But that was exactly the sort of rule Ferguson believed in observing in the breach. He slipped his right earbud in, then angled himself against the side of the plane. His neighbor in the seat next to Ferguson could only hear his side of the conversation; so long as he was careful about what he said, there'd be no problem.

"Ferg," he said, pressing the send button in his pocket.

"This is Van. You get the information from Corrigan?"

"Yeah. You see where they went down?"

"I have GPS coordinates," said Colonel Van Buren. "Thing is, Ferg, they're too close to the camp to get them without someone there noticing. We have to hit the camp at the same time."

"When's that?"

"We're looking at nine your time in Tripoli," said Van Buren. "We may be able to push it up. We're waiting to hear on a tanker. It's a little more than four hours from here to where the camp is. We'll be ready to take off shortly. The problem is really on the other side, picking us up."

It wasn't clear from satellite photos whether the landing strip would support the weight of a C-130. Staging helicopters in for a pickup would take considerably longer, because of not only their speed but also the need to refuel. Van Buren was working on a plan that would have C-130s and helicopters as backups, so he could switch if necessary. But that involved bringing the helos in from Egypt. They were still trying to finish the arrangements.

"When are you meeting Atha?" Van Buren asked.

"It's his call. I won't grab him until I know you're close. Just in case he has some way of warning them."

"Thanks, Ferg."

Of course, that would work both ways—if Ferguson waited too long, the camp might warn Atha. But it was a risk he'd have to take.

Ferguson tapped his phone to kill the transmission. He turned to the woman in the seat next to him. She smiled.

"You're using a phone, right?" she asked.

"That or I'm talking to myself."

"I do both on planes all the time," she told him.

Even so, Ferguson waited for his seatmate to go to the bathroom before calling Guns and Rankin. Guns answered.

"Ferg?"

"What are you doing getting shot down without me?"

"Sorry, Ferg." Guns explained the situation; they were about ten miles from the camp, on the other side of a ridge that separated it from the desert.

"Can you guys wait until about ten or so to get picked up?" Ferguson asked. "Be better for this side of the operation."

"No sweat."

"Be square with me, Marine." Ferguson made his voice very serious. "Yes or no?"

"Yes."

"All right. They'll call you when they're close. If things go to shit, holler. Otherwise stay under the rocks until they land."

The phone rang a few seconds later. Ferguson slid it out of his pocket far enough to see who it was.

"Hey, Madame Butterfly," Ferg told Corrine Alston. "What's going on?"

"That's my question for you."

"I'm about an hour out of Tripoli. You hear about Rankin and Guns?"

"Corrigan told me. They say they're OK."

"Rankin's not that good a liar, so maybe it's true."

"You have a rescue operation lined up to coincide with your grabbing Atha?"

"Yup."

"OK. Good." She paused for a moment, long enough for Ferguson to guess what was coming.

"I have another request," she said finally. "MI6 wants in."

"I don't know that song. Is it Irish?"

"Mr. Parnelles called and asked that you play nice with them."

"Yeah, see, it's not Irish. I only do Irish folk songs. I can give you a very good 'Finnegan's Wake.'"

"It's your call, Bob. And Mr. Parnelles says he owes you an apology."

"It's a really funny song. This guy dies, and they give him an Irish wake. Whiskey brings him back to life. A lot of puns, see, through the whole song. I'll sing it for you sometime."

"Thanks for the update, Ferg."

Ferguson checked his watch. It was a little past three, Tripoli time. He pressed the quick-dial for the Cube.

"Corrigan."

"No shit. Call that number I gave you the other day for Hamilton. Tell him to be on the five-thirty flight out of Naples for Tripoli."

"You sure, Ferg?" Only an hour before, Ferguson had told Corrigan that if he even mentioned Hamilton again he'd stuff a dozen stale British scones down his throat when he got back to the States.

"There are only two more flights today, Jack. He either gets that one or waits until midnight."

"Slott'll be happy."

"Yeah, well, make the call anyway." Ferg saw his seatmate returning, and pushed the button to hang up.

21

NORTHEASTERN SUDAN

"How long you figure before they send somebody else out to look for these guys?" Guns asked Rankin after he had finished dragging the last body into the plane.

"Hour, maybe two. We got the radio. We listen for them."

"Radio transmissions won't get through the hills. We had better radios than this in Afghanistan and it was always a problem," said Guns. "By the time we hear them, they'll be pretty close."

"Yeah." Rankin looked around the desert.

"We got two choices—we drive out further so they can't find us, or we go up into the hills," said Guns.

"Then there's door number three," said Rankin. "We scout the place for the landing team."

"I don't know about that."

"We scout the place, figure out where the defenses are. We're just sitting here, Guns. We might as well do something that'll make a difference. Shit, we'll be sitting on our butts until what? Nine, if we're lucky. By the time they're wrapped up and come looking for us, it'll be dawn."

Guns looked Rankin up and down, trying to decide whether he was really up to moving around or whether it was just the sedative—aka Jack Daniel's—talking.

Maybe a little of both.

"I'm OK," insisted Rankin. "Let's finish getting the bodies in the plane and go. We're sitting ducks out here anyway. Our best bet is to get closer to the camp."

"I'm not sure about this," said Guns.

"Come on, Marine. Don't be chicken."

Guns laughed. A blanket hugger calling a Marine chicken. Some things were just too funny for words.

Rankin got up. His head felt light, because of either the Jack Daniel's or the fracture.

"I'm just bustin' on ya," he told Guns. "We'd better get into the hills before they come for us, right? We don't know if it's one road or two roads or what."

"OK," said Guns.

"You're all right for a Marine," said Rankin.

"And you're all right for a jerk."

Rankin cracked up.

Definitely the whiskey, thought Guns.

22

Fresh off the airplane at the Tripoli airport, Ferguson strolled to the nearest bank machine, Rostislawitch's ATM card in his hand. He angled his head so the machine's camera couldn't get a clear shot of his face, then fed the card into the slot and punched the PIN code. He tried to withdraw a hundred dollars' worth of Libyan money—which didn't work, since the account was down to five rubles. He checked his balance, took the card, and slid away to the left, again being careful not to let his face be seen.

"It's so easy to put your money in, so hard to get it out," he said to an Egyptian woman waiting in line. She nodded in sympathy, even though she didn't understand all his words.

Outside, Ferguson got a taxi to the Alfonse Hotel. He handed over Rostislawitch's credit card to the clerk, reserving the room.

"Send some coffee up for me, would you?" Ferguson asked in Arabic.

"There are coffeemakers in the rooms," said the clerk, trying to sound helpful.

"Oh, I'm not going to drink that. You do have room service, right?"

"We do. Your accent—you're from Egypt?"

"Moscow. I spent time in Cairo as a boy."

"Ah. Very good," said the man, handing over Ferguson's card key.

The room was on the large size, with a thick gold bedspread ornate enough for Gadhafi to have worn as a robe, and plush velour-covered chairs. Ferguson scanned for bugs, then unhooked the cable from the television and hooked a receiver up so he could use it to monitor the two he'd left in the lobby and hallway. Before he was finished setting up, there was a knock at the door.

"Room service."

Ferguson went to the door, opened it a crack, and saw a waiter in the hall. His uniform made him look part Arab, part African; he had a long shirt with wooden beads around his neck, and an ornate, red tasseled cap on his head.

Ferguson unlatched the chain and stood back. As the waiter wheeled the cart across the threshold, Ferguson dropped a twenty on the floor.

The server glanced at it; the next thing he knew, he was facedown on the floor, Ferguson's knee in his back.

"Don't move." Ferguson reached under the man's tunic and pulled out the waiter's gun, a Walther P88 Compact.

"Nice weapon. I prefer Glocks myself, but you can't go wrong with a German gun," said Ferguson, getting up.

"Jeez, Ferg, quit horsin' around, huh?"

"You think anybody's buying that disguise, Ferrone? You don't look any more local than I do."

"What do you want? That's how the room service people dress. Take it up with the management."

"The hat's pretty cool," added Ferguson, helping Jimmy Ferrone up. Ferrone was the CIA's Libyan station chief. "I like the tassel."

"Long time no see," said Ferrone. "How are you?"

He held his hand out, but Ferguson was ready—when Ferrone tried to throw him, he reversed the move and spun him onto the floor.

"All right, you win," said Ferrone from his back. "I'm getting too old for this."

Ferguson snorted, then ducked down to the bottom of the cart Ferrone had wheeled in. There was another Walther P88, along with an MP5 submachine gun and enough ammunition for a small siege.

"What happened to the smoke grenades?" asked Ferguson.

"In the ice bucket." Ferrone stood up and straightened his clothes. He was about Ferguson's height and weight, and it seemed to him that he had kicked the younger man's butt not too long ago, or at least fought him to a draw. "You tapping into the security system?"

"No. I got bugs out quicker."

"Yeah? Something we can use?"

"You're not important enough." Ferguson checked and then loaded the pistol.

"Screw yourself, Ferg. What are you working on?"

Ferguson grinned.

"Yeah, all right," said Ferrone. "If you need more help, let me know."

"I'm good, Jimmy. Thanks."

Ferrone stuck out his hand. Ferguson shook his head. "I'm not shaking hands with you."

Ferrone turned to go.

"Hey, you forgot your tip," said Ferguson, pointing to the twenty.

"That's all right. Your coffee's cold."

23

NAPLES, ITALY

Kiska Babev's assistant called her just as the plane was about to board.

"Rostislawitch is at the hotel in Tripoli. He just checked in. Tried to get some money out when he landed. There wasn't enough in his account."

"Very good. Were you able to get a boarding list for the earlier flight?"

"Yes, and Ferguson wasn't on it. That doesn't mean he's not on his way."

"Antov, haven't I taught you never to state the obvious?"

"Yes, Colonel."

Kiska was just about to tell him that she wasn't angry when she saw a man walking into the gate area who looked familiar. He had sandy hair, a thin face, and dressed like a British college student gone to seed.

Familiar, but she couldn't quite place him.

Had she seen him in Bologna? Or before that, much before that?

British? Or German? Not American, a little too priggish with his clothes.

"Antov, what are the names of the British and German intelligence officers assigned to Italy?" she asked.

"Hold on, Colonel."

She watched the man, trying to remember. She'd been shown faces of various foreign agents before traveling, but that wasn't why he was familiar. It was further back than that.

"There are several dozen. You want me to read the names?"

"No. It's someone who was in Chechnya a year ago. A British agent, I think."

"Are you sure about Chechnya?"

"I'm not," she admitted. "Have someone at the airport take his picture when we land. Then follow him."

"You're stretched thin, Colonel." Her assistant began telling her about the problems he had encountered getting personnel into Libya; most of the people she wanted wouldn't be there until the next day.

"Just have the photo taken then," Kiska told him. "Get an identification. We'll see who he is."

"Yes, Colonel. It will be done."

A half hour into the flight, his gin and tonic finished—aircrew could never be trusted with martinis—Nathaniel Hamilton went to the lavatory and sat on the toilet. He took out his cell phone and broke it open, then reached into his pocket for what looked like a metal pen. He put the tip in his mouth and twisted, loosening it after considerable effort. Once the tip was gone, he pushed the plunger at the opposite end and pulled out what, in a real pen, would have been the ink cartridge. In this case, it was a collection of 25mm bullets, molded together so that they would appear harmless under an X-ray, especially to a harried security examiner. Hamilton extracted the bullets and placed each one in the cell phone, filling it up. Then he flushed the toilet, thoroughly washed his hands, and went back to his seat, apologizing to the rotund woman on the aisle and the man who looked like a dachshund in the center seat.

Hamilton stuffed a pillow behind his head, then took out his Tripoli guidebook and studied the city map. Ferguson's man had not told him where Ferguson, or Rostislawitch for that matter, was going to be. Even though Hamilton had a relatively clear idea of what would happen—obviously Ferguson had arranged for some sort of meeting between the scientist and Atha—Ferguson's lackey had neglected to say in his message *where* it was going to happen.

Hard to tell with the Americans whether that was on purpose or not, but given that he had failed to answer Hamilton's two requests for the information, it certainly appeared purposeful.

There were hundreds of hotels and restaurants in Tripoli, and the possible locations for clandestine meetings in the more usual suspects like back alleys and docks approached infinity.

Generally an operative like Ferguson would stick to a place he was already familiar with, especially if he didn't have time to set up beforehand. The problem was, Hamilton had no idea whether Ferguson had even been to Tripoli before, let alone where he might have worked there. Once again Hamilton was flying blind, and he didn't like it.

Hamilton paged through the book, refreshing his mental map of the city. More than likely, the meet would be a neutral place, public so that the Iranian would feel relatively safe. Ferguson had used hotels and restaurants in Bologna; since that was his modus operandi, Hamilton flipped to the restaurant listings and began looking at the entries.

The Tripoli Restaurant, owned by the Gadhafi family?

No. A connection with the government might be messy.

The Safari, featuring live animals as entertainment?

Too many distractions.

Ile de France? Ferguson hated French restaurants.

Hamilton flipped over to the hotel section. The Libyan Renaissance? Very high-class, very chic, the place to see and be seen for the restless, wealthy set.

No. Too much of a chance of a Paris Hilton type getting in the way of the action.

The Alfonse—once reputed to be owned by gangsters. Now *that* was the sort of place Ferguson would like.

Hamilton marked the page and continued down the list.

24

Atha was so anxious when they finally landed at the Tripoli airport that he left Ahmed and went straight to the Alfonse, the hotel where Rostislawitch had said to look for him.

The Alfonse's lobby was a pleasantly large space, with couches and chairs parked in different groupings to give a show of intimacy. There was a piano, some very thick rugs, and thin side tables. A wide staircase led to reception rooms on the second floor. The check-in counter was opposite the front doors, albeit separated by a good eighty feet.

Atha went to the desk and asked if Rostislawitch had checked in; the clerk said he had but would not reveal his room number. Atha started to argue, but before he could say anything the man picked up a phone and held it out to him.

"Call his room. The operator will connect you."

Atha looked around, trying to see where the operator was, but couldn't. He got a computerized voice telling him the guest he had called was unavailable, but he could leave a message.

"This is Atha. I'm in the lobby," he said, then hung up.

Atha went over to the Steinway piano and sat on a sideless couch next to it, which gave him a good view of the hallway leading to the elevator. Arms crossed, he tried to lean back on the couch, telling himself to relax though he knew it was hopeless.

Upstairs, Ferguson opened his suitcase and took out the hair coloring kit, adding some gray highlights to his temples and sideburns—just a touch, the way he remembered his father when they first moved to Cairo. Then he took a fake moustache, fiddled with it a bit, put it back, selected a beard.

Too much.

The Fu Manchu looked good, but that wasn't particularly Russian.

He went back to the beard. Ferguson didn't mind if Atha thought it was a disguise; he just didn't want him to connect the man wearing it to any glimpse he'd had in Bologna.

A pair of thick-rimmed glasses, his hair slicked back, a thick wool sweater—the overall effect was Russian, with a slight nod toward Berlin in the sixties.

The video feed showed Atha was still sitting alone in the lobby, rocking back and forth impatiently. Ferguson decided that he couldn't keep the Iranian waiting much longer. He stuck the Walther under his sweater, tucked a magazine of bullets in his left boot and a smoke grenade in his right, then went down to play Let's Make a Deal.

25

CIA BUILDING 24-442

Thomas Ciello had used the scripts Fibber had given him to map out Kiska Babev's travels based on her credit card expenditures. That had allowed Ciello to find possible connections between two of the T Rex assassinations, one in Seoul, Korea, where she had visited a week before a murder, and one in Turkey, when she had been in Romania a day later.

The fact that the connections were tangential didn't bother Ciello; any experienced intelligence agent would be careful about leaving a trail that directly matched with a murder he or she committed, and an assassin with a reputation and track record like T Rex's would be even more thorough.

But what did bother Ciello was the sheer paucity of records, tangential or otherwise.

He loved that word, *paucity;* it reminded him of the 1953 Pawtucket UFO incident, where the lack of information about a scheduled aircraft flight that disappeared from radar scopes for three minutes and thirteen seconds could *only* be explained as an alien abduction incidence, a fact proven by the lack of information about the incident.

In this case, the lack of information suggested not that he was dealing with a UFO incident—Ciello knew he could not be so lucky—but rather that he was missing a great number of accounts. Clearly, Kiska had other credit cards that he was not yet aware of. If he found them, he reasoned, he would undoubtedly find more definitive proof that she was T Rex.

And when he found it, he would be able to expunge—another of his favorite words, though not linked to a UFO case—the dark cloud hanging over him for his alleged misidentification of the nature of the Bologna attack.

Corrigan, of course, thought that two connections, along with the air trip to France, were proof enough. He had sidetracked Ciello with other assignments, telling him to dig up information about Iran's biological research labs and Libyan hotels. But finally, scut work done, Ciello began trying to puzzle out how to find the accounts.

Comparative searches—looking for similar expenses—were useless in this case, because the accounts were used so sporadically that the pattern they established matched three-quarters of the bank's accounts. He had to work the other way—he needed to know Kiska's other aliases.

Ciello couldn't come up with anything that wasn't already in her file. It was fairly easy to forge documents in Russia, so Kiska could be literally anyone. The problem for most people when they adopted a phony identity, however, was that they needed some way to keep track of it. That was why many agents who used different names to cloud their identity kept their first name or some variation; it was much easier to remember.

Kiska's cousin in the mental institution had six different accounts, all apparently used by Kiska. Her parents, who lived nearby, had one—which was clearly not used by Kiska, since the charges were all made within a fifty-mile radius of their home.

Ciello felt his back tightening up again and decided he had best take a break. He got up from his computer and stretched gently. Then he lay down on the floor, arms over his head, legs straight out. He closed his eyes.

The harsh overhead lights of his office shone through his eyelids. The white spots hovered together, like a fleet of spaceships spinning together.

Friends.

Or rather, other patients.

Ciello jumped up and began entering the address of the nursing home into one of the search scripts for the bank companies.

26

TRIPOLI, LIBYA

Ferguson walked out of the elevator and turned right past the back of the grand staircase. He swung around past the restaurant, avoided the maid cleaning the carpet with a vacuum that looked fifty years old, and headed toward the Steinway piano. He pointed his gaze straight ahead, oblivious to everything around him. He passed Atha, then spun around quickly, pointing at the Iranian's face.

"Anghuyu Jahan, you are here to see Dr. Rostislawitch," he said in Russian.

Atha said in Farsi that he didn't speak Russian. Ferguson pointed at Atha, turned his head left and right to look around, then sat down in the chair across from him.

"Do you speak English?" said Atha.

"I can speak English," said Ferguson, injecting a heavy Russian accent into his voice. "You are here for Dr. Rostislawitch. Your name is Anghuyu Jahan. You have people call you Atha. You are not to be trusted."

"Wait just a second."

Ferguson leaned forward. "No, Mr. Atha, as you call yourself, you wait. Who do you think you are dealing with? Just a professor from a laboratory? What do you think?"

Atha was not about to be bullied. "Tell Dr. Rostislawitch when he is ready to talk with me, he can communicate in the usual manner," he said, rising.

"I suggest you sit down, Mr. Atha," said Ferguson, showing his drawn pistol.

The Iranian frowned. "What is this?"

"This is a discussion to see if it is worth Dr. Rostislawitch's trouble to meet with you."

"Why did he want me to come to Tripoli?"

"Because someone tried to kill him in Naples," said Ferguson.

"Who would want to kill him?" said Atha sharply.

"Perhaps you can tell me."

"I don't deal with the *mafiya*. It's bad for business."

"What is the *mafiya*? What is it?" said Ferguson, his voice just a notch too loud. "A figment of a newswriter's imagination. I am just a business consultant." Ferguson slipped his gun back in his belt and modulated his voice. "A friend."

"How do I know you're not FSB?"

"Perhaps I am."

Atha scowled, but behind the mask he presented to the Russian he began to relax. This was a businessman with whom he could make a deal. The arrangements made more sense now—the scientist wouldn't have thought about holding back an essential ingredient on his own, but a man like this, probably fronting for other men, a network, would. And he would have wanted the meeting to take place here, in Tripoli, where the authorities could be counted on if necessary. Italy would be too problematic.

It also explained what had happened on the dock in Naples. Of course. He should have realized that a man like Rostislawitch, all brain, would need some brawn to complete a transaction. More than likely he was part of some sort of network; very possibly they had made these sorts of deals before.

The only question was how to make sure he wasn't cheated. He'd dealt with the type he saw across from him before; you couldn't show weakness, but on the other hand, if you were too antagonistic they became irrationally angry.

"Maybe, if Dr. Rostislawitch is willing, we can make an arrangement to our mutual benefit," said Atha. "But I have to talk to him."

"That can be arranged. If it is worthwhile."

Ferguson looked over and saw a blond-haired woman coming through the door—Kiska Babev.

Impeccable timing.

"What?" said Atha, immediately sensing something was wrong.

"The Russian FSB. Very inconvenient."

Before Atha could say anything, Ferguson jumped up and jerked Atha with him to the right. A loud pop echoed under the piano. Its strings vibrated loudly, and suddenly smoke began to fill the lobby.

"Fire!" yelled Ferguson in English as he pushed Atha toward the hall. "Fire!"

A woman who had just come down the steps began to scream. At the desk, Kiska turned and caught a glimpse of someone running away, but the smoke was so thick she couldn't make out if they were man or woman. Kiska began to choke.

"The blue car across the street," Ferguson told Atha as they reached the side hall.

Atha, unsure whether this was real or a performance, tried to slow his pace, but Ferguson wouldn't let him.

"The car. Now. Quickly," Ferguson said, pushing Atha through the door. He switched to Russian, calling the Iranian a fat toad who was going to get them killed.

The car was parked across the street where Ferrone had left it earlier. Ferguson opened the doors with the remote key and slid in, bumping his legs on the bottom of the dashboard because the CIA station chief liked to drive right on top of the wheel and had left the seat that way. Ferguson cursed—in Russian, and in character—and started the engine. As soon as Atha closed the door, he peeled out.

"I don't believe any of this," said Atha.

Ferguson yanked the wheel hard, turning down a narrow side street. He mashed the accelerator, then slammed the brakes and took another turn.

Atha's fingers fumbled to connect his seat belt. By the time he had gotten it buckled, Ferguson had turned back onto the street in front of the hotel. He drove to the corner, then pulled over. A pair of black Mercedes had driven up in front of the hotel; large men, obviously concealing weapons beneath their coats, were waiting near the door. The blonde Atha had just seen inside—Kiska, though he didn't know her name—came out coughing with another woman and a man. They got into the cars and sped off.

Ferguson pulled out from his spot, running the light as he hit the gas.

"What are you doing?" asked Atha.

"Following to see if they go to the Russian embassy. You want proof that they are FSB."

"That won't be necessary," said Atha. "Let's go somewhere and discuss our business."

27

NORTHEASTERN SUDAN

"The truck has not returned yet. If the plane was shot down, they should have found it. If not, they should be back."

Dr. Navid Hamid looked up from his computer. It took considerable effort to comprehend the Palestinian's words, not because they were spoken in a foreign language—Dr. Hamid had learned Arabic as a child—but because he was absorbed in the scientific language of bacteria and DNA. He had been studying information published by one of Rostislawitch's associates on the techniques they had used to manipulate the genes in E. coli. Understanding the papers was difficult, even for Hamid, though it was written in French, which he was fluent in.

"The airplane that flew over the camp was not shot down?" Hamid asked.

"It was hit. We saw smoke. But what happened we do not know

for sure. The men we sent out to look for it have not returned. It was three hours."

"Why did you wait so long to tell me?"

The Palestinian did not like to be berated, especially by a man who spent his days inside and did not understand the difficult strain of running the camp.

"There was much else going on, and you said you should not be disturbed."

"They don't have radios?"

"The radios don't work over the ridge."

Dr. Hamid rubbed his eyes. "Send someone."

"As you wish," said the Palestinian, starting to leave.

"Wait. Tell Muhammed we are ready to prepare the buses. We will be leaving this evening."

"I thought Atha said to wait until morning."

"No." Hamid rose. As he read the papers, there was no way to alter the bacteria strain in the way that Rostislawitch had claimed he'd done; introducing a second virus mutation consistently failed. It had to be a bluff. "We'll move as originally planned: the first bus leaves at nine."

28

TRIPOLI, LIBYA

Thera couldn't quite understand Ferguson's Russian. She covered the phone and waved across the hotel room to Rostislawitch, who was sitting glumly in a chair, watching the audioless television.

"Come here," she said in a stage whisper. "It's Ferg. Talk to him in Russian."

"*Zdrástvuitye,*" said Rostislawitch, picking up the phone. "Hello."

"Professor, the meeting is on. One hour. At Laxy's."

Rostislawitch looked at Thera. "Laxy's?"

She nodded.

"We'll be there," said the scientist.

Thera took the phone and hung up. Laxy's was an exclusive club on the waterfront that had been used as a meeting place by gunrunners and similar businessmen since it had opened in the late 1990s. Libya's rapprochement with the West had cost it some of its sparkle, but its reputation was still sufficiently tattered to draw a large and disreputable crowd.

It was also one of several places in the city the CIA had bugged. Ferguson had worked there before, so he was familiar with the layout.

"You have to wear the bulletproof vest," Thera told Rostisla-witch. "The sport coat and shirt will be brought from the embassy in a few minutes. They'll go right over it."

Thera helped him put on the vest. Her touch felt good against his arms and sides, reassuring, as if she were taking care of him.

"Atha will shoot me?" he asked as she stepped away. It was funny—he didn't actually feel afraid. If he was shot, then it was only justice.

"I don't know what's going to happen, Artur. Atha will probably threaten you. Don't worry. You tell him that your associate has the virus and will handle the business from now on. Answer whatever technical questions you have to, then leave to let Ferguson handle the arrangements."

"All right."

"When the meeting's over, we're going to go to the embassy, OK? It's the safest place for you. Then you can decide what to do."

"I want to go home."

"That might not be wise."

"What else can I do?"

He meant it as a rhetorical question—Rostislawitch was resigned to his fate; whatever happened to him, including death, was simply his penance for taking the material, for being willing to let so many inno-cent people die. But Thera interpreted the question literally, and told him that he was bound to be in demand with drug companies and large food concerns, or he could get a job teaching at a university. The CIA could help.

"A man like you has so much knowledge," she said. "There will be many offers."

She was such a good girl, he thought. So optimistic.

"I think I would rather go home," he told her.

"It'll be up to you," said Thera, disappointed. She picked up her sat phone to call the embassy. "Let's get through this first."

29

OVER THE MEDITERRANEAN SEA

The pilot of the MC-17 laid out a course that would get them over the southern Libyan desert without their being detected by the Libyan radars; they weren't worried about being shot at, but wanted to avoid any possibility that Atha might be on the lookout for an American combat transport. To get around the radars, the big plane flew at tree-top level for about a hundred miles, executing a number of tight turns along the way. Finally, as the sun was just going down, the pilot began climbing to a higher altitude. Colonel Van Buren looked out the window on the flight deck and watched the sunset; from where they were, it looked as if they had flown over it.

With the possibility of a long night ahead of them, Van Buren decided to go down and talk to his men. The bio/chem protective suits weren't particularly comfortable to sit around in, and the colonel decided it was important to emphasize to each man how important the suits were to avoid contamination. The officers and squad leaders had gone over this, of course, but Van Buren sensed that a personal word from him might carry a little more weight, and possibly prevent unnecessary casualties. He made sure his own suit was zipped tight except for the headpiece, then went down and began talking to the elite teams sitting in the hold of the plane.

Van Buren was about a third of the way through when he was called back upstairs to the command center. Corrigan was on the line.

"Ferg says go as soon as you can," said Corrigan.

"We're on our way. Should be a little over two hours."

"Godspeed."

TRIPOLI, LIBYA

After an hour of driving around Tripoli, Hamilton realized he was unlikely to find Ferguson this way. There were simply too many choices, and Hamilton didn't know the city well enough, let alone Ferguson, to narrow them down. Finally he pulled into a parking lot near the water and tried to come up with another plan. He called Ferguson's number and got his unctuous assistant, who assured him that Ferguson would contact him "when the time is right."

"Is there a special hotel I should stay at?" Hamilton hinted. "Or one to avoid?"

"Up to you."

"Oh, quite," said Hamilton, hanging up. Then he realized that ignorance was often a very valuable weapon.

And where did one find ignorance, if not in the intelligence community?

"I say, this is Nathaniel Hamilton. I'm in town on some company business," he told MI6's top resident Tripoli officer over the phone a short time later. "Looks like I may have to deal with some Americans. What is their favorite hotel?"

"The Hilton, Libya Regal, the Marriott. Not in any order. Any place with a good bar," added the resident. He offered to drop around for a few drinks and give Hamilton a backgrounder on the city if he wanted, but he didn't have time for that.

"I've been doing a good deal of traveling, so I'm going to check in and tuck myself in for an early night," he said. "But maybe tomorrow. I'll come round the embassy at noon or so. We'll have lunch."

"Very good."

"While I'm thinking about it, are there any other places that the Americans like to, uh, do business at? I'd like to scope them out beforehand."

"What sort of business?"

The resident had committed a faux pas, asking the sort of question one never asked of another officer on assignment, since of course it could not be answered truthfully. Hamilton ignored it, commenting instead on how difficult it could be to work with the Americans.

Realizing his mistake, the resident told Hamilton that he'd personally seen the Yanks use a number of places, including a club named Laxy's that was a hangout for the gunrunning crowd, and a small hotel lounge on the south side of the city called the Oasis.

"Very good," said Hamilton. "Well, then, I'll just be ringing off. Make sure to keep lunch open tomorrow. It'll be on my expense account, not yours."

"Very good."

"Oh, one more thing—I would like to pick up a weapon if possible. I feel rather naked without one."

"Do you really feel that's necessary?"

"One never knows."

"I don't suppose it will be a problem. Would you like me to bring it tomorrow?"

"I'll just pop around and pick it up. Then it's off to bed. Remember—lunch tomorrow."

"Looking forward to it."

Obviously a man who had been out in the boonies too long, Hamilton thought as he hung up the phone.

31

Rankin tightened his right hand on the truck's steering wheel to fight off the pain as he drove up the trail. It came and went in odd bursts—his arm would feel numb for a while, then all of a sudden, without even being jostled or smacked, the pain seemed to explode.

"Truck coming," said Guns.

"They'll think we're their friends," said Rankin. "Until we're close."

Guns checked the AK-47, making sure he was ready to fire. Rankin took a deep breath as the other truck got closer. The winding path through the mountains was too narrow for both trucks to pass.

"Let's do it," said Rankin. He turned the wheel hard, throwing the truck into a slide perpendicular across the roadway. Guns brought the rifle up and blasted out the front of the guards' pickup. Then he threw himself backward over the seat, following Rankin out the other side.

Both men crouched behind the pickup, waiting for more gunfire. When there was none, Guns started around the back end of the truck, while Rankin crouched near the front. He held the AK-47 in his right hand, cradling it against his hip, as he cautiously looked around the front of the truck.

"Damn!" yelled Guns from the rear, jumping up as he saw a dark figure running up the hillside. Guns fired a burst and then started to follow, but the man had too much of a lead.

Rankin checked the truck. Two men lay dead in the cab, their torsos riddled with Guns' bullets.

"You are a pretty good shot," Rankin said after Guns gave up the chase. "For a Marine."

"You think we oughta try and catch him?" asked Guns.

"I don't know. Took us damn long to get this far." He glanced at his watch. It was past seven. "I think we let him go and keep trying to find the camp. Give Van the heads-up."

"Call in."

"I'm not calling Corrigan every five minutes," said Rankin.

"Call in anyway." Guns went up ahead, scouting the road for signs of the man who'd gotten away. He was somewhere nearby, but Rankin was right—they couldn't both look for him and find the camp. They'd already lost several hours on the tangle of paths and half paths in the hills.

The road was too narrow to turn around. Guns got in the back of the truck they'd blasted while Rankin drove backward, looking for a safe spot to turn around. They found one about a quarter mile away, a pull-off around a bend—which also gave them a view of the canyon, and the camp at its end.

"There it is," said Guns. He jumped out and worked his way down and around the ridge, trying to get a better view. By the time Rankin found him, he was lying on his stomach with his field glasses.

"No fixed guns or anything like that," said Guns. It was getting dark; even with the glasses Guns had a little trouble making out the camp's layout.

"Hold on; hold on," said Rankin. He took out the phone and called Corrigan, then began relaying what they saw. Buses and trucks were clustered near a pair of small buildings at the northern end of the camp. People were lined up around a table near them. Torches were being lit, and their shadows flickered across the desert sand.

"What are they doing?" Rankin asked.

"I don't know."

"Rankin, are you sure you don't see any missile posts?" asked Corrigan. "We need to know for Van."

"There are no launchers around," Rankin told him. "They got us with a shoulder-launched weapon. You tell them to jump from altitude and they'll be safe."

"Van and his people are less than a half hour away. Just hold tight."

"Hey, Rankin, check this out," said Guns. "Looks like they're getting on the buses."

32

Patrons entered Laxy's by walking down a wide staircase made of long, flat stones. Water ran down a shallow channel at the center of the staircase, pooling on a landing at the middle where the stairs pitched around to descend into the cavernlike main room. A separate waterfall filled the entire right-hand wall of the stairs. The mist and sound made it seem as if you were entering a secret underground oasis in the middle of the desert.

Inside, the lighting was low and indirect. Couches and tables were located around panels faced with stone veneers, adding to the ambiance as well as privacy. A small orchestra played in the front corner, filling the space with strains of American music from the 1930s and '40s, songs that evoked an era of romance. As in most other places in Tripoli that catered to foreigners, liquor was served freely. The servers were all women; they wore low-slung miniskirts beneath sheer tops that teased patrons with a clear view of the fancy embroidery on the women's bras.

The food, though overpriced, was excellent. It was almost very Western; it was said that one could not find a better filet mignon in all of northern Africa, and the salmon was flown in daily from Scotland.

Atha had been to Laxy's two or three times before. He wasn't surprised that the Russian had chosen it; Rostislawitch's associate would surely think it was out of the way as well as exotic. Russians usually used hotels on the northwestern end of town for business, and with the FSB looking for them it would make very good sense to head to a place more often associated with Westerners.

The Iranian wasn't as worried about the Russian intelligence service as he was about closing the deal. He was willing to give Rostis-lawitch what he'd originally been promised, but coming up with more money at this point would mean going to the minister. Worse, it could easily involve a delay of a day, if not more. The minister would like that even less.

But while Atha had every incentive to get the deal closed quickly, he had to project the image of a man who was not in a hurry. He ambled down the steps into the club, going as slowly as he possibly could, glancing around to see if he might recognize someone. He smiled at anyone who came close to making eye contact, throwing his shoulders back and forth as if he owned the place himself.

The act amused Ferguson, who went ahead to the table without him. It was clear Atha was worried about making a deal. As soon as the Iranian sat down, Ferguson began probing him for information.

"And when we complete the arrangements," Ferguson said, laying his Russian accent over his English, "how do you plan on using our product?"

"That is none of your concern," snapped Atha.

"Of course not. But one becomes curious."

"Curiosity is not an admirable trait in our business."

Ferguson gestured to the waitress, and told her to bring them a bottle of chilled vodka.

"I don't drink," said Atha.

"Some tea then?"

"Nothing."

"Two glasses. He may change his mind." Ferguson shooed the girl away. "My curiosity is not idle. I am asking because maybe we have an opportunity for other business."

"Such as?"

"Lab equipment. It may be easier for us to obtain certain things than it is for you. You don't want to arouse suspicions. Plus, our prices can be very competitive. We can arrange delivery to Tripoli, Tehran, or anywhere, practically. The desert? A seaport? Not a problem."

Atha's eyes flickered ever so slightly at the word *desert*.

"I have no need for equipment now," he said. "But in the future, if the price were right, I might be in the market for some things."

"Such as?"

"Often I am looking for spare parts. Items for airplanes. Special ones that can be hard to obtain."

"I have more sources than you can imagine."

"Let us see how this goes first. Then, maybe, some more business."

The drinks arrived. Ferguson turned his glass around, then drained it.

"How far do you have to transport the material?" he asked.

"Not very far."

"It has to be handled carefully, you know. If you're taking it by car—"

"I'm well aware of the precautions. Where is the scientist?"

"Scientists are on their own schedule." Ferguson took the second glass, twisting it on the table once more before downing it.

Atha sensed that the Russian was simply stringing him along. He thought back to the hotel, examining what he remembered, trying to decide whether it had been staged. He didn't think so, and yet it was certainly possible.

Was the Russian working for the FSB?

It was possible. But in that case he would simply have arrested him at the hotel.

Or kidnapped him. The Russians had no authority here, though that never stopped them.

"I hope he comes soon," Ferguson told Atha, using the phrase he and Thera had settled on as a signal. "I have some other business to attend to."

"What sort of business?" asked Atha.

"Personal business," said Ferguson, refilling his glass.

33

As Rankin and Guns scrambled back toward the truck, another vehicle came up the road toward them from the camp. When he saw the truck, the driver stopped, and another man got out to inspect it.

Guns raised his rifle to fire.

"No," said Rankin, stopping him. "They'll hear the gunfire. We won't make it down to the camp."

The man who'd gotten out of the truck examined the broken window, then called to the other man. One walked up the road; the other came in their direction.

Crouching by the side of the road, Guns tried to calculate if he could reach the other man before he managed to grab a gun. He was only fifteen yards away, but the rough terrain would slow him down.

"Cover me while I charge him," Guns told Rankin.

"Listen, that's not going to work. I'm having a lot of trouble using just one hand to fire," said Rankin. "I have a better idea. Go back that way and cut up behind him. I'll moan."

"What?"

"I'll pretend like I'm hurt. When he comes down to investigate, jump him."

"What about the other guy?"

"He's too far away. It's dark. Come on. Go."

Guns slid down a few feet, then began backing around the curve.

Rankin turned around so his face wouldn't be visible from above, and then began to moan. It took several loud "args" before the man who was on the road heard Rankin and decided to investigate.

"What are you doing?" yelled the man in Arabic. "What happened?"

Rankin continued to moan. Finally the lookout started climbing down to see what had happened.

Guns launched himself at the man, clipping his head and pushing him over. He lost his balance and tumbled into him, and together they slid down the ravine. Rankin, worried that Guns would roll all the way down into the cavern below, dove at them but missed. Jarred, Rankin's arm shrieked with pain, and he began to groan for real.

Guns got his feet in front of a rock and stopped his slide. He leapt up and hooked the lookout by the back of the neck, hauling him to his feet. The man kicked at Guns but got mostly dirt; he launched a roundhouse that caved in part of the guard's cheekbone. Then Guns picked him up and threw him back against the rocks, knocking him out.

Guns and Rankin scrambled up to the roadside. The first man was nowhere in sight.

Guns started to walk up the path.

"Forget him. Come on, let's go," said Rankin, trying to shake off the pain as he climbed into the truck that had just stopped. "We have to stop the buses and trucks now. Come on. Get the other truck. Come on."

34

TRIPOLI, LIBYA

Kiska Babev was huddled with the head of the Russian FSB's Libyan office when a young clerk knocked on the office door and entered with a folded piece of paper. Impatient at the interruption, Kiska rose from her seat, intending to get herself a cup of tea from the sideboard. As she turned, she found the clerk standing at her side.

"It just arrived for you, Madame Colonel," said the young woman. "A fax. We're trying to trace it."

Puzzled, Kiska unfolded the paper. The message was printed in large block letters:

Laxy's.
Six p.m.
—Ferg

"Is it important?" the head of the office asked.

Kiska crumbled the paper and threw it into the wastebasket at the corner.

"What is Laxy's?" she asked.

35

TRIPOLI, LIBYA

Thera had the driver go around the block twice, making sure that it was clear. When she finally decided they could go in, she took one last look at Rostislawitch, fixing the bulky suit over his frame.

"OK," she told him, but as he started to get out of the car she pulled him back. "Take this," she said, passing a small pistol into his hand. "Put it in your pocket. If you need to, use it."

"I've never fired a gun," said the scientist.

"Use two hands. Hold it like this. There's a safety catch here. Slide it before you shoot. All right?"

He nodded, staring at the gun. Thera considered moving the catch off for him, but worried that he would accidentally shoot himself when grabbing for the pistol.

"In you go," Thera said, nudging him from the car. "Walk all the way to the back. Ferguson will be at the far table on the right. Remember the video—he has a beard and glasses now. If there's a problem, I'll be very close."

The scientist nodded.

"Don't worry," added Thera. "Ferg has everything under control. He always does."

Rostislawitch felt the blood rush from his head as he got out of the car. He started walking slowly, gradually gaining speed, though not composure, as he reached the door. He was sweating profusely under the bulletproof vest. He saw the water on the steps next to him as he descended into the restaurant and worried that he was going to slip.

Rostislawitch ignored the man at the maître d' lectern, walking toward the back as Thera had directed. His eyes had trouble adjusting to the low light; he saw shadows instead of people. The place was a lot more crowded than he thought it would be; every table seemed to be full. He looked right, and saw a man with a beard and glasses, smiling at him.

"Doctor." Ferguson rose deferentially, and told him in Russian how good it was to see him. Rostislawitch replied automatically that the pleasure was his.

"We should speak English for our partner," said Ferguson, gesturing toward Atha as he sat down. Ferguson poured Rostislawitch some vodka, but the scientist didn't touch it.

"What is this virus?" demanded Atha. "How does it work?"

Rostislawitch's mind blanked. He couldn't understand the question.

"Do you need a technical explanation about the virus and how it prepares the bacteria?" asked Ferguson. "Is it important?"

"Why did you sabotage the bacteria?" Atha asked Rostislawitch.

"Why did you take it?" said Rostislawitch. "You did not pay. How did you know where it was?"

"I always intended on paying," said Atha. "I just needed to hurry things along. I have time constraints. You do not understand this. You scientists think in terms of centuries. I have hours."

"Do you know how dangerous it is?"

"That's not your concern."

"Thousands—millions of people could die."

"If you don't want to do business—" Atha started to rise. It was only partly a bluff; Rostislawitch's attitude and tone angered him.

"Now, now, let us relax," said Ferguson. "Sit, please. Have some vodka. Are you sure you won't drink?"

Atha scowled, but sat back down.

"You're doing great, Doc," Ferguson told Rostislawitch in Russian. "But don't be so angry. Relax. Just keep him talking."

"Aren't you insulting him by insisting he drink?" asked Rostislawitch. "He's Muslim."

"You think so?" Ferguson smiled. That was the general idea.

"How is this virus to be used?" asked Atha. "What is its purpose?"

Rostislawitch looked over at Ferguson. When he nodded, Rostislawitch began explaining that the process would be familiar to anyone experienced in modifying bacterial DNA; the virus was custom-designed to make the proper modification. He gave the Iranian a few lines from a graduate lecture in the subject, staying away from the complicated chemistry.

The explanation was sufficient to convince Atha that the scientist wasn't bluffing.

"When you give it to me, then you will get your payment," Atha said abruptly, cutting Rostislawitch off in midsentence. "Where is it?"

"It's available," said Ferguson. "Let us talk price."

N athaniel Hamilton pulled the rental car to the curb near the entrance to Laxy's. The routine was getting old—go in, have a walk around, fail to spot Ferguson, leave. But the alternative was to simply sit in his hotel room and wait for Ferguson to send for him, as if he were a tart on call.

Oh, it was going to be so lovely to kill the son of a bitch. The money was almost not a consideration.

Almost.

Hamilton took out his satellite phone to call his room and check for messages before going into the club. As he dialed, a pair of black Mercedes drove up in front of him. The cars had plates from the Russian embassy.

A half-dozen people got out of the cars, five bulky men and a tall blonde. They looked up and down the block; then the men formed a wedge around the woman and headed into the building.

Clearly Russian agents, thought Hamilton. Maybe Ferguson was here after all.

Thera slipped the headphones into her ears so she could hear the conversation between Atha and Rostislawitch. She could just barely see the stairs from her table. Green and Griffen, two of the Special Forces soldiers dressed in civilian clothes who were backing them up, were sitting at a booth catty-corner across from her. Another pair of soldiers were farther back in the club, closer to Ferguson.

Thera's sat phone buzzed with a call. It was the Cube.

"Thera, Ferg's not answering his phone," said Corrigan.

"No kidding. Why are you calling him?"

"Ciello just worked it out—Kiska Babev *can't* be T Rex. She was in Georgia when Dalton was killed. The stop in Paris was just to set up some sort of alias. Ciello has her credit card charges. She never left the city and was out of town long before Dalton got to France."

"All right," said Thera.

She pushed down the phone's antenna. Before she could figure out a way of telling Ferguson, she saw Kiska Babev and five other Russians walking down the steps at the restaurant entrance.

Two million more, or there is no deal," Ferguson told Atha. "American dollars, of course."

"I can't do it," said Atha. "I just can't."

"Call whoever it is you're working for," said Ferguson. "They'll pay."

"I am working on my own."

Ferguson made a face to show that he didn't believe Atha. "Well, then you pay. It's certainly worth it."

"No."

"Then you won't get the virus. The bacteria you have is worthless."

Atha thought the minister might be willing to provide the extra money, even though he would grumble about it.

The alternative was to call the intelligence people at the Iranian embassy and get them to help him force the Russians to talk. But that might be tricky—too much force and everything would be ruined.

"If it is the office of the President," said Ferguson, leaning forward, "I have a friend who works there."

"It is not the President," said Atha. "How would you have friends in Iran?"

"I have many friends. Even among the Revolutionary Guard. And the Education Ministry."

Atha felt his breath choking. What if the Russian cut him out of the deal?

No. Impossible. He was the one with the camp.

"Let us say, for a moment, that we agreed on the price," said Atha. "I would need the material quickly."

"You'll have it within twenty-four hours of payment."

"Far too late," said Atha, shaking his head.

As Ferguson shrugged, he noticed Kiska Babev heading a pack of FSB officers in his direction.

"What a pleasant surprise," he said loudly in Russian, rising. "Colonel Babev, what brings you to Tripoli?"

Kiska glared at him.

"Artur Rostislawitch, why are you in Tripoli?" Kiska looked across the table at Atha. "You—who are you?"

"Doesn't speak Russian," said Ferguson, still speaking Russian.

"I don't know what sort of game you're playing," she said to Ferguson. "But I don't like it."

"I'm not playing a game. I'm conducting a business transaction."

"What?"

"The education minister of Iran has authorized this man to buy Russian germ warfare material."

Atha didn't understand a word they were saying, but he knew it was time for him to leave. He started sliding out.

"Sit down," Kiska told him in Russian.

"Doesn't speak Russian, remember?" said Ferguson.

"Sit," she said in English. She emphasized the point by raising her hand, revealing the pistol she was holding.

Hamilton, at the door, saw the Russians standing around Ferguson's table. Things looked far too placid for his taste, almost amicable.

He decided to remedy that. He took out his pistol and fired into the air.

The gunshot was like a switch, silencing the gentle buzz that had pervaded the place. For a moment, all of the patrons sat, stunned.

Then someone screamed.

People began running for the door. A man at a table in a corner—a member of Hamas who was meeting a financer—rose and pulled out his gun. He saw someone moving toward him; believing it was a Mossad agent, he shot him dead.

Ferguson pushed Rostislawitch to the ground. Atha tried to get by, but one of the Russian agents threw him down.

A Libyan who'd been hired as a bodyguard for the Hamas member began firing a submachine gun. One of the Russians returned fire; then the rest followed suit. The bullets flashed over the banquette and couches, ricocheting with bright sparks off the stone walls.

Ferguson took hold of Rostislawitch and pulled him with him as he scrambled out into the aisle between the tables. He kicked a smoke grenade behind him to cover their retreat, then pushed Rostislawitch down, low enough to evade the gunfire.

"No, Ferg, you're not going anywhere," said Kiska, pointing her gun at his face.

"The Iranian is the one you want," Ferguson told her. "He stole the bacteria with the help of the *mafiya*. Your scientist has been helping us get it back."

"I find that hard to believe."

"That's why he didn't go to you in the first place," Ferguson said. "Because you thought he stole it."

"You're lying."

"Better grab the Iranian before he escapes," said Ferguson, pointing behind her. "He's got the material with him."

Thinking Ferguson was simply trying to divert her, Kiska hesitated before turning around. By the time she did, Atha had nearly disappeared into the smoke.

"Grab him!" she told the others. "Go."

As soon as Kiska turned, Ferguson pulled the scientist with him back into the smoke billowing from below the table. They crawled past a row of couches into the kitchen. An alarm began to sound over the gunfire and screams outside.

"You with me, Rosty?" Ferg asked, pulling him to his feet near the table used to prep salads.

"What are we going to do?" asked the scientist.

"The back door's this way," said Ferguson. He'd used it before. "But get down!"

Ferguson pushed Rostislawitch down as a spray of bullets from an AK-47 ripped through the kitchen door, clanging against the hanging pots and the stove. Flames leapt from a damaged burner, and within seconds the stove and a nearby work counter were on fire.

"We're going to have to go back out the front," Ferguson told Rostislawitch. "Sorry. I didn't think we'd be having this much fun."

Rostislawitch gripped the pistol in his pocket as Ferguson pulled him back toward the doorway. They hit a thick patch of smoke and he began to cough. Ferguson and Rostislawitch crawled out of the kitchen and down the side of the room near the bar. The gunfire had mostly stopped, but now pieces of the place were exploding or crashing to the floor as the fire gathered force, feeding on the flammable sound insulation used on the ceiling and some of the banquettes.

Ferguson ducked down toward the floor, avoiding the worst of the smoke as he got his bearings. The lights shut off; the flames behind them tinged the darkness red.

A face loomed out of the blackness.

"This way," said Nathaniel Hamilton, holding a handkerchief to his mouth and nose. "Out the side."

"I hate going out the servants' entrance," said Ferguson.

"Suit yourself," said Hamilton, raising the pistol in his hand.

36

NORTHEASTERN SUDAN

Rankin put his foot down on the gas, accelerating as the first bus in the convoy started to move. The road was wide enough for two cars to pass; the shoulders were deep with sand. If he could crash into the bus before it got too far from the others, he could jam them up temporarily, slow them down long enough for the soldiers to arrive. But he was a hundred yards away, much farther than he'd hoped. Not only might the lead bus separate from the others, but it would have plenty of time to pick up speed.

Ferg would just plow right into the bus, and somehow walk away. That was Ferg, larger than life, completely invincible. The luckiest SOB on the planet.

Unlike me, thought Rankin. He pushed his head down closer to the wheel. The truck bounced on the hardscrabble road, threatening to jerk out of control. His left arm was worse than useless, throbbing with pain.

The bus driver began to veer to the left, toward the soft dirt at the side of the road. But he was too late—Rankin yanked the wheel hard, spinning the truck into a one-eighty and piling into the front quarter of the bus.

Behind him, Guns spun his truck ninety degrees across the roadway, skidding into the bus immediately behind the one Rankin hit. The bus's back end fishtailed across the road and tipped down, wedged against the pickup.

Rankin, stunned by the impact, sat dazed in his truck, his whole body now wrapped in pain. I have to get out of here, he thought to himself, but he couldn't move.

Guns jumped from his truck, the AK-47 in his hand. In the flickering torchlight he saw two men running toward him. Something blinked red from near their midsections. They were shooting at him.

He fired a burst from the gun and both men went down.

Rankin couldn't move, and couldn't figure out why. Finally he realized he still had his seat belt on. He pulled it off, then reached for the door. It wouldn't open.

It would open for Ferguson, wouldn't it?

Rankin was obsessed with him; they all were. That's why Rankin was so pissed off at Ferguson—he was lucky and sarcastic but, most of all, good at what he did. Better than Rankin would ever be.

Better.

So what?

Rankin wasn't used to anyone being better than him, that's what. The officers he served under—they weren't better than him, not at what he did.

But Ferguson *was* better.

He was going to have to live with it.

Rankin pushed at the door again. The only way to get it open was to use his left shoulder. He gritted his teeth together, closed his eyes, and pummeled against it. The door flew open and he tumbled onto the ground.

Guns kept firing to keep people back, sending short bursts into the ground near them. He didn't see any other weapons, but couldn't take too many chances. He backed toward Rankin, who was lying on the ground near the truck, cursing and moaning all in one breath.

Dr. Hamid had just started mixing a new batch of the infected juice when he heard the crash. He secured the bacteria cultures, then ran from the hut. People were pointing toward the buses, crying, wailing.

"What is this?" he said, starting to run past the tables where the juice was being given out. He saw that some of the buses had crashed into each other, and into a truck—two trucks.

There were gunshots.

Hamid looked up, and saw a wedge-shaped shadow in the sky. It was hard to see in the dusk, and at first he didn't know what it was. Then he saw another, and another.

Parachutes.

He turned and ran toward the lab building.

Watch it!" yelled Rankin, spotting one of the camp guards running toward them with a rifle. Rankin fired his pistol at the man, who threw himself down. Before the guard could bring his rifle around to fire, Rankin fired again. This time he hit the guard square in the head.

About time I hit something, Rankin thought to himself.

"Parachutes!" said Guns. "Van's here."

"We should find the lab," said Rankin, starting forward.

Guns grabbed him. "They're full of poison, remember? We can't touch them."

"Yeah. Yeah. I wasn't thinking."

One of the cottages blew up in a tremendous explosion.

"Trying to destroy the evidence," said Guns.

"Too late for that," said Rankin, looking at the people standing forty yards away in the dim light near the wrecked buses.

37

TRIPOLI, LIBYA

Ferguson threw himself into Nathaniel Hamilton's midsection as the MI6 agent fired. The two fell backward, rolling against one of the half walls that separated the bar area from the tables. Hamilton, shocked that he had missed, tried to push his gun closer to fire again. But Ferguson was too close to him.

Rostislawitch saw the gun in Hamilton's hand and froze. Ferguson and the British agent wrestled themselves against the half wall, each man trying to pummel the other as the smoke curled around them. A piece of the ceiling dropped down, burning. It just missed them.

The rocks that lined the club's wall were not actual rocks, but rather Styrofoam imitations. The fire had reached a point where they began to incinerate. When the flames first touched them, they caught with a fizzle, the painted skin literally boiling. Then the interior of the "stone" would burst with a pop. Finally, the mastic that held them in place caught on fire and blue flames consumed the wooden structure of the wall.

Rostislawitch shook off his shock. He had to do something, he knew, or he and the American would be killed. Rostislawitch saw the gun in Hamilton's hand and thought he could pull it away. Jumping up, he grabbed the man's arm, wrestling it away from Ferguson's body. But the British agent was considerably stronger than the scientiest had thought, and continued flailing at Ferguson.

"I hate you, Ferguson, you bastard," said Hamilton, pushing against him. Hamilton fired the gun again, though something was clamped to his arm.

The gun's loud report shook Rostislawitch, and once more he froze, petrified, his arm hooked around Hamilton's forearm.

For Ferguson, the second shot was a catalyst, a call for the last reserves of his strength. He pivoted his right leg down and drove himself harder into Hamilton, pushed his weight against the Brit's arm. Then Ferguson saw Hamilton's jaw a few inches from his head. He tried to bring his right arm up to smash it, but Hamilton had it pinned to his side. So Ferguson did the next best thing—he tucked his head down and then butted full force into the not-so-solid English jaw.

Hamilton felt a shock of pain run from his chin through his molars to his tongue and skull. The side of his tongue had gotten caught between his teeth and began bleeding. He tried to fire another shot, but before he could the wall behind him gave way and his whole body felt as if it were on fire. He tried to wriggle from Ferguson's grip. To Hamilton's surprise, it worked; he rolled to his stomach to crawl away.

Instead, he felt himself being dragged backward. Ferguson had grabbed him by the legs.

"You bastard," Hamilton shouted. He twisted to fire at Ferguson, then realized the scientist was still wrapped around his arm.

Ferguson saw Hamilton's arm starting to move and let go of his legs. He leapt up into the smoke and fire, aiming his heels toward the Brit's wrist. Ferguson's left heel missed in the smoke, but his right snapped five bones in the Englishman's hand. Hamilton's yowl was louder than the sirens outside.

"Side stairs," Ferguson told Rostislawitch. He grabbed Hamilton's feet again. The fumes from the fire were a putrid, toxic mix that took his breath away, and he began coughing so badly his stomach turned.

Rolling on the floor, Rostislawitch saw Ferguson and Hamilton moving toward a small blue square. The scientist started crawling after them, swimming on his hands and knees in the haze. They went through the bar into a service area. A whiff of fresh air revived him, and he began scrambling forward.

Ferguson pulled Hamilton, still shrieking, up the four steps to a small patio area at the side of the building. He let go of the renegade MI6 agent and collapsed against a chain-link fence, gulped the fresh air. He was about to go back inside when Rostislawitch came crawling up the steps.

Writhing in pain, Hamilton cursed Ferguson. "You're a cool son of a bitch, aren't you, Ferguson?" he said over and over.

"Who paid you to kill me?" said Ferguson, still trying to clear his head.

"Three million pounds, Bob Ferguson, for screwing the Syrians out of their nuclear material. Three million fuckin' pounds."

"I would have thought more," said Ferguson.

One of the waiters from inside had been trapped by the flames. Ferguson heard him calling for help near the door. He looked at Hamilton, curled into a ball, then leapt back down the stairs. A large piece of the bar, fortunately not on fire, had collapsed on the man's legs as he tried to crawl out. Ferguson wrenched it away, then picked the man up and took him out over his shoulder. He was so woozy when he hit the stairs that he began to trip. He pirouetted around, managing a semi-soft landing with the man against the chain-link fence surrounding the patio.

Ferguson looked up and saw Hamilton pointing a cell phone at him.

"What are you going to do, quick-dial me to death?" said Ferguson.

"Hardly. You bastard." Hamilton pulled himself to his feet. He extended the disguised gun toward Ferguson. He was unsteady; he'd have to shoot for the heart.

But it would feel good, very, very good, killing him.

"I'd do this for free," Hamilton told Ferguson. He looked down at the cell phone's number pad, moving his thumb to the space button to fire.

Before he could, a bullet from a Baikal MP-445 compact struck him in the side of the temple. Fired at close range, the bullet not only shattered his skull but pushed him over, sending him crashing into the fence next to Ferguson.

Kiska stood behind him. She moved her pistol in Ferguson's direction.

"I want the scientist, Bobby," she said.

"He gets to make that decision, Kiska."

"I can just shoot you and take him." She pointed her gun at Ferguson's head.

"You could," he said.

Rostislawitch, remembering the pistol in his pocket, started to reach for it.

"I can shoot you as well," she told him, pointing her gun down at him.

"Actually, I don't think you should shoot anybody," said Ferguson. He moved his right hand out from behind his back, making the .45 more conspicuous. It was pointed at her head.

"Is it a standoff, Bobby? You kill me and I kill you?"

"Maybe," said Ferguson. "But I'm going to guess Captain Helfers there is probably faster than both of us."

Helfers was standing a few feet away, his Beretta trained on Kiska's head.

"He's a Russian citizen," she told Ferguson. "He can't escape justice."

"Did you take the Iranian?" Ferguson asked.

"We have him. You want him?"

"No. I think he belongs with you. I think he was your target all along. When the smoke clears, I think it will turn out that the FSB actually set up the entire sting," said Ferguson. "I think you used the scientist to lure the corrupt Iranian businessman here. I don't think the CIA was involved at all. Or MI6."

Kiska frowned, though she had a feeling that what Ferguson was proposing would, ultimately, make a lot of sense. It had in the past.

"Who is he?" she said, pointing to the man she had shot.

"Nathaniel Hamilton. Also known as T Rex. I wish you hadn't shot him. But *c'est la guerre.*"

"If I hadn't shot him, you'd be dead, Bobby."

Ferguson, who'd had his gun ready, disagreed. But he didn't like arguing with a lady.

"You're probably right," he told her.

"You owe me another one, Bobby," said Kiska, lowering her weapon. "I expect to collect someday."

"You know me. I always pay my debts."

38

Thera felt her heart jump as Ferguson and Rostislawitch emerged from Laxy's. She shouted to them. Rostislawitch ran to the car; Ferguson strolled behind, as if he had not a care in the world.

"Take us to the hotel," said Ferguson, getting in the back. "My friend needs a shower."

Rostislawitch reached into his pocket and took out the pistol to hand it back to Thera.

"Careful where you point that, Doc," said Ferguson, grabbing it.

"I—thank you. Thank you. Thank you."

"There is something you could do for us," Ferguson told him. "Tell us everything you know about the Russian germ program."

"I don't think I should. No. I don't think I could."

"Thing is, Doc, they're going to assume you did anyway. They probably won't prosecute you, because we'll give Kiska the evidence to back up my version of the story, and they wouldn't want to risk that coming out. Kind of make them look bad. But they won't let you do anything important, either. They're not completely stupid."

"I'll have to think," said Rostislawitch.

"Totally up to you," said Ferguson. "Don't let the fact that we saved your life enter into your consideration at all. Because it is irrelevant."

Ferguson started to laugh. The others couldn't figure out why.

"What happened to Kiska Babev?" Thera asked. "Did you get the message?"

"What message?"

"Corrigan called. Thomas Ciello figured out she wasn't T Rex."

"Oh yeah, I knew that."

"You did?"

"I've been telling you that. T Rex wasn't after Rosty. T Rex wanted me."

"You?"

"Sure." He pulled off his coat and began undoing the bullet-proof vest he'd been wearing. He hated wearing them, but then, he hated being shot even more. Hamilton's first bullet had hit him square in the chest, right over his heart—he could still feel the pain. The bruise would be with him a long time, but it was considerably better than the alternative.

"Why was he hired to kill you?"

"I guess the Syrians are a little pissed off about the fact that the nuclear material they bought a few years back never made it to Damascus."

"So who is T Rex?"

"It *was* Hamilton," Ferguson explained. "Unfortunately, Kiska shot him in the head. It wasn't her fault, though. She didn't think I had a vest. Or a gun. If it were me, I would have preferred in the kneecaps so we could bring him home. Not going to bother Parnelles, though." Ferguson pushed his legs out, trying to stretch. He was tired; he needed about twenty-four hours of sleep before he'd feel human again. "I knew Rosty wasn't the target. Killing him isn't that hard. He lives alone, lives in Russia. Piece of cake to kill him. No offense, Doc."

Rostislawitch forced himself to nod.

"T Rex didn't mind a lot of blood, but he always took the easy way out when he killed someone. He only used car bombs because the victims had bodyguards or were generally on their guard. Rosty was too easy. The trick was to make us think he was the target. That was pretty clever."

"How long did you know it was Hamilton?"

Actually, Ferguson hadn't been positive it was Hamilton until he showed up in front of him at the restaurant. He also didn't know how much of the Iranian plot Hamilton himself had known, and while he suspected that he had purposely set up his preparer to lure Ferguson here, he couldn't be sure of that, either. But he just shrugged without answering, as if he knew the whole story, and had from the very beginning. Explaining things took away much of the mystery, kind of like a woman without any clothes.

Now that he didn't need to be on his guard, now that they were done and others could watch out for him, fatigue rolled over Ferguson like a tsunami wave. He closed his eyes, drifting. The song he'd heard in the background of the club played in his head. It was Cole Porter, an old love song. The music swelled and he got up to dance.

Ferguson turned to find a partner, and there was Thera, dressed in a long gown, pearls draped from her neck. He was in a tux.

"Shall we dance?" he asked.

"I'd love to," she said.

He took her hand and swirled her once, then held her close. And in the dreamworld that had suddenly descended on him, everything was perfect.

39

WASHINGTON, D.C.

"The site is secure," Corrine Alston told the President. "The decontamination teams are another two hours away."

"The bacteria has been contained?"

"We think so. Two of our people were at the edge of the camp. They're going to be isolated, but we don't think they were infected."

"A cure?"

"We hope they weren't exposed," said Corrine. "The Russian scientist is cooperating. But the strain is resistant to antibiotics. The people who were exposed may very well die. At a minimum, they'll be very sick."

"That's unfortunate," said President McCarthy.

"Dan Slott is arranging for medical care to be flown in."

McCarthy got up from his desk and walked to the small globe at the side of his office, spinning it around slowly until he was looking at Iran. "We're going to announce the Iran nuclear treaty tonight, Corrine. Very good work."

She felt a little embarrassed to be thanked, since she had had almost nothing to do with it.

"Ferguson and his people, and Colonel Van Buren, they really did a fantastic job," she told the President. "And, I should mention, T Rex—the assassin who killed our CIA officer two years ago—he's dead. He was a renegade MI6 agent."

"MI6?"

"Yes, sir."

"Sometimes you can't tell the good guys from the bad guys, can you, Miss Alston?"

"No, Jonathon, sometimes you can't."

McCarthy didn't say anything else. Corrine, with more work to do, left the President staring at the globe.